THE TINSMITH

THE
TINSMITH
TIM BOWLING

BRINDLE
& GLASS

Brindle & Glass Publishing Ltd.
brindleandglass.com

LIBRARY AND ARCHIVES CANADA CATALOGUING IN PUBLICATION
Bowling, Tim, 1964–
The tinsmith / Tim Bowling.

Also issued in electronic format.
ISBN 978-1-926972-43-5

I. Title.

PS8553.O9044T55 2012   C813'.54   C2011-907279-3

Editor: Jack Hodgins
Copy Editor/Proofreader: Heather Sangster, Strong Finish
Design: Pete Kohut
Cover image: Confederate soldier: John Cairns, istockphoto.com
Texture: George Bosela, stck.xchng
Author photo: Theresa Shea

Brindle & Glass is pleased to acknowledge the financial support for its publishing
program from the Government of Canada through the Canada Book Fund, Canada
Council for the Arts, and the Province of British Columbia through the British
Columbia Arts Council and the Book Publishing Tax Credit.

The interior pages of this book have been printed on 100% post-consumer
recycled paper, processed chlorine free, and printed with vegetable-based inks.

1 2 3 4 5 16 15 14 13 12

PRINTED IN CANADA

For my sister and brothers
and the river that shaped us.

Urge, urge and urge,
Always the procreant urge of the world.
—Walt Whitman

In all the relations of life and death,
we are met by the color line.
—Frederick Douglass

PART ONE

I

September 17, 1862, near Antietam Creek, Maryland

As the darkness continued to lift, Anson Baird, an assistant surgeon in the Union Army, knelt in a shallow, broad hollow off a rutted dirt road. Uneasily, he unpacked his rolled muslin bandages and small glass bottles of chloroform and whisky, but no matter what tasks he concentrated on, he found it hard to leave the dream world of the night entirely behind.

It had been as black a night as any he'd ever known. At some point in the early hours of the morning, in a steady, dripping rain, the crack of a picket's rifle had forced him to climb stiffly out of his bedroll and peer into the darkness. But he had seen nothing except the bundled black forms of the soldiers sleeping—or trying to sleep—nearest to him. In fact, the night was so dark that Anson could barely recall the terrain— a bucolic valley of limestone ledges, the Potomac River to the west, a winding creek to the east, a long and dusty turnpike running away to the south, past several farms and a small, square, whitewashed church. Ordinary enough, except for the two great armies bivouacked less than a mile apart with only that dusty turnpike running between them.

Anson shuddered. After a year's volunteer service, during which he'd experienced the brutal realities of several battles and hundreds of operations, he was no longer simply a sleepy country doctor, fond of the *Georgics* and prone to fanciful thoughts. And yet, now, he could imagine that turnpike stretched taut in the dawn air, like a dew-dripping thread with two massive spiders poised at either end to advance their terrible appetites toward one another. The startling, grotesque image properly belonged to the vague dream world of broken sleep, not to a real night on the real earth where a man, if not for the danger of being shot, could walk out across a rolling pasture to an orchard, pluck a ripe apple or peach from a bough, bite down, and taste the tang of juice on his tongue.

A wave of homesickness washed over him—for his quiet little practice and his solitary bachelor ways that a year's military service had almost reduced to phantasms, memories that some other man had once lived as sensual experience. Almost. For Anson still held in his palms the smooth curves of the small mahogany globe his late father had given him upon Anson's earning the two-year medical certificate from Haverford College, he still breathed in the wet fur of the Labrador retrievers that always shared his parents' home, each successive dog named Fetch because his father sought always some foil against mortality, and, finally, he still saw the glorious, broken-cloud spill of apple blossom along the deeply grooved lane he had walked so often as a boy to visit his grandparents.

Family. History. The simple comfort of such continuance. For what other reason should a man leave his home to bloody his hands and trouble his senses in the service of his country?

The last of the darkness had almost dissolved, and now Anson could see more clearly. Stretching away along both sides of the hollow, the deep columns of men prepared for battle. Many soldiers used the fronts of their uniforms to wipe the heavy dew off their muskets, while others adjusted their knapsacks, putting the canteen and haversack well behind, to give free access to the cartridge box. Closer to him, Anson watched a skinny private named Orson chew furiously on a piece of hardtack. Other men smoked. Behind the troops, horses whinnied continuously and the mules employed to haul the artillery wagons brayed just as often. The animals doubtless wanted their morning feed, but Anson suspected they wouldn't get it. The sight of mounted orderlies galloping along the lines with orders for their regiments confirmed the imminence of battle.

With a sigh, Anson stood and tightened the flannel band around his waist. It didn't help his nerves that he was still stricken with the common plague of the Army of the Potomac—what the soldiers called "a case of the shits." Ever since the swamps and miasmas of the Virginia fighting in the spring, he had been forced to minister to his own intestinal sufferings. But no matter how large the doses of calomel or how many opium pills he swallowed, no matter how much the flannel band fought off the infecting cold, he rarely knew any relief. A dozen times a day he had to bolt for the nearest ditch, the cramps almost crippling him in his hunched progress. It hardly inspired faith among the similarly plagued to see their surgeon, a man of thirty-five years, old enough to have fathered many of them, caught in the ignominious throes of the malady. But then, Anson knew what most of the soldiers thought of medical men: "quacks" was a mild epithet, and "butchers" a more common one.

He turned and saw his orderly wringing his hands, as if to drain a sponge. Even in this dimness, Anson could tell the young man's lips were trembling.

"It will be all right, Felix," he whispered, leaning close. "The worst is the waiting."

The orderly did not turn. "No. It isn't."

To Anson, such a small slap of truth felt like a hard blow, for he had not expected it. Fear, and any kind of battle experience, made all platitudes of comfort banal—he supposed even as simple a boy as Felix understood as much. Anson chose to settle into the safest place: himself.

"Laudo, laudas, laudat, laudamus, laudatis, laudant."

He had begun to call up his Latin during the long hours of surgery following his first battle. The simple memory work helped keep him awake, and, besides, the classical age possessed a rare calm—its violence, ennobled by its poets, somehow put this War of Rebellion into a more comfortable perspective.

Sharp cracks of musketry sounded somewhere to the west. Now in the grey air, the patchy ground fog broke at the soldiers' legs. Some of the men pointed to the sky ahead of them. Anson looked up. Not far beyond the southern edge of the woodlot, a thick river of coal-black smoke rolled straight heavenward, ominous in its motion; it seemed almost like a living creature. The rebels had likely set some farmhouse or barn on fire for tactical purposes. Anson dropped his eyes to the woodlot, a few rods ahead of the troops. Beyond that colourful stand of oak, hickory, and beech—a stand no more than a hundred yards in length—lay a gentle, bucolic landscape of head-high corn fields, low pasture fences of stone and Virginia rail, and several farmhouses and barns nestled against abundant orchards. And less than a mile away to the south, if all the rumours were accurate, waited tens of thousands of rebels.

An officer barked orders. The musicians' brass and drums shivered and rattled in preparation. All at once the pearl sky flared and ripped. Shells crashed to the earth like cord upon cord of wood being unloaded. The motion was sea swells. The soldiers shifted, foot to foot, their taut faces already drained of colour. Anson watched one heavily bearded man open the case of a cameo locket, whisper into it, then snap it shut with an almost fierce resolution. But his movements, and all others, were weirdly silent now. The men rippled slightly, like grass underwater. Some sloughed off their knapsacks entirely, and in doing so seemed tiny, even more vulnerable. How many lead balls might those knapsacks have deflected or slowed to a less deadly impact? Anson shuddered and made to turn away from the line.

But just then, the line began to move, like a chain made of flesh and muscle. The soldiers advanced as steadily and slowly as the black river of smoke above them. Soon blue and white coils shrouded the treetops and swallowed the troops—a few soldiers emerged in glimpses. As dawn broke, visibility decreased.

Pressed into the earth now, his head just above ground level, Anson peered into the tattered air, waiting for the first retreats of the wounded or the first advance of the enemy, hoping the two events would not occur together. He had given orders for the stretcher-bearers to clear the field, but where exactly was it? And when should he motion the bearers forward? The woodlot loomed like an iron gate between him and the battle. He heard the rippling and *whish-whish-whish* of musketry between the concussive explosions of the artillery, breathed in the battle's rolling smoke, watched men plunge toward it, but could only wait to see the first staggering effects.

Minutes passed quickly, slowly. The wood was but a dozen rods away, far too close should the enemy surge through. But if that happened, at least a retreat would come first, some small advance warning of the need for Anson to gather his supplies and fall back until he could better do his duty in the field hospital a mile to the rear.

He did not fall back. The wounded appeared, blue shadows helped by other blue shadows; the ripping of artillery seemed to tear the shadows out of the smoke itself. Anson jumped up and ran forward; he shouted at the stretcher-bearers to go into the woods. If they waited much longer to aid the fallen, too many men would leave the lines, damning the Union's cause and rendering his own charges almost useless. He shouted again, and to his surprise the men sprinted for the woods.

Within minutes, he saw Everitt and Cole emerge from the smoke. Moving their heads like horses struggling against the reins, they staggered to the hollow; all Anson could see of the soldier on the stretcher between them were his dangling arms.

"Put him here!" Anson shouted into the din. Failing to hear his own voice, he gestured to a spot below the lip of the hollow, which was itself no more than two feet deep and thirty wide—a meagre protection, but better than nothing.

The stretcher-bearers lifted the wounded soldier off the stretcher and onto the ground. Anson immediately dropped to his knees to shelter the man from a spray of dirt and rock thrown up by a shell.

The soldier, a man named Rufus Troy, was near Anson's age, with a thick beard matted with dirt and a hairline so receded that the shocked and trembling face, greasy as butter around the black smudges of gunpowder, loomed unnaturally large. Troy's lips glistened red, as if bloodied, and his dark eyes, though fluttering with pain, never completely closed. Through chattering teeth, he gasped, "Foot . . . it's my foot."

Anson pressed a flask of whisky to the man's mouth and watched the Adam's apple throb four times in rapid succession. Then he gently removed the fragments of boot and inspected the wound. The left foot had been shattered, likely by a shell fragment, and resembled a dirty, bloodied sack filled with shards of chalk. Despite the urgent need to act as quickly as possible and to stay focused on the present, Anson's thoughts raced ahead to the work he'd do at the field hospital. The foot would have to come off, a very difficult procedure he'd attempted only once, albeit successfully. He'd have to disarticulate through the ankle joint, saw off a thin slice of the end of the tibia with the malleolar projections. Grimly, Anson splinted the leg as best he could, then waved an ambulance-man over, all the while running the operation through his head. The trickiest part, by far, was shelling the os calcis out of the heel pad. If that wasn't done properly . . .

But he also understood that the circumstances of battle might not even bring this soldier into his presence again. Mere seconds after the ambulance-man had borne the soldier to a nearby wagon, another victim of the conflict, this one much younger and a stranger, collapsed over the lip of the hollow, almost scattering Anson's precious supply of bottled chloroform.

For two hours the artillery pounded and screeched: it let up only long enough to allow the crackle of musket fire, shouts of men, and severed neighs of horses to penetrate the sudden, eerie silences. At one point, out of the frayed rags of the battle, several cows lumbered straight toward Anson. Blood hung from them in broken strings and ropes, their heads swung wildly, their eyes resembled lead balls sticking out of fresh wounds. Anson threw himself over the body of the wounded man on the ground in front of him as the cows bellowed past, a sudden flash of light throwing their red-frothed hides into a vivid relief that lasted but a second. Then he raised himself from the oblivious soldier and, with his index finger, pushed into the messy hole beneath the clavicle, searching for lead. The soldier—a young man with corn-gold hair and beard—gasped as Anson's finger probed deeper without success. But where, then, was the exit wound? As gently as possible, Anson turned the soldier onto his side. From previous experience, he knew that the trajectory of the minie ball was erratic; so much depended on the angle of deflection by the bone. In this case, the ball must have remained within the upper chest or neck, for he could find no corresponding exit wound. Frustrated, he ordered another ambulance-man over and then turned to the ginger-haired youth on the ground with the lead ball lodged in his lower maxillary and the eyes soft and brown as a newborn calf's.

Anson's sense of time vanished. Rapidly, he dressed wounds, dispensed whisky and opium, and made snap decisions about which of the wounded needed to be placed in the nearby wagons and hurried to the field hospital and which could walk the mile back on their own. Choking on the sulphurous smoke, his voice hoarse from shouting orders to Felix and the stretcher- and ambulance-men, Anson saw only the blurred faces of misery and pleading bob up out of the din and swirl of motion. Once, after tightening a tourniquet on a fractured arm, he looked at the sun. It burned dully, a smudge of yellow beaten thin by the battle smoke and the clouds of dust kicked up by fresh troops rushing forward. The day itself seemed checked—certainly time did not progress in the usual fashion. For twenty minutes afterwards, all the soldiers brought in by the stretcher-men were either dead or well on their way to death—and presumably these had been the best candidates for survival. God alone knew what condition of suffering the stretcher-men had determined to be hopeless—soldiers blown to pieces, headless, limbless, their insides on the outside. Judging by some of the wounds—bones shattered by minie balls and shell fragments, bones that would be impossible to repair even under peaceful circumstances, Anson knew his surgical skills would soon be required at the field hospital a mile to the rear.

Around seven o'clock, a longer lull in the fighting occurred. An officer on horseback emerged out of the threads of smoke, his severely drawn, Spanish-dark face like an unexploded shell hanging in the air.

"We've got 'em now, by God! They'll soon be on the run!"

A stretcher-man dropped into the hollow. The wounded man who thudded to the ground behind him screamed, "Shoot me! Please, God, kill me!" He clutched his left leg. It flailed like a corn stalk in a breeze.

A neat formation of drawn faces with sickening grins marched past beyond the mounted officer. They all turned to the wounded man's screams. The officer pulled the reins and spun around.

"Give 'em hell, boys! They can't hold out much longer!"

Then he kicked the horse's flanks and disappeared.

The soldier was a hopeless case. Anson poured chloroform into a cloth and silenced the man's screaming, then ordered the stretcher-man to get up off the ground and take the soldier to an ambulance. No response came. Anson began to upbraid the man for shirking when he noticed the trickle of blood over the eyelids. He crawled over and put his ear to the man's chest. Nothing. Mercifully. Head wounds almost always proved mortal.

"Felix!"

The orderly scrambled over, swinging a pail like a censer. His long face chalked the air.

"I'll be needed at the hospital," Anson said. "You'll have to handle this yourself. It's quieter now."

But even before the orderly responded, the artillery barrage began again and a shell screeched nearby, bursting and showering the hollow with dirt. Shouted exchanges could not be heard. The smoke clotted. Everything swam through it. For ten minutes, Anson crouched in the hollow, shaking. No wounded arrived. He wondered if all his stretcher-men were themselves killed or wounded—no doubt some had run off. Their absence decided him: he could do more good at the hospital. If only the artillery would let up. Several times he rose, prepared to sprint, but each lifting of his body seemed to trigger an even greater explosion. Again and again, he shrank back down.

At last, when adrenalin heaved him out of the hollow, he joined a stream of soldiers fleeing the fight.

"They're through the corn!" a limping youth screamed into Anson's face just as the artillery noises gave way to long rolls of musketry. "We can't hold 'em!"

Anson paused. Men fell and rose all around him. The smoke looped in ropes and chains. Suddenly his choice took on a greater significance, became the cause itself. It seemed that his retreat, no matter how practical, was akin to leaving the field and the day to the rebels. And so, when a single soldier rushed past him toward the fight, Anson decided. He stopped and turned. A longhaired soldier clutching his side as if to hold it together shuffled along, his boots

11

barely lifting off the ground. Anson realized that the man stood a better chance of survival if his wound was tended to immediately, and so, after a brief dumb show of explanation, he hoisted the soldier onto his back and staggered to the hollow.

By the time he reached it, the smoke had thinned and fewer men were emerging from the woodlot. It seemed the retreat had been halted. The wounded, however, continued to limp and crawl in, many with bloodied tourniquets of cornstalk on their shattered limbs. They begged for water or death, their faces blackened with powder. Anson read the requests in their eyes, on their lips. When he shook the last drop out of the last bottle of whisky, he resorted more and more to opium pills—and when those ran out, he relied on the faith of his parents, on their unswerving trust in the mercy of God.

Most of the stretcher-men had vanished, along with Felix. The wounded came under their own power or with the assistance of comrades. Anson recognized some soldiers from his regiment, but most were strangers. He didn't know exactly when he'd noticed—perhaps by the fourth or fifth case—but he saw now that it had been this same tall, broad-shouldered young man in a uniform a size too small for him who'd been bringing the fallen over the crumbled lip of the hollow. Anson noted a curious lack of strain or panic on the soldier's face, though perhaps he was only numb with fear. The right cheek showed a large, rough wound, as if the skin had been scraped with a knife, but otherwise the young soldier appeared unharmed. He did not hide the wound, but he had a pronounced habit of ducking his head as soon as scrutiny lasted more than a few seconds, an action that seemed modest rather than devious.

But Anson looked at this man's face often enough over the next frantic hours that its features became vividly fixed in his memory: large, slightly bulbous eyes, a full, wet mouth, the bottom lip jutting out a little, and pale skin that yet had a curious dark cast to it, much the way that the moon, Anson thought, no matter how bright, always suggests the presence of darkness. Regardless of that impression, which did not so much unnerve as intrigue Anson, the youth's grace was striking. With surprising ease, he carried his wounded comrades either slung over his shoulders or cradled in his arms—and when he placed them down, his care was most evident. His expression, tight with exertion, never altered. Nor did he attempt to communicate. There was an odd deference to his behaviour that reminded Anson of something he'd seen before, and recently, but he could not place it. The youth, waiting for Anson to dictate by a nod of the head where he should lay the latest wounded man down, suddenly gave an involuntary shudder under the intensity of Anson's gaze and ducked his head. Then, placing the soldier gently on the ground, he raced back into the smoke and fire flashes, without even a rifle for protection.

Caught up again in his duties, Anson forgot about the tall soldier. The noise and smoke continued unabated, with troops rushing forward in columns and falling back again in bloodied fragments, the frantic motion accompanied by sporadic cheers and the terrifying peals of the rebels' yelling. Several times, the yells cut so sharply through the din that Anson expected a grey wave bearing faces fierce with the lust to kill to roll over him. But always the yells faded, the grey wave broke elsewhere, and the tall, calm, long-limbed soldier brought in another fallen comrade.

Some men, Anson knew from previous battles, shirked a more dangerous duty by helping the wounded—fit soldiers who accompanied the fallen out of the fight often found reasons not to return, or at the very least they returned as slowly as possible. This tall soldier, however, always rushed back to the lines with his fighting blood fully up. Perhaps he killed rebels with his bare hands. He appeared capable enough; his hands dangled thick and knot-tight at his sides. And by nine o'clock, during another strange lull in the battle, Anson knew that this fight was terrible, often a hand-to-hand affair. One soldier said that he lay on the ground beneath the powder smoke and shot at the legs of rebels as they passed a few feet in front of him. So perhaps the tall soldier did kill without a rifle. And yet, there was that faintly familiar humility, that long shudder, as if he'd been caught doing something wrong. Anson couldn't dismiss it entirely. He kept expecting to see the shudder again.

Oddly enough, however, once the shooting and shelling had stopped over the broken landscape and the cries of the wounded for water echoed dismally through the woods and across the pasture fields and orchards, the tall soldier had vanished.

Anson gathered the remainder of his supplies into his kit and stepped out of the hollow. The trees in the near woodlot were smoking, splintered sticks through which a staggering figure sometimes emerged. The ground flowed with torn smoke. A wounded horse neighed miserably as it kicked two legs at the sky. The cry of "Water! Water!" never stopped. Blue shadows crawled like flies toward the rear, some grey shadows among them. Most of the tall stalks of a vast cornfield nearby were gone, the stubs scorched black, the few leaves spattered with blood.

After helping to load some wounded onto a wagon, Anson left orders for the other ambulance-men regarding where to concentrate their efforts, then trudged for a half-mile under the risen sun to his bloodier labours at a barnyard northwest of the hollow. It was a strange, disorienting journey, with every twenty paces over the shelled earth bringing a new assault on the senses. Passing an orchard of broken-limbed trees, Anson suddenly breathed in the powerful aroma of ripe peaches. But just as he was enjoying the experience, the peach scent faded, replaced by the foul stench of death rising off a mangled horse. Twenty paces on, close to a trim little farmhouse, several swarms of bees poured like smoke out of a cluster of wooden box hives. Everywhere the collision of nature and war struck Anson with a gloom that made his steps feel more weighted down than usual.

The battle in his part of the field raged until early afternoon, then slackened. His regiment was out of it by then; he heard reports that more than half of the men had been killed or wounded, including many officers. While labouring in the barnyard, Anson was aware of the guns continuing to pound in the south, toward the little creek. From time to time, he'd look up from an operation to see a flash of orange light on the horizon. Occasionally, individual cracks of rifles, sounding closer than the thunderlike roll of the artillery, pierced the still fields around him and kept help from those wounded still lying in the zone between the armies, which, as far as Anson could tell, had reached a stalemate. Even in his situation, with the surgery relentless, Anson felt the tension in the air; the imminence of renewed full-fledged fighting was palpable. But here in the north, in the churned fields and broken orchards around his barnyard, the big guns remained silent as the afternoon dragged on and the yellow sun climbed free of smoke threads and burned hotter, increasing the wounded's desperate thirst as well as Anson's sense of helplessness; he simply could not do enough to ease the suffering.

As the daylight dwindled and the sun hung bloodily in the smoke of the last fighting, Anson noticed that the palm of his saw hand was blistered. Blood, intestine, and brain splattered his apron. His supply of Latin verbs ran dry.

He stood in a barnyard of flattened grass and operated on a door wrenched off a nearby house and laid out upon four oak barrels. His catling knife, bone saw, and other instruments sat on another barrel just to his right. Twenty feet away, William Childress, another assistant surgeon, bent over a body, his right arm rising and falling in the fading light as he cut through an arm or leg bone—the grating sound, low and dull, remarkably akin to that of wood being sawn, filled the barnyard and made everyone present temporarily unaware of the artillery and musket noises still coming from the south.

Several dozen wounded soldiers lay on the heavily trodden ground, forming a loose line leading up to the operating table. These men were either still in shock or medicated for pain—they posed little problem, though occasionally one resisted the surgery so strongly that hospital stewards were needed to hold him down on the table. It was the others—the slackers, the lightly wounded, members of the Quartermaster corps—whose open-jawed curiosity created a disturbance. Their silent, morbid gawking weighed down Anson's arm each time he explored a wound, poking a finger deep into torn tissue to remove bits of cloth or dirt or, if he was fortunate, a lead ball or other piece of killing weaponry.

The wound before him was bad, the kneecap shattered and the tissue shredded. Anson chose a spot several inches above the wound and fastened a tourniquet. He picked up his amputating knife from the basin of bloody water and as rapidly as possible cut through the tissue to the bone, then peeled the flap of skin back. Aware of all the eyes of the waiting wounded turned to him, he took up his saw and, placing the blade firmly against the bone, moved his arm back and forth in a steady rhythm.

Around him he heard a sudden commotion as another ambulance wagon arrived, blood dripping through its floorboards. A voice from inside cried, "O Lord O Lord O Lord" without pause. The horse neighed loudly. Someone shouted, "Whoa! Whoa there!" Shadows spread over the ground. The smell of blood and chlorophorm blended with the musk of manure and earth. There came a sharp cry, then a low groan. The dull sawing sound, steady as bee hum, persisted in Anson's ears, as if divorced from the motion of his arm. He paused to wipe the sweat from his eyes, then wiped his hand on his bloody, gore-covered smock and returned to his task.

Finally, with the useless leg dangling from his hand, he turned toward the ever-lengthening line of wounded. Men of all ages, from hardly-more-than boys to grey- and white-bearded veterans, lay or sat on the ground in loose clusters, their shirts either open or off, their eyes heavy. Several soldiers couldn't keep their jaws from opening and closing in rapid succession; they resembled baby robins waiting to be fed. Far beyond the clusters of wounded, a burst shell threw up smoke and earth. Anson's stomach lurched. There'd be little rest this night. But, God knew, there'd been little real rest since he'd enlisted and left behind his somnolent bachelorhood and drowsy practice of mostly sore throats and mild catarrhs and the occasional broken bone, almost always clean, from a fall off a horse or a barn roof. For one thing, there'd been too much to learn, too many vile city diseases to fight, too many new ways to remove flesh and bone and muscle in order to preserve life. And for another thing, there'd been too much death. That was the worst of it. At home, it was easy to believe in the natural course of God's plan—birth, youth, age, and finally a kind of gradual sunset out of the mortal condition. Even when a baby was stillborn, or a woman died in childbirth, or someone met with a cruel accident, the event was rare enough not to violate the natural laws. But war . . . it hadn't just violated, it had destroyed the past fifteen years of Anson's comfortable abidance in the unquestioned verities of continuance. In any case, how could there be rest during a rebellion, when one side of the body was attacking the other?

He looked down at the lower leg in his hand, as if his thoughts alone had severed it from a body and put it there. And yet he did not doubt the necessity of the fight to keep his country together. No, that was without question. Even so, it was wearying, unpleasant work.

He flung the leg onto a pile of limbs and heard it land with the usual splat, as if he were piling fruit. The sound sickened him anew; it was always a harsh reminder of how infrequently he could keep the wounded whole. Heavily, he turned back to the damaged body on the table and sutured the arteries, his needle pulling the silk thread tight.

"Next!" he called and waited for another wounded man to emerge from the horrified lineup.

Darkness fell at last. The battle sounds ceased, replaced with a steady, echoing lament of suffering. Lanterns bobbed in the fields as hospital stewards and stretcher-men continued to search for wounded. Anson worked with his back to a great gambrel barn, its four sloped roofs giving it a queer, giant bat–like quality whenever he turned and faced its massive bulk. If not for the powerful, comforting scent of alfalfa wafting through its hayloft window, the barn would have seemed a gruesome observer of Anson's surgeries. Instead, he used the scent of hay, faint though it was, threatening to dissolve completely in the mingled musk of chloroform, blood, and manure in which he stood, to carry him home to his grandparents' farm. There, at harvest time, many men had worked in the fields, swinging scythes.

This peaceful reverie of reflection never lasted more than a few seconds. Eventually, Anson would look up to see his half-dozen fellow surgeons bent over in the barely sufficient light of sperm-oil candles held in the unsteady hands of exhausted assistants. Sometimes he would be called over by a colleague to consult on a particularly difficult operation, but mostly the surgeons worked independently, with Josiah Rawley, the regimental surgeon, patrolling from candle to candle when he wasn't busy cutting into flesh and bone himself.

Meanwhile, out in the dark fields, the sharp cracks of pickets' rifles kept help from reaching those soldiers who had fallen in the contested ground between the armies. But without the constant shrieking and pounding of shells, the worst of the killing was over, and Anson's body responded. Several times he dashed from the operating table and relieved his bowels in the pasture, where at least the spread manure made his foul contribution less apparent. The cramps intensified as the night wore on, and the energy spent in these evacuations soon brought back his fits of violent coughing.

Once, returning to the table where an anaesthetized man with an arm fracture lay in readiness for amputation, Anson encountered Rawley, the barrel-chested career army man whose silver-grey beard and pallid skin gave him a ghostly appearance in the candle flickers.

"For heaven's sakes, Baird, don't be so dainty, man!" With a sweeping motion of one arm, he indicated the black, fetus-curled figures of the wounded nearby. "This is no time for niceties. Go in your breeches if you have to!" Then he slapped Anson on the shoulder and, with a broad smile, said, "It's always you bachelors who are so fussy. You need a good woman to take care of the manners for you."

Though Anson was not sure how a woman could make his diarrhea any less unpleasant, he took his superior's point—with the ever-increasing miasma of odours (blood, shit, smoke, vomit, chloroform), no one was going to remark on his excretions.

And it was true: with each hour, more stragglers came in from the great battle, many suffering from shock and loss of blood. Some managed remarkably to reach the hospital under their own power, while others were helped in either by comrades or by one of those men deputized for the duty. As such men were mostly drawn from the ranks of shirkers or were soon needed to help out as nurses, the fresh supplies of wounded inevitably dwindled toward the early hours of the new day.

By then, the piteous cries of stranded soldiers, for water, for their mothers, or for death, decreased. Anson clutched his stomach and leaned on the operating table with his other hand. In the candlelight, his hand appeared savage, pale skin showing under the blood smears and gore; it looked as if he had cut it off and forgotten to toss it on the nearest stack of limbs. But his feet troubled him the most. They were swollen and aching, and no matter how he adjusted his weight, he could find no relief.

Then the rain began, lightly at first, sending up a gentle chorus of patters among the tree leaves and on the barn roof. But quickly the light shower became a downpour and operations had to be performed inside the barn. Now, as he sawed into bone, his shadow loomed grotesquely on the beams and stables and stacked hay. His arms, black and several times larger on the planks, moved with a creeping, spidery motion that he could hardly bear to witness. Anson knew that others noticed this as well and likely couldn't draw their eyes away. Each time he laid his amputating knife against skin, he imagined he was cutting into a huge indrawn breath.

Finally, he lost count of the amputations and of those who perished on the table before he could begin. Some had already died before they were lifted into place. Other waiting wounded were regularly pulled out of the line as corpses. In the brief pauses between operations, Anson heard the sound of digging just outside. At one point, Samuel Cossins, another assistant surgeon, appeared in the gloom and shadows with a chart in his hand. He wearily but methodically checked every wounded man—and there were hundreds sprawled in the barn—seeking their identification for possible use in his growing registry of graves. Anson almost envied him his miserable work, for at least it did not involve this relentless sawing of bone.

The rain fell softer, the thin drops tapping the boot-slopped ground outside the open barn door. With difficulty, Anson fished around in a gaping thigh wound, seeking to ligate an artery to stop the bleeding. Blood gushed over his hands. He swore beneath his breath and continued to reach with the silk thread; it was like trying to set a hook inside the belly of a fish. Finally succeeding to tie a loop around the artery with one end of the thread, he left the other end to dangle out of the wound. Later, he would be able to check to see if the loop had rotted loose by pulling on the dangling end. When the loop pulled away, if a blood clot had formed and closed the vessel, his efforts would have succeeded. If no clot had formed, there might follow an even worse, secondary hemorrhage. This had happened once to another surgeon at Bull Run, and the patient had died.

Anson wiped his bloodied hands on his apron and briefly shut his eyes.

et, si quid cessare potes, requiesce sub umbra.
huc ipsi potum uenient per prata iuuenci,
hic uiridis tenera praetexit harundine ripas
mincius, eque sacra resonant examina quercu.

He opened his eyes and looked around. There was no sacred oak in sight, nor swarms of bees humming from it; not even Virgil could have imagined himself away from such misery. Wounded men so crammed the interior of the barn that if he'd taken two steps in any direction, he would have trodden on one of them. Their shock-pale faces crowded close as mushrooms. He felt the piteous gazes of what seemed to be an entire regiment.

Near daybreak, in an effort to keep himself going, Anson walked into a corner of the barnyard where a hospital cook had a large pot boiling over a low fire. He asked for a cup of coffee and a piece of salt pork, and after drinking and eating, he decided to stretch his legs by going for a walk—he could not remain near so many dead and dying for another minute and still keep his freshness and alertness for the surgeries. A little time to himself might translate into a cleaner, more efficient procedure with an improved chance of recovery. Perhaps a walk might even ease the aching in his feet. Quietly desperate, he swallowed two more opium pills. Then he selected a large tree on the lightening horizon as his destination, stepped cautiously around the sleeping and moaning forms on the earth, and tried to clear his mind.

From what he'd heard, the battle had been a victory, even if, from his vantage point, it didn't look like one. Some of the wounded had grumbled that they could have whipped the rebels for good if they'd been allowed to, but most felt that they'd given a fine account of themselves and that the Republic had won the day. The uneasy night, pitch-dark but for a scattering of watch fires and horrible with the cries of the wounded, had not created a victorious atmosphere, nor had the clusters of grimy-white hospital tents that had sprouted like mushrooms in and around the barnyard.

The dawn Anson walked into was just as uneasy as the night had been. He realized with a start, as he almost tripped up against a dead horse, that the battle could be resumed at any time. Soon the drummers would call the fit men to readiness. Another half-hour and there'd be enough light for the artillery to fix on their targets. Anson quickened his pace. Somehow the tree had become a necessary objective—it almost seemed that, if he could reach it, he could stop the battle from continuing.

He walked for several minutes over the churned earth, only cast-off knapsacks and clothing showing evidence of the battle. But soon he came among mangled bodies and tipped-over wagons, dead horses, smashed limbers, even more scattered remnants of shirts and coats. The field had the ominous stillness of a garbage pile—any movement seemed likely to release a horde of rats out of the darkly bleeding edges of the departing night. Already the stench of decay forced its way through the lingering powder smoke. Anson kept his heavy eyes on the trunk ahead—the tree, like most others in the area, had been struck by shells, denuding it of most of its branches. But one thick branch, in particular, pointed almost straight upward, like a regimental flag. Focusing on it, Anson could almost conjure up the whiff and tang of ripe apples, almost summon up those two bucolic autumns of his youth when he'd taken his medical certificate, not far distant, in Pennsylvania. Such a long time ago . . . another world . . .

Stepping suddenly into a hole, he stumbled and fell to one knee. This set off another violent fit of coughing that he could not quell. Terrified, he listened to his coughs echo through the stillness like musketry.

But nothing moved or sounded in response. Cautiously, Anson stood and then limped the remaining yards to the tree. As he leaned against the trunk, breathing in rasps, he heard something a little way to his right—a breathing almost as laboured as his own and, in between each breath, the sound of an object being dragged. Pressed hard to the trunk, one hand clasped to his mouth, Anson peered into the grey-black air. Seconds passed. Then a strange shape emerged, the figure of a huge, deformed man dragging a smaller body, its feet bumping over the earth, its head indistinguishable—it might have been a headless corpse.

As Anson stared, poised to defend himself somehow, or to run if necessary, the giant figure stopped almost directly beside him. Slowly he turned his head. Anson stepped back. It was as if the head of the corpse had been propped on the giant's shoulder. With the two heads now pointed in his direction, Anson suddenly felt his muscles relax. Then he had another surprise—the giant's slightly bulbous eyes, his clear brow and full mouth, the large scrape on his cheek, were all familiar. This giant was in fact the tall, young soldier from the morning before, the one who had brought so many wounded into the aid station.

"Let me take the other man, soldier." Anson moved around him to where the dragged figure lay motionless on the ground.

"Thank you, sir."

The voice was calm, even-tenored—it occurred to Anson that he had not heard the soldier speak before. But then, the din of battle did not leave much opportunity for conversation. Now the pre-dawn stillness carved attention around each word.

"The hospital's back there." Anson pointed. "But I should just look at these men before we start." He bent to the figure on the ground. The uniform was shredded, the bare head small. Blood caked the eyes and bridge of the nose. He was little more than a boy. And he was dead. Probably had been dead for hours. When the tall soldier placed the other man on the ground, the limp body emitted a low groan. At least this one isn't a corpse, Anson thought, and with a finger he gently probed the gunshot wound in the neck. It might be only a flesh wound, but the loss of blood could be dangerous. This man was middle-aged, stocky, rough-bearded. Anson figured he must be as heavy as an anvil.

"What's your name, private?"

"Sir?"

"Your name?"

The tall soldier blinked slowly, then said, "John."

"John? What's the rest of it?"

Before the soldier could answer, a voice called sharply, "Don't move!"

Anson turned and saw two soldiers—likely pickets—aiming their muskets at them.

"It's all right. I'm a surgeon. We're taking this wounded man to the hospital." Anson indicated the body lying at the tall soldier's feet.

The pickets stepped closer. After staring at Anson's bloody smock, they nodded in unison and withdrew quietly into the last darkness.

"Just the one man, sir?"

Anson sighed. "The other's dead. A burial party will take care of him. Was he a comrade of yours?"

"No. But I reckoned he'd make it."

The darkness lifted rapidly. A pink tinge appeared on the horizon of low hills. Anson knew it was foolish to remain in the open. He ordered the tall soldier to take up the wounded man and follow him. Together they crossed the debris-strewn battlefield. Just as they reached the first white cluster of hospital tents near the barnyard, a drum roll rippled through the stillness.

"Baird! Where the hell have you been?"

Rawley's face was florid, his lips pulled back, revealing his incisors. "I told you not to leave the table! This isn't your cozy little practice back home." The blood splattered on his hands and forearms and smeared across his brow explained more than his words why he was so angry. And with a glance at the waiting wounded, Anson realized that every moment he'd been absent was a moment that couldn't be spared. He turned to tell the tall soldier where to deliver the wounded man, but both the soldier and his burden had moved on and were soon lost among the tents.

"Now that this blasted rain's stopped, we can go back to operating outside," Rawley said. "And work fast, dammit. We might be moving out anytime."

Recovering his instruments from the barn, Anson plunged back into his duty, joining the dozens of surgeons, stewards, and soldiers deputized for hospital detail who scurried about the barnyard, setting up the wrenched doors and oak barrels for surgery. Hours passed in a blur. The day grew warm, then hot. Sweat poured into his eyes, trickled through his moustache and beard. He hardly noticed that the sounds of battle had not resumed. No artillery pounded the earth, though sporadic musket cracks continued through the early morning. At one point, looking up from his table, Anson noticed two soldiers going through one of the viscous stacks of arms and legs. They reached in gingerly, then tossed limbs off to the side. Anson hurried over.

"What are you doing there?"

The men looked up sheepishly. One, corn-haired and freckled, with rubbery lips, immediately lowered his head again. His companion, who wore a beard dark and sharp as a spade under cheeks of a vivid red, spoke up mildly.

"Sorry, sir, it was only Jim's fancy. He's got it into his head to have his arm back. You see . . ."

The man's embarrassed hesitation irritated Anson. "I can't see anything if you don't tell me."

"Well, it's this way, sir." The soldier's cheeks seemed to drain of colour and immediately flush red again, as if he were continually dying and returning to life. His grey eyes fluttered. "Jim's a seaman, and the arm he's missing has his favourite tattoo on it. And Jim, why, he's afraid if he don't at least study it a while, he won't remember it exactly so as to get it made again just right."

The corn-haired soldier looked up, scowling. "But I don't see as how he 'spects us to know which one of these is rightly his. You can't tell the blood from a tattoo nohow."

"Mebbe we should just pick one," the bearded soldier said, the red in his cheeks almost reaching his eyes. "Jim's pretty sick. He might not look hard enough to know the difference."

Speechless, Anson turned heavily away. Just then, a violent commotion erupted in a near corner of the barnyard. A stocky civilian on a large white charger shouted at Josiah Rawley.

"I have the right to recover my property!" He yanked on the reins, but the more he did so, the more the horse seemed to react to the violence of his words. "And if it's in that barn, I aim to find out!"

"This is a hospital!" Rawley brandished his amputating knife. "And I am its commanding officer. No man's going to search for anything here unless I say so."

"Then say so before I go ahead and do it anyway. I've got a government contract here to round up dead horses and I'm going to need all my niggers to get the job done."

"Well, then, come back when the fighting's over. As far as I know, neither army's going anywhere just yet. Your dead horses will stay dead."

The civilian, a squat man in English riding breeches, glared out from under his slouch hat. He had a scruff of reddish beard, like a tilted crescent moon, running from ear to ear, framing what to Anson was one of the ugliest faces he'd ever seen. The cleft in the chin was dark and thick and gave the whole jaw a cloven hoof quality. The eyes were black and shining, tiny patters of grease. Briefly, the man curled his thin lips back and revealed a pair of sharp incisors. Then, with a curse, he savagely spurred his mount and charged straight at Rawley.

To Anson's amazement, his superior officer didn't move out of the way. He simply widened his stance and leaned forward slightly, as if about to whisper a secret. With a wild, pealing neigh, the horse rose up, mud flinging off its hooves. Its rider's grin almost split his face in two. Anson imagined the top of the skull was about to tear off at any second.

Once the horse quieted and dropped to a standing position, its graceful white head yanking from side to side and up and down without rest, Rawley spoke.

"If you're not careful, sir, your property, if you find it, will be gathering up your fine charger with all the other poor beasts. I suggest you water the animal."

The civilian leered out of his half-oval of beard as if out of a ring of fire. His voice came like a shout smothered by gunshot.

"And if you're not careful, I'll have my niggers dump you in a trench with all the rest of this rotting Yankee flesh."

With a sharp snap of the reins, he reared the horse around and sped off westward. For a half-minute, Anson watched the man sink on the darkening horizon like a stone. Then a familiar voice brought him around.

"Come on, back to it now." Rawley buried his right shoulder into a scattering group of civilian onlookers, many of whom appeared to believe that their contribution to the Union cause amounted to standing around and gawking. There were at least a dozen of them, and they'd likely come down from the surrounding hillsides after the battle, as nonchalantly as if they'd chosen to stroll after a picnic. But the ladies, at least, in their feathered hats and wide-hipped gowns, were shocked enough to hold perfumed handkerchiefs to their noses. Anson could hardly abide the presence of civilians, but then, the war was still new to most people, still a matter of romance to be followed like a theatrical production. Try as he might, however, he could not appreciate the civilians' looks of horror, for in these lay only the common sense human response to misery and death. To anyone, surely even to a general, the battlefield now was horrifying.

He approached one of the men, a particularly delicate-seeming fellow in a clean linen suit and straw boater whose pinched face wore a curious mixture of superiority and disgust.

"As long as you're here," Anson said, "you might as well pitch in. You could take water to the men, at least." He pointed to the ever-growing group of wounded lying flat on their backs or seated at the edge of the barnyard.

The man's nostrils dilated as he glanced at the wounded.

"Thank you, no," he said. A crack of a rifle sounded in the far distance. The near-simultaneous loud groan of a soldier who was being lifted onto Anson's table made it seem as if the man had been struck again. The sound backed the civilian away. He spoke softly to a pretty young woman with long flaxen hair who stood near him, her eyes wet, her chin trembling.

"Come, Dora, I've seen enough to write my article."

A journalist! As far as Anson was concerned, there was no lower breed. But as he was about to call the man a scavenger, the pretty woman stepped forward, pushing back the ruffled sleeves of her gown.

"I . . . I would like to help. I had no idea of what . . . of . . . oh, it's awful. Please, tell me what I can do."

Softened, Anson led the woman over the manured ground to where a steward was tearing strips of cloth for bandages.

"This lady wishes to help," Anson said. "Find her a suitable task, Clavett, please."

The steward, whose face was like sodden paper with two large ink blotches on it, spoke dully. "Help? What for, miss? You ought to go home and take all these useless dandies with you. They're only getting in our way."

The young woman bridled. She lifted her chin and spoke with resolve. "I do not intend to be in the way. I intend to be of service to these poor men."

Clavett smiled at Anson, then said, "All right, miss, I guess you're in earnest. I'll find something for you to do. Even if you just visited with the wounded, that'd be a mercy to them."

A mercy. Anson could no longer connect the word to its meaning. Mercy was what happened back home when an old and respected member of the community died in bed after a long illness. Mercy was what had come to each of his parents in turn, what should come to all souls in the fullness of time. He knew he could never think of mercy like that again. Not here. Not in a place worse than any nether world he'd read about in his beloved classics. Anson watched the young woman slip away, like Persephone, except with blood and not the seeds of pomegranates soon to besmirch her palms. Placing a hand to his side to fight off another piercing cramp, Anson made his way back to his operating table.

The stench grew by the hour. The gases of decomposition were being released from the dead still lying in the field, and the heat only made matters worse. Anson swayed a little from the pain in his stomach. His feet ached. His shoulders slumped heavily. And yet the damaged bodies kept appearing on the tables, the same quick decision about whether to amputate was made, the smell of chloroform no longer dulling the sickening odour flowing off the amputated limbs. Anson's strength for pulling lead out of wounds, when he could find it at all, had dwindled to almost nothing. He muttered phrases of bucolic Latin to try to stay alert.

It rained heavily for an hour in the afternoon, but they did not move the tables again; tarps and blankets were set up on poles to shelter the area of the surgery. In any case, Anson barely knew how the day unfolded outside of his own unceasing tasks. A sudden increase in the lines of groaning men he understood vaguely to be the result of a truce for exchanging wounded—a positive development from the human point of view, but Anson disliked the extra work. He wondered if he'd ever be done with cutting through tissue and sawing through bone. Exhausted, sickened, he berated the well-dressed onlookers, including a few women clothed in their most delicate finery, for not offering assistance. But they seemed to be in a state of mute and motionless disgust. With considerable gratitude and relief, Anson greeted the tall soldier's sudden reappearance.

The young man hadn't been there a few minutes ago, and now he was. And the result restored Anson's vigour. Almost as soon as he set another wounded man down on the table, the soldier took up a cloth and administered the anaesthetic. He did so firmly and without fuss, seemingly unmoved by the patients' fears and struggles. In the general miasmic atmosphere, with men groaning and crying out and awful stenches flowing across the torpid forms on the ground and in the crowded canvas tents of the barnyard, Anson felt himself lifted by the young soldier's steady presence, his lean face, surprisingly calm-looking despite the rough, broad scar on one cheek that suggested some act of violence. When time permitted, he vowed that he'd find out the man's regiment and secure for him a commendation.

The day ground on. Now some of the wounded, with the protection of shock having given way to severe pain, lashing the nerves and burning like hot wires, begged to have a limb removed. Anson ceased putting down his knife or rinsing it between surgeries; he simply held it between his teeth as another soldier was placed on the table. Then he explored yet another wound—most were serious fractures caused by minie balls, and it was difficult often to find the track of the lead, the entrance and exit wounds being wildly disparate. His fingers probed with increasing roughness as fatigue weakened him. The tall soldier's assistance became vital. He proved remarkably adept at calming agitated patients with nothing more than a calm, steady look and a firm grip. Before long, Anson asked him to hold his fingers on arteries during the amputations; the soldier's composure made the application of tourniquets unnecessary.

As dusk fell, Rawley decided not to move the tables back into the barn because it was overcrowded with wounded. Sperm-oil candles set up on barrel tops burned a faint, flickering light. Anson, for his part, was relieved to remain outside, despite the stench and insufficient lighting; the sense of vastness conveyed by the night and stars helped keep his duty in perspective. No matter how difficult the work, how exhausted his body, he knew he was but a single man with limited power. Besides, he had already observed that the open air seemed to help the wounded somehow, perhaps because the wind dispersed the miasma.

The young soldier, too, with his firm hand, made the long night bearable. Even on a few occasions when Anson began to make mistakes, the soldier lightly coughed or shifted his body. Once, when Anson uncharacteristically began cutting away too much tissue from around a bone, he even spoke.

"I've noticed that you generally leave more skin than that."

Anson shook his head, wiped his eyes, asked for the candle to be lowered.

"Thank you," he said after a few seconds. "You've just saved this man a great deal of grief."

The soldier pulled back with the candle, his face briefly rivered with the light.

The work continued. Anson came to depend heavily upon the soldier's help, but the surgery was relentless. Some time after midnight, Anson paused and looked up from the table. From far across the fields, beyond the woods, came a low rumble and tramping, the sound of troops on the move. What did it mean? Anson turned, but the tall soldier wasn't there. A new man, just as young, very pale, his face a wilting blossom, looked down at the wounded man in amazed disgust.

"The man who was here before you," Anson said. "Where did he go?"

Backing away from the table, as if terrified that he'd fall into the wound, the new man—Anson vaguely recognized him as a musician from his own regiment—said, "I don't know. I was just told to come over here. Sound asleep I was too. Haven't slept in days. It ain't fair."

Anson made a brief prayer for strength, clutched at his stomach for the hundredth time, and returned to work.

By the time another daybreak approached, he noticed his cutting had become less efficient, more ragged; he could not help it. Pain flared across his shoulders, down his spine—the rheumatism back in full force. Latin was only a dead language now, as dead as everything else around him.

"Here's another, Sam," he said to the assistant surgeon in charge of registering the dead as he lifted a body from the table.

The surgeon's reply was drowned in a burst of shouting, followed by the pounding of a horse in gallop. Anson looked to the east. The sky had lightened slightly but he could see nothing against it. The dark seemed oddly still, alive with unseen forces.

"What in tarnation was . . ."

"Shh! Listen!" Anson said.

The pounding of hooves surrounded them. Anson whirled. Voices shouted the air into fragments. Then a dark mass exploded a few feet to the left, a terrible long screeching neigh ripping down the sky.

"Don't shoot, you damned fool!" someone ordered.

Anson stared toward the clusters of grimy tents, each one full to overflowing with wounded. In fact, much of the overflow still lay on straw inside the barnyard fence rails, very much in the horse's path. They'd better shoot it, Anson thought, scrambling toward the tents, or it's going to trample somebody.

A torch blazed up, rolled like a burning eyeball through the dark. Someone shouted for it to be doused. A few swinging lanterns emitted a dull yellow light. In its muted glow, the powerful charger reared up, kicking its front legs. The shadowy forms of men flung back and forth.

Then Anson saw it. Briefly but vividly. A rider lay along the horse's neck, his bare head a shifting stain against the white hide. Then the horse and body plunged into the surrounding dark once more.

Seconds later, a shot rang out, crisp, resonant, like a single toll of a church bell. The living dark grew placid. Slowly, out of the silence, crawled the familiar groans of the wounded, for whom a runaway horse meant nothing, not even a chance to put them out of their misery. Anson heard low voices not far off, and walked painfully toward them on swollen feet.

A group of soldiers stood loosely around the regimental surgeon. Even in the dim lantern light, Josiah Rawley's gaunt face glowed savagely. In his hand he held a pistol—his arm rested across his chest with the pistol set on his opposite shoulder. It was a curious, statue-like posture, but Anson could see how exhausted his superior was.

"I gave an order not to shoot," said a young major, stepping up to the surgeon.

"My apologies." Rawley lowered his arm from his shoulder. "I didn't hear the order."

Startled, the major simply nodded. Then the whole group turned its attention to the dead horse.

"Sir." The major addressed Rawley in a grave tone. "I think you'll want to take a look at this."

Anson followed a few more paces into the darkness, then knelt beside the surgeon over a body on the dew-damp ground.

The light came on, grey and thin. The lantern shone less vividly by the minute.

The dead man was not in uniform. He lay flat on his back, one arm tight against his side, the other flung out, as if to point at the terrifying approach of death. His cloth shirt hung in shreds over his chest and his breeches were down around his thighs, the long leather belt almost completely detached from the waist. In both his clenched hands sprouted clutches of horsehair. Anson recognized the wild, laughing grin that covered the man's scratched and bloodied face. It was as terrible a death mask as he'd ever seen, but the body contained a grimmer secret: the man's genitals had been hacked off—only a bloody stump of gristle remained.

"Like somethin' a Indian would do," a soldier said calmly. "Only we ain't in Indian territory."

After a brief examination, Rawley determined that the man had died of severe blood loss. Then he suggested that the major take the matter up with someone higher in the chain of command.

"This man's a civilian," Rawley said grimly. "He had a contract for gathering up dead horses."

They all looked at the fallen charger, which had collapsed into almost a perfect kneeling posture, its eyes shut as if in a gentle sleep. But blood drenched both flanks and spotted its neck, destroying all thoughts of gentleness.

No one spoke for a moment. Their breath hung faintly between them. Then a man with a long, thick beard parted in the middle stepped into the light. He did not wear a uniform. Instead, his thick chest appeared between the open sides of a long woollen coat that reached almost to his boot tops. When he spoke, his voice resonated with a heavy Scots brogue, which nevertheless contained a curious jocular quality. Overall, he gave the impression of the sun breaking through a dark bank of cloud.

"It'll be a fine day. If ye don't mind, major, I'd like to do a study of the horse before ye take it away. I canna think who has the contract now, but if the animal could only be kept like this . . ."

The man lowered himself to his haunches and squinted through a gap between the thumb and forefinger of one hand.

"What are you on about, man?" Rawley bristled.

"Aye, if ye can give me a few hours, I'll just bring the wagon up." He stood and backed slowly away from the horse, his hand still over his eyes.

"You have no authority to be here," Rawley said. "'This is a hospital and civilians are suffered here only when I . . ."

The Scotsman turned. Calmly, he said, "My authority comes from General McClellan." He held out a small card, one of the fashionable cartes de visite.

Rawley squinted at it in the oyster-coloured pre-dawn light.

"Photographer? For the army?"

"That's right."

Rawley seemed on the verge of either spitting or yelling. "And what blasted use to the Republic is a photograph of a murdered slave owner's dead horse? I suppose you'll be wanting the corpse left here too."

The Scotsman smiled. He had a broad, strong face. The skin around his eyes crinkled as he stroked the forked ends of his beard.

"Nay, that won't be necessary. There's no ee much of the sublime in that. If he were a soldier? Nay, not even then. I dinna ken the public is ready for something quite so terrible."

"Baird, we have work to do." Rawley turned and stomped off.

After a last wondering look at the dead man, Anson followed.

At his back, he heard the young major give orders for the body and horse to be left.

Once again, Anson resumed his operating. Somehow the murder renewed his strength, made his commitment to life even stronger, his sense of duty to the Union even more important. Certainly the daylight improved the accuracy of his incisions.

Even so, the tall soldier's reappearance early in the morning reassured him.

"Ah, John," Anson said cheerfully. "Come to lend a hand again? Good man."

The soldier's face hovered in the air, the cheeks, brow, and jaw blackened with dirt, no doubt from burial detail.

But the detail must have rattled him, for his composure was gone. His large hands trembled, he glanced up regularly in alarm, and he did not speak at all. From time to time, he lightly touched the wound on his cheek and paused, as if remembering something. His lips were flecked at the corners with dried spittle and he kept holding his bare forearms out before him and turning them slowly over, as if searching for a wound that hadn't broken the skin. But he helped as best he could when called to it, and Anson was generally too preoccupied to worry over the tall soldier's altered behaviour.

❖ ❖ ❖

The morning of the 19th proved very fine, clear and warm. Most of the able-bodied troops had assembled in readiness for an advance or attack, but that still left a small army of wounded in the tents and farm buildings and on the ground near the operating tables. Along with everyone else, Anson learned of the enemy's departure from the field. The marching and wheel-grinding audible through the night and past daybreak were exactly what they sounded like—a retreat. But Anson did not know whether that meant victory for the Union—he could hardly think so, given the carnage. Nonetheless, the retreat encouraged him. The last thing he needed was a fresh supply of wounded.

A pungent, putrid smell of rot consumed the day. The thousands of dead soldiers still lying in the field bloated and turned black. Their bowels emptied. And since most of the men also suffered with Anson's malady, the air became diarrheic, thick and foul enough to seem almost solid. The civilian onlookers soon retreated—at least most of the fine ladies and gentlemen picnickers did—those who had crowded the hillsides to watch the battle two days before.

But when Anson, unable to sleep and unable to remain amid the suffering, again headed for the large tree on the horizon, he noticed that other civilians had embarked on work of their own. He stopped a short man in a bowler hat rifling the pockets of a dead Union soldier.

"You! What are you doing there?"

The man straightened up, his white-gloved hands empty. He grinned wolfishly, then dabbed a lace handkerchief to his nose.

"The smell is very loud today, sir. Very loud, indeed."

Anson looked at the dead soldier. His young face was almost coal-black. A mass of flies crawled over his smashed torso. The boots had been removed from his feet.

"What were you doing to this man?" Anson tried to put anger into his voice, but the effort left him spent. He barely maintained his balance.

"Oh, I was touching him only in his service, I assure you. He might be one of the sensible ones with a coupon, you see."

"A coupon?"

The man lightly brushed a fly away from his pink mouth and pointed to an ordinary-looking wagon a short distance behind him. His reedy voice carried an odd mixture of enthusiasm and pride. "For the embalming. If he had possessed the foresight, for the sake of his loved ones back home, to have purchased one of Mr. Greaver's coupons, then his corpse would have been preserved and shipped home in a lovely zinc-lined coffin." He kicked at the body, raising a handful of flies. "But alas, he did not avail himself of the opportunity when it was presented to him. Others, no doubt, were wiser, more considerate of their families."

Anson followed the man's gaze over the rolling, ravaged fields. Clusters of negro contrabands were busily recovering corpses for burial. A few dozen feet away, a long line of dead Union soldiers appeared like a festering snake on the torn ground. Two civilians stood over them. Some kind of black apparatus—like a survey tripod, only bulkier at the top—was set up nearby, a few feet from a delivery wagon draped in a tarp. Anson recognized the burly, bearded Scotsman from earlier. What had he said he was? A photographer?

Remembering daybreak's runaway horse, Anson turned and walked back in the direction of the barnyard. It took him several minutes to find the spot. When he did, he discovered that the mutilated corpse was gone, though the charger remained in its gentle kneeling posture, its flanks and head swarming with flies, their buzzing as loud as bee-hum. Anson wondered if the Scotsman had taken the study he'd wanted. Sadly, he knelt and stared into the horse's face. Somehow its closed eyes seemed dimly alive with terror still. No doubt some investigation of the murder would follow, now that the Rebels had retreated. Anson breathed deeply and the effort set off another violent bout of coughing. He raised his hands to his mouth. His own blood mixed again with the dried blood and pus of the hundreds of wounded he'd tended over the past two days.

When he recovered, Anson sensed that he was not alone. He stood and, looking through watered eyes, saw the blurred image of a soldier. In a few seconds, the image solidified.

"John?"

The soldier said nothing, merely stared hard at the air. Though blood had spattered his face and his torn uniform resembled a splotch of stains, something more than fatigue and sadness haunted his eyes, something Anson knew he did not feel himself. It wasn't fear, but an unequivocal plea for assistance.

"Is there something wro . . ."

Before Anson could finish the question, two officers rode up swiftly. The older man, a sergeant with a spare, dark face and a neat goatee, dismounted carefully, as if exiting a rowboat. Bloody muslin bandages swathed his right shoulder. He grimaced as he studied the ground around the charger. Then he said something inaudible to the younger man, an unwhiskered, red-cheeked lieutenant who immediately swung down from his horse with fluid ease.

"I did leave orders, sir. Obviously they weren't followed."

The sergeant turned.

"What do you men know about this?"

Anson wiped sweat off his forehead with the back of his hand. "Sir?" His voice came out in a croak.

"There's supposed to be a body here. Of a civilian. He'd been killed in a . . ." The sergeant paused, as if aware of the absurdity of his forthcoming phrase, under the circumstances. "In a gruesome fash-ion." His eyes roamed the field briefly. He cleared his throat and spat.

"It was here," Anson said. "This morning."

"Hell, I know that. But why isn't it here now?"

"Perhaps a burial party picked it up," the lieutenant said.

The sergeant grunted. "Christ. As if I don't have better things to do than to care who killed a goddamned farmer who was fool enough to stay around here during a fight. Have his niggers been rounded up, at least?"

The lieutenant nodded.

"Probably some reb killed him for his boots. They sure as hell didn't leave any on our boys." The sergeant squinted hard at the tall soldier. "Are you wounded, son?"

"He's on medical detail," Anson said quickly. "I'm a surgeon."

The sergeant frowned.

"After the battle," Anson continued. "During it, he brought many wounded into my aid station from the front lines."

"Is that so?" The sergeant appraised the tall soldier coldly from head to foot. "That's the best fit they could find for you, is it?"

The tall soldier's chest strained at the fabric of his uniform; several long tears in the sleeves and the thighs of the trousers exposed his skin.

"He used most of his uniform for bandages," Anson said. "This was the best replacement we could find."

The sun burned fiercely. Shadows lay bunched at the officers' boots; they seemed to stand in pools of blood. The creak of a wheel sounded nearby. Anson watched the photographer's wagon bump over the battlefield like a wounded crow. Sunlight glinted off a few buttons and bayonets of the dead. A group of ragged contrabands bearing shovels over their shoulders trudged between the bodies. Anson could easily picture the weary endurance etched in the sweat-slickened faces of the runaway slaves, their skin as black as the earth that crumbled off the shovel blades.

The flies buzzed, louder and louder. The officers' horses flicked their tails rapidly.

Anson stared after the contrabands, seeing their faces hanging like charred petals at the edges of every important and unimportant movement of the troops. The faces were always there, present but forgettable, linked like a chain that had risen out of the soil to attach itself somehow to the army, a chain of faces—desperate, hungry, miserable, yet somehow radiant with hope—that seemed to grow as silently and inexorably as the stars at the onset of dark. And though Anson had never really focused on any one face in particular, its look was familiar to him, with its almost unbearable aura of suffering mixed with resolve. Suddenly, with a shock of recognition, Anson knew that he had focused on that aura, that he had seen it and identified it and yet not comprehended the truth of his own senses and instincts. He looked at the tall soldier.

The man stood as if guyed to the torn earth, except for the one arm that he kept lifting from his side and gazing at, turning it like meat on a spit. Flies crawled over the blood on his forehead and one stuck like a hardened tear to one eyelid over one slightly bulbous eye. But the tall soldier did not brush the flies away.

From far inside the earth Anson could hear the contrabands' shovels turning the bloodied ground. Then the scraping sounded across the horizon and he looked for the source of it without success. But when he brought his gaze back to the tall soldier at last—who still hadn't brushed the flies away, who wore them just as a scarecrow wears its stitches—Anson heard the scraping again. And he knew it for the terrible longing that it was, not for the peace of the dead but for the struggle of the living.

The sergeant scowled. "We'd better find that body, lieutenant. Or find out for certain what happened to it. There'll have to be a report." He spat again, then nodded at Anson while raising a hand to his bandaged shoulder. "Perhaps this was some of your work. I don't wish to keep you any longer from continuing it."

Now Anson himself couldn't move. But it was a kind of exhilaration that paralyzed him. He forgot the ache in his spine and in his swollen feet because now he understood more than the guilt of the tall soldier standing at his side. In the foul, clotted air of the slaughter of two great armies, Anson suddenly tasted and swallowed the truth, which wasn't only a window flung open on the battle's murk and smoke and blood, but a window flung open on the depth of his own commitment. And when he finally moved closer and looked into the soldier's eyes, his open, unblinking eyes set in the scarred and dirtied face, the man's expression had truly become a reflection of Anson's own. All at once, Anson saw that he and the soldier were not separate at all, except that one face—in the slightest jutting of the lower lip, the slightest bulging of the eyes, but more in the sheer terror of the expression—was negroid, another link in the war's great dragging, breeding chain. Now the abstract cause assumed a living form. And that form needed protection.

Without analysis or logic, with the deepest call of instinct, Anson understood that he had been chosen to provide it, if not by some divine power, then by the ineluctable and curious justice of circumstance. The dead Latin stirred in his blood, sprang to life on his tongue. But it was plain English he uttered.

"Let's go, John. We have work to do."

II
September 18, the battlefield at Antietam

Alexander Gardner studied the mutilated body for a moment, and stroked the forked end of his beard as he considered whether such a gruesome corpse—and of a civilian too—could be of any artistic or commercial use to him. It would be one thing to display photographs of dead soldiers in a New York gallery, quite another to exhibit a large stereo view of some farmer who'd had his manhood hacked off. Then again, war was war, business was business, and there was no telling what the public might stomach, or, indeed, even relish. As for art, well, Gardner understood the perils of playing that game too cannily. Best get to work and think about art, the public, and the other incidentals later.

He lowered himself to his haunches and made a small frame by placing his hands around his eyes. A disbelieving voice sounded from above him.

"You canna be serious, Alex. For Christ's sakes, man, leave it alone."

"Jim, you surprise me. I dinna peg you for a maidenly sort." Gardner flashed his assistant a big grin, just so he wouldn't take offence. He knew James Gibson was a touchy one, but he also knew there was no one he'd rather have with him in the field. Gibson was a gifted man with the camera, and no mistake. And he could work quickly with the plates too, which was even more important. His assistant didn't know it yet, but Gardner aimed to take most of the studies; he had to be the one behind the lens. There might never come another chance like this.

Gardner handled the body by the legs, not wanting to touch the head, which was grinning and greasy as a gargoyle soaked in oil, and hoped that his fellow photographer would rise to the challenge. He was no more maidenly than a Glasgow publican, after all.

"Come on, Jim. They'll be back for it soon. I only want to shift it a little ways. Till the sun's up."

For the truth was, Gardner had seen a mass of dead rebels not too distant. He realized that he and Gibson could dump this body among the rebels and nobody'd be certain to come near it, at least not for hours. By then, there'd be light enough. And he'd have his first prize stereo of the great battle: Slave Owner's Terrible Last Moments. Or something akin to that. It wasn't the time for thinking up fancy titles.

Gardner noticed Gibson look past him. His eyes measured the progress of the light. All around them in the large, churned-up field, the low groans and gasps of wounded men broke into the monotonous droning of the flies, faded away briefly, then started up again.

"We'll be seen," Gibson said. "And if we're caught, Alex Gardner, you'll no ee get any studies of dead soldiers. That's what we're here for, isn't it?"

"Ach, you'd think you were the dapper Brady himself with your fussing and worrying. I'll do it myself. Just bring up the wagon, will you. There's little doubt the Rebels have gone, what with all that ruckus in the night, but we'd better be sure before we go any closer to where the worst fighting happened."

Gardner could see his assistant's nostrils flaring, but he suspected that the quiet all around them, not to mention the dead, checked his tongue against a slanderous rejoinder. He only grunted and pointed to the horse. "And what about that? Just look at the animal, kneeling there like it was in the stable at Bethlehem. You'd no ee take it for dead. That'd make a fine study."

He was right, of course. It was a handsome white charger, its front legs gracefully tucked under its blood-soaked body, its noble head turned to the side. The poor creature looked to be living still, unlike the hundreds of others scattered around, most of them tangled in their reins so tight that they might have been tangled in their own bloody guts. But Gardner hadn't time for dead horses now, no matter what they looked like.

"They willna move the man's horse," he said. "It's him they'll soon be after. And they can have him too, just after I get my study."

Gardner quickly looked around. It was still dark enough for cover and he wouldn't need more than ten minutes. Keeping his hold on the legs, he dragged the body toward the dead rebels, deliberately avoiding its ghastly expression. If not for the heavy smell of blood, he thought the corpse might open its mouth and shout at any second.

No one saw him as he moved slowly toward his goal. He knew then, with Lee reportedly in retreat and the sun rising, that fortune was truly on his side. It would be a bonny day, the exposures would be wonderful. Even here, in a position behind the front lines, and in the grey dimness, he could see what a terrible carnage had occurred. It did not leave him unmoved. But sentiment, for a soldier or a photographer, was a luxury to be enjoyed when the work was done. And his was only starting. Fast work it would have to be too. With the Rebels gone, the army would waste little time in clearing its dead from the field. Already Gardner was gagging on the stench. It hung so putrid and solid that he knew no burial party would linger over their duty.

When he reached the sprawl of dead rebels, he paused for a while to consider them. Already some were bloated, their hands and feet twice their usual size, their faces black as any negro—one wore a fountain of bloodstains from throat to forehead, another, likely caught in the act of preparing to reload, had the end of a cartridge clamped between his teeth.

The light came on steadily. Gardner hesitated, one hand on the rough bottom of his long beard. He thought it an odd matter that this same sun, responsible for blotting out all traces of individuality from a man, for staining and corrupting his face, should also be the agent for preserving his last earthly appearance forever. He placed the body carefully between two rebels, building a sort of breastwork of their corpses to hide the civilian from sight. Then he turned to the east and squinted at the wagon's ponderous approach. A low, broken mist like a ghostly fence wreathed the torn earth. Except for the groans of the wounded, all was still. Then Gardner realized why his assistant moved the wagon so slowly. Even from many rods away, he could hear the faint clinking of the glass bottles of chemicals inside the wagon—it was a shivery, graveyard sort of sound, and for a moment it unnerved him, even more than the piteous complaints of the wounded.

The moment passed. Gardner deemed it advisable not to remain near these particular dead. In an hour, he and Gibson could begin in earnest. But he knew there were portions of the field that contained more dramatic photographic possibilities. It was, after all, extensive, covering over a square mile from the woods and fields in the north to the fight at the creek bridge in the south. The day before, watching from the hillsides, he had seen that the fighting had been fiercest along the pike, in the vicinity of the little whitewashed church. And early reports had mentioned a great slaughter in a cornfield as well as along a sunken road. Later, should time permit, he would return here to make a study of the mutilated slave owner. Ha! If this day did not mark his break from that popinjay Brady, it would be no fault of Providence! Here was glory worthy of any man's craft. And yet, when he considered the violations performed on this body, when he regarded the bloody pulp at the groin, all thoughts of glory seemed meaningless. But he who lives by the cruel hand dies the same.

The shadow of Gardner's horse fell on the dead man's face, turning it as black as his Rebel comrades'.

Jim whispered down. "If you're quite finished rearranging bodies, Alex, I could use a last cup of coffee before we start."

Gardner nodded. By the time Jim had had his coffee, perhaps back at the hospital where the cooks would doubtless have pots on permanent boil, they'd know for certain that the Rebels had retreated. Then it would be time enough, and light enough, for glory.

After walking a hundred yards south, the two photographers came upon a grim scene. Gardner was thankful for the slow approach of the light, else he might have been duty-bound to record the misery of that foul barnyard. The wounded and the sleeping lay mixed in among the dead, so closely that the bodies formed one large body that groaned, wept, snored, vomited, cried out in agony—no foot of earth was uncovered but for the area around the surgeons' tables. Large canvas tents greasy with shadows stood in the field outside the barnyard fence. Several wagons were being emptied of supplies—blankets mostly, but also bandages, bottles of pills, and liquids. Apart from the surgeons, the few men who were moving at all were moving slowly, as if fighting through molasses.

As Gibson hitched their horse to a rail and headed toward a leaden-faced negro cook stirring a pot, Gardner stepped up to one of the operating tables. A ragged, pointy-jawed soldier lay there, his eyes like raisins pushed into lard. His thin lips either trembled or muttered a prayer, Gardner couldn't tell. A sort of cone was placed over the soldier's nose and mouth and some liquid dripped into it. Then the surgeon, a bearded man of middle years with a strong nose and prominent brow, both already besmirched with blood, took a double-edged knife from between his teeth and bent closer to his patient. Soon the surgeon's head and that of his assistant, a very tall, long-limbed soldier in a ripped uniform, hovered so close over the anaesthetized figure that Gardner could not be sure who held the knife. Even when the sawing of the thigh began, it seemed that both men moved the implement. Gardner didn't hear them speak at all. But when the sawing was done—a dull, disturbing sound that made Gardner grit his teeth—the surgeon and not the assistant turned with the leg in his hand and looked straight at the photographer.

Ah, had he been beneath the cloth at that moment, with enough sun to let it stream through both lenses, Gardner knew he'd have captured a face that revealed the very meaning of warfare. True, it was an ordinary enough face in respect to the features—the nose and brow, though fine, were not exceptional, and sunken cheeks and bloodshot eyes were sadly familiar in most men of the time. But the feeling behind the eyes, the sense of a barely controlled agony, made all the more remarkable because the eyes did not seem to take anything in! Oh, what a stereo he'd have made from that face. Though the surgeon looked right at him for several seconds, Gardner was convinced the man was not seeing him. He drifted like a sleepwalker to a tall pyramid of bloodied, fly-greasy limbs and rested the leg on top as if careful to maintain the balance of the whole. When he drifted back, he limped slightly, perhaps out of sympathy for the soldier whose leg he'd just removed. Gardner decided, then and there, that he'd find this surgeon again, either this day or the next, and get him to pose. But the dead had to come first.

This thought brought the stench in even more powerfully. Over by the tents, a sound of retching, deeply drawn out, almost made Gardner ill himself. He pulled his flask from his hip pocket and took a long slug of whisky to cleanse his palate.

He heard the drummers begin to call the troops to the day. Their rippling rhythm straightened the gravediggers up and stirred the able-bodied soldiers, who rose like spirits among the dead and wounded. Despite the preparations, Gardner heard rumours from hopeful soldiers that Lee had indeed retreated in the night. He found Gibson and said, "Let's start here. We'll just go back, take a few studies of dead soldiers and that unfortunate property owner, then go up to the front with the burial parties. I'm sure we can ask them to stop their work long enough to get our exposures."

Gibson grumbled something about wasting time, but Gardner ignored him. Maybe it was the whisky, or the rapidly improving quality of the light, but his confidence was riding high. Conditions could not have been better. No man in the country—certainly not that half-blind Brady back in New York waxing his moustache tips—was better qualified and ready for this chance. Except maybe Gibson and Timothy O'Sullivan, but they were both taking Gardner's orders here. He knew, as well as Robert Owen himself had ever known the devilish machinations of the leisured classes, that he had enough time for everything if he just put himself in harness and set to work.

Even so, Gardner started that ripe morning in haste. Gibson, now that he'd had his fortifying coffee, proved every bit as eager, and together the two men were like children after butterflies in a meadow, except these butterflies were already pinned and still. Gardner decided right away to use only his stereo camera. That way, the gallery would have the most options for selling prints—stereo views, cartes de visite, and the big Imperials Brady's nobs liked so much. And Gardner didn't intend to take more than a single exposure from each angle; there was just too much ground to cover.

As soon as he'd settled on his first study—a Reb officer flat on his back with the brains spattered over his blackened face and his belly swollen like an observation balloon—he set Gibson to sensitizing the plates. Gardner knew it would be at least seven minutes before his assistant threw back the big tarp and scrambled out of the wagon, so he had just enough time to pick up a nearby rifle and stick it in the officer's open hand. He couldn't get the officer's fingers closed around the stock—they were too stiff—but it was a useful touch nonetheless.

The sun crept over the nearby tree line now, gushing light over the field, so Gardner fixed the camera and aimed it at the body. Then, with a long breath to calm himself, he stepped under the cloth and focused.

And there the dead officer was, black-faced and swollen, his dirty grey uniform open at the breast, the rifle in his hand. Only, of course, he was upside down, and it seemed for a few seconds that the dead officer floated out of a torn cloud, a terrible vengeance in his cold rifle.

Gardner ducked out from the cloth just as Gibson stepped backwards from the wagon with the plate fixed in its wooden holder. He shut the door and hurried over, his face tense.

"Come on, man!" Gardner urged, knowing full well that even an extra second could dry the collodion and render the plate useless.

"Do you want me tripping, Alex? I canna go any faster." His voice was a strained rasp already, and Gardner thanked the Lord for it. Say what he would about the man's cussed cantankerousness, James Gibson cared as much as Gardner did about getting the job done.

Gardner took the plate holder from him. Then he moved the focusing frame out of the way and put in the holder—it took him a little longer than usual to attach it to the camera, his hands trembled so. But he drew another deep breath and slid the front panel out of the holder, exposing the plate to the inside of the camera. Now came the moment of truth! He removed the two lens caps and he almost swore that he could hear the light flooding through—it was like a torrent of water every time, though he knew well enough that he heard only the blood pounding in his temples.

If the battlefield had been still earlier, it was frozen now as Gardner counted out the exposure. One, two, three . . . slow down, easy . . . four, five . . . go even, Alex, boy . . . eight, nine. Those fifteen seconds were the longest of his life. When the last number finally passed his lips, he replaced the lens caps and the holder's front cover. Then he looked up.

"Jimmy! Are you set?"

It was a foolish, unnecessary question, but Gardner put it with a smile. In fact, he couldn't wipe the joy off as he strode to the wagon.

"Don't be so daft, man," Gibson said. "Just give me the plate."

Gardner handed it over carefully. "We'll have to sink them all in glycerin till tonight. There's no ee time to heat them now."

"Aye." Gibson plunged back into the wagon, yanking the tarp behind him. Gardner could hear his assistant cussing a blue streak as he tied the tarp strings to his ankles, but he wasn't worried. Gardner knew that safelight couldn't be any safer even if he himself was the man working in it. Besides, he had to move the camera.

So an hour passed, unchanged but for the increased activity in the field. Several burial parties—a few consisting of negroes—dragged Gardner's potential studies away and placed them in shallow graves; individual soldiers out searching for comrades sometimes found them, picked them up, and moved away soberly to find whatever better resting places might be available. The photographer rushed from one body to another, all the while thinking that everything was happening too fast, that he couldn't delay going to the front lines any longer—there were bound to be even better studies there—but how long before the routine procedures of the army destroyed them? In his excitement, he took little interest in the activity around him.

Sometime before noon, however, Gardner witnessed a strange scene. A dozen yards to his left, a man in a fine suit and bowler, his hands in white gloves, was being threatened at knifepoint by a monkey-faced little fellow naked from the waist up. The two stood over the dead Rebel officer whose study had begun Gardner's day. Cautiously, he moved closer.

Monkey-face's lips pulled back to reveal mostly gums. A lock of oily hair hung over one yellow eye. He held the knife in his fist. "You git yore dad blamed paws offa this one. It's mine. Touch it again and you'll be dead on the ground too."

The gentleman yawned as he reached into his breast pocket and removed a small pistol. His neat moustache quivered slightly. He held the gun straight in front of him, his arm fully extended.

"I strongly suggest, my good man, that you find another officer." He sniffed, and scowled. "There are certain to be plenty for all. But this one's now the property of the Horace Greaver Embalming and Fine Casket Company."

Monkey-face brought the knifepoint so close to his face that it seemed he planned to put his own eye out. He squinted. "Greaver, you say? That the feller with the humpback? In the tent yonder?"

The gentleman grinned, exposing his sharp incisors. "Humpback? I believe you're referring to one of the metal canisters."

"Hunh?"

The gentleman sighed. "It's not a hump. It's one of the tanks for draining blood. Or for pumping the . . . ah . . . continual life into these distinguished fallen."

Monkey-face shrugged. "Wal, whatever it is, that feller said he'd pay good for officers brung into his tent. And I aim to git that money."

The gentleman, still grinning and holding the pistol out, said, "It seems we are working for the same fine establishment. And as I am not on commission . . ." He pocketed the pistol. "You may remove this hero from the field. But I warn you, there are competitors less patient than I. You would be wise to find a more . . . ah . . . persuasive weapon." He made a graceful sweeping gesture with one arm. "I'm certain a man of your obvious discernment can find something amid the armoury here gathered."

Monkey-face spat. Then, putting the knife between his teeth, he bent and took up the dead officer by the armpits.

The incident's open, naked demonstration of money lust appalled Gardner, but not for long. When he reflected on his own considerable worldly ambitions on this battleground, he couldn't exactly condemn others who also sought to improve their fortunes. After all, the fighting was over and the dead could hardly complain. With undiluted resolve, Gardner returned to the tripod, ducked under the cloth, and focused. Two dead Rebels, one's head leaning on the other's chest; he could perhaps come up with a title about dead brothers.

Dead Rebels? Gardner suddenly remembered. When he stepped out from the cloth and saw that Gibson had not left the wagon with a fresh plate, he looked to the south where he had hidden his "treasure." Human crows wandered everywhere, picking at corpses for one reason or another. Some negro gravediggers chanted low, in an unmelodic rhythm; above the sound, Gardner could hear each spade thrust in the earth. Where exactly was that line of dead Rebels?

Then the photographer saw a soldier bent over the bodies. Though Gardner stood fifty yards away, the soldier seemed closer; he was wrapped in the bright sunshine, carved by it into prominence, like the image on a print. And he was dragging a body out of the line!

Gardner took two quick steps forward as a shout formed and then died on his lips. Behind him, he heard the tarp draw back. A fresh plate! Now, of all times. Gardner looked at the camera, at the two Rebels posed fraternally on the gutted earth. Suddenly the awful reek of death washed over him, as powerful as the collodion on the plate. He swallowed deeply and almost staggered against Gibson as he rushed up.

"What is it, Alex? You canna be woozy like I am, man. It's a regular ether bath in that wagon. I almost passed out on this one."

"He's taking the corpse!" Gardner pointed, his mouth open.

Gibson put a hand over his eyes, as if he couldn't look at the world anymore except through some kind of lens. He shrugged.

"What of it? You'll never get Brady to print that one anyway. He probably won't even print the dead Federals."

"Brady? He's no ee the only one who can make and sell prints. You might be willing to work for him all your born days, but I dinna come to this country to be taken for a fool. What's the point of following the army if you're just going to let Brady make all the money off your talents? Wake up, Jim. We've got enough here to make a start on our own. Whatever Brady won't print and sell, all the better for us!"

Gibson handed Gardner the plate. "All right, captain," he said, referring to the honorary stripes Gardner's friendship with McClellan had earned him. "But you'd better hurry with this one before it dries."

At that moment Gardner knew James Gibson was with him and his fortune was made. It had taken only the saying of it.

Gardner dove back under the cloth. The world flipped upside down again. When he later returned to the light and started counting out the exposure, he could see, across the bereaved and scavenging, across the dead and wounded, the tall, long-limbed soldier carrying a body on his back toward the woods. By the time Gardner had whispered fifteen, the soldier had vanished into the trees.

❖   ❖   ❖

The stench worsened as the sun climbed. The droning of flies made a steady, sombre chorus over the fields, but it was loudest inside the enclosed space of the wagon, which sat in the heat-crinkled air like a block of black ice that melted without getting smaller. Gibson complained mightily.

"I canna keep the sweat from dripping off my forehead onto the plate. And when I can manage that, the damned flies get crawling all over it. You're just lucky, Alex, I can bring you anything worth using."

He liked to exaggerate, did Jim Gibson, but Gardner knew too well the delicate and frustrating problems he faced. So Gardner offered to sensitize a plate while he let his assistant take a study of some colonel's dead horse. Gardner soon regretted his generosity. Being inside that wagon was like being on the surface of the sun itself. He'd never known such breath-smothering heat. Sweat gushed out of every pore of his body, and he'd have almost preferred the stench of the festering flesh outside than the giddying fumes of the collodion. If the fumes weren't bad enough in themselves, they attracted so many flies it was nigh to impossible keeping them off the plates. Gardner's respect for Gibson grew immensely as he struggled to keep his dripping head away from the plate while savagely shooing flies away with his hands. Had they reversed roles for the day, Gardner doubted they'd have managed even half of the studies that they eventually made. Of course, he wasn't about to let Gibson know that. Fortunately, when he pushed past the tarp with the plate and walked dizzily to the camera, Gardner found his assistant in even worse shape. He had one hand over his nose and the other on a flask of whisky pressed to his lips. When he'd done drinking, he gave Gardner a ghastly, white look and said, "If it's all the same to you, Alex, I'd prefer the wagon. I dinna know how ye can stand it. It's like swallowing great gobs of pus out here."

By the time the two photographers reached the slaughter along the pike road near the whitewashed little church with the thatched roof, they had their system worked out. Soon enough they didn't even talk anymore. The light poured over the bloated corpses and smashed limbers, and the white church shone like a gull's wing against the black woods. A bonny day for photography. But Gardner knew he'd be a cold and heartless man if he hadn't paused amid all that carnage and considered the truth of what lay before him: brave men had died horribly, boys from modest backgrounds mostly, farm boys and fishermen and workers on both sides, dying for their beliefs while Brady's fine friends nibbled on squab and made grand noises about sending the Rebels back to Richmond. Gardner almost hated himself then for his excitement—nay, his joy—under the cloth. And yet, he thought about what his images might mean to a public far removed from the war's reality, and that spurred him on. Mostly he didn't even have to embellish; the dead were affecting enough, even if, as the day wore on, only Rebels and horses remained on the field. The burial parties worked quickly. Often Gardner had to ask them to take a break while he made his exposures, for any movement would blur the image. They obliged, no doubt out of curiosity at the photographer's presence, but not for long. Gardner couldn't blame them. It wasn't a ground well suited for lingering.

Gardner did not think of his stolen corpse again until later in the afternoon, when, recrossing the battleground of their first studies, which still resembled a massive broken tabletop left uncleared after some giant's hideous orgy of feasting, he and Gibson stopped once more at the fenced barnyard surrounded by greasy tents for some fortification. Little had changed. The surgeons still cut into bodies, the wounded lay about in solid piles of moaning agony, the graveyard with the plank headboards had grown just outside the fence beyond the cooks' tent. A few women, looking strange in their feminine apparel, placed cold cloths on foreheads, dispensed water and food, and generally comforted as best they could. Their courage and sense of duty so moved Gardner that the raspy voice at his ear startled like gunshot.

"Have you just come from out there?"

Gardner turned and recognized the bearded surgeon he had observed on his earlier visit. If the man had looked ravaged then, he seemed little more than nerve endings now. The torn sackcloth of his face, the eyes swimming in blood, the forearms so gore-caked that he might have just dipped them in a vat of guts: Gardner could hardly believe the surgeon possessed the strength to speak. He pointed weakly toward the battleground. Gardner nodded, half afraid the wake of air from his small gesture would knock the surgeon down.

"The tall soldier. The one who was helping me. You didn't see him?"

The urgency in the man's voice alarmed Gardner. He could hardly tell what answer the surgeon hoped for, but Gardner gave him the truth.

"I did. At least I believe so. I was some distance away."

The surgeon grimaced and clutched his stomach. "Excuse me, sir. One moment." He opened a small bottle, shook a pill into his hand, and quickly swallowed it. "What did you see exactly?"

The question took Gardner aback, but he saw no reason not to answer. "I saw him carrying a body into the wood."

The surgeon grabbed Gardner's elbow. His grip reached to the bone. "That man has done noble service. He has saved many from a lingering, painful death. If you are asked about him, I urge you . . ."

A cry of pain from behind spun him around. When he turned back and looked in Gardner's eyes again, he spoke in a hoarse whisper.

"Don't mention to any officer that you saw him carrying a body. By my oath, I ask this out of humanity . . . and . . . justice. If you believe, sir, in what the Union stands for, I urge you . . ."

"I don't understand. Why would an officer ask me about him? Many soldiers are carrying bodies today."

And then, with a jolt, Gardner recalled what body it was, and the manner of the death, and he was almost ashamed to admit that he saw his chance and took it. But the camera was not a toy, no more than a bible was a plaything to a preacher. And this surgeon, his weary, pained face, would make a wonderful study. Gardner struck a bargain.

"Agreed. But I have a single condition. If at some point I wish to make a study of you, you will pose for me?"

Already the photographer felt he had trapped a kind of ghost in his camera—something in this man seemed to flow out of him. He conceded listlessly to Gardner's bargain and they shook on it. The photographer wondered how he could ever forget that firm handshake of blood and pus. The surgeon did not appear to notice Gardner's lingering gaze, however. Only when he turned away did Gardner see that the surgeon held a severed lower leg in his other hand—it seemed to lead him like a child back into a nightmare.

Gardner was to get his study two days later, at a different field hospital, a mile to the south of the previous one. Apparently the bearded surgeon had moved as well, and stood awkwardly amid a group of half-collapsed canvas tents barely covering several dozen wounded. Smoke rose from a nearby cook fire. Gardner heard a rough snoring. A light breeze blew the usual death stench over the ground and tents. By then, the photographer had heard tell of an investigation about that mutilated corpse. Apparently, the dead man had been of much use to McClellan and Pinkerton in their gathering of information about the enemy. It was, according to rumours Gardner had heard, a delicate matter, given that Maryland had not yet committed to either side in the conflict. But no one asked the photographer anything. And the truth was, by September 21, Gardner was so puffed up with the success of his venture, and so immured to the misery and carnage all around him, that he gave little thought to that one farmer's corpse.

And yet, when he bid the surgeon be still as he ducked under the cloth, Gardner was certain that, just over his study's shoulder, peering out through a thin pillar of smoke, stood the very soldier whose actions had motivated the bargain he had struck with the surgeon. But when Gardner stepped out from the cloth, no soldier remained. And he half-doubted, despite all his subtle craft, that the exposed plate would capture anything but a flattened cornfield running away beneath a blank and pitiless sky.

III

September 19, the battlefield at Antietam

In the middle of a charred, broken field a hundred yards north of a barn serving as a Union field hospital, Horace Greaver swatted impatiently at a buzzing cluster of flies. If only the blasted lazy fools from the Quartermaster corps, he thought, would stop bringing in useless corpses, this day looked promising and profitable indeed. Dozens of corpses had been brought from the battlefield to the side of his large, black tent, and the fetid air told him many more would be arriving. Ah, but these lazy fools . . .

"If they don't have a coupon," Greaver said, "I don't want them. This one's no good to me. Take it back where you found it." He pulled the brim of his worn bowler down over his bespectacled, watery, bloodshot eyes and turned away from the slack-jawed teamster's assistant.

"Back? But I just drug it from clear over there, by the crick."

"Did you even look for a coupon first, as I instructed you?" Greaver drew an invisible tiny square in the air before the man's eyes, then angrily snatched it away. "Don't waste my time. If you can't be bothered to look for coupons, then at least bring me officers. Preferably Union. But Rebels too, if the rank's high enough. The higher, the better."

Greaver pulled a watch and chain from his vest and squinted at it. The truce for exchanging wounded had been on for nearly an hour. Soon he would set about exchanging the dead Rebel officers he'd managed to recover for any Union officers that his Confederate counterpart had collected. While it wasn't impossible to collect a fee from a grieving Southern family for the safe return of their hero's preserved body, it was altogether easier to restrict such dealings to the North.

He returned to the naked corpse set up on a few bare planks propped on two large wooden barrels. With the last of the blood already drained through the jugular vein, Greaver set about raising the carotid artery. He drew an imaginary line from the chest to a point midway between the jaw and mastoid process, all the while contemplating the exchange fee he might reasonably demand from the Rebel embalming surgeons. He could receive up to $80 per corpse for an officer in the North, so perhaps he should demand half that amount for any Rebel officers, should their embalmers run out of Union corpses for trade, of course. That would likely happen, since it was hard to imagine any Rebel being as organized and efficient as he was. Why, he had at least ten men out searching the battlefield, with Tomkins, that cool devil, acting as a manager. Just let the Rebels compete with that!

Greaver wiped a drop of sweat off his broad, fleshy nose, removed his glasses, and puffed on the lenses before placing the glasses gently back on. Then he turned the dead captain's head to one side and, from the opposite side, made an incision about an inch and a half long just above the clavicle bone, near the juncture with the sternum. After cutting through the muscle, he found the small gap between the sternal head and clavicular head of the mastoid muscle, separated the fascia, and pushed the muscles to one side till the vessels appeared. He worked quickly and coarsely. Time was against him. The black seconds whirred inside the steady fly hum. But delicacy, in any case, was not required. Roughly he dissected the sheath of the exposed artery, inserted the needle underneath, and raised it to the surface. Then he slid a thin sliver of wood under the artery to hold it in place while he used two pieces of thread to tie a loose surgeon's knot.

Damned glasses! Greaver removed them again and mopped his brow. The day was warm. He thought about stopping for a glass of water, but the dead were stacked like cord wood by the tent and, just as he paused, another of his hired workers approached through the haze bearing yet another corpse. Horace muttered into his sparse whiskers but could not repress a feeling of exultation. There was much money to be made in this work, as he'd predicted. And even more money than if he'd won a commission from the army to provide all their embalming services. It gladdened him that now he'd failed in that attempt, since to work independently would prove far more profitable.

He neatly looped his glasses over his ears and bent to take up his bulb syringe. The artery hadn't emptied of blood yet, due to the suddenness of death, but Greaver didn't have time to waste on cosmetics—if the skin looked too flushed, so be it. Preservation was more important. He grinned as he inserted the drain tube into the internal jugular vein and started the draining. His solution, which he had perfected just before the battle, worked wonderfully. Indeed, it was a joy to insert the injection needle into the carotid and work the bulb syringe, shooting the perfect strength of bichloride of mercury through the vessels. A few pints at most for a private, a few quarts for an officer, and the body would remain as natural-looking as if asleep; and it would remain that way for no less than two weeks. Beyond that, Greaver guaranteed nothing—so much depended on the weather.

He hummed a little as he worked, forgetting all about the temporary employee approaching over the battlefield. Only, at a subtle sideways glance, Greaver saw that it wasn't one of his hired men; it was a Union soldier he'd never seen before, a very tall one. Greaver shrugged inwardly and returned to the corpse. Finding its blood flush in the cheeks satisfactorily low, he rubbed his hands on a cloth, pretending a greater busyness than was required. He did not yet address the man standing a few feet away, who had just lowered a body to the ground. Instead, Greaver took the captain's few personal effects— some letters, a college ring, a small photo of a child—and placed them in an open, zinc-lined coffin. Taking a pencil stub out of his vest pocket, he carefully wrote the deceased's name on the lid, along with the address of his parents—somewhere in Pennsylvania, this one—not too far to travel, as the crow flies. Greaver intended to lift the captain and place him in his coffin, just to gain a further advantage by making the newcomer wait. But the man's stillness disarmed him; the soldier just stood above the body, gazing at Greaver with unblinking, bulging eyes. Usually, if you made a prospective seller wait long enough, you established more authority when it came to prices, but Greaver had a good instinct for people—living and dead—and this seller wanted something more than money. Even so, Greaver had a very intimate relationship with time, and no man had the power to hurry him.

He stepped over to the corpses on the ground and picked out the next one for the table. Wearily thinking of how much he'd have to sweat to lift the corpse onto the table, he decided to approach the tall soldier instead. Before speaking to him, Greaver noticed the stripes on the uniform of the corpse the tall soldier stood over. In fact, Greaver noticed the stripes even before he noticed the grey fabric surrounding them.

"A Reb colonel," he said, unable to keep the impressed tone out of his voice. To mask it, Greaver lowered himself stiffly to his haunches and considered the old, white-whiskered face. It would be a pity to trade such a noble corpse back to the Rebels. Perhaps it would be worth the risk to do the embalming himself and find some way to recover his fee from the family—no doubt they'd appreciate Greaver's skills more than most, given the regal bearing of their patriarch.

The embalmer stood, straining with the effort. Suddenly the sky darkened as clouds scudded across the sun; the air tasted of rain. Greaver lowered his eyes and the same unblinking gaze burned into him. The soldier was well over six feet and wore a uniform tight across his broad chest and shoulders. The uniform was torn in many places, like the shirt of a scarecrow that hadn't scared off many crows. The powder burns were so thick on the soldier's face that they almost seemed the beginning of a beard, and one of his cheeks was roughly scraped. And he was young, perhaps twenty or so. Only he didn't seem young at all. He gave the impression that he'd been walking battlefields to sell corpses ever since the beginning of time. Greaver shuddered as the soldier nodded toward the corpse at his feet and said, "I'll trade."

Trade? Greaver scowled. What on earth did the man mean by trade? Perhaps he had lost his wits in the fight. Best just to humour him.

"Put him on the table," Greaver said.

The soldier picked the body up as if it was a sack of dust and placed it on the planks. Then he stood by as Greaver made a closer inspection. The colonel's hand, when held to the light, was most intriguing—the inner flesh of the fingers had not turned opaque yet. The embalmer reached into his vest and removed a small mirror; he positioned it over the colonel's mouth. No breath blurred the glass. Greaver pressed his ear to the colonel's chest. Nothing. He must have taken his time dying, since the battle had ended almost two days ago now.

"Freshly dead." Greaver narrowed his eyes at the soldier. As the man seemed too dense to understand the implication, Greaver added, "*Very* freshly."

The soldier's blank expression did not change. His arms hung loosely at his sides. Greaver noted the large hands—they twitched every few seconds. They were obviously hands that could do great damage. But, after all, what did it really matter how the colonel had died? If this soldier had finished him off, he'd probably just done the Rebel a favour.

"I can give you a dollar," Greaver said.

The soldier's upper lip curled slightly. He shook his head and spoke in a deep, anxious voice.

"Have you . . . did anyone bring in a body, not a soldier . . . it had been cut."

Greaver glanced over the battlefield. He might require Tomkins's assistance if this soldier's madness turned violent.

The soldier placed his twitching hands near his groin. He stammered. "Cut here. Cut off."

"Well, now . . ." Greaver pushed his glasses back up the bridge of his nose with one plump forefinger. "I don't recall such." He turned his head slowly toward the dead colonel. "But this one. Even though he's not one of ours and I might not be able to collect on him, I can offer you two dollars." Perhaps the thought of money would bring the soldier to his senses. After all, even a madman needed to live.

When Greaver turned his head back, he almost struck the soldier's chest. The man had moved closer. His huge eyes narrowed. And as they kept narrowing, they seemed to shut out the light. But it was only the sky doing that, the dark clouds suddenly stalling overhead.

"A hard bargainer, sir, very hard." Greaver attempted a smile as he fished in his leather purse for a more appropriate bill. "But I won't say unfair. A colonel's a colonel, and worth the price." He couldn't keep a quaver out of his voice. The soldier stood so close that Greaver could smell him—sweat and earth and . . . chloroform? Unmistakably so. What did this mean? Was he out walking the battlefield, poisoning the wounded?

Inwardly, the embalmer gave another great shrug. He had seen much that did not reflect well on the human species. And, in truth, he could not say chloroforming wounded men to death might not be a kind of mercy.

The first drops of rain fell. Greaver passed the money to the soldier, who took it and stared at it in wonder. Then he let it fall to the ground. "Are you sure?" he said. "A man with small eyes and red hair all around his face? Grinning?"

Despite his apprehension, the embalmer could not repress a chuckle. A grinning dead man? But his mirth passed quickly. He turned his chuckle into a cough and scanned the field for Tomkins.

The soldier's lips parted slowly. His tongue slowly crossed over his large top teeth. The sight made Greaver even more uneasy. He stepped back, cleared his throat, and said, "I pay only for soldiers. No one else."

The tongue stopped, vanished.

Then the soldier fixed his gaze on the metal canister filled with the captain's blood. The rain continued lightly. From the distance came the singular retort of a rifle, which oddly extended into the barking of a dog. But Greaver listened only to the light tap of raindrops on the metal canister; water joining water, he thought soberly, wishing the soldier would go away, wishing he had said he wasn't buying any more bodies, coupons or no coupons. Not from this man. Greaver couldn't understand his energy. The energy of the dead, though also mysterious, at least belonged to some other realm. He did not confront it except to stay the mortal rot with herbs stuffed into orifices and mercury shot into vessels. And he did not like to confront the enemy of any living thing he could not read as easily as a corpse.

Without another word, the tall soldier backed off. His departure seemed to take the rain away. For the light drops ceased to fall. Greaver shivered the whole length of his body as he watched the soldier break into a loping run and shrink to a black mark near the distant woods. Then the embalmer removed his glasses and wiped the sweat from his forehead. At last he returned to the regal body stretched out on the planks. A few raindrops had settled in the wrinkles below the slowly sinking eyes. Horace Greaver was not a fanciful man, but he couldn't shake the idea that the Rebel colonel was crying.

IV

September 21, near Sharpsburg, Maryland

Four days after the great battle, Anson Baird had been reassigned to
a large encampment of tents filled with Rebel wounded, more than a
mile to the west of his previous field hospital, across the dusty turnpike
and a half-mile south of the little white Dunker church that had been in
the centre of the fiercest fighting. His labours remained unpleasant and
unending. He stooped in and out of the sagging canvas tents, checking
wounds and amputations for infection, trying to cool fevers, changing pus and bloodstained dressings when supplies of fresh bandages
were available. His eyes were sore and bloodshot, he shook constantly,
and he coughed until he thought his bones would fracture. When he
slept—infrequently—he suffered terrible nightmares in which whole
armies of horses were tossed alive on great blazing pyres of railroad ties,
and then awoke to the stomach-churning reality of an ever-thickening
miasma that enveloped the whole landscape.

Only one thing sustained him in his daily rounds, one small contribution he had made to the cause outside of his expected duties. At
his lowest ebb, when yet another amputee did not survive, when a

hemorrhage proved unstoppable or a wound blackened or a face set into the awful devil's grin of lockjaw, he thought of the tall soldier and his spirits lifted just enough to carry him to the next tragic, mundane moment. To save a life by cutting off an arm or leg was necessary and unpleasant; to save a life without taking up an instrument at all was something he had not expected, and it felt like a blessing. In fact, the knowledge of the tall soldier's escape from the army's investigations of the farmer's gruesome death and molestation became as much of an addictive drug to Anson as the opium he swallowed.

It wasn't difficult, what he'd done, at least not on a practical level. A young soldier new to the regiment had fallen in the fight, and no one would miss him. The army's recordkeeping was, to be charitable, incomplete. And so, within just a few days of the battle, a runaway slave with no other name besides John became, in the army's records, a Union soldier named William Sullivan Dare. Though the deceit initially troubled Anson's sense of honour, he soon accepted it as a necessity for the greater good. But there was a problem.

The newly named William Dare still required medical attention and was in no shape to understand that he'd been given a new identity, a chance to move on with what remained of the army as something more than a white-looking contraband. The shock of killing his former master had unhinged his mind, and so Anson kept him hidden from prying eyes, covered with blankets in a tent full of dying rebels. Ever since Anson had become his protector, the tall soldier had done little but shake and gaze at the empty air as if it flashed a steady stream of pictures. He pulled at his scraped cheek and mumbled incoherently. A few times he sprang bolt upright and cried out, "The mulatto! He's come!" Once, he shouted violently into Anson's face, "It's a lie! He's a liar!" Anson could make no sense of these sudden exclamations, but they were infrequent and caused little trouble or notice amid the groans and cries of the men around him. Besides, the tall soldier grew less agitated day by day, and that, more than anything else, strengthened Anson as he made his rounds. He had been so saturated with death and misery, had felt so deeply in his own body the relentless onslaught of physical suffering, that the mere thought of preserving one life and setting it on a clearer, if not exactly safer, course proved a continual elixir to his spirit.

Late on the day of the 21st, however, after he had bent and emerged from yet another tent of moans and decay, Anson received a jolt. From twenty feet away, a man standing upright behind a tripod was staring at him. Anson shrank from the sight, though at first he was not sure why.

"Ah, doctor," the man said, walking forward, his broad face jovial, trailing a beard thick as smoke. "I've come about that study at last."

Study? Anson blinked into the sunlight. Behind him a patient snored heavily, the sound like tearing canvas. Anson's thoughts became clear and he remembered, with a quickening pulse, who the bearded man was.

"I can see you dinna remember our bargain." The Scotsman smiled and pushed his long hair back from his face. But Anson felt threatened anyway. This man—yes—this man alone could have suspicions. Did he? His expression seemed innocent enough. Anson shivered, started to walk out from the group of tents onto the grass.

"Nay, doctor, if you dinna mind." The Scotsman held up one hand, the fingernails black, as if rotting. "If you'll just be so good as to stand right there. Still as still. That's right. I won't be but a few minutes."

Anson stood completely unprotected as the man hurried back to the strange-looking wagon all hung with tarp and spoke a few words into it. Anson struggled to calm himself. How could the photographer suspect anything?

The Scotsman ran to the tripod, a small object in his hands. He busied himself about the camera. Then, holding up one hand again, said, "Just like that, just exactly there," and slipped under the black cloth.

Anson's eyes shifted from side to side. This man was reading him, possibly discovering the truth about the tall soldier's changed identity. And if so, well . . . Anson's forced, weak smile broke. Out of the corners of his eyes, he watched for motion, afraid that Dare would choose just that moment to emerge from his shock.

The black cloth shook and the Scotsman reappeared. Again, he worked rapidly around the camera. Then he sped to the wagon, as if yanked back by an invisible rope. More words, but Anson couldn't hear them. The tarp moved. A hand appeared, disappeared. Then the Scotsman strode toward the tents, still smiling. But his soft eyes had a questioning, curious cast to them. He stopped a few feet before the first tent, his long coat opened in two behind him like great wings, his legs apart, firmly braced. Anson couldn't shake the sense that the man had become a tripod and camera himself—he seemed to investigate and record, he seemed like a small god. Anson glanced to one side. No one was there. He exhaled slowly.

"I've not seen you since . . . ah, when was it? . . . at the other hospital, in the barnyard."

Anson clutched his side. If the man was leading up to something, why didn't he just get on with it?

"I wasna sure I'd be able to take your study, after all. I've been busy, and then I thought perhaps when some of the army moved, you'd have moved with it."

"No. I had to stay behind." Anson lowered his eyes to the tent in front of him.

"Ah, of course, of course." The Scotsman relaxed his stance, exhaled through pursed lips. "I've no right to talk about being busy to you, have I? You dinna look as though you've slept much, doctor."

Anson scowled. Was the man suggesting he had reason for his conscience to keep him awake?

"I'll no ee keep you then. I've my own work to do, though it's not as important as yours."

The Scotsman seemed sincere enough. Even so, Anson breathed easier as the burly figure turned to go. But the man took only a few steps before stopping and turning back.

"Ah, doctor? About that body?"

Anson's heart thumped and turned over. If Dare should appear now . . .

"You remember?" the Scotsman continued.

Anson nodded and looked along the line of tents. Still no one appeared. The thin smoke of a fire drifted on the heavy air.

"The army's still after it. Seems the man might have had some important papers on his person." He paused and leaned forward, his coat tails flowing out like the ends of his cloven beard. "I hope that soldier who was helping you so much with your surgeries has gone with the troops that have left. I was not more than two hours ago privy to a conversation that might prove uncomfortable for him."

Anson touched his stomach instinctively but only blinked in response.

The Scotsman continued with a visible shudder. "I was at the embalmer's tent. Unpleasant fellow, clammy-looking as death itself. Must be from the work. Anyway, two officers were asking him about that slave owner's mutilated body. I rather think they suspected him of trying to cash in on it." The Scotsman's thick moustache bristled. "And I canna blame them. There's some here would rob the dead of their souls if they thought they could make a dollar from the sale." He paused, let his eyes roam over the dozens of tents. "The embalmer . . . I heard him mention a very tall soldier who'd been quite active bringing him bodies. I didna think of it at the time, but seeing you again, doctor . . . I was reminded, you see."

Another cramp almost doubled Anson over. But he remained standing, sweat dripping into his eyes, stinging them. He cleared his throat huskily.

"The soldier you refer to"—his voice, booming out, half frightened him—"he left with his regiment yesterday."

The Scotsman smiled. His whole face became a camera, the lenses wide open, reading, reading.

"Ah, that's a good thing, doctor. I'm pleased to hear it. I'm no friend of the propertied myself, and when they're slave owners, well . . . my sympathies would be of the abolitionist bent, you see."

He knew something, then, but what? Anson heard a low groan of misery from behind him. It might have come from his own mouth. He had lied again and knew he would continue to do so if necessary. But how much did the Scotsman really suspect?

"My apologies, doctor. I must take full advantage of the light that's left."

As quickly as that, he bowed slightly, gripped the two sides of his coat together, and strode away.

Anson watched him climb up onto the board of the wagon. Then a strange, glassy clinking began as the horse moved forward and the wagon slowly shrank to a black smudge along the pike road. Eventually Anson brought his gaze back to the greasy shadows in the clustered tents—a mass of cocoons filled with putrefaction. Somewhere inside one of them breathed the tall soldier he had given new life. Anson realized it would be best if the newly minted William Dare moved on as soon as possible.

V

September 19, the battlefield at Antietam

Horace Greaver's mood had turned as foul as the air. He still smarted from the failure of the truce the afternoon before. With his wagon containing three Rebel officers neatly solidified with mercury and resting naturally in lovely zinc-lined coffins, he had bumped across the battleground to the still-contested area where the Federal and Confederate surgeons gathered and exchanged wounded. The sun dazzled off the broken muskets and sabre tips, then sank inexorably into the bared flesh of the dead.

He climbed stiffly out of his wagon and approached a Rebel surgeon who was busy directing stretcher-men. Clearing his throat loudly, he said, "Pardon me, sir. Horace Greaver, embalming surgeon, at your service."

The willow-thin man looked up, his eyes dark as bruises on a transparent apple. He glared a few seconds, then turned back to a soldier trembling on the ground.

"I realize, sir," Greaver went on, offended by being disregarded but not wanting to let the offence interfere with business, "that you are

65

engaged in your most important and honourable duties. If you could just direct me to your embalming surgeon?"

To Greaver's amazement, the Rebel snapped up like a branch released. His nostrils flared whitely.

"We do not have such . . . such *individuals* in the Army of Northern Virginia." He melted back toward the earth.

Gardner removed a handkerchief and mopped the sweat from his brow. As always, a cluster of flies hovered around his hands. He did not know how to proceed. The Rebel's unexpected scorn, as much as his information, had left him both impressed and winded. But when he concentrated on the lost profit—a colonel, fully preserved!—he felt dizzy. He tried to explain.

"I am sure, doctor, that the families of the South are anxious to have the bodies of their loved ones returned to them. In my wagon, I have the beautifully preserved corpses of three of your officers, and I am willing, for a fair price, to put them into the hands of whoever is responsible for seeing that the soldiers of your army are returned to their homes."

It hardly seemed possible to Greaver, but the Rebel's face flushed. His jaw worked rapidly but no words came out. Then he put two fingers into his mouth and whistled, short and sharp.

In the near distance, a group of Rebel soldiers turned at the sound. Greaver quickly understood the surgeon's intention. With haste, he returned to the wagon, climbed in, puffing heavily, and snapped the reins. He did not look back, but he could imagine the lead balls sinking into his flesh, almost feel the blood draining from his vessels.

But no sounds followed him. After five minutes, reassured that there was no pursuit along the dusty turnpike, he slowed the horse to an amble and began to calculate his chances of getting payment directly from the Southern families. How would he manage it? No doubt they'd be willing to pay, Rebels not being so different than Northerners in their customs of death. But how could he collect? Or, for that matter, be sure to get the bodies shipped with a guarantee of delivery? If only he had access to the president, Greaver was sure that Mr. Lincoln would do everything in his power to see that the embalmed Rebels made it home safely. But not all embalming surgeons were treated equally; some, like Dr. Holmes, had influential contacts. Greaver, on the other hand, was left solely to his own devices. And he had to face the hard facts: the truce had turned into a debacle of lost profit. A colonel! And he'd spent two hours injecting him too. A lovely job, all to no avail.

Now Greaver stood in the comfortless shade afforded by a thin tarp, injecting a couponed Union private through the armpit, and encouraged only by the fact he'd paid that mad soldier nothing for the colonel's corpse. Still. Waste! This particular loss gnawed at him like a maggot in a festering wound. Of course, there was still considerable profit to be made from the Union officers alone—he would do well from this battle, very well indeed—but the loss rankled, as if he'd been the victim of a confidence man. But that soldier had been too mad to play tricks. No. Greaver could not deny it: what truly bothered him was that he, a graduate of the two-year diploma in surgery, had not known that the Rebels had no embalmers.

He drew in a deep breath of decay, pulled at the soldier's cheek, found it satisfactorily stiff, and decided to suture the incision. As he did so, he heard horses rapidly approaching.

Tomkins emerged from the tent, twirling the waxed ends of his moustache.

"Officers," he said. "I fear, doctor, that this does not augur well."

Greaver grunted and stepped away from the table. He whisked a few flies away, put one hand over his thick lenses, and watched the three horses draw near. Just beyond them, as if pulled in their wake, came a wagon much like his own. One of his competitors, no doubt, sniffing out an opportunity. But Greaver knew he had nothing to be concerned about from the officers. The president himself favoured sending embalmed soldiers home. Even so . . . even so, he knew that Tomkins possessed a rare instinct for trouble, which was why he'd vanished into the tent, withdrawing like a damned snake into its hole. Greaver grumbled and covered the corpse with a blanket. If Tomkins wasn't so useful, Greaver had a mind to tell him that his services were no longer required.

The officers arrived, well striped and fine looking, one young and one old. They'd make attractive corpses someday, Greaver mused, nervously eyeing them as they dismounted. The third rider was very different. Small and darkly clothed, his tiny eyes darting above a pointed nose and tight mouth, he had the appearance of a wet otter and even seemed to slide off his horse. But the two officers turned in unison and briefly conferred with him. Then, soberly, they strode toward Greaver, their spines as upright as the sabres at their sides.

The horses nickered softly. From the near distance floated a high, tinkling sound, almost like cow bells. Except for the stench and corpses, it was all very bucolic. The senior officer—more than a colonel but not a general: Greaver had not yet made a thorough study of the command insignia, just enough to know the top price when he saw it—had a prominent cleft chin and heavy side whiskers. He was at least sixty. His voice had a pleasing gravity, and he stood very still.

"We have information that you have been embalming more than soldiers here. That you've been embalming civilians."

If not for his admiration of the officer's tone and carriage, Greaver would have been stunned by the statement. As it was, it discomposed him enough that he shifted his weight from one foot to the other before replying.

"Sir, your information, I'm afraid, is inaccurate. That is to say, I'm willing to perform my services, as a general rule and at a very fair price, for anyone in need of them. But here . . ."

The embalmer looked slowly across the battlefield, his dramatic gesture grossly interrupted for him by the sight of the horse and wagon that had almost reached his tent.

Two men were seated on the board, the tinkling sound grew louder.

"Here I have not encountered a member of the public in such need."

Greaver stared at the wagon. What competitors were these to ride so brazenly into his operations? His temples throbbed. He wanted to call out to Tomkins for assistance, but that would be as effective as calling to the bodies in the coffins.

The otterlike little man stepped forward. He was barely taller than a small boy but well into middle age. A few white whiskers showed in his trim beard. His air was both cool and tense, as if he knew what was going to happen but not how others would respond.

"The information is reliable," he said. "You have had in your possession the body of a farmer named Orlett. Who brought it to you? And where is it now?" He pointed toward a stack of open coffins, the zinc reflecting the sun in daggers. "Here?"

"Gentlemen." The throbbing in Greaver's temples moved behind his eyes. He touched his glasses delicately but did not remove them. The officers, motionless, glared. Greaver heard the wagon stop nearby, the clatter of men getting down. He could not define the greater threat. After all, the army wanted embalming surgeons. Hadn't he already done much service to the families of the brave men fallen in the nation's cause? Not as much as others, perhaps, but then, he had only begun. No, he could not perceive the officers as a threat. The otterlike man and the men from the wagon, on the other hand— Greaver did not like them spying on his operations. No doubt they wanted to look at, perhaps even steal, a bottle of his special embalming solution.

"Gentlemen, I assure you . . ." Greaver stepped to one side of the trio and started toward the wagon. The younger officer, red-mouthed, blue-eyed, stopped him by holding out one gloved hand.

Now Greaver grew indignant. Civilians indeed! Had he come to this battlefield, risking his own life, to use his skill on civilians? Why, he could have stayed safely in the city and done that.

"I assure you that I have preserved only soldiers, and many officers included, under this tarp. These hands"—he held them out—"have touched no one else."

The officers and the little man bent their heads together in a cloud of whispers. Greaver seized the opportunity to look for the wagon men. To his dismay, only one appeared; what about the other? Greaver turned so quickly toward the table under which he kept his bottles of fluid that he became dizzy. He put his foot down hard to regain his balance, and the sound brought the three heads up.

Very dignified, the older officer said, "We will make a careful search."

Despite himself, the embalmer almost smiled. That'll flush Tomkins out of his hole.

But the satisfaction was fleeting. An amused voice boomed out from behind him.

"Hello, Pinkerton. Are you finding a nest of spies among these corpses now?"

The man at the tripod had suddenly come up, his long coat open, his full beard split at the bottom. The laughter in his eyes dazzled like the sunlight on zinc.

The little man scowled. He looked at the burly, jesting figure and spoke low. Greaver could not hear the words. But the heavily bearded man did not stop smiling as he nodded.

"Aye, I thought you'd have your eye on that business. But you weren't there, Alan. It was quite a sight. If it hadna been so dark at the time . . ." The bearded man paused and then made a dismissive gesture with one hand. "There's plenty of killing here as it is. One corpse, more or less, canna change the war. But listen, Alan . . ." He gripped the other's elbow and put his great buffalo head very close. "I need to use the wire. I have to get more plates sent. Right away."

The little man frowned. "I can't promise, Alex. If you haven't noticed, that was a great battle yesterday. Communication with the White House is of the highest priority."

"But, Alan." The bearded man's voice rose. "One message! Very short!"

The younger officer appeared from behind the stacked coffins and tapped Greaver's shoulder.

"Come with me," he said.

Greaver followed, his head swivelling back, still drawn by the bearded man's passion, a passion Greaver understood and respected—ambition. The tremble in the voice, the fire in the eyes: fortunately, the man was not an embalmer. Greaver had figured out that the tripod was a part of a camera, that the reference to plates indicated photography—he knew a little about the latter, as he had considered having a carte de visite made for business purposes. Indeed, once these mistaken officers departed, perhaps the bearded man could be persuaded to take a portrait? Perhaps even of a body being prepared for the eternal rest? Ah, but the cost. It might be prohibitive. Especially with the Rebel officers not being sold yet.

But Greaver had to contend with the two Union officers first. They stood ramrod still, eyes as cold as somatic skin, looking down at the lid of a closed coffin.

Greaver walked up slowly, stopped, and unlooped his glasses. The day was too warm; he couldn't keep the sweat off his lenses.

"One moment, gentlemen." He pulled out his handkerchief. A moment later, his glasses back on, the officers as motionless as what lay in the coffin, he read the words he'd written on the lid: *Colonel. Army of Northern Virginia.* Greaver straightened up. The silence was broken only by the cheeping of a bird. "Yes?"

"Open it," the older officer said.

"I beg your pardon?"

The younger officer, equally serious, said, "Do you expect us to believe that you're in the habit of embalming the enemy?"

"But, gentlemen . . ." Greaver shaded his eyes from the sun as he looked up at them. His hat gave little protection; he felt the greasy rim of it on his brow. The otterlike man sidled up. His shadow stuck leechlike to the others.

Greaver felt dizzy but managed to gather his thoughts and express them slowly. "If I was hiding a body, would I inscribe such words on the lid? That would be foolish. And I am not, gentlemen, a foolish man."

"Do you mean to say," the older officer said, "that there's really a Rebel colonel in this coffin?"

Greaver flushed, taken aback. It did look foolish, embalming enemy soldiers and not being able to trade them. He should have known better. But, after all, he was bound to take a few missteps in his first great battle. "Yes," he said, thinking quickly, "I thought perhaps, during the truce, I could use the colonel to recover one of our fallen officers."

"Very noble of you." The younger officer wore an ugly sneer. His voice hardened even more. "Open it!"

Reluctantly, Greaver started for his tent to get a crowbar. Perhaps he could even pry Tomkins out of hiding with it, get him to do the work.

But the little man said, "That's all right. It won't be necessary." He spoke once again in whispers that Greaver couldn't catch. The officers, stone-faced, finally nodded.

The older one said, "This Rebel officer, how did he come to you?"

Ah, of course. Greaver had known there was something suspicious about that tall soldier. Eagerly, he said, "A very tall soldier, not in my employ, you understand, brought him to me. I didn't trust him at all. The body was still warm."

The air snapped around the three listeners.

"What time was this?" the little man said, taking a notebook out of his pocket.

"Let's see, let's see." Greaver pulled at his lower lip. "Early in the afternoon of the day after the battle. That is, yesterday afternoon, gentlemen. Yes, just when the rain started. I remember the rain."

The little man lifted his pencil off the notebook. "This soldier who brought you the body? Describe him."

Greaver wracked his brain. The soldier had been extremely tall, his uniform ripped. What else? His eyes bulged. He was threatening, unbalanced. But already the embalmer's image of the man had faded, as if the rain had washed it away. He sighed heavily.

"He was tall, well built. His uniform was ripped. I didn't trust him, gentlemen."

"You didn't?" the older officer said. "Why not?"

Oh, dear, Greaver thought, this is not going at all well. These men will not like to hear how my business is conducted. "Yes, you see, I offer payment for the bodies brought to me. But he did not want money." The embalmer scrambled to defend his practice. "It is, ah, a small expense for the privilege of preserving our soldiers and sending them home to their families."

The younger officer wrinkled his nose. A touch of red came into his fair cheeks. "There appears to be no end to your noble deeds on behalf of the Republic."

Greaver was not bothered; he had grown used to people's distaste for his profession. But he had expected the army to appreciate the comfort he provided; it was no small thing for a soldier to head into battle knowing that, if the worst befell him, he would not lie in a mass grave away from home. Greaver stood a little taller. In the near distance, he saw the photographer tinkering with his tripod again. Yes, a portrait taken in the field, if not too expensive, might prove very useful for business.

With dignity, he said, "If that is all, gentlemen, I have much work waiting for me."

The younger officer suddenly pulled his sabre out from the sheath at his side and placed the tip only inches from Greaver's nose.

"You filthy scavenger! You goddamned greedy sonofabitch!"

"Lieutenant," the older officer said calmly but did not move.

The otterlike man chuckled. He stepped forward as the younger officer lowered his weapon.

"He didn't want money, you said. What did he want?"

Greaver, swallowing rapidly and trembling, could not hear any birdsong. A sort of low moan drifted over the fields. He slowly opened his eyes, which he'd closed desperately on the snake-head of the sabre's tip.

The bearded man stood there, grinning broadly, his stance wide and steady beside the little man. "A very tall soldier, did you say? In a ripped uniform?"

The little man nodded. "Do you know something about this, Alex? You've been out here since the battle."

"Aye, Alan, but my head's been mostly under cloth, you see, and the world's a tad topsy-turvy then."

He spoke rapidly, gave a forced laugh. Eyes wide open, Greaver gazed at him. Why, he did know something. But what was there to know? It was all very confusing, and Greaver hated to be on shifting ground. He waited. The photographer pulled at the rough ends of his flowing beard. Finally, he shrugged.

"I've seen a lot of soldiers, tall and short, living and dead. I canna remember one that's special for any reason that might interest you in your work, Alan."

The older officer grunted. "I believe we've wasted enough time here, Pinkerton."

"Perhaps." The little man's eyes narrowed. He looked slowly around him, his gaze settling on Greaver's coffins. Then, as loudly as he had yet spoken, he said, "Did you remove the papers from the body?"

Greaver blinked. His lips parted. All the shadows on the ground rushed toward his feet.

After ten seconds, the photographer burst into laughter.

"Nice try, Alan. I believe it would have worked too, if the man wasna telling the truth."

The little man did not smile. "And I believe you're wanting fresh plates, Alex? I believe you're wanting the use of the telegraph?"

The photographer sighed. "Yes, but you canna blame me for my good nature now, can you?"

"Time and place. I'm sure you've heard the expression?"

Then he and the two officers turned and strode away, the little man moving his feet almost as rapidly as he moved his eyes.

"Well, now, doctor," the photographer said once the others had gone and the sound of horse hooves broke the silence. "A curious business?"

Sweat blurred Greaver's lenses once more, but he did not remove his glasses. Everything confused him so much more than life and death. Cold skin, sunken eyes, no smudges on a hand mirror, no sound in chest or wrist. Incision, raised veins and arteries, drain, inject. Into coffin. Name, address. Collect fee. Why should a man attempt to see clearly except in the execution of his talents? Greaver studied the blurred image before him. A curious business? Did he mean embalming, or the missing body? And taking photographs of dead soldiers—that seemed the opposite of providing comfort to the bereaved. Why should this man, this photographer, be free of suspicion? Ah, only because he did not do the necessary, unpleasant work of actually preserving the dead in their material form.

Uncannily, the photographer picked up the train of Greaver's thoughts.

"You canna expect others to understand, doctor. When you work with the dead, in such a place as this, you might be accepted, but not loved." He leaned back, made a square over one eye with two fingers of each hand. "The army survives on intrigue. They might even be in the business of making it happen. Never mind. I was wondering, doctor, if you'd mind posing for a photographic study?"

Greaver brightened, Already, the pounding of the horse hooves had faded. He unlooped his glasses and puffed on the lenses. Wouldn't Tomkins be impressed! A carte de visite, in the field, preserving a corpse! It was a surprising and marvellous world, full of opportunity, once the shadows sped away from your feet and you could listen to the lovely flow of liquid through a syringe, hour after hour. After wiping his lenses clean, Greaver looped them over his ears, and the world dazzled, all of it zinc-lined, at his service.

He licked his upper lip with the tip of his tongue, gracefully cleared his throat. "Perhaps, sir, we could come to some sort of a bargain."

The photographer held his grin still for several seconds. Then he laughed so loud that Greaver was certain the dead still out in the fields all sat up to enjoy a final earthly joke.

VI

September 21, near Sharpsburg, Maryland

Three days after his fight with Orlett, when the worst of the shock had worn off, when he was able to blot out the images of the blood-coloured fringe of hair around the overseer's leering face and drown the desperate lie flung from that foul mouth, John returned to himself. He lay in a square, sagging tent crowded with groaning, gasping men on their way to death, judging by the stench of it that pressed against his eyes and lips, a stench as bad as what he remembered hogs giving off as they squealed before the knife.

At first, he could not tell where he was or who the dying men were, but by lying still and listening, he soon understood his situation. The accents and uniforms told him he lay among wounded soldiers of the South, and he assumed that he was still near home, where the great battle had been fought and where the overseer, Orlett, had died. But the why of his situation remained a mystery. He was neither a Rebel soldier nor even wounded. He lay motionless in the ceaseless fly drone and watched the grimy canvas over him brighten and darken with the hours.

That gradual change—and the play of shadow as the kind-faced, sad-eyed man moved among the groaning forms, dispensing whisky and pills and soft words—took him further back, to the beginning of his memories. Outside Daney and Caleb's shack, that huge pile of sawdust, soft, with some wood chips in it, layered in it like the feathers in a goose. A pile he had to tilt his head back to see the top of. In the rain, watching that pile turn from yellow to almost blood red. Then, holding some sawdust in his hand taken from inside the pile. Its paleness like his own. He'd stare at the dust in his hand, trying to capture exactly when the colour changed. But the blood red just happened, as if he'd closed his eyes. The sawdust would be heavier, just a little, like rape seed. He'd stick his hand back into the pile, plunge it deep to where the dust was still yellow and dry and light. If it rained hard enough and long enough, the whole pile changed and he'd sit beside it, drenched, breathing in the sweet, wood-scented air, blinking up to catch the flight of a trilling oriole—its song behind his eyes— but he couldn't hold it like the dust. He couldn't feel it that same way. Only the dust . . . the colours changing . . . the weight . . . his hand plunging deeper, till it came out like Caleb and Daney's, darker than any blood, even the hog's blood in the barn, but spreading over him like that hog's blood, like the light over the fields . . .

Now a shadow passed, hovered. A broad hand, slightly damp, lowered to his forehead, a kind voice asked if he'd like some water. He closed his eyes, and it was Daney instead, her smell—of sweat and earth, the moist wool of the shift she'd made for herself, and the tang of okra.

She sat on a plain bench in the dirt-floored, rough-lumbered shack with mud stuck in the chinks of the walls, shelling peas into a tin pan and laughing at Lute, the yellow hound at her feet, sighing and whining in his sleep, sometimes waking enough to snap at the flies circling in the syrup-thick air. Daney's laugh was deep and rich—the way a river would laugh if it could, Caleb always said. Daney laughed more than the other slaves, but it wasn't always an easy laugh. John hadn't known when he first understood the difference, when he had learned that a laugh could be a weapon too. Daney always said she could bear anything so long as her children were not taken from her. And she never used her laugh as a weapon inside the family. Not once. She was a stout, strong, yellow-skinned woman with a wide gap between her front teeth. Her hands were quick, small skillets of melted butter. Her bosom was large and soft from many years of nursing, and she had a way of turning and looking over her shoulder just exactly when you didn't want her to see what you were doing. Caleb adored her. He said, "You g'wan, you talk to Daney, she knows," more than he said anything else. But Caleb didn't say much. He was starless black and tall, and the bones showed sharp in his long face. He liked nothing better than to take the young children on his knee and sing them songs about grasslands and lions that had been sung to him by his grandfather.

John did not stay with Daney and Caleb in their shack in the slave quarters a half-mile down the dirt road to the fields. He did once, but that was a long time ago, when he could sit by the sawdust pile and watch it change. For years he had stayed at the big house in a neat, pine-scented room off the kitchens and had done the tasks of a house servant, but he worked hard in the fields and barn too when needed. Some said the master kept him at the house exactly because he was so light-skinned, they said the master felt embarrassed having such a bright nigger living with the darkies; it might seem to the other white folks that he didn't know and respect the difference. Once Jabeth the freedman snickered out of his wrinkled, peanut-shaped face and said that maybe the master's embarrassment meant a lot more than skin colour. But Daney had shut him up fast. She had laid her sewing by and crossed her bare forearms and said that she'd been on this farm a long time and there was no goings-on she didn't know about. Later, she told John that he'd been bought and brought to the farm from Baltimore when he was but a baby and nobody knew who his father and mother were. Later still, when he was old enough, she told him that his parents were probably sold at auction the same time he was, and probably into the South to work on a cotton or tobacco plantation. It did no good to think about it, but it was important to know the truth so you wouldn't get any wrong ideas about what being a slave really meant. She said, it doesn't matter how easy your life might be now, but when you're a slave you'd better know change will come, and most times it's hard. But it was no good thinking on it too much. Weren't she and Caleb always so good to him and the master as kind as could be expected? He ought to be grateful that he hadn't been sold into the South too. He should thank the Lord every day that his lot was as good as a slave's could be. Even when he was hired out at times, and only ever a few miles away—to Sharpsburg or Shepherdstown—didn't the master choose good situations where a slave could learn woodcraft and tinsmithing and other useful skills? Yes, Daney insisted, he ought to be grateful that things weren't a lot worse.

By then, by the winter of 1859, John was sixteen and not a boy anymore, and he could listen to the talk of the white folks and the blacks too and know that nothing caused more excitement than the possibility of a war breaking out. Sometimes it was all anyone talked about. John understood that it made the white folks angry and nervous; they mostly didn't see how any good could come of it. The master sometimes asked him after such long and heated talks if he wasn't happy with his lot, if Daney and Caleb and the others weren't happy too. Didn't he treat them well? Hadn't he always done so? They wouldn't have any reason to run off, would they? As time went on, the master asked such questions more often, and he grew increasingly agitated, his voice almost pleading, his eyes wet. His skin looked like a china doll's with cracks. And the tracks were always glazed with tears, the thin lips always trembling, the sparse white hairs on the tiny, bony chin a sign that the master wasn't looking after himself proper anymore.

For his part, John did not know what to think about a war. When he listened to Daney and some of the other blacks, he could feel their excitement and hope for freedom inside himself, a kind of warmth, as of a change from winter to spring. Daney said that a war would change everything for the better, that it would lead to the promised land. And she laughed more. All the black folks were happier, even after a new overseer was hired and punishments for misdeeds, such as not working hard enough or fast enough, were increased. Some of the free blacks in the area, though, were sullen. Jabeth said that if he'd known freedom was coming he would have just waited and not spent his hard-earned wages on something that he was going to get anyhow. But Caleb didn't like the talk or even Daney's laughs. He said there was nothing that important that ever came easy, and if those fool niggers thought the white folks was just going to fold their hands and bow as the black folks packed their belongings and walked away, well, he wasn't that much of a fool. And besides, where was there to go? Daney said he was just getting old and tired and it was a good thing she had enough life in her for both of them when the time came, as it surely would. Caleb never argued about that. If Daney said a thing would happen, he didn't question it.

But when John stood before the master, or when he walked slowly among the visiting farmers with a serving tray in his hands and listened to them argue that a war fought over slavery would be a foolish waste of money and lives, a desire for peace and stability rose up in him even as his circumstances remained largely unchanged.

But even with life going on much as always, the outbreak of war had seemed closer every day. As the newspapers heated up with opinions (Jabeth always relayed what he read) and gossip among whites and blacks reached a fever pitch, the master about lost his senses. He became convinced that the blacks were plotting to rise up and take over. For the first time, he let the new overseer, Orlett, take full charge of discipline on the farm. Food was held back: meat was rarely given and each black received only a peck of corn a week and had to grind it into meal by hand. But Caleb was skilled at trapping animals in the woods and good at teaching those skills too. So the families didn't suffer overmuch from want. John knew they felt the change, though. Mostly they feared what could happen and not what was happening. Even though Daney never doubted that freedom was coming, she knew how right Caleb was about white folks. And the master's behaviour troubled her. She said, just lie low and don't give any cause for trouble, our time's coming and all we has to do is bide it and wait.

So John worked harder in the house and especially in the fields on those rare occasions when the master sent him there. Because he did not like the way the new overseer studied him. His eyes had a hawk's hunger and patience and he licked his thick, red lips as if waiting for a chance to uncoil the black snake whip from around his shoulders. So John never let up, never talked back. Besides, he knew he was strong and growing stronger and he loved to drive the oxen and cut wood and gather in the harvest and help with the corn shucking. And he enjoyed being with the field hands, for he rarely spent time in the slave quarters, preferring to stay around the big house and listen and watch.

One night the master had several guests over and they got to talking about their favourite subject: what to do with the niggers now that war seemed sure to come. Enoch Brand from over near Hagerstown laughed out of his ruddy face with its lips flapping like a horse's and told the master that if he wanted to get anything at all for his property he'd better sell it quick while he still had a chance; otherwise, his property would just walk off on him, it had happened already, he'd heard tell of a plantation in Calvert County where the niggers set fire to all the buildings before they left. Oliver Kendrick, who farmed up near the north woods, scoffed and said, just let them try, they know they won't get very far here. And the master trembled like a soaked hound and said he wasn't so sure about that, hadn't his slaves been getting more difficult, every month, one woman he'd owned for years seemed to laugh at him all the time even though her face showed nothing. That's how it starts, Enoch Brand said, they get to thinking they have a right to be free and they might just as well be free, you might just as well count your losses right then and there.

After the guests had gone, the master called him into the dining room. The room always impressed John, no matter how often he entered it. The gleaming warmth of the long walnut table and scroll-work-backed chairs and of the tall liquor cabinet calmed him even as the fancy oak and glass chandelier took his breath away.

The master sat at the table, his left hand holding a tall wineglass, one finger of his right hand tracing the glass's rim.

"John, I want you to tell me everything that's being said in the slave quarters."

To John's surprise, the master's voice shook more than usual, like his right hand, and his pale face seemed as fragile as the china plates stacked on the sideboard just beyond him.

"Especially what Daney and Caleb say. They're up to something, I know it."

Upset, John looked away, up to the chandelier. But all the little hanging glass lights trembled as if they were tears that belonged on the master's face, and so John felt no protection from the sudden surge of anger that he tried in vain to hide. The thought of spying on Daney and Caleb was as unthinkable as it was unnecessary.

The master tightened his grip on the wineglass. His trembling jaw suddenly set, his blue eyes lost their watery blue and narrowed.

"If I do not get the truth, I'll let Mr. Orlett do what he will. Do you understand?"

John nodded, swallowed dryly, and retreated slowly at a wave from the master's right hand.

In the hallway, he stood a moment before the full-length wall mirror, studying his own face as if he could read what he should do there. But, as always, he found only his own confusion, his pale skin like the master's, and the slight bulge to his eyes and the thickness of his bottom lip that he understood made him a servant. Daney and Caleb, he knew, were plotting nothing, and, as it turned out, after weeks spent around their shack and others, John discovered no news to report. The master grew increasingly agitated, he took more and more to drinking wine until his cheeks wore a constant stain, like the bruises in a windfall apple. Something was bound to happen. John knew it. Everybody seemed to know it.

The week before Christmas, cold but no snow. The hog-killing time. One morning the master called all the blacks together in the barnyard—Caleb and Daney and their six children and the five other families, about thirty folks in all, little children to the very old. John watched the breath flow from every mouth. The blacks shivered and wrapped their bare arms around their shoulders. Letta's small child cried and she hushed it fast. Nobody else said a word. The smell of hogs' blood thickened the air.

The master came out with the overseer, a short, stocky man with a large cleft in his chin and always a red ruff of whiskers framing his face like a half-circle of caked blood and a sparse clutch of hairs at his Adam's apple. His cheeks showed white and patchy-red in the cold, like slices of bloody ham. He tapped a rawhide whip lightly against his thigh and kept grinning the way a dog does when it's running. At every word the master spoke, the overseer twitched like a giant muscle.

The reason for the gathering was made plain enough. The master stood with one gloved hand on his hip, the other gloved hand holding a cane, and scanned the crowd of blacks slowly. But when he spoke, his eyes were raised, as if seeking an answer from the pink-streaked sky.

"A hog's been stolen. And if it's not returned by sundown, if the thief doesn't confess to the crime, you'll all be punished." The master lowered his eyes. He dabbed at the corners of them with a white handkerchief before continuing. "I know I've always been too easy on you, too fair. It was your late mistress's desire, and I've honoured it. But when you take advantage . . ." He paused to catch his breath, leaning on his tall cane with the bronze knob shaped like a horse's head. His breathing was still audible, but he managed to control it. "Even so, if the thief confesses, I'll see to it that you don't all suffer for the crime." He turned to the overseer and nodded.

The overseer pointed with his bullwhip in the direction of the shacks, and the downcast blacks, almost as one, turned to leave.

"John," the master said after the other blacks had gone, "I want you to find out." His old face was sickly, the cheeks sagging and bright red, his nose and eyes running. "I'm warning you too, if I don't have that thief by sundown, I will recover my loss." He paused, his gloved right hand trembled as he slowly raised it. Beside him, the overseer's breath flowed like a panting dog's. "If I have to, I'll sell Jancey. I'll have Orlett take her into the city tomorrow."

John's heart constricted. Then a rush of hot anger almost made him shout. But he swallowed the sound and stared at the overseer without blinking. Now it had come as Caleb predicted, and he knew there was no other choice. He hung his head and confessed that he'd taken the hog.

The overseer kept right on grinning and tapping his thigh with the whip. But the master spoke kindly.

"That's not true, John. I know it isn't. I didn't realize that she meant anything to you. But it can't be helped. I admit, she's a handsome girl, but that's why she'll bring a good price at auction. I don't wish to sell her, you understand. I have always looked after my people. But I will not be made a fool of in my own home, I will not be laughed at."

John insisted it was true, that he had been hungry and wanted meat. He tried to describe the theft but it was no use; he had no wiles for lying.

"Sundown," the master said. "Come, Jacob, we have matters to discuss."

The master walked away. The overseer spat on the frozen ground and followed.

❖ ❖ ❖

Caleb was in the barn, cleaning up after the killing. His faded, one-strap overalls were bloodstained, and even his hovering breath had a bloody smell. For a while they didn't speak. Then John swallowed hard and in a rush told Caleb everything. After a long pause, during which the old man rubbed his grizzled chin and slowly opened and closed his eyes like an owl, Caleb said, "I didn't think we'd get all de way to free without they'd be trouble."

He laid the shovel by.

"Dey ain't no hogs missing either. He jes need something to be missing. You go on and tell him I took it. Don't argue now. You go on and tell him, you hear. Isn't anyone should take a whipping to protect her but me. Isn't she my child? You go on and tell him."

"But, Daney," John started to say.

Caleb rested a thick hand on John's shoulder and smiled. But the smile was weak, the skin under the old man's eyes bunched and flaccid. He spoke, however, with a fierce resolve.

"You jes leave that to me. You go on and tell him I took dat hog. Dat way, he won't spect I'm jes trying to protect her. He trusts you. Sometimes I think he even believes you'se his own blood kin. It ain't no fault of yours, it's like he forgets, and why wouldn't he, being a widow man all these years and lonesome. You go on and tell him I took it. He'll believe it 'cause he wants to. He wants to believe you're not like dis black nigger and all de others. He trusts you. Go on now. Don't fret. It had to come and maybe dis will be de end of it."

John didn't believe Caleb about the ending, but he went back to the house and told. And just as Caleb said, the master believed him. Fumbling to undo a button at his collar, his tusk-white hands trembling, he gave up, sighed, and said, "I thought it might be him. Well, now. Thank you, John. Go into the kitchen and have Charlotte fry you some bacon, you've earned it."

He didn't want the bacon. He went outside instead and took several long, gasping breaths of the cold air and prayed that whatever was coming to Caleb wouldn't be so terrible. Caleb had been whipped before; most of the blacks had known at least a few lashes from the new overseer. But this was bound to be the worst punishment yet, and Caleb wasn't young anymore even if he was still strong and a good worker.

A hog's fast, frightened screech split the air. The day moon over the barn was the mottled colour of the overseer's cheeks. Beyond in the field a hawk dropped like a stone and rose up with a vole in its grasp. He walked on to the shacks.

The news was already out. From Charlotte probably. It didn't matter. Daney's face was all tears, she shook the whole length of her body.

"John, you know it isn't true. How could you lie like that? You must have done it." Her wide face broke. She yelled, "You did and you're trying to protect yourself."

Caleb held her against his chest and hushed her but she would not listen. She turned her head away from Caleb and continued. "You've never had to face this before and you're afraid. Well, we'se all afraid, but that don't turn us into liars." She stared at him, her eyes widening. "You jes trying to prove you as white as he wants you to be." She dashed her face against Caleb's breast. Caleb motioned him to leave.

Outside, moments later, Caleb said, "It's hard, I know, but it's better if she believes it, if everyone does 'cept us. It's our only chance. You wanted to take de punishment and you're taking it. Dis is harder dan what I'll get, but when it's over and done with, I'll tell her, jes her. If dey all know, den de master will know. And what happen den? We jes got to wait it out."

When John hesitated, water coming to his eyes, Caleb stepped closer and placed a small, worn leather pouch in his hand.

"Whatever happens," he said, "don't you forget one thing. Dat woman nursed you, she's as much of a mother as you've ever had. Right now she's jes scared. Dat's all."

John stared at the leather pouch; it was feather-light but seemed to pull his eyes down and hold them. When he managed to look at Caleb again, the old man smiled.

"Dose are your milk teeth, son. At least de ones you brought to Daney when dey fell out. She figured she had a right to keep them because of all de sharp nips you give her when you was nursin'."

John opened the pouch and emptied three tiny teeth into his palm. They were grey-white; two were square and cracked, another pointed and smooth. He could not believe they belonged to him, that anything remained of his boyhood self that he could touch. All of a sudden, he was overwhelmed with fear that he would drop them in the dirt and lose them. Carefully, he returned the teeth to the pouch, then slipped it into his trouser pocket. His eyes blurred with tears.

"You go on now," Caleb said. "It'll be all right. We jes got to wait it out."

Then the old man walked into the shack, leaving John alone, the leather pouch strangely warm against his thigh.

He felt a hand on his brow and opened his eyes. A heavily bearded face, with deep grooves extending from each side of the broad nose to form a triangle with the upper lip, hovered over him. The lips were full and pale pink. When they formed into a smile, a thin gap showed between the man's front teeth. He spoke softly but directly and held out a canteen.

"I know it's soon. Much too soon. But it has to be now. Here, have some water. And listen. Do your best to take this in."

He paused and looked over his shoulder toward the flap in the tent. The shadows of branches and leaves flickered above him, and one of the wounded men snored brokenly—it could have been any hour of any day.

"You have to go with the troops. As a soldier. Do you understand? You can't stay here. An investigation has started. They'll find you, and the civilians will know who you are."

John had struggled to raise himself on his elbows, but he found the thin blanket over him as heavy as lead. He took the canteen and tipped it, and a splash of lukewarm water doused his cracked lips and his chin.

Opening his mouth, he found he had nothing to say. He nodded instead.

"You have a new name now. Listen carefully. You are now William Sullivan Dare. He was a young soldier, new to the regiment, who was killed in the battle. From Maine. You're that soldier now. Have you got it? William Sullivan Dare."

John blinked rapidly. It was hot, sweat ran off his forehead into his eyes. From a distance came the trill of a bugle.

"William Sullivan Dare," he mouthed.

"Yes, good." The kind-faced man leaned over and gently placed a blunt, trembling hand on his shoulder. "You won't have to go until you're strong enough. But the sooner you start thinking of yourself as William Sullivan Dare, the better."

A long, rattling gurgle suddenly filled the dead air of the tent. Alarmed, the kind-faced man rose off his haunches and, grimacing, crossed over to the source of the sound.

"Oh mama mama, where are you? Help me oh help me."

The accent was Southern and heavy. Another long, gurgling rattle followed the words.

"I'm here, son," came the voice of the kind-faced man. "Rest easy now. That's right. You just rest your head on my lap and everything will be fine."

Now when the rattle started, it cut off in midstream and silence rushed in to wash it away. After a few seconds, John heard a sob of anguish, brief, deep, as if drawn from some well far in the earth. When the kind face reappeared, tears lay in the grooves on each side of the nose and in the large brown eyes the colour of creamed coffee. But the voice was not broken.

"And let your beard grow, at least as much as it can. That ugly wound on your cheek won't matter much now, but later it might draw more attention than it's worth. And whatever you do, keep your own counsel. A soldier's silence, especially after a battle, isn't much remarked upon."

The kind face hovered a short while longer, then drew slowly away.

John touched the faint hairs of his beard and the torn skin under them. As soon as he did so, time blew open and he was back there again, a slave again, on the farm along the Smoketown Road, near Antietam Creek, with the others.

❖   ❖   ❖

The daylight dwindled. John stood at the edge of the barnyard, amazed. He'd never seen so many people there, blacks and whites. There must have been a hundred of them, all standing in the long shadows between the back veranda of the master's house and the barn. The blacks had been made to come, to profit from the example, but the whites were there for reasons that he didn't know. The overseer, Orlett, carried an oil lamp as he walked briskly forward out of the crowd of whites, mostly men John recognized but several that he didn't. There were even a few white women present, their faces almost completely obscured by bonnets drawn tightly at the throat. Caleb stood in front of the overseer, stripped naked with his hands tied behind his back. The overseer looked slowly around with that dog's grin and then with one kick knocked Caleb down before the whipping post. Then he placed the burning lamp on the ground and said, "Get up, nigger." Caleb got up, his face blank. The overseer untied Caleb's hands and ordered two blacks, Jeb and Darius, to lift him just off the ground as the overseer stood on a milking stool and roped Caleb's wrists to the post high above his head so that his toes barely touched the ground.

The crowd of whites near the back veranda parted slightly, and the master stepped into the light. He wore a hunter's cap with fur flaps at the ears and a knee-length coat that looked as thick as a hide. Even with all that protection, his cheeks and nose were a vivid red. His breathing was just audible in the silence, and each white puff of breath seemed to weaken him. He leaned on a tall staff as he spoke, his soft voice trembling, then growing strained and high.

"I don't like having to do this. You know I don't. But I can't have thieving here. Maybe you've been hearing rumours and believing them. You ought to know better. If there's a war, it will come and go and things will go on just the same as before. So you'd better get the foolishness out of your heads and be good niggers and do your work. All right, Jacob. John? Where are you, John?"

He was standing closer to the blacks but a little off by himself. Still he could hear Daney breathe like a scared horse and see the girls bite their lips and gaze straight up at the horizon. All their faces shone wet. He knew what the blacks were thinking about him, but he tried to put it out of his mind and look ahead to when the whipping would be over and Caleb would tell Daney the truth. At first he did not hear when the master called his name. Then he walked forward a little and said, "I'm here."

The master came and stood near him and addressed the whites. "This boy has been loyal to me, he's the one I was telling you about." A low murmur of voices spilled through the dark a few seconds before the master said, "I want you to stand close here, John. All right, Jacob, you may proceed."

The overseer stepped a few paces back as he uncoiled the bullwhip from his waist. The lamplight flickered, brighter now as the darkness came on. The overseer's breath faded. He grunted as he reared back and lashed out. A loud crack like a frozen branch. Caleb cried out and all the blacks drew breath at once, as if the whip flayed their own skin. The overseer expertly gathered in the whip and made another pass. Caleb didn't cry out so loud this time. On the third lash, he made only a gasping sound. The blacks' faces glistened in the yellow lamp glow. Some of the whites smiled, but most had stone faces. Before the whip fell again, one said into the silence, "Runaways'll get worse." Then fell the crack of the whip and the grunts of the overseer and the gasps of Caleb as his body twisted a little and the blood from his flayed back rolled down his back and buttocks and legs and dripped onto the ground.

The master did not order the whipping stopped. He stared like a lost child into the crowd of blacks straight at Caleb's family, at Daney, who was crying and silently laughing too, her mouth open, her teeth shining at the lamplight's edge. The lashes kept falling. The blood dripped faster. The overseer's shadow snapped across the ground. The master wouldn't take his eyes off Daney. After a long while, when Caleb no longer made any sound, the master said, "Check his pulse, John, I'm sure he can stand the whole fifty."

John did not move. If he touched Caleb now, his hand, too, would be a lash.

"John! I told you to check his pulse."

The eyes of the whites struck him like hot coals, and he knew the overseer wanted only one chance.

So he stepped up to the whipping post on trembling legs and put his ear to Caleb's chest and listened for the old man's life. All he could hear was the blood, the pulse coming up out of the shining pools on the ground. He thought about lying, but the overseer stood too close, close enough to hear Caleb's blood in the vein.

He told the master that there was a pulse.

"All right, Jacob."

The overseer took up a bucket from behind him and lifted a soaked rag out of it. The tang of salt filled the air as the overseer slapped the rag onto Caleb's back. Caleb gasped and bucked slightly, then hung still. The overseer flung the rag back into the bucket. Then he reared back with the whip again.

Later, when the lashes had finally stopped and Caleb was cut down and lay senseless and prone on his stomach, his back a solid shining red, it seemed the punishment was done. The overseer stood motionless, his shoulders slumped, his breath ragged. Not even the whites had anything to say. Most were looking down or had their heads turned to a neighbour. The crowd had tightened into a closer circle.

The master still stared at Daney and she still laughed without making a sound. Some of the whites showed their guns on account of the tense silence flowing out of the blacks. A breech clicked, loud as a breaking branch. The master never even turned when he said, "All right, Jacob."

The overseer stood over Caleb for a few seconds, his shadow long on the ground, like a plank between the blacks and the whites. Then he reached down and yanked Caleb's head up by the hair and pulled it against the post. When he nailed the ear to the wood, using just three sharp hammer blows, the sky darkened and the lamplight blazed. And when he took out a knife and sliced the ear off, Caleb's body slumping again to the ground, full night rushed in and swallowed Daney's laugh and the master's stare. For a second the red blade of the knife caught the lamplight. Then the master said, "That's enough, you can all go back now." And he went and joined the whites heading toward the house, which rose in the gloom like a cliff.

Robert and Tom, Caleb's oldest boys, came and lifted their father off the ground and carried him away. Soon just the overseer remained in the lamplight.

"If the nigger's young," he said, "there's something else that gets cut. You hear, bright boy. *Don't go thinking on that girl too much. He* almost believes you're not a nigger like the rest. But I'm not fooled. I know what you are. Yellow. I saw it from the very first day. Skin doesn't fool me. I see right past that. I know you. And the day's going to come when he knows it too."

He spat into one of the pools of Caleb's blood and strode away.

❖ ❖ ❖

He had nowhere to go. Unwanted in the shacks, he lacked the stomach for the big house. So he shivered in the barnyard and watched the tomcats slink out of the shadows and sniff at the shiny pools of Caleb's blood until he couldn't stand it anymore and chased them away. Closer to the post, he saw the mangled flesh of the ear, the little splotch of blood on the ground beneath it. The longer he stood there, the more the ear looked like an eye gazing at him through red tears, trying to see who he was beneath his skin.

Finally the silence became too much and he tried again to think of where he could go to get away from it. There wasn't anywhere. He shivered in the faint moonlight, relieved at least that Jancey wasn't going to be taken away and sold. He could be alone for a time, knowing that he and Caleb had prevented that. Daney always said that she could bear anything so long as her children were not taken from her. But he wanted the alone time to be short.

Instead, it drew on. Caleb lay insensible after the whipping and the master ordered the overseer to leave him be.

"Take him a bit of blood pudding, John," the master said. "That'll revive him. Just so long as he doesn't think it's from the hog he stole, mind. But I doubt he'll steal another just for a bowl of pudding, not after last night. Caleb's not stupid. He was always quick to learn."

Then the master turned to the overseer. "I have to let him recover, don't I? He's no good to me if he can't work."

The overseer nodded and left the room.

"Go on, John, get a bowl of pudding from Charlotte. And have a bowl for yourself. You were right to tell me. No good comes from letting crimes go unpunished."

So he went into the kitchen and asked for one bowl of blood pudding. "For Caleb," he pointed out when Charlotte ignored him. "Master said for me to take him some."

Charlotte was a fat, frowsy-haired woman about ten years older than he, and she had always been especially nice before. Caleb had told him to watch out. "She got her eye on you," he said with the sad smile he always wore when he talked about relations between men and women.

But Charlotte's eyes were flint-hard as she gave him the bowl. He took it and stepped outside into the bright sunshine. It was a cold morning, and the frost was only just lifting. The hogs screeched down at the sheds. Orlett and the male hands would be there. He decided he'd join them, show that he wasn't so favoured that he didn't have to work.

He walked along the dirt road to the shacks. The squat Dunker church glowed whitely far ahead of him, and the woods loomed dark black beyond. Jabeth said he'd heard of runaways hiding out there for months at a time. "Whar you think yore coons go?" he said. "And those stalks with no cobs on them? They's always some poor nigger running through here now. Pretty soon, when the war come, you won't be able to hunt no game at all for all the niggers and patrollers gettin' in yore way."

It was quiet at Caleb's shack. Daney would be sewing clothes with the other black women. If Caleb had come to himself a little, they could have a private talk. Maybe he could remind Caleb to tell Daney the truth. He knocked softly and waited. When no one came, he opened the door and stepped inside.

Sunlight fell in long splinters on the worn planks. At first, he didn't see anyone in the small space, but as his eyes adjusted to the gloom, he noticed Caleb lying on a low bed in one corner. Next to him, on a wooden stool, sat Jancey, her head in her hands, her dark hair hanging loose. He cleared his throat, but she did not look up. For a few seconds he stood motionless, wondering whether he should leave, but the smell of the pudding reminded him of his errand. As he stepped toward the bed, the floorboards creaked and Jancey sprang to her feet, her eyes wide.

"Master wanted me to bring Caleb some pudding." He lowered his eyes, afraid of her beauty. She was but fourteen, tall, yellow-skinned like her mother, with a handsome figure even the faded calico dress couldn't hide. Sometimes, it was true, he found himself admiring the curves of her breasts and hips, but he always brought himself up short. Daney and Caleb still spoke of Jancey as if she were a child, and he did not want to upset them. Besides, he wasn't much older than her; he hardly understood the feelings in his own body.

She had relaxed slightly by the time he looked at her again.

"Put it on the table," she said and pointed.

The table was beside the bed. As he put the bowl down, he took a closer look at Caleb. He lay on his stomach, his torn back uncovered and smelling of some mixture of herbs. The skin was raw and pink-ridged in places, the black like burnt bacon. Caleb appeared to be asleep.

"How could you do it? How could you?"

Her voice broke and large tears filled her eyes.

"You know he didn't steal no hog."

He forced himself to meet her gaze. He yearned to tell her the truth, but it was as if Caleb spoke to him, saying, Not yet, it's not safe yet, just wait.

He listened. His lips moved but no words fell from them.

"We thought he was going to die," she said. "He's too old for such a whipping. Mama said she'd never seen so many lashes. If Tom and Robert hadn't got hold of her, she'd have run out and grabbed the overseer's arm."

He swallowed hard. "How is he now?"

Suddenly her whole body stiffened.

"What you care? You got what you wanted. Ain't no marks on your back."

It was time to go. He wished he could do something for Caleb, but nothing occurred to him. As he turned to the door, it burst open and the overseer, Orlett, strode in. The shack filled with the ferocious barking of the large bull mastiff straining at the leash in Orlett's right hand. In his left, he held a shotgun. Behind him stood Cray, the huge mulatto that the overseer had brought with him when he'd arrived at the farm. This man was younger than Orlett and powerfully built; his head sat like a cracked boulder on his shoulders. From the largest crack an uneven group of dull teeth stuck out. The skin around the cracks was light brown and he had ears the size of jug handles. Because he had been away on an overnight errand on the night of the whipping, his presence now seemed especially disturbing.

The overseer appeared to laugh as he surveyed the room, but it was impossible to tell because of the barking. At a sharp jerk of the leash, however, the mastiff quieted and sat bristling on its haunches.

"Well now, I didn't figure you'd pay much heed to my advice, but I figured you'd last a mite longer than one night."

With the dog growling at his side, Orlett walked over to Jancey. She was panting, her arms crossed over her chest, her wrists together near her throat, the way Caleb's had been together. Orlett let the leash drop to the planks and told the dog to stay. Then he reached up and ran a blunt finger along Jancey's jaw line. "Very comely," he said. "Almost as bright as you, boy. Generally I like them darker, but a man must always be prepared to make exceptions." He turned to the mulatto. "Cuff him to the bedpost, Cray." Both the snarling dog and the gun were pointed at John as the mulatto carried out the order.

"Take off that dress, girl," Orlett said. "Come on, now. Or I'll rip it off for you." A few seconds later he smacked her across the cheek with the back of his hand. She cried out and cowered against the wall. The cuffs dug deeper into John's skin and the bed shifted a little. He shouted at the overseer.

"Shut him up, Cray."

Expressionless, the mulatto kicked out. Pain flared in John's skull, down along his spine. The room whirled. Faintly he saw the overseer wrestling with Jancey. Orlett held her to him from behind, his arms around her waist. "Cray, make some space on the bed, will you."

The mulatto stepped up to the bed, took Caleb by the shoulder and rolled him onto the floor. Caleb groaned as he hit the planks.

Orlett hurled Jancey onto the bed, then stood laughing above her. "Damned if I couldn't use another set of cuffs. But the day a nigger wench can outwrestle me . . ." He ripped Jancey's dress straight down. Her screams came loud and then muffled as he clamped his hand over her mouth.

On his knees directly below, John could not fail to watch. To look down was even worse, for Caleb's head with the mutilated ear was only inches from him. The cuffs ground in deeper and deeper as he strained.

Orlett struck the girl again. Then again. She quieted. Then came the click of a belt unbuckling. The overseer's breath quickened. Jancey cried in gasps. The overseer climbed onto the bed.

John shouted and the mulatto kicked him in the stomach. He lost his breath. His jaw unhinged as he fought to regain it. The smell of herbs rose thickly off Caleb's back.

Seconds passed. Suddenly a piercing shriek rent the close air. A flurry of motion crossed before him and launched itself at the bed. The overseer shouted in pain. Jancey's crying quieted inside the sound.

"Bitch! Get off!"

The dog's barking fell like blows as its jaws snapped at the bodies on the bed, Daney's arms scything the air as she struck the overseer again and again. Orlett, on his back, held his arms over his face for protection and shouted, "Bitch! Goddammit! Cray!" Jancey cowered on her knees, tight against the wall.

Through blurred vision, John sensed the mulatto's slow, methodical movements toward the bed. There was a sharp crack, the shrieking stopped. The barking continued beyond it. Caleb gave another groan.

Daney lay sprawled senseless beside Caleb. Her bare arms bled from where the dog's teeth had sunk in.

"Cray, you damned fool. If you've gone and killed her . . ."

"She ain't dead," the mulatto said calmly. "I jes cracked her on de jaw. Dey's nothin tougher dan a nigger woman protectin her chile."

The dog's barking grew even more fierce. The overseer snarled.

"Shut up, King! Shut up!"

The dog did as it was told. The shack grew quiet except for the indrawn short crying breaths of Jancey, who now lay half-naked, curled into herself. The overseer slid off the bed, stood, and buckled his breeches. He stared at the girl and said, "You better get used to it, you and your sister both." Then he lowered himself to his haunches and grinned and put his face very close. He stank of liquor and goose fat and dog fur. Several long bloody scratches ran from his eyes down through the short grizzle on his cheeks and chin to the sparse hairs at his throat. "You see, boy, what messing with women leads to. I was only giving you the advice a father'd give his own son."

John collected all the spit he could and spat in Orlett's face, but the overseer just laughed and wiped the spit away with his sleeve. "You know you're a nigger now. You know what it means. I'm the best thing that's ever happened to you, boy."

Orlett heaved himself to a standing position. He told the mulatto to undo the cuffs.

"And don't be thinking of running either. The second I find you're gone, that's when these niggers will start paying for your absence."

He laughed his dog's silent laugh. "You might as well eat that bowl of pudding. You might as well get used to the taste of blood cause that's what a nigger's life tastes like. Cray, kindly pick that nigger bitch up. When she comes around, she'll need to get back to her sewing. And you. You get yourself to the barn."

The overseer shouldered his gun, pulled the dog's leash, and left, Cray following behind with Daney over his back like a sack of wheat. Now it was just John and Caleb and Jancey again.

On his knees still, he stared at his torn and bleeding wrists. His breath flowed whitely but hid nothing. He saw what his life was without having to taste anything. It was the overseer's death. That was plain. No matter what else it would be, he knew his life would have to start with that.

As gently as possible he lifted Caleb onto the bed and placed him beside his weeping daughter. He covered them both lightly with a thin sheet. Then he headed for the hog pens to do his share of the killing work.

❖ ❖ ❖

The next day put the blacks into a panic of gossip that spread over the farm like a sickness. John understood the cause straight away. The appearance of a single strange white man always created a stir, even in the calmer years, but now, with the war rumoured to break out at any time and the master relinquishing more power to the overseer day by day, an unknown white man was more terrifying than any haunt the most superstitious black could imagine.

Being at the big house, John knew about the man first. And he knew the blacks had every reason to panic, for the man was indeed a slave trader. Early that morning, the master said, "John, there's a gentleman coming here to do business, and I wish everything to go smoothly. Serve the finest liquor and cigars. And be sure to cover up those wounds. Wear long sleeves. And stay away from the hogs this morning if you can't protect yourself any better than that."

John had not told of the overseer's actions, knowing that in a battle between the two of them, he could not win. Orlett had become the old man's most trusted support, on account of his running of the farm. Generally, too, the word of any white man was always taken over that of a black.

So in his fresh-washed apron he served the three men, the overseer obviously displeased by his presence. "He shouldn't be here," he said to the master. "We don't want this talked about."

The stranger agreed. He was neither young nor old, his face thin and grizzled, his voice and language not those of a gentleman. The roughness of his clothes was equally surprising; from hat to boots, his clothing was well worn and of cheap quality. But an exaggerated eagerness to please in his manner made the master disregard the man's physical defects. His name was McElvane and he had travelled all the way from Georgia.

That was all any black would need to know. Even if the master ordered him to leave the room immediately after he'd served the drinks, John had learned enough. Perhaps that was why Orlett only shrugged when the master said, "John understands this is private business. He won't speak of it."

The stranger ran a bony hand through his thin hair still damp with frost. He looked at Orlett just the way a dog looks for the command to go ahead and eat. Except for the ticking of the grandfather clock and a few bird chirps outside the window, the dining room stayed quiet. The cigar smoke swirled. Orlett blew a great cloud into the air.

"Yes," he said, "this boy can be trusted. This boy's the most trustworthy boy on the farm. He knows I know him."

Orlett's eyes sucked in the smoke.

"I'm sorry," the master said. "I did not foresee that I would be in this position. But the man who stands still while things change around him is not likely to come out ahead."

"Quite right, sir, quite right."

The stranger moved to the edge of his chair.

"Your timing couldn't be better," he said. "There's a great need for labour in the South just now. Mr. Wych of Columbia has instructed me to purchase as much good stock as I can. But, of course, good is the word. I don't want no bad niggers, nor no old and sickly ones neither. There's no profit in dealing in scrubs."

The master scowled. Delicately he picked a fleck of cigar off his bottom lip. "I leave you to discuss all that with Mr. Orlett. What I wish to know is the price you're willing to pay. I don't part with my property easily or gladly."

McElvane smacked his lips appreciatively after sampling the liquor. He said, "For a good field hand no more than twenty years old, a thousand at least and mebbe more. Boys over ten almost as much. Women and girls not so much, unless there's some likely breeders."

Orlett stuck his thumbs under his suspender straps. "And if they're good-looking wenches too, that's a premium as I understand it."

McElvane nodded. "There's buyers who'll pay tall prices for that, yes. How old?"

"Two of them. Thirteen and fourteen."

John's heart constricted. He closed his mouth tight to keep his breathing in.

"When you say tall," the master said, "what figure do you have in mind?"

The trader scratched his chin with a knuckle. "If the girls are good-looking and bright, mebbe four thousand for the pair."

Daney always said she could . . .

"John, please fill our guest's glass."

His limbs numbed. He moved without feeling himself move. She could bear anything so long as her children . . . He poured the liquor and withdrew.

Numbers were mentioned, of slaves, ages, skills. Their prices.

House slaves? John did not realize that *house slave* referred to him. He could not shut out Daney's face. It seemed to stare through the window. It seemed wet with tears, except they were as red as what had dripped off Caleb's ear.

The overseer pushed his chair back loudly and left the room. The trader smiled broadly at the master.

"Even if it don't come to war, you're right to sell now. Just the talk of war has drove the prices very tall. On the plantations, they want to increase production as fast as they can, before a war shuts down the shipping channels to Europe."

"Sometimes, Mr. McElvane, circumstances make these decisions for us. I've grown old. The world is no longer what I would like it to be."

The trader fidgeted on his chair. "Ah yes," he mumbled and looked at the door almost longingly.

John guessed at the trader's impatience for the overseer's return. Orlett's absence was unnerving. Why had he gone? Why had the day fallen so still, with not even the birds chirping anymore?

"These days," the trader said, "you can't judge no dependence at all in a man. There's a lot of sharps around. But I don't deceive any man if I'm awise of the fact."

"I'm certain you don't," the master said. "Mr. Orlett would not have invited you here if you were not to be trusted. We were prepared to go to auction in the village if necessary, but I prefer a more private arrangement farther afield. It is how I have always bought my slaves."

John could no longer keep his tongue. "Master, you're not selling Jancey? You said if the thief was caught that you would not sell . . ."

"Circumstances change, John. Of course I meant what I said, but the times are conspiring against us." He placed his cigar down as if it was made of glass. Just exhaling the cigar smoke appeared to tire him. "These decisions do not please me."

Orlett returned, his face tight. A long muscle throbbed in his neck. "I need to talk with you."

The master hesitated, then rose slowly. "If you'll excuse me, sir." He and Orlett put their heads together on the far side of the room. A minute passed.

"Search before you do anything else." The master finally lifted his head. "Use the hounds. But don't release them. There mustn't be violence."

The overseer scowled. "Four thousand dollars," he whispered fiercely. "Think on it. There's a faster way to recover them."

"Not yet." The master turned back to the trader with an apologetic smile.

McElvane's shoulders slumped. "I reckon the girls you mentioned is run off? I can wait if they're as prime as you say, but only if we come to terms on some others. If we don't, I got to get back on the road."

"Oh, we'll come to terms," Orlett said and gripped his own thigh hard. "You might as well come and have a look now. I've rounded them up in the barn."

"Jacob, you'll remember what I said?"

"Of course." Then the overseer said something low.

The master looked over at John. He looked for several long seconds. His eyelids fluttered. The blue veins darkened at his temple as he turned. Weakly he said, "You best go along too, boy."

As soon as he stepped outside, the mulatto jumped him and wrestled him to the hard ground, snapping the cuffs back on. The steel struck hard against his wrist bones. He gasped with the pain.

Orlett said to the trader, "The master here's been overly kind to his niggers. It's his habit, formed I believe by his late wife. I'm trying to save him from himself."

McElvane frowned. "Sometimes a man reaps what he sows. But I don't favour violence any myself. A good nigger don't need it and a bad nigger don't change on account of it."

"No? Well, I can't say that's been my experience."

John's chest heaved. He felt tears sting his eyes as he blinked hard at the master, in shock, unable to speak. Surely the master did not favour such violence toward him. After all, John knew himself to be different from the others—why else had he been chosen to serve at the house? But the master did not meet his gaze. He had already turned his back.

The overseer stepped into the barn. "Put him with the others, Cray," he said.

The faces were familiar, but not the fear and bewilderment on them. A dozen men, including Daney's two eldest sons, and three boys, the youngest barely ten years old, stood shivering in the straws of light falling through the chinks in the walls. John was both relieved and concerned not to see Caleb; the old man was probably too damaged to be sold. The boys wept, and Motes, who was nigh on sixty years of age, softly sang, "There's a better day a comin', will you go along with me? There's a better day a comin', go sound the jubilee." Even though the hog-killing was done, the air still had a bloody smell. Not even the manure of the stables could quash it.

The others wore handcuffs too, but also leg shackles attached to iron balls. And they were joined together by chains. When John was shoved into the group, a new smell hit him: the reek of fear, the rankness of bodies responding to the slave's worst nightmare. He could hear the unvoiced prayers, Oh, Lawd, don't let me be parted from my own. Suddenly he understood what Daney had always told him: he was no different, he was exactly the same. He understood it now in his body, in his own trembling, in his sweat, the hatred rising at the back of his throat like burning bile.

Hands on hips, a goose-quill stuck between his teeth, Orlett addressed them.

"You're going to be sold. But whether you end up in a good home depends on you. Mr. McElvane here represents important businessmen in South Carolina, and they don't want any bad niggers. If they get them, those niggers go straight to the rice fields. And the masters there aren't like what you've been used to. You've had it soft a long time. That time's done."

He turned to the trader.

"The men are all strong hands, no defects. You can look for yourself."

The trader walked slowly from man to man. He told them to open their mouths and show their teeth. He spent a considerable amount of time assessing their backs and limbs.

"Whip marks?" he said.

The overseer shrugged. "A few. And given only to harden these boys up a bit, to get them ready. They're not bad, just a little slow to work on account of they never had the right encouragement. Like I said, the master here . . ."

"I'll have to take a few dollars off."

"But these are prime hands. A few whip marks . . ."

The trader sighed as he leaned to Garney, the smallest boy, and pulled at his upper lip. "My employer doesn't want trouble selling what he buys. And whip marks make a buyer shy." He let go of Garney's lip. "Don't take on so, boy, there are beautiful homes in the South. It's a rich land."

When the trader stopped before him, John saw the man's confusion. Scratching his temple, he stepped over to Orlett and whispered something John couldn't catch.

"Yeah, him too," the overseer said. "Just the same as the others, even if he don't look it. He's a good worker, field and house. A few years ago, the master even hired him out for a while to a tinsmith, so he's got some craft."

John clenched and unclenched his fists. He could feel the blood pounding behind his eyes, in his limbs and chest; he could feel its heat. To calm himself, he tried to turn the pounding and the heat into a soothing memory of his tinsmithing work, into the rhythmic cutting of tinplate with shears, the steam rising off the solder and drenching his face with sweat. He had never felt so free and alive as when he'd been tinsmithing; even the thick chemical fumes of the work came to his nostrils now as a kind of springtime scent, full of hope. But he could not hold on to the memory. The rhythm of the shears became the pounding in his veins again. He kept his mouth shut tight, for fear of the blood spurting out through his teeth.

The trader shook his head. "There's folks won't take him for a nigger. And if he runs, how am I supposed to get him back? A patrol's not likely to bring him in."

Orlett squinted up at the flight of a barn swallow. He chewed on his thick bottom lip for a few seconds, dragged a blunt hand along his blood-red ruff.

"There's something I can do about that. Even if it takes a few dollars off, I don't mind. I promised the boy a new life, and I don't want to disappoint him. He's hankering to travel. No relations, you see. No reason to come running back here."

"What can you do about it?" the trader asked Orlett.

"I'll show you tomorrow. Can we settle on the others? I got to run those girls to ground."

They agreed to prices and the trader returned to the house, presumably to pay the master.

"Chain them with the woman," Orlett said to the mulatto. "Yeah, him too. We'll deal with him once we get the girls back."

Cray grunted an order and they all pulled up the leg chains and hobbled out of the barn.

John thought about running because he didn't have the chain or iron ball, but things had happened too quickly. Rage and fear confused him. He did not even have a sense of his chances. Besides, there was Caleb and Daney. It ate at him that Daney did not know the truth, and he had come to rely so heavily on Caleb's advice. He wondered what Caleb would tell him now.

They were put into a dark shed. A dry, musty smell of corn came out of a crib in the corner. In another corner sat the slumped, chained form of a woman.

As his eyes adjusted to the gloom, John watched the woman raise her head slowly. The old familiar smile of endurance lit up Daney's broad face. He had never seen so much scorn in it. To his relief, she directed the smile not at him but at the mulatto.

"Here comes the proud man. You proud of yore work, nigger?"

His face, large and ridged as the side of a squash, remained blank. "No'm. But I'm nothin' else neither."

Daney's laugh was terrible to hear. There was wild in it, but frightened wild.

"Nothin'? What kind of devil's talk is that? Every man's either gonna be proud or shamed. If you're nothin' to yoself, then you shamed, nigger."

The mulatto turned in the doorway, almost blocking out the light. It cast a thin glow around him. "Mebbe I is, but they ain't no irons on me, is they?" He slammed the door shut behind him.

"Oh, yes," Daney shouted, "you'se a free man, free to do the devil's work! That gonna get you nowhere but the fiery pit!" Tears streamed down her face and hung off her nose and upper lip. Her shoulders shook.

Against the wall, John hunched into himself and hoped she would not notice him. Fortunately Daney calmed herself and started to comfort the boys. All three were bony-chested, their ribs visible just under their coal-black skin. They wore only thin loin cloths, and tears dripped off the ends of their eyelashes and noses as they pressed together, their shoulders turned inward. Daney told them to have faith, that nothing was done yet, that they had to be brave.

"Ain't I got my girls safe away? They's always hope. Maybe the master will come to his senses and stop all this foolishness."

Beside her, Robert, her eldest son, whispered something and her face went rigid. For several seconds she did not move. John was almost glad Daney was chained to the wall because he could not be sure she wouldn't attack him. But when she finally moved, only sadness moved with her. He felt it wash through the shed in waves.

"They's no saving yoself by doing evil. Punishment come to all in time. To the white folks too. The Lawd takes care of that. I got no energy for hating him now. They's much worse around."

John opened his mouth to tell her the truth, but then an image of Caleb bloodied on the ground stopped him. He doubted that she'd believe him anyway. In the end, he fingered the leather pouch in his pocket, grateful just to be left alone. His mind whirled. He had to clear his thoughts. The master was selling his blacks, including him. This had been done before, a few times, but always locally, never to a trader from the South. Occasionally a black on another farm had been sold down the river, but the master always tried to sell his people in Maryland. This time was obviously different. And he knew from the reaction of the others how terrible a fate it was to be sold into South Carolina or Georgia or anywhere in the South. He had heard of the cruelty of the rice and cotton plantations, of blacks worked to death under the scorching sun. Was this where he was bound? If so, how could he save himself? Then a kind of indignation stole over him. He was not like the others, no matter what Daney said. His pale skin had led him away from the shacks—or so Jabeth had insisted. Surely that paleness would save him now? He looked at his arms. The skin was not black, and yet his hands were cuffed. They were cuffed. The cold weight of the steel returned him to the one question that mattered: how could he save himself?

Bodies slowly shifted, a chain clinked. Some of the men had moved so that Garney could crawl up into Daney's lap. She laid her cheek against his; their two wetnesses seemed to glow in the dim light. Softly she spoke. "Honey, don't you fret, nobody but the Lawd know what's comin' and the Lawd is promised to deliver us out of our bonds, chile." She kissed his cheek and he quieted. But she could not hold Garney in her arms, she could not wrap her arms around him because they were chained to the wall.

John could feel the frustrated yearning in her to soothe the boy with the touch of her hands. It flowed through the dark, stale space. It touched his own body, then fell away like a breeze and left him even colder. Now she hummed into Garney's neck and her bosom rose and fell. The beating of her heart must have added a weight to the rhythm of her song, but neither sound had any ease in it. Her eyes moved too quickly for the heartbeat and the humming. She kept looking at the door, then back at Garney.

The door would open on them and it would not bring their deliverance. If he understood that much, then Daney did too. But her terrible hope distracted him from his own fate. He could see the girls running, their pretty faces scratched by branches, he could see them turn in terror at the baying of the bloodhounds. But maybe they were not alone, maybe something else had been arranged. One of the free blacks might have agreed to help. He looked at Daney and saw that Garney had gone to sleep in her armless embrace, his head lifting slightly with each great breath of her body.

Some time later the door opened and the overseer stepped in.

"I've got something to show you," he said and moved aside as the mulatto shoved Daney's girls ahead of him. They were gagged with burlap strips that made the terror in their eyes more apparent. Daney screamed. As she struggled to rise against her chains, Garney slid away from her. "Noooooo! Lawd noooooooo!" She kicked her legs on the planks until it seemed her shoulders pulling forward with her weight must tear out of their joints.

Tom and Robert shouted at the overseer, but this only made him laugh.

"I expected a harder time of it, but I guess you niggers have had it so easy for so long that you don't even have it in you to run. I could probably unchain the whole lot of you and give you two hours to start and still have you all back in this shed by sunup. Cray, kindly give that boy there a reminder of how much I favour silence."

The mulatto ambled heavily over to Robert and punched him, hard and fast, in the face. Blood spurted from Robert's nose. Daney's screams intensified.

When they subsided again to moans, the overseer said, "You've all been sold now, so I've no cause to worry about the shape you're in. Besides, where the trader's taking you's no short journey. You'll have time to heal before you're sold again."

The girls' muffled cries spread through the air. On hands and knees they crawled to their mother. Daney's neck tightened until the sinews threatened to snap.

Orlett ordered the mulatto to pull the girls up. Cray did so mechanically, easily. "There's a better day a comin'," sang Motes with his head lifted and his eyes rimmed with tears. "Won't you come along with me?" Daney's girls went limp, all the fight drained out of them. No wonder their hands hadn't even been tied. The overseer slapped them both on the backside as the mulatto took them by. Daney moaned, a froth of spittle on her lips, and shook her head from side to side. The boys were sobbing heavily again.

John sprang up and launched himself, his hands forming a cross before him. But the overseer saw him coming. He jumped aside and expertly stuck one foot out. The planks rushed up to meet John. His face hit hard. Before he could even roll over, Orlett pressed a boot down so hard on the back of his neck that he could barely breathe.

"Goddammit, Cray, why isn't he chained like the rest?"

"You never told me to."

Orlett cursed. "Do it now then."

"Don't have no mo' irons."

"Then go and find some, for chrissakes! And take the girls with you while you're at it. There's time tonight to deal with this boy too." The overseer kept his weight pressed down hard.

Daney's moans rose to screams again as the mulatto drove the girls out of the shed. Then, with the door shutting out the brief light, she suddenly fell quiet. Only the boys' snufflings could be heard.

John's neck flashed with pain. He struggled to twist his head sideways an inch to allow a little air into his lungs. Daney's voice reached him dully. She was pleading with the overseer.

"If they got to go, let me go with them. I'm a good worker. You know it. Please let me go. I can pay you. I have some money. I'll give it to you and you can let the trader take me away for nothin'. Please, I got to go. They jes babies still. Please, massa, please, I'll do anything only let me go with them. They jes babies."

John wanted his neck to snap and he wanted even more to rise up without cuffs and wrap his hands around the overseer's throat and squeeze until he saw the tiny eyes bulge and turn the same red as the red on Caleb's back.

The overseer said nothing. But now a different sound, even more terrible, filled the shed. Motes was weeping in great, heaving gasps. The shame of it surged through John's body. He readied himself to focus it into one desperate act of strength when the door opened again and the iron snapped around his leg. The pressure came off his neck. The mulatto grabbed him under the shoulders and yanked him up.

The overseer looked straight at him, as if Daney's pleading had deflected his hatred. "I can't let you go out into the world, bright boy, without the world knowing what you are. And I want you to know too. Bring him, Cray."

In minutes John was back in the barn, his hands chained to the wall, his legs also shackled together. The mulatto had stripped him. The cold bit into his skin, but John promised himself that he would give no satisfaction. He imagined Caleb going to the whipping post to protect his family and Daney pleading to do the same. He would not give the overseer anything but hatred. And yet he wanted to live. Life was more precious than ever because it meant the future and the future meant his hands around the overseer's throat.

Even when they tightened his chains and applied the first coat of tanning to him, he understood that worse was coming. Tanning wouldn't last; it was merely a gesture. He knew it, Orlett and Cray knew it. Something deeper than the surface of the skin was involved. The fear came into him and he could not stop it. His stomach swayed, his groin tightened. He closed his eyes against the flickering oil light, heard the hiss of the coals.

When the iron sank into his cheek, he did not think he would survive the searing pain. Then he did not think at all. There was no thought except the pain, no sight except the pain, no sound, no past, present or future. Only the pain.

He did not know how long he lived inside it. Or when he passed out of it and woke to it again. The barn was dark and quiet. He shook the whole length of his naked body as he watched his white breath float up to the rafters where an owl ruffled its wings. Something scurried in the straw. A strip of moonlight fell straight down and just missed his feet. They were dark in the darkness. His thighs too. He could not see his arms or his hands chained behind him. But he felt the darkness on him, inside him, beating there. With relief, he became aware of his genitals. Then he returned to the pain. Whatever they had done, they had done to his face.

He lay in the soft night sounds of the barn and stared at the strip of moonlight. The overseer was right. As he lay there, John knew exactly what he was, and he knew also what that meant. Between the pain on his face and the desire for the future to hurry to him, he passed the hours until cock-crow.

As the darkness lifted, the mulatto returned. Expressionless and silent as always, he undid the wall shackles and drove John, still naked, the hundred yards across the frozen mud, then the crisp, tinsel-like grass, to the big house.

The overseer sat at the kitchen table, his face greasy with egg and bacon. Behind him, Charlotte gaped, her hand pressed to her cheek.

"Give him some bacon," Orlett said to her.

The mulatto shoved him into a chair. John did not look at either Charlotte or the plate when she brought it over.

"Go on, eat," the overseer said. "You got to keep your strength up. Unless you want to die of starvation even before your new life starts. What's the matter? Don't you want to know what it's like to look like a nigger same as the others?"

But the overseer's voice was tired, his face pale. His hands shook a little. Still he found the strength for goading.

The words, however, did not touch John. He thought better of refusing the food. The bacon smelled wonderful, and he knew the future he dreamed of was not possible if he did not recover. But his hands were still cuffed. With difficulty, he took a fork in one hand

and stabbed at a strip of bacon and raised it to his mouth. But he was weak and the bacon dropped to the plate before he could put it in his mouth.

Orlett said, "Don't just stand there, woman, feed the nigger."

Charlotte did as she was told and, not meeting her eyes, John began to chew.

The overseer watched him closely. But John was more concerned with his nakedness, and he pulled up to the table as near as possible so that Charlotte would not see his lower body. He ate the bacon with increasing appetite and gratefully drank the water that Charlotte held to his mouth. His cheek throbbed with pain, especially when he chewed. The muscles in his face seemed torn. Charlotte gaped at him; sometimes she even missed his mouth with the forkful of bacon.

Finally the overseer told her to stop and to go and get a handglass.

"You might as well have a good look at yourself," he said. "You won't get the full benefit just staring into a flooded rice field." He grinned and wiped his mouth with the back of his sleeve.

Charlotte returned.

"Hold it up to him," Orlett said.

At first John was not going to look; he was going to stare right past the glass. But curiosity got the better of him. As well, he did not want to give any satisfaction. He vowed to look and not react.

"I know you know your letters, boy. That's what comes of being an idle nigger."

The truth was, he recognized some letters and could read a little, but he was not proficient. The master had not wanted any of the blacks taught. But there were enough books around, and the opportunity to look at them, that he had begun to figure out the symbols. One time Jabeth had taught him some of the sounds. But then Jabeth had become frightened for him. "When you free," he said, "den de readin do you some good. Only trouble for you till den."

John looked at his face in the glass. It was light brown. Two letters were branded into his right cheek: one was shaped like a snake, the other like two sticks growing out of the ground at opposite angles.

He studied them, confused.

The overseer chuckled. "Me and Cray didn't have time or room for the whole word, but the meaning's clear enough. You do know your letters, don't you?"

He knew that the snake shape made a snake sound. From that, he reasoned out the word. It wasn't nigger, so it had to be the other. But it didn't matter what they'd burned into his skin; he'd get rid of it just as he'd get rid of the tanning. In time. In time he'd get rid of the overseer too. Daney was right about the future. There would be deliverance. But she was wrong to trust to anything but herself to make it happen.

"Well, what do you think, nigger? A new face for a new life. Ain't you going to thank me?"

John had long since stopped wanting to tell the truth about Caleb and the hog. It wouldn't matter anyway. The overseer's hatred went far beyond any simple cause. Some whites were just like that. Evil. There was no sense trying to understand it. What he did understand without trying was that the evil had to be destroyed. And he couldn't do it now. He looked at the overseer and kept all expression from his face.

Orlett belched and pushed back his chair. "Put him in the shed, Cray. The trader'll be here soon. Then we'll be done with him for good."

The mulatto gripped John hard on the shoulder.

He rose and, without resistance, picked up his leg chain and walked to the door, dragging the iron ball.

An hour later, all the sold blacks were brought into the barnyard. The sun glinted off the barrel of the overseer's gun and off the harness buckle of the trader's horse. The horse neighed and snorted a great breath. The trader dismounted as if his joints pained him. He squinted into the bright sunlight. Almost reluctantly, he studied the blacks, most of whom were crying silently. Orlett had ordered the mulatto to keep the other blacks locked up to avoid any prolonged scenes of farewell. And that extra bit of cruelty seemed almost worse than Caleb's punishment. From somewhere a low wailing of misery, like a dog's howl, drifted on the air.

"The blacksmith will be along directly," the trader said and paused before Daney. He scratched his head, then took a small pad from his pocket and studied it.

Orlett stepped forward. "I don't know how she managed it, but she got to the old man somehow. Like I told you, he's soft on niggers."

McElvane scowled. "No, that's not it. I knew she was coming. He told me about her wanting to go and said that I wasn't obliged."

Orlett raised an eyebrow.

The trader said, "I figure that having her along'll make the trip easier. It won't cost much to feed one more. But I don't think I marked her down here. Must have forgot."

The overseer cleared his throat and spat. "I don't see any likely market for a old woman past breeding, but it's your business."

"It is that rightly." The trader moved along the line and came to a stop in front of John. "What's this?" he said with a wince.

Orlett laughed. "He won't be taken so easy for white now."

McElvane sighed and scratched his earlobe. "I told you I don't favour violence. A nigger's either good or bad. If he's bad, the violence makes him worse. If he's good, the violence can turn him bad."

"Well," the overseer said bluntly, "you've already got your receipt."

"It's like I told your boss, you can't judge no dependence at all in a man." The trader hung his head a few seconds and then gathered himself and faced the overseer. "If he weren't a prime number one, I'd leave him and you'd be explaining to your boss why I was asking my money back."

"I've done you a favour," Orlett said. "Now if he runs, you'll be sure to catch him."

"Mebbe so." The trader screwed up his face.

"Well, your buyer will be awful glad of those letters."

"Mebbe." The trader looked toward the road. A horse and rider approached from the village. "Here's the blacksmith now." McElvane turned and addressed the blacks.

"I've paid tall prices for you and I'll try to see that you go to good owners. But I don't want no trouble on the way. What's going to be done is going to be done and if you're good niggers everything will be fine." He walked to his cart and removed a mass of chains and shackles. Orlett kept his gun trained on the blacks until the rider dismounted with his tools and began joining the blacks into a coffle. Daney and her girls and four other women were merely tied together with a rope about the size of a bed cord, which was placed like a halter around the neck of each.

"I'd cuff the mother at least," the overseer said, "if you don't want trouble."

"I's goin' with my chillen," Daney said, some of the old power returned to her face and voice. "Why'd I run off now?"

The trader paid no attention to Orlett. He just watched as the blacksmith methodically fitted each of the male blacks, including the three boys, David, Garney, and Anesto, with an iron collar padlocked around the neck. A chain of iron, about fifty feet long, was passed through the hasp of each padlock, except at the two ends where the hasps of the padlocks passed through a link of the chain. In addition, the blacks were handcuffed in pairs, with a short chain about a foot long uniting the cuffs and their wearers, alternately, by the right and left hand.

Cuffed to Robert, John felt no special wrath in the closeness, nor did their bondage unite them in any way except the physical. He experienced only a dull, low thrum of mingled despair and hatred, the former more powerful until the overseer approached the coffle of women, looked Daney straight in the eye, and announced that Caleb was dead.

"So there's no reason to come back here on his account," he said as Daney dropped to her knees, pulling her daughters down with her, and covered her face with her hands.

With a surprising show of energy, the trader marched over. "Our business is settled. You go on. You're no help to anyone here."

Along the chain John felt the tension in Robert's body as he reacted to his mother's wails. Tears streamed down his cheeks, but he kept his jaw raised and rigid.

The overseer spat on the frost-hard earth. His thin hair blew back in wisps off his skull as his white breath rose over him and broke apart. The smile on his raw-boned face was crisp.

John could not keep looking at him. His chest burned with the desire to kill. To ease it, he looked beyond the overseer to the back porch of the house. In the frame of the doorway stood the thin figure of the master. Leaning on a cane, his head bare, he looked like stone-struck water. In a few weeks he had aged a dozen years. As John watched,

Charlotte came and led the master away. Even from across the barn-yard, the misery showed on her face, which hung in the open doorway a moment, like a last autumn leaf, and then fell back out of view.

The trader stood above Daney and shifted from one foot to the other. He scratched the back of his neck. For several minutes he let the women cry out their grief. Then, taking a watch from his inside pocket, he frowned and bent to the rope. Pulling on it firmly, he said, not unkindly, "Come on, now, didn't I agree to take you?"

Daney always said she could bear anything.

The sun dazzled on the frost.

She fell quiet.

So long as her children . . .

The line of women rose as one.

"Go sound the jubilee," Motes sang softly into the birdsong.

In two heavy lines they commenced the journey south.

❖   ❖   ❖

The doctor's name was Anson Baird, but John could think only to call him "doctor." He stood beside John now in the putrid air outside the tent and spoke quickly, almost imploringly.

"It doesn't matter to me what happened with the dead man. I know you by your service on the field. A man owes me nothing who gives so freely of his courage and strength. Do you think your having been a slave changes that? I imagine you were driven to it. I don't need to know. You were a slave, but now you're white enough to get away clear. For good. Do you hear me? This is a chance that doesn't come to many. Act like a soldier among soldiers, as you've already done, and you'll be taken for a soldier. Keep clear of the contrabands. If you're among them, someone might look close, as close as I did."

John squinted into the setting sun, which spilled its bloody light across the rolling hills of battle-churned earth. A hundred yards away, pressed up close to the dark woods along the Smoketown Road, a mass of blue-clad troops sprawled and squatted and strode among a settlement of tents. Nearer, close enough for him to hear their low chanting, three black men dragged a dead horse by its legs along a stubbled, blackened cornfield toward a massive bonfire. Everywhere he looked, John saw another dead horse or a shattered wagon or a torn coat or knapsack. But the bodies of men had all been shovelled into the ground. With Caleb. Into the ground.

The bonfire crackled and spat and white smoke poured off its top like a horse's rippling mane. From down among the troops floated the sad notes of a harmonica.

And the overseer too. With his bloodied ruff of beard. Into the ground. John's pulse quickened as he studied the ravaged landscape for the mulatto's vengeful charge. But it was only dead horses he could see, only chanting and the sad music he could hear. Into the ground with his pathetic lie about John's blood. How could he be white and not know it? He couldn't be. And even if it were true, he had no way to prove it. Not even the kind-faced doctor would believe him. But it wasn't true. It wasn't. He was black enough to love Daney and Caleb and the others. So he was black. Orlett knew it. But there was no trick the overseer wouldn't use to weaken a man. Only Orlett was dead now, and his death had made John a man, a man with a new name and a different future. He felt the doctor clap him on the back.

"I'll give you my address. I want to know how it goes with you. And if we both survive, perhaps I can be of some service."

John took the extended hand and shook it. "Thank you," he said quietly.

The doctor smiled. The red sunlight played over his tired face. "May God keep and protect you," he said.

And John, who was to think of himself now as William Sullivan Dare, put his booted feet into the dirt of the Smoketown Road and did not look back until he had blended into the worn and tattered blue of his new life. By the time he turned, the doctor had already gone.

PART TWO

I

July 1881, New Westminster, British Columbia

The smell of money rising off the river and drifting into the hotel bar almost made Jacob Craig smile. Instead, he touched his aching molar with the tip of his tongue, then sipped at his drink as he considered the company he'd called together: four Scotsmen, three Americans, two Englishmen, and a Swede. Most were seated around the bend of the long bar counter, though a few stood, heads tilted down to catch the conversation. This time, Craig allowed himself a brief smile through the pain. His competitors looked just like gulls perched on a cannery roof; one or two birds were always too restless to settle completely.

But these gulls had ordered drinks. Whisky all around. No, not quite all—Henry Lansdowne was a teetotaller, an odd fact given that the man's brother was famous from Victoria to far up the Fraser for his resemblance to the squat bottle of a particular brand of Scotch that he favoured. A man could enter almost any saloon in the province and ask for "a drap o' Tam Lansdowne" and there'd be no confusion. But the older brother had earned a different reputation and a very different nickname: most called him "Squire."

Craig let the alcohol gather in one cheek and swallowed it with half his mouth. Then he looked along the counter at the two Englishmen and smiled inwardly. Farmers. Sheep for the fleecing. It gave him some small measure of national pride to know himself superior to the English Lansdownes. Besides, he knew about the debt they'd been steadily accruing and suspected he knew even more about it than the older brother did. They were easy enough to control without that knowledge, of course, but the extra advantage never hurt. He could see the worry writ bold as moonlight on the stockier brother's face. It was a pleasing sight. How men could dig themselves into such holes, Jacob Craig never understood. But that they did so made things all the better for him.

The cigar smoke thickened, and as the party moved to the sparsely furnished drawing room with a window facing the river, the smoke trailed after them like a Chinese dragon. The Swede, Ben Lundberg, boomed out a laugh as he clapped Marshall English on the shoulder. In an hour, English would be too drunk to count his own fingers. By the end of the meeting he'd be excusing himself to vomit out the window. Craig doubted the American would last much longer in the salmon business. A Californian, he'd already lost one fortune during the stock market slump two years before, keeping only enough to invest in a cannery. But the high livers never endured. Craig had seen dozens come and go already, and this business wasn't a decade old.

Ben Lundberg was different. In truth, Craig found it hard to take the Swede's measure. Most annoyingly, the man's success came from his ability to finance his operations with American funds—and the source of these was difficult to ascertain. If a man was prey to Victoria interests, as in the case of Thomas Lansdowne, there was nothing Craig could not discover about him. Lansdowne's wife, for example, was an hysteric, if the agent Smith could be believed.

The other Americans, Adair and Wadhams, were also indentured to the eastern banks and could be controlled. Adair, a bachelor, liked to frequent the whores at Madam Tong's in the north end of town, and that would be the end of him eventually—women, unless you wedded them, were a drain on finances, and they often remained so even after marriage when a man was weak, as most were. It was another advantage Craig held over other men; he'd sooner ride a squaw for nothing than waste money and energy on romance.

He watched the frown on Henry Lansdowne's face tighten to a grimace as the men, all seated now in horsehair armchairs around a long table, poured themselves more drinks out of the several whisky bottles in front of them. A fire crackled in the grate opposite the wall with the window, but most of the light in the room came from the wooden chandelier hanging close above the table, the sound of its hissing gas unusually loud in the rare cessation of talk and laughter. Henry Lansdowne's obvious displeasure in such company in such a room would have made Craig laugh if he'd ever felt the inclination. It was a good thing he never had, for the coast literally crawled with his own former countrymen, and in a company of Scots jollity was dangerous.

Craig peered over his glass at Alexander Owen and felt that he was looking at his own reflection, only it was colder because he could not be sure what thoughts lay behind it. Owen sat comfortably, his legs crossed at his boots, his vest unbuttoned, a barely discernible smile on his sun-weathered face. He raised his glass slowly, as if it contained something he could sell instead of drink. Owen would not be driven out, he was as fixed on this coast as any of its rivers. In fact, he might have to be brought along. Or perhaps there was enough wealth in the new province for at least two sons of Hibernia to make their kingdoms.

That could wait: there was a more pressing concern. Craig took a discreet puff of his cigar, then leaned back in his chair, picking flecks off his lower lip. His surprise guest was due to arrive at any moment. Then the business of this business could begin.

Tobacco juice pinged off the brass spittoon in the corner. The gaslight flickered with each burst of conversation as the men's shadows leapt along the bare wood walls. Despite the cigar smoke, the smell of the river, heavy as wet dog fur, dominated the room. Craig's blood quickened at the smell. He turned and stared a moment at the dark square of open window. It was almost as if the river was going to pour in and drown the men in coin. The salmon were gathering by the millions, and each precious one was money in his purse. And with what he had learned in Victoria—a gift from the Maker, no less than that, an act of providence he would never have thought to pray for, had he time for prayer—Craig knew the most difficult American would soon be history.

"Come now! Come now!" the Swede shouted, standing up from the table, a stub cigar like a blossom in the corner of his gap-toothed grin. "What is dis all about, Craig, hey? It's not like you to spend money on drink for no good reason."

The voices subsided, leaving a brief quiet into which Henry Lansdowne coughed like an old maid. "Yes. I think we'd better come to the point. Some of us have land to work tomorrow."

"Relax, Squire," English said with a sloppy grin plastered on his thin, pointed devil's face. "You're not one of them. A swamp hardly counts as land."

Boisterous laughter washed up and died against the elder man's sober countenance. A glass clinked. Wadhams, still smiling, struck a match. His paleness was like the belly of a dead salmon left too long in the sun. Favouring spirits was one weakness, but not being able to handle them was even worse. At least English remained composed after spilling the surplus into a roadside ditch or out of the nearest window. Craig suspected that Henry Lansdowne, if he ever drank, wouldn't lose his sobriety. And if the man had been a Scot, no doubt he'd have controlled his finances in the same way. But then, not all Scots were cut from the same cloth. Braddock and McKay, for example, sitting side by side, prim as schoolmarms when a moment ago both were slapping their knees and throwing their heads back to get the Scotch down faster; they'd do all right in a good year and they'd survive in a bad one at least a few times, but they lacked the fierce mettle to rise to the top and stay there. Lyon and Laidlaw, the remaining Americans, were no different, cautious and carefree by turns. All of these men, however, possessed to some small degree one dangerous quality: the volatile, mercurial nature of their fortunes made them, in the end, unpredictable. And this remained a frontier place, despite its still-fresh status as a province. The nights were very dark. Miles and miles of emptiness stretched away from the banks of a savage river and ran into thick forests. Craig feared no one, but he trusted no one either. A man required a plan, the nerve to put it into motion, and the wisdom to operate things at some remove.

He looked through the wisps of grey smoke and the yellowish light at the powerful, slumped form of Thomas Lansdowne. Legend had it that he and his brother had been on the first coach to cross the United States into California after the Donner party. Physical courage in Thomas Lansdowne was a palpable fact. It would take a fool to challenge such a man directly, even when he was in a good mood. Now he sat brooding among the company, resembling a barrel of powder whose fuse was burning down. It almost pleased Craig to think that his news would lighten Thomas Lansdowne's burden.

Suddenly Craig felt Owen's slate-cold eyes upon him. He drew his shoulders in against that unflinching grey assault and waited. Owen's words were always few and always as clear as the sun striking the salt ocean. It was impossible not to admire him. Who else would have thought of packing salmon in one-pound flats instead of talls, then charging the English a dollar more per case? And Owen, as far as Craig could discover, never borrowed; he simply used his own profit to expand. He'd been a fisherman himself too, and that seemed to have given him a profound understanding of the creature's behaviour. All the appetite of a gull, all the patience of an owl: that was what the Swede had famously said of him. But witticisms didn't adhere to Owen; he wasn't part of the world from which they came.

Owen leaned forward in his chair and, when he spoke, it was impossible to see any movement of his mouth in the thick, red beard. But the words were as clear and loud as if shouted from the heavens.

"You have five minutes, Craig."

Everyone stopped, as if listening for some great clock to begin ticking. When, almost immediately, three quick raps came on the door and it pushed open, even Craig, who was expecting the new arrival, blinked confusedly at the short, slope-shouldered man standing there in gumboots with the yellow light reflecting off his bald head. His thick, white side whiskers and flushed, fat face might have been genial if not for the piercing scorn of his gaze and the aggressive ease of his manner.

"Good evening, gentlemen," he said as he strode over to the table and softly, in that curious, lulled accent of a Southerner, so different from the harsh burr of Owen, asked Laidlaw to hand him one of the whisky bottles. Upon receiving it, the newcomer, with a practised flourish, took a swig, then appraised the company with an obviously superior air.

Craig swiftly read every reaction in the room but one. Most were perplexed by the stranger's sudden arrival. Henry Lansdowne was displeased, Ben Lundberg's face was as open and welcoming as a sunny morning in the heather, and Thomas Lansdowne remained locked in his own worries. Owen, of course, was granite. Craig could almost believe that Owen somehow knew what he himself knew—not only who the stranger was, but what important information he held. But it didn't matter. What mattered was this man's, Daniel Fayette's, background, and how his knowledge of race and blood would remove the one salmon canner, excepting Owen, who stood in Craig's way. If Owen somehow already knew the truth about the uninvited and unwelcome William Dare, he'd act on it in like fashion soon enough. But no—this was Craig's discovery, and he was going to enjoy revealing it.

He introduced Fayette to the company. The Southerner toasted the men's fortunes in the upcoming salmon season, then said, once the glasses were down again and he had settled himself in an armchair at the head of the table, that he was surprised that any of the men succeeded at all if they didn't do a better job of controlling the industry.

Blank looks all around followed his words, all except for one face that didn't alter. But wasn't there some slight stiffening of Owen's jaw? Craig allowed himself a sigh of satisfaction.

"Craig has informed me of recent conflicts here on this fine river," Fayette continued, after licking the whisky off his lips with his tongue. "And I must say, I wouldn't have known how to advise you if we hadn't travelled to the Victoria waterfront a few days ago. Craig, you see, was in the midst of persuading me to invest in this canning business, but I'm a man who must know all particulars of a venture before I spend my money. This one particular, however, seems to have escaped your notice."

Again Owen's chilling gaze probed Craig's face. All right, all right, Craig thought, let's get on with it. His impatience came as much out of embarrassment as anything. Did the damned fool American really have to talk so openly about investment? He cut in. "We happened upon Dare at the Kerr warehouse and—"

"Craig. If you please." Fayette stood, hand on hips, and with a haughty gaze said, "I can't expect you British fellows to know any better. And God knows not all of my countrymen"—he spat the last word out, paused briefly, and continued—"are any less ignorant in these matters."

"What's this about Dare?" Thomas Lansdowne said and rose. The river smell seemed to tightened around him. A powerful muscle in his neck throbbed.

Fayette curled his lip. "It's one thing if a man makes business difficult for you. That's unavoidable. In fact, as I see it, that's the whole nature of business." He shook his head sadly, and looked at each man in turn, even Owen, whose coolness wore perhaps the slightest red tinge of temper. Did it? Ah, but he had a Scotsman's blood after all.

The night hovered at the open window. In came the long creak of tide against piling, the clotted mix of mud and brine. The shadow of someone's shoulder and arm shifted like a slow stain on the wood.

The curl in Fayette's lip grew more pronounced. "But it's something else when you let a damned nigger get the better of you."

The ensuing silence was like a drawn breath before a shout. Craig scanned the faces; they looked as blank yet amazed as a caught salmon's—the same eye-gape, the same unhinging of the jaw, the same struggle to recapture their familiar element. Thomas Lansdowne's mouth hung wide open and his head swivelled quickly from side to side, as if to say, What? Who? But the other canners were equally confused. Most were clenching the arms of their chairs, and Lyon, the hatchet-faced American, sat so far forward he looked as if he were about to fall across the table. Even Owen's thick eyebrows had lifted slightly before he returned to his usual display of bored indifference, the digging under his fingernails with the blade of a tiny knife.

Not surprisingly, it was the Swede who shattered the silence with his damnably cheerful, thickly accented voice.

"A nigger? Billy Dare? Oh, dat's a good one you said dere. Dat man's trouble all right, but he's no more a darky dan me. Hell, he's almost a Swede!"

Laughter followed, but it was nervous, subdued. Fayette stopped it entirely with a short, harsh laugh of his own. "That's your problem right there. You think being a nigger's as simple as having enough black in your skin. If you'd ever lived among them, you'd know better."

Henry Lansdowne stood, his eyes narrowed, his lips drawn tight. The grey streaks in his full but neatly trimmed black beard gave him the look of a prophet. But there was nothing rousing in his manner; he was too English for that kind of drama.

"I am no friend of Dare's," he said. "But I do not like a man's character to be impugned on such thin evidence as you offer, sir. And even if it were true, not all of us have such an unchristian hatred of our fellow beings."

"That's nothing to me," Fayette said and kicked some mud off the sole of one leather boot with the heel of the other. "You can believe what I say or not. And you can act on it or not. All I know is, I watched this fellow, Dare, long enough to know him for what he is. It took but a minute. I don't care if his skin's lily white. Only a nigger moves like that, only a nigger posing as a white man acts as if the light of heaven's going to reveal the truth about him at any minute." He jerked a thumb in Craig's direction. "And from what I hear about the habits of this Dare—living alone, won't co-operate with anyone, doesn't even build himself a decent house—well, I know a nigger for a nigger even if you gentlemen don't."

Thomas Lansdowne whispered fiercely into his brother's ear as Marshall English gracefully excused himself from the table. The sound of his violent retching at the window seemed to clear the air of its shocked quality. When he returned, a little pale but not otherwise affected, he said with a shrug that there was no mistaking the colour of the night anyway. "It's damned black out there. I sure hope the fish can see where they're going."

But the company was in no mood for jesting. Owen, his legs crossed, one hand stroking his chin, quickly put things into perspective.

"Doubtless this is all very interesting, Craig, and perhaps we can use the information. But white, black, or yellow, Dare is a problem. The question is, what are we going to do about him?"

"No difference!" Fayette's eyes widened as he leaned his sweat-slickened face forward. "Craig, you expect me to put money into an industry where a nigger can cause trouble and it doesn't matter that he's a nigger? Hell, even a well-behaved nigger'd be bad enough."

Before Craig could respond, Ben Lundberg, who'd clearly had enough of the Southerner, said, with a grin like a carnival clown's, "Hey, how do dey make a white nigger like dat anyway? I tink somebody's maybe not minded too much about dat skin colour with his breeches down, hey."

Fayette shook his head and sighed as the laughter ebbed away. "There was a time when a man could do what he would with his own property. I'm not denying a nigger wench has certain attractions."

Henry Lansdowne's face flushed. His Adam's apple worked feverishly, as if something had lodged in his throat.

"We are not slaveholders here," he said. "Your immoral appetites are your own affair and will be dealt with come the Day of Judgment. We do not welcome hearing of them."

"Just a minute, Squire," said Braddock, taking a plug out of his vest pocket and biting off a chaw. "We're not all quite so godly as you. If Dare is what this man says he is, then I think it does matter."

"Gentlemen . . ."

The one word came cast in ice. Owen uncrossed his legs and turned his face slowly from one to another.

"I don't have time for discussions of the finer points of morality. But I believe there is a way we can use this information. Dare's backers will no doubt consider the matter of his blood to be a cause of some— shall we say—hesitation. In the event that this proves otherwise, I will see to it that Dare causes us no further trouble this season."

Craig couldn't resist the bait. He felt uncomfortably like a boy in a schoolyard listening to an older boy talk about carnal matters. "And just how do you intend to do that, Owen?"

The grey eyes under the heavy eyebrows made Craig shiver; there was a quality of imminent predation about them.

"It's a clear matter of law and order. Of British law and order. Is this not, after all, British Columbia? Let's just say that I have a certain influence with the magistrate, a man who can have Dare locked up for a week or two."

"Ye canny bastard," McKay said.

Fayette scoffed. "Law and order? It's a wonder any of you can succeed at all in business. When a nigger causes trouble, there's no need for courts. A whip and a rope is—"

"A mere variation," Owen said.

Now the shiver was a chilling ague. Craig swallowed drily.

"Enough!" Henry Lansdowne stood. "You would think the Lord had no senses for detecting such evil. I will be party to no such plan, Owen. Yes, Dare has been difficult. But I do not know that he deserves this uncharitable plotting. In any case, I will not be involved." He turned and nodded at his brother, who sat, boulder-still, staring at the Southerner.

After several seconds of uncomfortable silence, Henry Lansdowne coldly bid the company a good evening and left the room.

Thomas Lansdowne cleared his throat and faced Owen.

"You mean to have Dare arrested when the season is at its peak? On what charge?"

"The man believes a large stretch of river is his own personal property. Now he's using a shotgun to keep other boats away. In most civilized countries, that's criminal behaviour."

Ben Lundberg grinned and rubbed his close-cropped blond hair. "But maybe dis is not so civilized a place here, hey? You are always so civilized, Alex Owen?"

The Scotsman looked for an instant as if he might smile. Instead, he finished the whisky in his glass and said, "I come from a Christian country and was born of Christian parents. So indeed I must be." He stood and it was like the easy uncoiling of a snake after a long bask in the sun. "Gentlemen."

When Owen had gone, Marshall English scratched his head of tight black curls, then reached for a bottle on the table.

"It's all too involved for me. But I feel a little sorry for Dare, to be honest. With the likes of Owen and you, Craig, gunning for him, I don't see as he has much of a chance."

"You're sure he's a negro, then?" Thomas Lansdowne said quietly, his broad hands, as if of their own will, forming a noose over his stomach.

"Tell me something. You ever had a real close look at him? Ever looked him in the eyes? No, I didn't think so. He won't let it happen. There's enough nigger blood in him to show if you had a good, close look." Fayette cleared his throat and spat on the rough plank floor. "I noticed he wore a thick beard. And if his hat was pulled any lower, you wouldn't know he had eyes to see with."

Lundberg's grin flashed wide and wet as a knife cut. "So Billy Dare has a beard? What does dat prove, hey? I see him close up one time, close enough to see how he's got this long white scar sticking out of the top of his beard on de one cheek. When I asked him about it, he looked straight at me, like a man should, hey, and said it happened in de war between the states. Didn't sound like a lie to me, and I'm used to hearing lies, especially in dis canning business, hey, Craig?"

As always, the Swede's jolly, insinuating tone crawled under Craig's skin. He sucked silently at his molar and said, "You can't deny Dare keeps to himself. Like he's got something to hide."

The Swede clapped his free hand to his forehead. The force slopped the whisky out of the glass and onto his fist. He licked the back of his broad hand and laughed. "If every man around here who wanted to be left alone was a nigger, we'd have more niggers dan dey have way down south in Dixie."

The joke fell flat. All the men stared at the thick air in front of them, as if Dare's face might emerge from the tobacco smoke at any time.

Finally, Daniel Fayette shrugged and placed his hands open on the table. "Believe what you want. But I know a nigger when I see one. Bring me a bible and I'll swear on it if that'll make you feel any better."

Craig noticed Thomas Lansdowne's wondering expression, bald and pathetic as a newborn bairn's. But it didn't matter what Dare's blood meant to any other man; the fact was, Craig needed Dare to be more than white; he needed him transparent. He needed to see through him to imagine the field for the larger battle. And there was only one sure way to see through a man, and that was to remove him entirely. It didn't matter that Dare seemed to have financed his operations alone, that he was not beholden to Victoria or eastern interests.

It didn't even matter that his blood was now certain to convince the others to drive him out. The point was, Owen had stolen the show again; it was as if he had brought the news about Dare being a nigger. Somehow Craig felt defeated at the very brink of triumph. He could no longer deny the obvious: Owen wouldn't hesitate to treat a fellow Scot any different than he would treat an Englishman or a nigger.

Craig lightly clenched his teeth and let the pain flow from the molar into his jaw. Now more than ever, he needed to clear Dare out of the way.

II

July 1881, the mouth of the Fraser River

Dr. Anson Baird stood on the wet, wooden deck of the sternwheeler slowly churning its way through the sandheads of a muddy, coagulant river and took in his surroundings. On the near bank, a low marsh of vivid green and brown rushes and grass and mud stretched away to the south for miles. In the opposite direction, to the north, rolled the broad expanse of the rivermouth so wide that not even a black smudge of treeline appeared to indicate the other bank. But beyond that, above the hidden trees, a range of deep blue mountains whose snow-clad peaks dissolved straight into the grey sky was almost striking enough to dwarf the powerful river. If he had been a younger man, Dr. Baird imagined that he could have tried his luck in this fresh, green part of the world.

He drew a deep breath of the brinish air and tried to orient himself. It was certainly a curious sensation to stand in the steady drizzle, inside the repetitive *whump-whump* of the large paddles, and to watch great black flocks of ducks and geese and other game birds rise with the boat's progress, like clouds of soot or dust, so silent as to be non-existent if you drew your eyes away. And then, on the river itself, the dingy white sails of dozens of small fish boats scattered here and there, apparently at random, contained their own unnerving silence, the silence of the memories Anson Baird could not repress, even though he tried, if only for the sake of honouring this beauty that was entirely new to him.

Once the rain had blurred his glasses and he had removed them, the rising flocks became shell bursts and the sails of the fish boats took on the same grubby white sag of the hospital tents at Antietam. It was no use. He had travelled this far from home because of the war, and no amount of natural splendour could divert his mind or his spirit from the fact. All the way up the coast on the steamship, as the green of the forests and the blue of the waters turned greener and bluer and then the rain ran the colours into dull greys and sharp blacks, Anson had not been able to lose himself fully in the observation. Not even over the past few days in the bustling city of Victoria, a port half-wild with frontier ambition and half-asleep with English gentility, could he step outside of the long, bloodied shadow of his nation's terrible conflict. Nor—and he had to face the truth again—could he step outside of the smaller and somehow equally dark shadow of William Dare, the man who had cabled to request his presence here, the slave boy who had looked white enough to pass for white but who never claimed to be anything but black and who, according to the telegram Anson had received a month earlier, needed help. The details were scant, but since William Dare had not asked before now, not once in almost twenty years, for Anson to come to him, it was easy for Anson to decide. A man was no friend, to others or to his own sense of loyalty, if he hesitated at such a summons, regardless of the unpleasantness, past and present, he might be forced to confront.

Now, with the sloppy mercury of the Gulf of Georgia at his back and the paddlewheeler's first port of call somewhere in the blurred murk ahead of him, Anson felt the war enter him physically, as it often did. He coughed violently into a handkerchief and clutched the wet railing with his bare hand. A sharp cramp under his ribcage bent him over slightly, and he almost squeezed his glasses, still held in his hand, hard enough to break them. By the time he had recovered, the paddles had stopped turning and the strange chorus of the ordinary world—rainfall, wind, the reel of gull cry, the trill of a songbird— brought him back to the present. Slowly, he positioned his glasses on the bridge of his nose and considered where he'd arrived.

The place had a peculiar name: Chilukthan. But it resembled any other landing the doctor had seen along the coast: several dark pilings and a wharf of lighter-coloured cedar planks, a few square, flat-roofed buildings, an A-roof barn and a house of rough lumber set just behind it, beyond it an earthen dike about fifteen feet high and a hundred yards long. A broad slough, fifty yards wide at the entrance and gleaming dull silver against the muddy flats, ran south from the deepwater channel of the river and disappeared beyond another dark house about a half-mile inland, if you could properly call the swampy morass "land." Along the slough banks, ranged far apart, a half-dozen giant coniferous trees, their dark green boughs fringed with silver-black raindrops, stood forlorn, each somehow as dominant as the one shattered tree on the battlefield under which he and Dare had first met, before the boy had even become Dare. Anson shut his eyes and willed himself to leave the war in the past, where it belonged. When he opened them again on all the drizzling grey, he saw a rowboat approaching, a thin, dark figure pulling steadily at the oars. Anson shivered—the sight was grim, but at least the figure wasn't standing upright like Charon, with a long pole in his hands. Suddenly, from over the dike, a strange thunking sound began, harsher and less regular than the sound of the paddlewheeler.

Before Anson could think what the sound might be, a nasal voice made him turn.

"What do you think of the place, doctor? Only a dozen families, give or take a few, a couple of bachelors, but a man has prospects here."

The speaker—short, thin, rat-faced, but exceedingly dandified under the circumstances (he reeked of hair oil and wore an expensive tailored coat over a bold orange suit)—never ceased to talk of finance. All the way from Victoria across the Gulf of Georgia until at last Anson had retired to the deck, this peacock of a booster had sung the praises of the new province of British Columbia. And why shouldn't he? According to his own proud song sheet, he was a fiscal agent for an English concern interested in expanding the salmon canning industry.

At first, Anson had welcomed the man's conversation. After all, William Dare was himself a salmon canner and it would be useful to know something of the challenges he faced. However, over the course of the three-hour journey, it became clear that the agent was obsessed with numbers and hardly interested at all in the practical details of running a cannery; he couldn't even explain anything about the salmon themselves. Other than mentioning, in a callously offhand way, that Thomas Lansdowne, one of the two brothers who founded this settlement, had lost a daughter of fifteen years to typhoid the summer before, the agent offered little useful information. Besides, he was pompous, and Anson's tolerance for pomposity had died, along with so many other things, a long time ago.

"I have no prospects in this place," he answered. Taking another deep breath of the rich musk of mud and brine, he marvelled again at the distance he had travelled from Pennsylvania—by rail to San Francisco, then by steamer to Victoria, and now, at last, by paddle-wheeler and skiff to his final destination.

The agent lit a cigar and drew on it in immense self-satisfied pleasure. "Come now, doctor. I've met a great many of your countrymen. In fact, British Columbia is as American as it is British, speaking purely from the perspective of business, not culture, you understand." He exhaled an acrid little cloud, which dissolved his pinched features. "Americans, if you don't mind my saying so, have great instincts for prospects. That's what makes your country so successful."

Anson resented the cigar smoke. The river smell was new, distinct, flavoured perhaps by the great salmon runs he had read about. Tobacco smoke was as common to him as the smell of blood.

"I do mind," he said below his breath and thought, Did so many die in misery, attempting to tear our country apart or hold it together, only to have this preening, pale-handed Englishman blithely call us all the same? Anson stepped away from the railing, out of the cigar smoke.

The agent chortled, following. "Just you wait, doctor. A man of your education and talents, in a land like this, just ready to boom. Why, in a few weeks, I'll wager you'll have your hand in a dozen concerns. I might even be negotiating with you on the price of tinplate. Yes, sir, with your keen interest in the salmon, I'm certain you'll be pricing tinplate for cans soon enough."

The skiff reached the side of the paddlewheeler and moved slowly along to the stern. At the deckhand's request, and with some difficulty, Anson descended the rope ladder into the skiff, the dark figure extending a long, narrow, and surprisingly firm hand to help him. Introducing himself as Henry Lansdowne, the man shook Anson's hand firmly but did not smile. His face was woe-heavy, much wrinkled, the eyes wet and black and about as sad as any Anson had ever looked into—only the wispy white smoke of side whiskers afforded any colour to the features. Anson understood at once that here was a more typical sort of Englishman, the sort who preferred to keep even his silence to himself.

As the agent struggled to board the skiff, cursing and gasping as his feet sought the next rung of the ladder, the day suddenly erupted in shrieks. Anson turned to face downriver. The whole horizon was blackened with birds winging rapidly over the marsh.

Once landed, the agent's mercantile bonhomie did not abate; he seemed oblivious to the violent din of the flocks, even though they filled the sky beyond his face and shoulders like a living storm cloud. He merely smoothed his ratty whiskers with his gloved fingers and proceeded to calculate the likely amount of cases in the coming season's salmon pack.

"I hear rumours of the run being very lucrative, Lansdowne. You'd best keep your Chinese busy at those shears. You can't have too many cans this summer." Ah, so that was the sound coming from over the dike, the sound of tin being cut. Anson was about to inquire about particulars, even if it was only a matter of the agent rattling off more prices and statistics, but he didn't have the chance.

Henry Lansdowne, arranging luggage in the skiff, cut matters short. "It's my brother, Thomas, you're here to see. He handles the cannery business." With that, he lowered himself behind the oars and pulled for the wharf. His expression did not change, but Anson noted the tautness in the jaw and neck muscles. Henry Lansdowne was not a young man—Anson reckoned him ten years senior to himself.

Perhaps Lansdowne's three-score age, combined with the heavy sadness and welcome aura of silence after the agent's ceaseless chatter, made Anson favourably disposed to the man.

Even though the rain had stopped, the day's gloom deepened. Unable to push its light through, the little smudge of sun gave up and retreated behind the scudding grey. Other than the creak of the oarlocks, followed by the plash and gurgle of the oars, and every minute or so another punching thunk of the shears, silence descended on the river. Even the rat-faced agent fell quiet; he shrank into the tailored shoulders of his coat and stared at the afternoon's fresh pall as if it was a personal affront. He blew longer puffs of cigar smoke and tapped a gloved hand on the gunwale.

It was a short passage, the shortest of his whole journey, but the doctor crammed a wilderness of reflection into it. In a way, he had lied to the agent by saying that he had no prospects in this place. The truth was, he had helped to finance Dare's cannery operations from the first year, 1874, and he held shares in the venture, even though he did so out of friendship and not with any expectation of increased wealth. To date, the returns had been modest at best, but it was a young industry with a bright future. Anson's understanding, limited to what he'd overheard while travelling the coast and to the sparse information in Dare's rare correspondence, was that this year, the high point of the salmon's four-year cycle, should be the most productive yet.

But it didn't much matter to him, except in his sincere hopes that Dare would do well and perhaps make a permanent life here. Anson Baird prided himself on self-knowledge—to lie to yourself seemed to him the very height of folly. He was well into middle age, a widower with no children, and the illnesses that had ravaged him during the war would not grant him a long life. These were the facts. Others—especially that of Dare's most recent communication, a telegram reading, "Difficulties here stop come as soon as able stop," explained merely his physical actions. The larger issues of his solitude and poor health had already made him a dispassionate observer of the various madnesses of men. The war had preserved the union and freed the slaves—Anson had done his part, and he did not lack for pride in the contribution. But all madnesses after the surrender at Appomattox seemed small and petty by comparison. What mattered now was what he had accepted as his purpose at Antietam—to preserve one good man's life in a world indifferent and even hostile to virtue.

They reached the wharf. As Anson climbed out of the skiff, another great clatter of bird-cry rolled across the southern horizon just beyond the dark, peaked roof of the house, which now looked to billow black smoke. Anson paused, stricken by the astonishing violence of the flocks. If he were superstitious, he might have considered the event a bad omen. But the sheer mass of dead flesh he had known left him more than skeptical of unbodied fancies, including God. Anson kept such doubts to himself, however. His patients would have neither understood nor appreciated them—and why upset a man who'd asked for your help?

As soon as the agent had set foot on the wharf, he clutched his collar around his throat and ducked his oily head. "I was told there'd be a hotel this time," he muttered. "I'm accustomed to decent lodgings when I'm on business."

"My wife keeps a good house," Lansdowne said from the skiff. "You can board with us. Or you can return to the boat and find lodgings in New Westminster. I understand there are several hotels there that cater to those of more refined tastes."

His scornful tone did not elude Anson, but the agent appeared not to notice.

"Perhaps. What time does the boat leave? I need to discuss business with your brother first."

With impressive dexterity for a man of his years, Henry Lansdowne put his hands on the wharf and swung himself stiffly over the edge and into a standing position. Not even taking a deep breath, he immediately said, "My brother is working in the fields and will not stop until this evening. If you wish to talk with him, you must lodge here for the night. Or, if my wife's housekeeping is not to your standards, you are free to shelter where you can."

The agent looked dubiously skyward and tugged at his lapels. The great clatter of bird-sound had faded almost as rapidly as it had come—now the trickle of tide below and the whisper of wings above brought the day more comfortably together. Anson looked at the house—dark, square, a short walk from the wharf down a tilted gangway through a field of mud and slickened grass. Just to the southeast carved the pewter slough. Another house, equally dark, rested squat on the slough bank a half-mile distant. The wind carried a sour, brackish smell off the muddy bank. It seemed an unlikely place for a man to make his fortune.

Anson took up his bags and said, "I'm looking for the home of William Dare. Is it far?"

Henry Lansdowne hesitated just slightly. "Crescent Slough. Best to go by boat, but the tide's against you now. Have to wait till morning." His liquid eyes hardened to wet stone. "Are you expected?"

Anson admonished himself, remembering the telegram. The difficulties Dare had mentioned could refer to anything or anyone.

"Yes. But he didn't know exactly when I'd arrive." Anson shifted uncomfortably, lowered his bags to the wharf. It hadn't occurred to him that he'd have trouble actually getting to Dare's house. Was he to hire a skiff and row there himself?

"I can take you tomorrow," Lansdowne said. "He doesn't come to the Landing often."

The agent, who had been waving a cloud of mosquitoes away from his face, suddenly went still.

"Dare, did you say?"

Annoyed with himself, Anson simply nodded.

"If you don't mind the question, doctor, what could a man such as yourself want with a man such as that?"

Anson stepped forward. "What do you mean? A man such as what?"

The agent glanced at Henry Lansdowne and then away.

"Oh, nothing, nothing at all. Dare is just, well, he's a little rough compared with yourself. How do you know him exactly?"

Anson could see no sense in answering, especially as the agent's tone was almost excitedly curious. So, when the thunking of the shears sounded again, he allowed the noise to end the conversation. In the silence that followed, he bent and picked up his bags.

The agent shrugged slightly and flicked his burning cigar onto the wharf. "Damnable insects! I've had enough. I could use a drink."

Lansdowne scowled. He stepped on the cigar butt with his boot and strode off toward the gangway.

"A cheerful chap," the agent said. "He suits the place. But there's no money to be made in the soft parts of the earth, eh, doctor? Come on, we might as well get indoors before the rain starts."

Anson nodded and looked upriver where he adjudged Crescent Slough to be, given his host's slight hand gesture. In the near distance, a ramshackle collection of shelters, constructed of driftwood and planks of uneven sizes, sprawled under three trickles of white smoke. A long dug-out canoe rested half out of the tide, its brightly painted bow vivid as a smear of lipstick against the bank reeds. Nothing moved except a lone mongrel that loped along the sloppy tidemark, stopping to sniff every few feet. Anson looked away from the dog. The overcast pressed greyly on the tin-coloured water, as if to contain the force of the tide. The rain now fell again in wisps. From the distant fields drifted a low moaning. Anson coughed twice, each one like a seizure, leaving him shaken, teary-eyed. When he could see clearly again, just as he started to walk to the gangway, he saw a boy and a girl approaching along the slough bank. He stopped, blinking rapidly several times. He'd have been no more surprised if a boy and a girl had stepped out of a woodlot at Antietam. The sight calmed him, as the presence of children always did. A place could not be so desolate with children in it. If Elizabeth had only given him a son or daughter. Well, it was best not to dwell on such things. He'd known many men who'd be only too happy as childless widowers instead of what they were—the heroic dead, remembered less with every passing year.

Anson watched the children's slow progress for a moment. Then, lighter of heart, he followed the other men up the gangway.

III

Several hours later, Anson lay on a hard, narrow bed in an unadorned upstairs room of Henry Lansdowne's house, listening to the night sounds through a partly opened window. For a while the hooting of an owl kept up a steady, ghostly rhythm. Then only the sucking of the tide at the pilings thirty yards away disturbed the silence. The night carried a powerful smell of wetness—mud, river, earth, with something brinish mixed in. It was heavy, anaesthetic. Anson almost succumbed to its weight on his face several times, but then he recalled Henry Lansdowne's tight expression at the dinner table and opened his eyes wide again.

If such a man so strongly disapproved of salmon canning, that did not bode well. At the very least it gave, to those "difficulties" Dare had mentioned, a greater gravity. And when Thomas Lansdowne had arrived, his burly, stumplike figure so incongruous below a face restless with anxiety, it was as if the walls of the house had collapsed and left them all standing separate and vulnerable in the elements.

Anson had excused himself shortly after the meal, out of courtesy, knowing that business was to be discussed, but he also longed to escape the tense gloom. It was no exaggeration to say that Henry

Lansdowne despised the rat-faced agent and his cigars, nor that he resented his younger brother's inviting such a man into their lives. On several occasions, he had made pointed references to farming and ranching as the foundations of community, references that raised his brother's chest like a billows. Oblivious to the Lansdownes' unspoken disagreement, the agent praised the younger brother for his foresight. "A man can do nothing greater for British Columbia," he had said, "than to invest in the salmon. It's silver gold." No one had joined him in the chortling pleasure he'd derived from the phrase, but that hadn't stopped the agent from repeating it.

At that point, fatigued from his journey and depressed by the atmosphere, Anson had decided that a few hours with Virgil's *Eclogues* would be recondite.

A long shriek pierced the stillness, then faded away in a choked strangle. A wildcat of some kind. Anson recalled the terrifying cries he'd heard in the swamps of the Peninsular Campaign and sat up, aware of his heartbeat; it was stronger than usual. He took his left wrist in the opposite hand. Of course it was natural that he would think of the war while on his way to see Dare for the first time since 1866, when the former slave and soldier had spent a few days at Anson's home before heading west to make a fresh start for himself. And yet there was something in the heaviness of the air, in the fraternal tension between the Lansdowne brothers, that made him feel he'd crossed some invisible line and re-entered the past. But how could it be? He wasn't even on American soil.

Difficulties, the telegram had said. What difficulties, other than the approach of death, could there be after what they'd endured together, after the torn bodies they'd tried to repair? Yes, he had lent Dare money, but that was nothing to the help the man had given him at Antietam. That service had changed Anson Baird's idea of himself, had brought him face to face with the fundamental questions of honour and justice. Yet as the long shriek rose and fell again, the word "difficulties" reeked of blood and chloroform and deceit. No war ever ends, Anson thought, seeing Odysseus, hooded and plotting, as he returned to his home ten years after the fall of Troy. But Anson was no Odysseus. Dare was not his son, there was no Penelope, no kingdom.

The only parallel was the memory of death and the palpable sense of violent change. Cold sweat formed on Anson's temples. Slowly he brought his feet down to the bare wood floor and stared at the window.

This darkness had a weight unlike anything he'd experienced, yet it was disturbingly familiar. He didn't want to know why, but the answer drifted to him through the thin opening between the glass and sill, one word like a light-dazed moth: Dare. Anson rubbed his eyes, could almost feel the blood slosh behind them. He stood and began to pace.

"O mihi longae maneat pars ultima uitae, spiritus et quantam sat erit tua dicere facta!"

But recitation was futile. The ancient language wore blood- and pus-stained dressings, and each word dropped on the cold wood like an amputated limb. Anson stopped before the window. As he stared through it, he thought the glass might shatter any moment. Out of old habit, he reached into his pocket for a bottle of opium pills, but he had not taken opium for years. The struggle to stop, for his wife's sake, had almost killed him, but Anson had not savoured the drug in this way for a long time, not even after Elizabeth's death, when grief so easily could have weakened his resolve.

He remained at the window and watched the sky turn pink over a blue-black mountain range to the north. He stood until his feet ached and the cattle of the Lansdowne brothers began to low in the fields. A terrible familiarity had wrapped itself around his heart.

Dare. It was, after all, a false name, the name of a dead farm boy that Anson had given, out of an impulse he'd never regretted, to a run-away slave fortunate enough to look white. Dare. The name dropped from Anson's lips just like Latin, a word in a dead tongue. He wondered why the household did not wake at the sound. Anson closed his eyes as light moved swiftly over the river and marshes.

When the air greyed outside the window and the first pips of bird-sound drifted up from below, Anson could bear it no longer. Moving quietly, he put on his coat and boots, tiptoed down the hall past the Lansdowne's bedroom, walked softly down the stairs to the front door, and left the house. Outside, the musky smell wrapped him like a buffalo robe. Other than the intermittent lowing of cattle, bird pips, and river trickle, the pre-dawn was silent. Anson negotiated his way through the muddy field to the dew-slick gangway, walked to the edge of the wharf, and looked at the river. It was very broad, several miles across; he could see nothing but water. The agent had explained, in his boosterish manner, that millions of salmon swam right past this very landing on their way inland to spawn—a man could throw a net off the wharf and fill it in minutes during one of the big runs. And this year, he had said, a glint in his eyes, was expected to be very good indeed; there was no telling how many fish might choke the river.

Anson stared at the water and tried to imagine so much animal energy below the surface. But it was unimaginable. The river was dark, roiling. As the minutes passed, the surface grew lighter, became a rich brown, and moved faster, judging by the branches and what sometimes seemed to be whole trees on its surface. Anson stepped back from the edge. This was no eastern river; its wildness was far beyond the ken of his experience. His resolve to find a boat and row upriver in the direction of Crescent Slough weakened.

He looked nervously up the bank. Somewhere in that short grey distance, Dare was sleeping. The idea was no more fathomable than the idea of millions of fish pouring themselves against the river's flow. How rarely Anson had known his friend to sleep! In fact, he couldn't recall Dare's face in repose—always he had been awake, taking things in, helping, moving before being asked. It had been the same during those few days after the war, when Dare, at once grateful for Anson's friendship and restless to be on his way again, seemed never to relax. And to think of how much he had travelled since Anson had first lost news of him—a few months after Antietam, when ill health had forced Anson to resign his commission, though not before Dare was safe, as safe as a man could be while fighting a war. Anson did not even know all the places Dare had gone—south and west with the Army of the Potomac, then afterwards to Kansas, San Francisco, Victoria, and now the mouth of the Fraser River—no doubt there had been other stops along the way. Anson wondered how heavily those years of constant motion would be mapped on his friend's face. Dare would have aged; he could not have discovered any way to stop the progression of the suns. No, not even Dare could have learned that.

Faint voices swirled out of the grey. Anson tensed. Rapidly the voices grew louder—a harsh, guttural tongue suddenly exploded in the air. A wide, flat skiff filled with men emerged out of the half-light and drifted rapidly toward him. One man stood, hunched over, in the centre of the dark heads—like a flower with its petals torn off. Anson rallied to the panic in the voices; the shouts had turned to cries as the river hurled the skiff along the bank.

In a moment the faces took on definition. All were upraised, open-mouthed. They belonged to yellow men, Chinese, judging by the long pigtails dangling from their dark canvas slouch hats. Briefly, and for the first time, Anson had encountered the race and its language in San Francisco, but this shock meeting on the Fraser River transcended race and speech.

The skiff sped toward him. The faces, young and old, gap-toothed and darkly shadowed, loomed so close that Anson could attach the flung gutturals to individual mouths. The man hunched over in the centre of the skiff held a long pole and swung it toward the wharf. He shouted continuously, his lips peeled back, his hat fallen to the back of his skull and staying there by means of a string around his throat. Each time he swung the pole, the hat jumped up, as if he had a small monkey clutched to his back.

Anson suddenly understood the reason for the terror. The tide was running so fast, and the skiff was just far enough out in the main current, that the man with the pole could not secure a landing. The end of the pole bounced futilely on the first planks of the wharf, each contact threatening to upset the man's balance and plunge him into the river. Two of the other men grasped the pole man's coat tails, flailing instructions with their free hands, shouting words as harsh as retches. Another man had scrambled into the stern, where he held his arms out to the east, as if to embrace the sun he didn't expect to see again. His movements only increased the terror. Two others leapt to their feet and stepped, bent over, toward the bankside of the skiff.

Afraid they planned to jump, Anson shouted, "No! Don't!" and waved his arms frantically, at the same time looking around for a spot where he could plant his feet. To grab the pole would not be difficult, but how could he keep himself from being yanked into the river? The pole hit the wharf a few feet above him and he squatted, ready to drop backwards, his boots braced against the slightly raised crossbeam at the wharf's edge.

The Chinese had seen him now. A few words of English exploded out of the strange consonants and vowels, the surprising clarity and force of them almost as great as that of the skiff when Anson finally seized the pole.

"You hold! Swing the bow around!"

A few seconds of slack followed as the pole swung in front of Anson like a scythe. He drew in a deep breath, tightened the muscles in his thighs. In the skiff, the men who had been holding the coat tails now wrapped their arms around the pole man's lower body. He, in turn, crouched even lower.

With a jolt, Anson jerked forward, his arms tearing at their sockets. But his boots held firm to the raised beam. Second by second, the pole slid through his hands. He felt a stab of pain in his wrists, felt the skin of his palms tear. He lowered his head and hoped his muscles would not snap like weak rope.

The bow turned. A thump sounded on the wharf. Anson looked up to see one of the Chinese scrambling onto the dock and reaching out his hands to the others to pull the skiff safely in. The tension in the pole decreased. Another pair of boots struck the planks. The strange words were still loud but no longer panicked. The tension decreased again. Anson's shoulders and chest straightened. He drew several deep breaths. The familiar, enticing smell of opium engulfed him. He stared into his hands. Splinters were driven into the bloodied palms.

English again reached his ears. The Chinese surrounded him and grinned so widely that their faces threatened to crack like vases. One man said, "Thank you. You saved us. Thank you, sir." Another man bowed, then reached out and shook Anson's hand in both of his. He did not appear troubled by the blood, but Anson grimaced at the contact.

Heavy boot steps pounded across the wharf. Anson looked behind him to see Henry Lansdowne approaching, his face as sad as it had been the night before.

To Anson's amazement, the thin Englishman barked out a few words in Chinese. All of the men but one cringed at the sound and turned away, busying themselves with the moored skiff. The remaining man's grin quickly vanished. He was about to speak when Henry Lansdowne held up a hand and silenced him.

"Are you all right, doctor?" he said with genuine concern.

Anson nodded and wiped his bloody palms on his trousers.

"I saw what happened from the window. You're stronger than you seem. I'm sorry I wasn't able to get here in time to help."

"I'm only glad that I was here myself."

"These damned Orientals. I don't know why they choose to work near water when they're so afraid of it. Not one of them knows how to swim."

Henry Lansdowne scowled at the remaining Chinese—Anson recognized him as the one who'd held the pole. Alone of the group, this man did not wear a pigtail, and his face was fuller, healthier; the others had the emaciated, bone-showing, and skin-slack faces of nutritional deficiency so familiar to Anson from his war years.

"Why would you get it into your heads to travel on such a tide? You should have all been drowned or washed out to sea. Were you trying to get home to China? That's no way to do it."

The lone Chinese almost jumped in his eagerness to explain. "Not our fault. He's crazy. He's gone crazy. Not like other white men. He used a gun!"

Lansdowne narrowed his eyes. Briefly, he looked beyond Anson, upriver. It was an almost imperceptible glance, but the silence that followed it could not be mistaken.

"He called us spies!" the Chinese continued. "He says we work for Owen. He's crazy! He says he will make more cans himself!"

Lansdowne said coldly, "He isn't crazy. Not about that. He can make the cans, right enough. And better than you can make them too."

He turned to Anson. "I'm sorry, doctor. You'll want to return to the house. This is more of my brother's salmon business. These men make the cans for packing the fish."

Anson clenched his hands, felt the blood stick.

"Spies?" he said to the remaining Chinese man. "Why would he call you that?" He knew from Henry Lansdowne's tight-lipped expression, if nothing else, that they were talking about Dare.

The Chinese shrugged. "He's crazy, that's all. He thinks everyone out to get him."

Vivid light flooded over the mountain range. Some sort of marsh bird whistled by. Its flight turned Anson's gaze upriver.

"Maybe someone is," he said, watching the Englishman.

But Henry Lansdowne did not take the bait.

"If you please, doctor. My wife will see to your wounds."

Anson looked at his torn palms. "Thank you. But I wish to go to Crescent Slough this morning. As soon as possible. If it's a matter of payment . . ."

The Englishman frowned. "Once my wife has looked after you, and the tide is slack, I'll take you. We don't charge guests for our hospitality, doctor."

Satisfied, though a mite embarrassed by his unintended insult, Anson began to walk away. But a strange impulse, a prickling on his nape, made him stop and turn back. Lansdowne and the lone Chinese stood very close together. The Englishman's lips were moving. Against the pale sky the two heads were silhouetted as clear as cut glass. Anson began to shake. He wished it was only because his old weakness had returned, borne to him on the sweating terror of the men he'd pulled to safety. Because that weakness was something he knew, and knew he could overcome if he wanted to summon the strength. But there existed a curious kinship between this conversation whose words he couldn't hear and the Latin he could no longer recite with equanimity. The sensation was curious, more so than if he had heard Virgil's poetry in the mouth of a Chinese.

Anson noticed the empty skiff. If a soldier in a torn uniform had leapt from it, a dead man on his back, he would not even ask him about his purpose. The purpose didn't matter, not as much as the consequence. And maybe that didn't matter either.

The thought of life's futility—not entirely new to him, but never before draped in such black colours in such a lonely place—put the river beneath his feet, the salt of some great untraversable distance on his mouth. With a sigh, Anson continued his slow walk back toward the house.

❖　❖　❖

Three hours later, as Henry Lansdowne steered the skiff into the wharf at Crescent Slough, Anson shivered at the eerie silence hovering over Dare's settlement. By the time he stepped out of the skiff onto a small, black wharf, even the almost-ceaseless gull cry above the river had stopped, leaving only the sighings and gurglings of the slight current, the drone of mosquitoes, and, every few minutes, the incongruously cheerful trill of a blackbird or robin. Anson looked up at the earthen dike, twenty feet above the wharf and stretching southward along the riverbank toward a cluster of buildings similar to those that constituted the Lansdownes' cannery. Similar but with some clear differences.

Dare's main building was several hundred feet long, low—perhaps a dozen feet high—open-ended at the riverside and without windows. And its lumber was almost blond compared with the dark planks of the Lansdownes' cannery, perhaps, Anson thought, because it had been more recently built. But there was something disturbing about this white building. It did not look new so much as scoured, like a beached whale that had been gnawed down to its skeleton by the elements. And it stood out dramatically, because all the smaller buildings—A-framed and also windowless, likely used, as at Chilukthan, for net storage—were darker and touched in places with a dark green slime.

"I'll wait here," Henry Lansdowne said and lowered his head toward the gnarled fold of hands in his lap. "Just in case. Fifteen minutes, mind. No more than that."

Anson shook off the foreboding caused by his first sight of the white cannery building and almost smiled. Just in case of what? That Dare might chase him off with a gun as well?

"Thank you. I'll come back as soon as I can to let you know if I'm staying."

His calf and thigh muscles still aching from his rescue of the Chinese, Anson climbed the gangway and, upon reaching the dike, surveyed the immediate vista.

In a hollow about fifty yards away, a plain-planked, two-storey house sat in a foot of muddy water surrounded by huge weeping willows, their yellow fronds motionless. Another fifty yards off to one side of the building, near a cluster of cottonwoods, a canvas tent had been constructed. No one moved near the house or the tent, and no smoke rose against the blue sky. Anson approached the house. A single window, facing riverward, was boarded up, with perhaps an inch showing between boards. Anson peered in, conscious of not wanting to make Henry Lansdowne wait the full fifteen minutes. As he did so, a dog began to bark fiercely inside, its dark shape sliding across the broken sunlight falling into a large room filled with junk. Anson stepped back, then braved the dog's noise by staring through the gap again until his eyes adjusted to the gloom. Now he could see clothing scattered everywhere, cooking utensils, what looked like animal hides and pieces of fishnet. The barking increased, more shapes slid toward the window. Then Anson noticed the figures seated on the floor; they appeared to be weaving something. A body unfolded itself from the shadows and called to the dogs in a strange tongue. The dogs quieted and the body vanished. Anson stepped back again in confusion. Why should Dare have allowed his house to become an Indian village? At Chilukthan, the Indians camped on the riverbank, on the opposite side of the slough mouth.

Then Anson remembered the tent, and the explanation came to him. Dare would not be the only veteran of the war who preferred camp life to more civilized surroundings. After years of living rough, away from furnished rooms with only a simple fire and simpler meals to afford any material comfort, many ex-soldiers struggled to adjust to society. Of course, in such a forlorn place as this, with society so lacking, a man like Dare was free to arrange his living conditions to suit himself. And besides, he *had* been a slave; there was no telling what degrading conditions he'd once known. In any case, Anson had never asked Dare about his enslavement; to have done so at Antietam would have been to pour vinegar in an open wound. And afterwards, it had never seemed useful or tactful to raise the subject in a letter.

As he started toward the tent, Anson even envied Dare that particular kind of domestic freedom; many was the time he'd felt trapped by genteel surroundings, not to mention genteel manners. For a long while after he'd resigned his commission, the opium had given him an escape, and finally his love for Elizabeth had made everything that confined him a rare and exhilarating openness. But his blood never ceased to quicken at the sight of a campfire.

Dare's fire was cold ash, however. And the tent, musty, stained green with mildew, was empty except for a few blankets. Anson decided to check out the cannery. If he did not find Dare there, he'd have to either send Henry Lansdowne back alone or go with him. While he understood the veteran's fondness for camp life, Anson wasn't entirely sure he'd like to forego the comfort and company of Chilukthan while he waited for Dare to come back from wherever he was.

On the earthen dike above the cluster of cannery buildings, he hesitated. The stillness below was somehow uninviting, but he descended and began to explore the dusky interiors, starting with the long, low building, which must have been new, since its walls exuded a powerful scent of cedar. But the freshness vanished as Anson stared at the long, waist-high wooden tables and sluices, the greasy bulk of silent machines, the complicated chains and gears and belts ominous in their static condition, like diseased animals waiting to die. The interior was a large, unpartitioned space, yet it felt cramped, oppressive. A strong smell of blood and salt rose off the planks, and several pieces of salmon—a severed tail, some gobs of red flesh—lay in the shadowy corners. Obviously the cannery had been working recently; even the machines gave off a burnt, acrid smell as Anson leaned closer to them.

In a smaller building, he discovered something remarkable: hundreds of thousands of empty, lidless tins, stacked fifteen feet high, right up to the rafters, gave a silver shock of brightness to the gloom. Anson stared at them in awe. How did Dare have so many? Perhaps this was the reason he could chase his crew away.

The doctor did not brood long over these questions. They seemed less important than the restless, shifting loneliness that prowled the wet rods between Dare's home and his cannery. As Anson stood by the tins, the breeze through the door brought a low whistling out of them, as though in warning. His skin prickled. Something alive in the emptiness of the whole settlement disturbed him. He had the eerie feeling that the machines were going to whir into action at any second and that the planks of the buildings and the dirt of the dike would be fed into them. The question of Dare's whereabouts had almost slipped his mind when he backed away from the tins and turned directly into the path of an elderly Chinaman holding a shotgun.

"What you want?" The Chinaman raised the gun before him, straight upright, and floated back a few steps, turning his head quickly from side to side as if convinced other white men unknown to him might appear at any second. Thin and tall, he wore a long pigtail and a faded blue smock. One eye was milky, likely blind.

Recovering from his shock, Anson grew irritated at the man's aggression.

"I've come to see your boss," he said. "Where is he?"

The Chinese placed the long nail of his forefinger to his wispy-haired chin. "Who are you? Do you know him?"

"I'm an old friend. From the United States."

"The United States?" The Chinaman grinned, revealing a front tooth that hung like a tiny ice pick and several gold-capped molars that seemed roughly jammed into place. "Maybe you a buyer, huh?"

"No. Listen, is he here or not?"

The Chinaman lowered the gun horizontally, to his waist.

"Gone to New Westminster. Back maybe one week."

"A week? Why so long?"

The Chinese grinned even more broadly than before. "Business. Fish almost come. Much work to do."

Anson wondered why this one man had not been forced away at gunpoint like the others, but he wasn't given the encouragement to ask. Almost as suddenly as he'd arrived, the Chinaman disappeared, fading away like smoke. The doctor had little choice but to return to the wharf and inform Henry Lansdowne of Dare's absence.

"You'll be wanting to stay on with us, then?" the Englishman said, his voice neither warm nor cold.

Anson turned and took a final look toward Dare's settlement. There still weren't any gulls keening above the cannery. The absence of the rhythmic sound of tin being cut suddenly struck him like the absence of the pulse in a body. The silence was gloomy, and not even the sunshine brought any warmth to the place.

"Yes," he said. "For a short time. But I intend to pay for my room and board."

The Englishman scowled. "If you prefer."

Anson sighed. What he would have preferred was to go upriver to New Westminster and find a hotel, but, somehow, he felt the need to stay closer to Crescent Slough. If the place itself wasn't so unwelcoming, he might have made himself at home in the tent. But he well knew what sleeping rough would do to his aching body.

Slowly he lowered himself into the skiff, almost ashamed by how relieved he was to return to Chilukthan. And yet, the silence made him even more anxious to see Dare and talk with him. There was something unnervingly final about it that needed to be halted before the silence spread all along the river and spilled over into Anson's own crowded memories; he did not want the past blanked out this way, no matter how much it might haunt him. For the past, after all, was nothing less than a proof of life. Without its tug, how was a man to know his blood still flowed through his body?

Henry Lansdowne unmoored the skiff and settled behind the oars. Somehow his silence was of a different kind, and Anson had no desire to break it. Instead, the doctor sat in the stern and watched the black emptiness of Crescent Slough shrink to the size of a cave mouth, to the size of a horse's eye, to nothing.

IV

Three days passed, leavened only by Anson's keen interest in Chilukthan's preparations for the next salmon run. Rarely had he seen such a combination of skill and speed as evinced by the Indian women on the main wharf who wove the linen fishnets. But the Chinese crew who soldered the cans in back of one of the smaller buildings especially fascinated him, mostly because their hot, repetitive work with molten solder and tinplate and muriatic acid was exactly what Dare must have been doing for years. Watching the Chinese through the crinkled air of extreme temperatures as they doused pig lead in large, fire-enveloped crucibles of brick, it was in fact easy to see Dare through the smoke and steam, sweating as he carefully applied his soldering iron along the seams of each tin. Along with the heat and the dull rhythm of the pressman stepping on the treadle that activated the cutting of the tinplate sheets into appropriate sizes, the cloying smells of the chemicals quickly disoriented Anson's senses. But he could not easily pull himself away. There was something mesmeric in the rapid movements of the Chinese as they waved their brushes of acid in calligraphy strokes and fed sheets of tin into machines, all the while grinning as if delighted to be doing any kind of work that kept them away from the river. The explosive clash of red flame against silver, the endless billows of grey smoke and dripping steam, the blurred faces appearing and disappearing in the heat-curdled air held Anson in a thrall he could break only when he felt himself on the verge of passing out.

Despite the fascinating diversions of the fishing preparations, however, and many hours spent in his room reading his well-worn editions of Virgil and Tibullus, Anson grew increasingly restless. For the first time since Antietam, Dare had summoned him for help, and in this instance it was with words, clear and direct, not with an escaped slave's red-eyed look of terror. The significance was not lost on Anson: because Dare had cabled, Dare's life must be threatened. And if his life was threatened, and Anson could not help, then more than their shared past was in peril; his nobler sentiments, his love for his country and for Elizabeth, would be committed at last to the same cold grave. Each moment that passed in which he did not begin to act on Dare's summons in some practical way gnawed at Anson's nerves, at his sense of himself as a man who could be relied upon.

He tried to hire an Indian to row him the two miles upriver to New Westminster, but they were all too occupied with their cannery work to oblige him. And in any case, Anson wasn't even sure that Dare had remained in that city. According to Henry Lansdowne, Dare most likely took a ship along the opposite bank from New Westminster to Victoria, because that was where a cannery crew could be hired. When Anson mentioned that he ought to do the same, the Englishman looked at him soberly.

"If he's gone to Victoria, he'll soon be back. The salmon are on their way, doctor. With respect, you are a stranger here and do not recognize the urgency. The salmon are a curious harvest, most unpredictable. They are not like the apples in the trees or even the potatoes in the ground. They live far out at sea for years before they are called back to the very waters inland in which they came to be. Theirs is a blessed and miraculous travail. It is much harder to be sure of their bounty."

"Then how is it that you know they are coming in such numbers?"

The two men had stood on the dike above the cannery at Chilukthan, looking north over the river. Henry Lansdowne rubbed a bony hand along the white side whiskers of one cheek. His voice, though low and somber, suddenly trembled with a distinct quality of awe.

"You ask how I know that the salmon are coming in such numbers? Doctor, I know as only a devout man knows his God. They are coming. Theirs is a cycle designed by the Lord, and He has made it Truth that in every fourth year, the salmon return in abundance. Even the Indians, savage though they are, understand this. And Mr. Dare . . ."

Anson's blood quickened. He waited for the insult, prepared to refute it, but it did not come.

". . . appears to understand the salmon's habits better than most. He'll be back before they are here."

Reluctantly, Anson accepted his host's logic. The wisest course, as so often proved to be the case, was the hardest course. And if it was so hard to wait, Anson consoled himself finally that waiting was the right thing to do.

And so, in the days that followed, he tramped the soft peat bogs, scaring up flocks of red-winged blackbirds, their scarlet bangles shaking like rose petals in the wind. Once, he had met Thomas Lansdowne's daughter, Louisa, along the way. She was a pretty girl of ten years, with long black hair and a winning, dimpled smile. The day had been blustery, and her hair had blown out behind her in a rippled stream. Anson had been gripped by a sudden, not unpleasant sensation that he had encountered the childhood ghost of his late, beloved wife, except that this girl, Louisa, while she possessed Elizabeth's same delicate cheekbones and rosy complexion, was more animated; it seemed, in fact, that her vital nature was straining against the very proprieties and gloom of the settlement. He had exchanged only the briefest of pleasantries with the child before she had skipped off over the peat, her small hand holding the straw bonnet to her head to prevent its flying off on the breeze.

Other than that rare encounter, Anson met no one, not even when he walked back and forth along the short dike—only a hundred feet long—that fronted Henry Lansdowne's property. Sometimes he walked a half-mile along the slough bank, to a point opposite Thomas Lansdowne's house, drawn there by the cry of crows building nests high in one of the great bell tower fir trees. Often, too, he watched the Chinese and Indians at work, and he always sought to keep out of the way of the industrious Lansdownes. But most of all, he tried not to place the silence at Crescent Slough alongside the image of Dare's terrified face at Antietam and the mutilated corpse of his murdered master. But the thick clouds of black flies and mosquitoes hanging over every foot of the settlement, as well as the palpable sense of anticipation in the air about the salmon's return, which was almost akin to the tension preceding a military engagement, only increased Anson's unease.

Finally, one morning, he stood trembling on the wharf in heavy rain, watching the progress of the paddlewheeler coming up the river from the Gulf. Large drops fell off his hat brim, blurring his view. But there was little enough to see. The wind had raised a chop on the black river, and the steamer's smoke plume immediately dissolved above the boat, which crept relentlessly up the channel, black as a bull pulling a plough. The dull thump of the paddles rose and died with the gusting wind. Anson willed it to arrive faster, eager to know if Dare was on board.

The black shape broadened gradually in the channel as the tide-weighted paddles thumped out the heavy minutes. It was a dismal process, and so the sudden apparition of Louisa running up the gangway lifted Anson's spirits.

She was, indeed, a regular whip of a child, crackling with energy, her dark hair and eyes vivid and shining like black fire. In the days since meeting her on the peat bog, Anson had grown very attached to the idea of her presence, perhaps too attached. For he had begun to pity her, and he was in no position to feel that way; he had no right, and no manner of helping even if he overlooked the insignificance of their bond. To be so filled with joy in such a joyless place! But perhaps the child's lot was simply the human one, and the reason he felt so removed from God.

"Dr. Baird! Dr. Baird! We're going to have a house guest! He's coming on the steamer!" The child's hair gusted around her bright cheeks, her words danced on the air.

Anson smiled. "A guest? What sort of guest? Another doctor?"

With a flutter of her hands, she pushed her hair back and leaned forward, blinking downriver into the rain. "I don't think so. Father didn't say." She chewed on her full bottom lip. "But . . ." Her eyes widened. "He's an American, like you."

No, child, Anson thought, not like me, a worn-out country doctor who suffers terrible nightmares when he can fall asleep at all, a veteran who served his country and his conception of God and now hardly believes in either. That kind of American doesn't generally travel the world. He stays home, among his people, quietly doing his work and waiting, like those under the grass at Antietam and Gettysburg, to be forgotten.

The paddlewheeler drew close enough for the dark water on the paddles to be visible. Smoke lay like a whipped cur along the stack. The rain bounced off the river and the planks of the wharf.

"Where's your bonnet?" Anson said. "You should be wearing one, Louisa."

She laughed and tilted her face up into the storm. "I hope he isn't a doctor. They worry too much."

She stood on her tiptoes at the very edge of the wharf. Anson was certain she was about to clap. But then her uncle emerged out of the weather, moving blackly and efficiently toward the moored skiff, and the sight of him automatically drew her back from the edge.

Slowly the paddles stopped their revolutions. Into the new quiet the rain swelled. Anson realized he had no desire to meet one of his countrymen. Such encounters were inevitably delicate, especially if the person was from the South. But, of course, he didn't meet many Southerners, and, in any case, he preferred not to discuss the war or current politics with Northerners either. Over the years, he had listened to patients who had served in the army, listened with sympathy to the catalogues of ailments that they'd picked up in the great conflict, and even held his tongue when some veterans complained that freeing the niggers hardly seemed an honourable accomplishment. Anson had heard such comments often enough and tried not to judge the speakers; usually they were suffering from old wounds and sicknesses, and then there was always the inexplicable sense of loss that followed a war. The ancient Greeks and Romans had experienced it too, and their battles had never been so momentous and violent in scale.

Well, whoever this American was, Anson recognized that he wasn't likely to be much involved with him. In fact, if Dare was on the steamer, Anson wouldn't even be staying on at Chilukthan.

To his surprise, this thought induced a wave of melancholy. He looked at the child again. How different his life would have been if he'd become a father! That responsibility would be enough to steady a man, to keep him working for the future despite whatever nightmares and plagues trailed after him from the past. Thomas Lansdowne, for example: he possessed an admirable resolve to succeed, a faith that Anson could hardly understand, though he deemed it the proper attitude for the head of a family. This child, then, was fortunate. He need not pity her.

They stood in silence as the driving rain weakened to a drizzle and Henry Lansdowne rowed evenly into the choppy channel to the steamer. Once there, he helped the passengers into the skiff and began rowing back again. Anson suddenly felt an overwhelming desire to flee. There was but a single passenger, a stranger. Dare had not returned.

As the skiff pulled closer, Anson's nerves began to fray. The passenger's appearance was disturbing. He was not young, so he would have knowledge and opinions of the war. But much worse than this was the one sleeve of the man's coat: it was empty and pinned to his chest. A wounded veteran, and all that remained to complete the dismal picture was the man's country. For Anson could not, even in his most patriotic moments, believe that the defeated Confederacy had gone away, at least not as a moral entity in the minds of its citizens.

He watched Henry Lansdowne moor the skiff and help the passenger out. Louisa ran forward but then turned to him, beaming. "Come along, Dr. Baird, come and meet our guest."

And for the child's sake, certainly not his own, Anson stood in the drizzle and awkwardly shook the passenger's gracefully extended left hand.

"Ambrose Richardson. A pleasure to meet you, sir."

The accent wasn't strong, but it was there, a mild lilt, a subtle music. By the time Anson had come close enough to the man to see his narrow face and pale blue eyes, receding hairline, and full handlebar moustache of pure white, he had expected the worst. Now the man, tall and compactly built, his long legs bowed, suggesting he'd spent considerable time on horseback, was scanning Anson's face, likely trying to estimate his allegiances and service record. It was wearying.

Falling back on his habitual courtesy, Anson asked the newcomer how long he planned to stay in Chilukthan.

"It depends," Ambrose Richardson said, removing his hat from where he'd expertly tucked it under what remained of his amputated limb. He shook the rain from the hat before settling it back on his head. "If I like what I see of this salmon venture, I might want to stay a while and watch the proceedings. I understand the fishing is quite the spectacle."

"Yes. I believe so."

"And are you here as well, doctor, as an interested observer?"

Anson smiled thinly. He could hardly explain, even to himself, why he remained. To help an old friend, a comrade-in-arms? Yes. But also, perhaps, to confirm the rightness of the war and to honour its dead. Anson realized he couldn't say so, and he wondered how much of the thought could be read in his face. Well, no doubt there would be other conversations. Dare was not on the boat; Anson would be staying on at Chilukthan, if not as an interested observer, then as a patient witness of whatever the resurrected past had in store for him.

"I've come to visit an old friend who lives nearby. But he's gone away on business. I'm waiting for his return." Anson looked at Henry Lansdowne, expecting some response in the form of a scowl or narrowing of the eyes, but the Englishman, surprisingly, was bent at the waist, speaking to his niece. Now the girl was indeed clapping; she could not contain her happiness, the words came rushing out.

"Oh, Uncle, really? Something for me? What is it? When can I see it?"

Henry Lansdowne hushed her gently, then rose.

"Mr. Richardson, if you'll just come with me. We've arranged for you to stay at my brother's home. Thomas will conduct you through the cannery when you've had a chance to get settled. Louisa here will accompany us." He nodded to Anson. "Good day, doctor. We will see you this evening? Mr. Richardson and our relatives will be dining at the house."

And with that, they were gone and Anson stood by himself once more, cold rain dripping down his neck, his body still shaking. He watched the two men and the girl enter the muddy field. Beyond them came the sound of wood chopping. The thick stand of trees just past Thomas Lansdowne's house loomed on the horizon. The axe blows fell heavily, in a dull, steady rhythm.

Anson realized that he couldn't stay much longer, but he had to wait for Dare's return. The rain that fell seemed even colder now. If Dare didn't come soon . . . But Anson didn't complete the thought. There was no need. He would stay as long as necessary. Looking across the muddy field, he imagined he saw his old friend against the light, just as he'd once seen the shell-smashed tree in the Antietam battlefield. But as Anson took a step toward him, Dare retreated, an image only, a trick of memory. And there was only the woodlot and the sound of the falling axe and the chilling feel of an old enemy's hand, the wrong hand, on his wet palm, so chilling it might have been the dead one, lopped off almost twenty years before.

❖　　❖　　❖

Dinner that evening began politely, calmly, with experienced, time-hewn faces around a table in candlelight, gracious if tentative conversation, the aroma of roast beef pleasantly circulating, the light clink of cutlery, the illusion of a decorous and genteel world tucked neatly between a wild, powerful river and a billion cold stars with heathen Chinese going about their mysterious rituals in their own illusory imaginings, whatever they might be.

Yet as he cut into the blood-tinged meat on his plate, Anson shrank from the lightly probing questions of his countryman, the alternately distracted and raptly attentive features of Thomas Lansdowne, and, most of all, the ghostly urgency of Edney Lansdowne to belong in the material sphere. For the woman, it was painfully obvious after fifteen minutes had passed, was still grief-haunted and barely able to stifle either tears or screams—Anson had seen the malady in women before, and it always defeated him, medically and morally. Looking at her, he could not abide the artifice of gentility; she wore her dark but grey-streaked hair in two severe braids, leaving a part like a long, white scar on her skull. Her brow was creased, her cheeks sunken and the cheekbones prominent, and the black of her eyes dull. Anson was appalled. The woman should have been home, resting, especially since she was clearly with child. But he couldn't bring himself to inquire after her health; to do so somehow seemed akin to attacking her. In any case, he kept expecting one of the family to relieve her of the burden of hospitality.

But Thomas Lansdowne, looking ill at ease and pulling periodically at the shirt collar around his thick, ruddy neck, was intently seeking Ambrose Richardson's impressions of Victoria. Was it not a thriving capital city? And New Westminster, the visitor would find, was equally prosperous.

The Southerner responded amiably, neatly dabbing at the corners of his mouth with a napkin. Yes, Victoria appeared lively, there was certainly considerable evidence of commercial enterprise. And then the blood on Anson's plate and knife appeared to shine.

"In a warehouse near the harbour," Ambrose Richardson said, "I almost made the acquaintance of one of your fellow salmon canners, Mr. Lansdowne. At least, I had him pointed out to me by the proprietor, but he was gone before I had the opportunity to speak with him. The name was Dare. He is familiar to you, no doubt?"

The Lansdowne brothers exchanged glances. Then Thomas Lansdowne cleared his throat and took a drink of water, his other hand clenched around a fork that he held, motionless, at chest height. Into the silence came the keening of the wind.

"Perhaps I'm mistaken in the name?" Ambrose Richardson blinked benignly at each of the brothers in turn.

"William Dare," Anson said, watching one of the candle flames flicker and go out, "is the man I've come to visit."

The Southerner smiled. "Well, now, if that's not a coincidence?

I wish I had spoken with him. But, as I say, the moment he'd been pointed out to me, he was no longer there. An energetic and industrious man. And one of the more successful canners, I understand. The proprietor of the warehouse said as much."

The air thickened. Anson looked away from Thomas Lansdowne's white-knuckled fist to his wife's uncomprehending stare—neither sight calmed him. In fact, he could sense his impatience and irritation rising.

Henry Lansdowne laid his knife down carefully and said, "Mr. Dare has made several good packs, I believe. But he's not exactly free with such information. He does not . . . that is, he is not a man to fraternize."

Anson had had enough of the cautious English equivocations. Damn it, what was going on? Here he was, politely dining with a woman caged in her own thoughts, whatever they were, and a wounded Virginian whose arm Anson might well have cut off in another age and place, and all the while he was fighting the desire to join a Chinese work crew for a long smoke of an opium pipe. The illusion had to cease.

"Dare has always been a private man. It's a trait that I've grown to appreciate more over the years, given its rarity. Men, as a general rule, take too great an interest in the affairs of others, wouldn't you agree?"

"But, doctor," Ambrose Richardson said, "you have very succinctly described the world of business." He winked at the Lansdowne brothers. "And if Dare is successful in business, he must, therefore, take a most considerable interest in the affairs of his competitors."

Anson bristled. He disliked the wink and the supercilious tone, but the stolid, closed faces of the Lansdownes bothered him even more. Turning to the elder, he said, "Is this true? Is this your impression of Dare?"

"My impression," Henry Lansdowne responded flatly, "is of no consequence."

"He is"—Thomas Lansdowne began with energy, ignoring his brother's raised hand—"rather more combative than private."

"Combative?" Anson's pulse quickened. "In what way?"

Ambrose Richardson said, "Sir, you are too sensitive. We must consider the company." He smiled across the table. "Business cannot be but a dull subject for the ladies. We must reserve such conversation for after this fine meal."

Reserve the conversation be damned, Anson thought. And if you're considering the ladies, you might have noticed that one, at least, is ill and not even listening.

"I've been here nearly a week, sir, and in that time any mention of my friend's name has resulted in a definite air of disapproval. Mr. Lansdowne says that Dare is combative. I think the accusation merits an explanation."

The Southerner flushed; his smile vanished into a tight line. "Doctor, if you do not have the manners to be composed when a guest at someone's table, you ought not to accept the hospitality."

"You've only just arrived, and you presume too much." Anson leaned forward into the candle flickers, staring hard at Thomas Lansdowne. "I believe this gentleman possesses the good grace to answer my question."

"Dr. Baird," Henry Lansdowne said calmly, "we know little of your friend. If we knew anything that would be of any use to you, of course we would have shared it."

Thomas Lansdowne opened his clenched fist and let his fork drop to the table. "You ask why I consider Dare to be combative? Well, you've met his crew. Does a peaceful man chase off his Chinamen with a shotgun?"

"What's this?" Ambrose Richardson said. "A shotgun?"

Anson crossed his arms over his chest. "And are you privy to his reasons? The Chinese said he thought they were spies. Now, would my friend, whom I regard as the most sensible and practical of men, dream up such an idea without foundation?"

Thomas Lansdowne pushed back his chair and stood. The veins in his neck bulged. He leaned hard on the table. "What do you mean by that? Are you suggesting that . . ."

"Sit down, Thomas," Henry Lansdowne said. "The doctor's not suggesting anything. He is, quite rightly, concerned for his friend. Dr. Baird, I am certain Dare will return soon. When he does, you can no doubt gather his impressions of the delta."

But this effort to defuse the tension failed miserably. Ambrose

Richardson had stood as well, his back very straight, his pinned sleeve completely still. "I would apologize, ladies, for the behaviour of my countryman, if indeed we shared the same country."

Ah, yes, Anson frowned, it was only a matter of time. He steeled himself for the fight, but a small gasp from across the table stopped him from responding.

"Edney, dear, what is it?" Mary Lansdowne reached a hand out to her sister-in-law, who was staring wide-eyed at the black window. Her mouth hung open, the fingers of one hand were splayed at her throat.

Then, from outside, came the rapid, violent barking of a dog.

"Here, Edney," Mary Lansdowne urged, "drink some water. Oh, Father, perhaps a little Madeira. To settle her nerves."

"I'll see to the dog," Thomas Lansdowne said and charged around the table, out of the room.

"Excuse us, gentlemen," Henry Lansdowne said, rising. "I must speak with my brother. Mary, take Edney to lie down."

"If there's anything I can do," Ambrose Richardson said, addressing Mary Lansdowne.

Anson rose and went to the stricken woman's side, feeling guilty that he had not acted sooner upon his observance of her nervous condition. She was pale, her pulse very rapid.

"May," she whispered. "Outside. Mary, I'm certain of it. It was she."

"Hush now, hush. Let the doctor tend to you."

On his knees beside her chair, Anson gently let her wrist down into her lap. "A small glass of spirits is sensible. See if you can get her to take a few sips before she lies down."

Edney Lansdowne gazed at the air. "May. Oh, child, what is it? What can I do?"

Distressed, Mary Lansdowne hurriedly helped her sister-in-law to her feet and gently led her away.

Two candles had gone out, dimming the room. The keening of the wind increased until it seemed to surround the house. But the barking, at least, had stopped. Anson returned to his chair at the table, thinking, of course, she's suffered the loss of a daughter who was almost a young woman, that explains it. And now, in her condition, she doubtless fears another loss, the two events becoming one in her mind; it's not uncommon, and, yet, it seems close to unbal-ancing her reason. I must speak with the husband.

Ambrose Richardson's continued presence took Anson by sur-prise, more so than his contentious manner.

"I would not think," he said, all pretence of manners dropped like a gauntlet, "that you'd have the gall to speak of interfering in other people's affairs, as if it were something that offended you. Your coun-try's interference in my country's affairs cost me a great deal more than my arm. You're fortunate that my losses have not deprived me of my adherence to the proprieties of civilized life. But I warn you, sir . . ." He pulled his shoulders back and glared down at Anson. "I'm no more apt to forget an insult to myself than I am to forget an insult to my country."

Anson rarely had any taste for such argument. The past, as it had often done, exhausted him. He had spent the better part of twenty years trying to escape the honest, killing errors he and his medical colleagues had perpetrated in the name of healing. All those surgeries performed in filth, all those wounded men lying in stables and barn-yards and manured fields, all those instruments cleaned in bloody water. It didn't help to know that they'd done so much damage in innocence, just as it certainly didn't help to know that victory had not put an end to the hatred between the two combatants. And Anson knew that he'd come to the aid of Dare for the sake of washing away the ugliest memories of that past; his friend was still the cure for futil-ity and despair, just as he had been at Antietam. There might not be a god or a country worth all that suffering, but there remained the idea of a certain kind of man, an idea Anson continued to put his faith in. If he did not, then there was no reason at all to respond to the hatred directed at him now.

He stood and, unblinking, faced the self-righteous Southerner. "When you threaten a man or his country, you must expect the conse-quences. I won't hesitate to defend myself."

"Defend?" Richardson's jaw trembled. "Is that what you call the war, a defence?"

"Yes. A defence of principles."

Richardson's cheeks flushed. His jaw and eyes went rigid. "I suppose you're referring to the negroes. And do you suppose, doctor, that you've done that race a great service? You think they're happier now, working for the great munificence of your wages?"

"I would imagine they are, yes. Better to do an honest day's work for yourself than to do a lifetime's work for someone else."

Richardson smiled unpleasantly, revealing a yellow cast to his teeth. "That's the trouble with your country, doctor. You make no distinction between work and money. It never occurs to you, does it, that a man might work for something greater than that?"

"If money means freedom, then it must be great indeed to those who are only allowed to earn it for others."

"Have you lived among them? Do you understand the first thing about what they value?"

Suddenly Anson saw a young, white-skinned man staggering across an open stretch of torn earth, his eyes swimming with terror. Money was beside the point. That young man had almost driven himself mad to earn his freedom. Anson had no more time for the Southerner's platitudes about slavery than he had for the Christian's blind belief in a merciful God. Dare existed outside of both positions. He assumed only one: that a man of character and courage deserved to be the master of his own life.

But before Anson could articulate the thought to Richardson, the Lansdownes returned.

"Our sincere apologies, gentlemen," the elder said. "We wished only to make a check of the property. The Orientals, and the Indians of the area, are generally to be trusted, but, of course, we can't take their movements for granted."

"Be thankful," Richardson said, still meeting Anson's eyes, "that you do not live among negroes. A country free of their treachery must indeed be a country of opportunity."

Anson looked down without responding. In a few seconds, once he had composed himself, he raised his head again. The bitterness, he acknowledged, was understandable. After all, his side had won the war and he had tasted the dregs of the victory; he could only imagine how much greater was the bitterness of the defeat. Suddenly, Ambrose Richardson, standing there in his honour, missing one arm and who knew what else, seemed a pitiable figure. Anson had no desire to continue the verbal gamesmanship.

He didn't have to. Henry Lansdowne said with surprising coolness, almost vehemence, "We do not sit in judgment, sir, but it would be best not to speak of your country's unfortunate history of enslavement."

"Brother," Thomas Lansdowne said as he stepped in front of him to address the Southerner. "It's been a trying evening. My wife, as you can see, is ill. Dr. Baird has, I believe, been too long among us and we have been perhaps too preoccupied with daily matters to be sufficiently hospitable. As well, the time of preparing for the next salmon run is difficult and puts us all on edge. An early evening, I think, is advisable."

This was the longest and most articulate speech Anson had heard from the younger Lansdowne, and it was remarkably effective. Ambrose Richardson soon deferred to it with a nod and a few curt words.

"I've not come all this way to discuss negroes with those who have no knowledge of them. You're experts on the subject of the salmon, and about the canning of them for market. That is why I'm here. Tomorrow you'll show me your operations and we'll discuss business."

He bowed stiffly, his arm across his waist.

"I'll walk back with you," Thomas Lansdowne said.

"And your good lady?"

Henry Lansdowne explained that he would accompany his sister-in-law home after she'd rested a while. Then his brother and Ambrose Richardson departed. Anson found himself alone with the elder Lansdowne. They stood in uncomfortable silence for a moment until the Englishman finally excused himself. Anson, understanding the man's embarrassment, waited briefly before walking into the front hall and putting on his coat. Then he stepped outside.

It was a clear night, the sky star-clustered, a small full moon shedding wan light over the fields and slough. The figures of Thomas Lansdowne and Ambrose Richardson, a dog at their sides, were just visible against the black backdrop of the woodlot. Anson lit a cigar as he watched them diminish, and inhaled gratefully. Though he disliked to admit it, he conceded that the Virginian had a point; it had been improper to confront the Lansdownes about Dare in that company. First, one of the ladies was indisposed. Second, he had only just made Richardson's acquaintance. Anson accepted that his timing had not been propitious. He blew smoke at the stars and stepped slowly along the veranda. Fifty yards to the west loomed the bulk of a ridge-roofed barn. Just beyond it, along the dike, began the cluster of cannery buildings, and beyond those there was only river and marsh. Much closer, thirty yards to the north of where he stood, the Lansdownes' gangway and wharf hung, tiny as children's toys, at the edge of the great muddy river.

Anson exhaled another plume of smoke and tried to orient himself. Two miles up the river, on the opposite bank, was the city of New Westminster. Dare's settlement was almost as distant, though on the near bank. It seemed hard to imagine any *single* human life, not to mention whole communities of them, out there in the thick, brinish dark. Anson gazed at it until the heavy sameness forced him to blink. If nothing else, he thought, a man had plenty of quiet for reflection here. Other than the intermittent hooting of owls and lowing of cattle beneath the wind, the night was still. The Chinese, of course, were by now well ensconced in their melancholic sojourns along the opium trail, and it was all Anson could do to keep his thoughts from becoming regretted actions. Dare had made life unexpectedly difficult for him, but perhaps the trial had a purpose, perhaps he was meant to endure it for a greater good he could not yet foresee. Even so, Anson was not sure that he should wait any longer for a Victoria-bound steamer. It might be a pleasant diversion to visit New Westminster, even if for only a week. Someone there might be able to provide more information about Dare's conflict with the two Englishmen; it couldn't be a large city, after all.

He put his hands on the veranda railing and stared at the red end of the cigar in his fingers. In the surrounding dark, the tiny light was like one of the soldiers' meek fires in the days after the Battle of Antietam. How fragile they had seemed after all the carnage, and how welcome too—ever since, Anson had never ceased to be attracted to a good fire; it seemed at once a refuge and an escape. In those long nights of misery, his hands and feet aching, his bowels loose and stomach cramped, his lungs filled with the spreading miasma of death, how powerfully the soldiers' weakest fires had fortified him. Between the comfort and hope inherent in the flames and the equally vital presence of goodness in William Dare's character, Anson had found his survival. Was he, then, to feel chagrined by his continuing loyalty? No, he would not apologize for that. But a man of his years ought to practise greater diplomacy.

He lifted the cigar to his lips again and considered the immediate future. Thomas Lansdowne must be warned about the perils of his wife's condition; she clearly required more than a few hours of rest. And Anson realized it was indeed advisable that he should take the next steamer out of Chilukthan, no matter which direction it was headed. In the meantime, he'd stay discreetly out of Ambrose Richardson's company and he'd limit his conversations with the Lansdownes, especially on the subject of Dare.

Satisfied, Anson flicked the cigar into the muddy yard and was about to return inside the house when he heard a faint, curious tinkling sound coming from the direction of the river. It was an eerily familiar sound, and at first he doubted that he'd really heard it. He strained to shut out the wind. Yes, there it came again, a glassy shivering. Anson closed his hands to keep them from shaking. All the calm he'd gathered from the cigar was evaporating with each repetition of the sound. He looked dully into the moonlit dark, expecting . . . what? He knew that glassy shivering, but it took him a moment to see the wagon in his mind's eye and the burly photographer with the heavy brogue and pointed questions. It had been some time since Anson had recollected that image. Ah, but it was too much, fanciful—the product, he knew, of futile brooding. A man could find the past everywhere if he wasn't vigilant against it.

Self-knowledge. Anson had never considered himself a fool, and he wasn't about to change. And yet, there was a reason for the patterns the mind assumed, just as there were reasons for the rhythms in nature. If he'd come to the delta of the Fraser River to find again the battlefield of Antietam, so be it. And why should that even be a surprise? In twenty years Dare had never asked for him to come anywhere, had only sent telegrams and brief letters regarding business matters after their last meeting, when Dare had stayed at Anson's home. So, out of loyalty and genuine faith in the man, Anson had come to this Canadian river. There was misery and tension all around him, his old longing for opium had returned, and a former enemy bearing the physical evidence of defeat had opened the painful wounds of his country's severance. Why should all this not be photographed like a battlefield? It would make a fine study of the dissolution of the years. Anson could see the grinning Scotsman making a square of his fingers before his eyes.

But the image faded. Anson knew he was not prone to fancies. So he left the veranda and walked around the house. The glassy sound increased as he crossed the field toward the wharf, and, walking up the gangway, he recognized the sound as piano music. He could not have been more amazed if there had been a tripod set up on the planks with a grinning figure poised to vanish under a black cloth. In different circumstances, Anson would have clapped his hands with joy at the unexpectedness of life, he would have gladly succumbed to humility before the mysterious workings of a greater power. As it was, the sight he came upon only deepened his dread, for it struck him as grotesquely out of place, like seeing children emerge from a woodlot at Antietam. His mouth filled with the smoke of long-dead ashes, Anson approached the unlikely congruence in the moonlight. But with each step, one amazement gave way to another. For as he reached the source of the sound, he felt easier in his spirit, liberated from the poisonous miasma of his own musings.

The girl stood in the middle of the wharf, her thin figure in the moonlight slightly hunched, her elbows extended to either side. Bareheaded, her long, black hair gleaming, she faced the river. But he knew she could not see it, for her view was blocked by the large wooden crate that had been unloaded from the paddlewheeler some days before and that Anson had assumed contained cannery equipment. Off to her right, stepping rapidly forward and back, poised as if to run, stood the girl's older brother, Edward, a reserved, handsome boy of twelve years. Near his feet lay the front side of the crate. Only when Anson had reached the end of the gangway and stepped onto the wharf did he notice that the boy held a hammer in one hand and a crowbar in the other. Even in the bright moonlight, his face looked ashen.

But Louisa did not lift her hands from the piano, which, as far as Anson could see, was a handsome instrument, the front of its high back ornately carved and almost gleaming, as if made of rosewood or some other special variety. The high notes swirled into the damp air, notes as delicate and pretty as the child who gave them life. Anson felt the tears come to his eyes. In such a remote and forlorn place, where beauty seemed mostly to exist in the surroundings, such music was a rare beneficence. Even the sucking of the tide at the pilings and the drone of the mosquitoes seemed quieted by Louisa's playing.

The boy, only a few feet away, suddenly dropped the hammer and crowbar and hurried to his sister. He grabbed both her elbows from behind. She gasped and the music stopped.

"That's enough, Lou," he said and then added in a whisper, "You're upsetting the doctor."

Anson, however, was smiling broadly and letting the tears press against his lenses until he finally had to remove his glasses.

The brother and sister, blurred now, waited. The lost music had drifted away with the current, which gurgled and sucked at the pilings. Anson tried to hold on to the notes. In a quavering voice, he said, "That's very pretty. Chopin, I believe?"

"I . . . I don't know," the girl said. She hardly even seemed a part of her surroundings, her face shone so vividly. Anson noticed that her fingers still played the air at her sides.

"You don't know? Well, I suppose the composer doesn't matter as much as the composition. But you play beautifully, Louisa. And at such a young age. How long have you been taking lessons?"

"She's never even had one," her brother said, and it was as if he'd turned all the moonlight onto the girl.

She lowered her eyes and said quietly, "Ed, you're forgetting Mrs. Parmiter. She gave me a lesson."

"That hardly counts. Two or three minutes was all it lasted before Mother came in and made you . . ."

The boy stopped and glanced over Anson's shoulder in the direction of the house. He frowned and all the sudden enthusiasm over his sister's talent drained out of his body as if he'd been punctured. Anson, still amazed by what he'd come upon, hurried to address the girl.

"Do you mean that you've never been taught to play? How is it that you can play Chopin?"

Her brother's enthusiasm flooded back. His broad, handsome face beamed.

"She has a gift. Mrs. Parmiter said so. She said Lou was a . . . a . . . what was that word, Lou?"

The girl did not look up. Her fingers twitched a little, as if the last of the music was dying out in sparks.

"Prodigy, I suspect," Anson said.

The boy nodded excitedly.

"And I suppose this is why there's a piano on the wharf?"

Neither child responded. Very gently, the boy had taken hold of one of his sister's hands. The tenderness of the gesture moved Anson deeply. These children had lost an older sister the summer before, their mother, still grieving, was clearly not well. Edward and Louisa, he saw at once, were close in a way that Anson, without siblings, had never known.

He smiled. "Your parents have recognized your talent and are encouraging it?"

"Oh, no, sir," Edward said. "I don't believe so. Mother doesn't like her to play and Father thinks it will be good for her to play hymns in the house. Mrs. Parmiter wants to give her lessons, but I don't think Lou will be allowed."

Anson nodded slowly. He could almost feel the sadness seep back into his face. To combat it, he put as much cheer as possible into his voice.

"Well, now, something will have to be done about that. Louisa, surely you wish to take lessons?"

"Oh, yes! More than anything!" The girl pulled her hand free, then clapped both hands together. The sound sent all the notes she'd played whirling starward again.

Anson, who had almost forgotten the infectious sensation of joy, suddenly recognized the oddity of the situation. "Why on earth is this piano on the wharf? Why hasn't it been taken indoors?"

The children blinked, as if they found the questions silly.

"But, doctor," Edward said, looking toward the cannery buildings, "it's the salmon season."

Anson frowned. "Yes, I know, but why does that . . ."

Louisa, in a peevish voice, explained, "Father and Uncle have no time for anything except work when the salmon come."

Feeling sorry for the children, and the girl in particular, Anson sought to recapture the joy of the moment before. With careful diplomacy, he thought he might be able to arrange piano lessons for the child.

"Perhaps I can help," he said. "I will see what I can do. No promises, but a talent such as yours, Louisa, is a very rare and special gift. You understand that?"

The girl pushed her long hair back and revealed a hopeful smile. Anson could not see the tears in her eyes, but he knew they were present.

"But the Chopin?" he said, suddenly curious. "Where have you heard Chopin before? Does your family have a gramophone?"

The girl shook her head and replied in a trembling voice. "At the Parmiters. Mrs. Parmiter was playing it. From a book."

From a book! Anson cupped his chin with his hands and murmured a brief paean in Latin. Finally, noticing the children's confusion, he laughed and pointed at the piano.

"Well, Louisa, I cannot be satisfied with such a brief concert. Will you do me the pleasure of playing that piece again? I don't know when I'll have another chance to hear something so lovely."

God truly works in mysterious ways, Anson thought, and as the music rose again, like a spring rain reversed and returned to the heavens, he could almost forget the murderous ways and the bloodied path he'd been forced to walk, away from the softly tolling certainties of his own childhood and youth.

V

The only thing interesting about a sunset, J.H. Craig mused as he stood on the wharf outside his New Westminster cannery, watching the agent's dainty approach up the gangway, is that it tells fools to stop working. A seagull flapped out of the red sky and unfolded like a dirty newspaper on the planks a few feet away. It screeched and started to peck at something. Briefly admiring of the bird's industry, Craig caught himself. He snarled at the bird and stomped toward it, waving his arms in small circles. Screeching louder, the gull flapped away. Craig bent to the red pulp of salmon flesh, disgust turning his lips thinner. Goddamned waste. Such a firm piece of fish belonged in a tin. He stood, gingerly brushing dirt off the piece, and watched the agent almost tiptoeing toward him. Belvedere Smith. A ridiculous name, but it suited an English gadfly more interested in fancy clothes than in the workings of a cannery. Still, he could be useful.

The agent's orange suit in the red sunlight made Craig wince. He did not wait for any pleasantries. "Well? Who is he? What's he here for?"

The agent wheezed a laugh out of his pasty, sparsely whiskered face. He looked like an underfed fox that the hounds had cornered, except that he was too stupid to even realize it. "Having your supper, Craig? I trust I'll merit something better."

Craig whistled sharply at a Chinaman lazing against a piling fifty feet away, and the toothless old man, wearing the usual blue smock, shuffled over.

"Get this into a tin," Craig said and handed the piece of flesh to the coolie. "And tell Kwan I don't want to see waste like this again. Or I'll deduct it from the contract."

A sharp pain flared along Craig's gumline. He glared at the agent, but the man was too stupid and too English, which amounted to the same thing, to take the hint.

"A week from now," Smith said and nodded southwest in the direction of the rivermouth, where the dingy sails of the returning skiffs could just be seen, "and you'll be up to your knees in fish that you won't be able to tin. That's what the Indians are saying."

"Whose Indians? Did you talk to Dare's? Goddammit, man, I'm not paying you for your predictions on the next run."

"All right, all right, just let me have a smoke."

The agent delicately bit the end off a cigar, lit a match and held the flame to the tobacco, and was about to fling the match away when Craig grabbed his arm.

"Not on the wharf. Can't you tell it's like tinder in this heat?"

The agent shrugged, inhaled deeply, and blew out a puff of smoke.

"Well?" Craig said. "Did you learn anything or not?" He sucked at his molar and tried to shut out the shuntings of the cannery and the gurglings of the tide so he could better focus on the agent's answer.

"He's American, a doctor from the east. Doesn't talk much, but he's definitely come to meet with Dare. And I don't think it's to discuss whether he should set up practice at Crescent Slough either."

"How do you know that?"

"Henry Lansdowne asked straight out. They wouldn't mind having a doctor at Chilukthan, you know. The Landing's large enough to support one." Belvedere Smith shook his head. "But not this doctor. He's not thinking of his prospects. At least that's what he told me, and I believed him. Worn-out chap, really."

Craig closed his eyes against the pain in his mouth. A doctor?

Perhaps he was the source of Dare's financing? Somehow or other, the damned nigger had the means to hire a new crew of coolies in Victoria. Now it looked as if he'd be ready for the big run after all. Owen, for all his shrewdness, hadn't been able to stop him. Then again, Dare hadn't been seen for days. Craig cursed under his breath. Not knowing what a rival was doing pained him more than any tooth could. He pushed his tongue hard against it and thought, Maybe this doctor doesn't even know Dare is a nigger. Inspired, he phrased the thought into a question and asked it aloud.

The agent smiled through the grey rings of smoke. "I never brought it up. I could tell it wouldn't have mattered. The doctor's one of these noble chaps, you can tell just by looking at him. A good American. Apparently he saved a bunch of Dare's coolies from drowning the first night he arrived."

"Yes, I know about that," Craig said. "So the Lansdownes didn't mention that Dare was a nigger either?"

The agent guffawed. "Henry Lansdowne? He takes the Lord's view of such things. And his brother, whether he likes it or not, follows suit. Anyway, I'm not so convinced that Dare is—"

"I don't care what you think about that. Just tell me about this doctor. You think he's a friend of Dare and that he's here to help him?"

"I don't see any other reason for him to be here. And he did ask a lot of questions about the canning business. About the salmon too. Seemed to expect me to know why the damned things come back to the river when they do."

The agent wheezed out another laugh; it ended in a snivelling gasp.

Craig had had enough. Dare on his own was already a problem that had to be removed. And Dare with help? Well, that meant there was no waiting for Owen's canny bribing of a magistrate. A more direct means of elimination would be necessary. And there were plenty of shiftless failures around who'd rather earn a dollar with a gun than with a set of oars and a net.

The white sails of the skiffs drifted closer. Craig could almost hear the lusty voices of the men crying out for a higher wage. Even the sun seemed to stick its bloodied hands into his pockets. He turned and started to stride away.

"Wait a minute," the agent said. "Haven't you forgotten something?"

Craig turned slowly back, one eye narrowed to a slit. "You've been paid. And too well for the service."

The agent tossed his cigar into the river. His skinny face was like a bairn's about to blubber.

"You promised me a meal, Craig. That was agreed upon."

"So I did."

Gleeful, Craig reached into his coat pocket. He could not believe he had almost forgotten. He pulled out two oat biscuits, dry as navy hardtack, and handed them to the peevish agent. The fool's face looked as doughy as the biscuits. But before he could even protest, Craig suppressed a chuckle at the base of his throat and walked away, already wondering how little he could pay a lazy Irishman to get rid of a nigger.

VI

Anson had no way to reach Victoria unless he waited for a steamer to stop at Chilukthan or else rowed himself upriver to New Westminster to board a Victoria-bound vessel there. While he seriously considered the latter option, he knew his health would not allow it. He had to accept the unpleasant fact: he was stuck at Chilukthan.

But stuck did not have to mean purposeless. Anson was determined to be of some use while he waited for the steamer or Dare's return. As long as Thomas Lansdowne's wife remained inadequately attended, the family's gifted daughter would suffer, perhaps would suffer all her life if a domestic tragedy destroyed her chance of realizing her talent. The very thought of such a desecration urged Anson over the fields with no break in his stride. Elizabeth had not given him a child, and the Lansdowne girl was no replacement for that loss, but if the years weighted a man's spirit, they also made clear his responsibility to his own character. He had come to the Fraser River to help William Dare. Before he left, he would do what he could to help the girl too.

He found the Englishman a considerable distance from his house, beyond the woodlot. Emerging from the trees, Anson felt as if he dragged the forest's intimate darkness with him, as if the trees them-selves housed human aspirations.

Thomas Lansdowne was even more violently red in the face than usual as Anson came up. His horse, yoked to a massive stump, pulled so that its eyes were moon-wide, and the Englishman, on his knees in the wet earth, grunted as he heaved his body against the black, sodden, many-rooted weight, trying to dislodge it from the mucky ground. He did not appear to notice Anson's approach. So Anson waited, staring across the flat, unvarying distance that hardly merited the name of "field." This was no easily broken soil. It was, in fact, hardly soil at all. Obviously the Lansdownes, in their diking and stump removing, were engaged on the noble work of the future. Anson respected them for it, but the future could not, should not, come at the expense of the present. If a man laboured for the sake of his children, he ought not to be allowed to neglect the wife who carried his child. Simply put, that went against nature.

With a grunt that was almost a shout, the Englishman threw his body against the stump just as the horse gained its position on the slippery surface. The stump shifted, a foot, two feet. Then it lodged firmly in the mud again. Thomas Lansdowne did not curse, he did not shake his fist at the heavens or slump down on his knees in defeat. Instead, he said, "Good girl" and marched up to the horse and slapped its glistening flanks. Still he did not appear to notice that he was no longer alone. He wiped the sweat from his face with a bare, ruddy forearm and squinted at the sun.

Anson took in the greyly smoking pile of already-dislodged stumps a few rods away and the three other giant stumps rising like whale-back from the ground just beyond Lansdowne, and his respect for the man's strength of purpose increased. It would be years before the plough would drag as smoothly through this earth as a whale fin through the ocean. No wonder Thomas Lansdowne worked such long days and looked so exhausted in the evenings. The farming, alone, would have defeated most men. But he was also heavily involved in the salmon business, which, Anson could already tell, was a risky ven-ture replete with both expected and unexpected difficulties. On top of all that, the man's wife was in no condition to help him.

"Is there something I can do for you, doctor?"

Surprised, Anson understood that he'd been staring at the Englishman without really seeing him. The voice, therefore, was like a handful of gravel tossed lightly in his face.

"Yes. Yes, there is." Anson, thinking of the girl and the music she had played, gathered his resolve once more. He spoke directly, his eyes catching and holding the Englishman's sun-reddened attention. "Your wife, sir. It's my opinion as a medical man that she's seriously ill and in need of considerable rest before the arrival of your child. I tell you this only because I realize that you have many responsibilities and demands and might not recognize certain symptoms of her condition that lead me to speak with you on the matter."

"I see." The Englishman again rubbed his forearm across his brow. Then he squared himself on the wet ground, his gumboots squelching softly. From downriver came the familiar, repetitive sound of the tin press punching out cans. It was like the throbbing of the sun or of the blood in the body, a common pulse mostly unnoticed but integral to all else. "Last night, doctor, you claimed that, in your opinion, men take too great an interest in the affairs of others. Isn't that so?"

Anson conceded the fact with a scowl but was not cowed. He was, after all, a medical man sworn to take an active interest in the health of others. If they chose to disregard his opinion, that was certainly their prerogative.

"I did say that, yes. But in this case I am not seeking to know anything. I am simply advising you, out of concern and experience, that your wife's in greater danger than you might realize."

Thomas Lansdowne spat on the ground. His shadow lay like a burnt trench behind him. "Danger?" The word hung heavily in the air, and it seemed to Anson that they both stared at it, as if it was a bird one of them was about to flush. He waited.

At last, the Englishman made a guttural sound of dismissal and crossed his thick arms across his chest. "And what do you know of danger, exactly? The east's a settled land. Many things that are commonplace here will appear dangerous to you, doctor. My wife is stronger than most men."

Anson understood the insult but let it pass. He knew it was a delicate matter to discuss another man's domestic affairs, and he and Thomas Lansdowne were not exactly on friendly terms to begin with. Even so, he had to quell the urge to scoff at the man's arrogant assumptions. Farming along the Fraser River might be hard work, but it was hardly dangerous in the way that Bull Run and Antietam had been dangerous. In any case, Anson realized that the discussion was not about him. And when he remembered that the gruff, forceful farmer had, in the midst of all his other responsibilities, been responsible for the piano's miraculous presence on the wharf, it was easier to remain calm. A man who would do that for his child clearly had more to him than the unyielding English coldness suggested. Before Anson could respond, in fact, Thomas Lansdowne spoke in a different tone, one verging on disbelief.

"Indeed, my wife is much recovered this morning. I left her in the company of your countryman. It appears his conversation has had an invigorating effect on her."

"I'm happy to hear that," Anson said and recalled that Ambrose Richardson had wanted to assess the cannery operations this morning. Surely he and Thomas Lansdowne had not done so at daybreak? But Anson felt the need to defend his medical reputation; he could not believe that the woman he'd seen in such distraction and distress the evening before could have recovered so quickly, no matter the excellence of the Virginian's talk. "However, I would not think that your wife can be out of danger without a considerable amount of rest."

"Ha!" The explosive laugh seemed to tear a scar in the sky, but it was only the sudden keening arc of a gull. "She'll have rest enough with all the chatter going on." Then, as if aware that he'd revealed more than was proper, he spat again and hitched his belt up with a firm yank. "We didn't come here to rest, doctor. My wife no more than I. If you've not noticed, this is rough country. Rest, when it comes, will come after."

The religious reference irritated Anson more than it should; he was long since sick of piety. "After will come sooner than you expect if she is not unburdened of at least some of her daily labours. I've seen it before. In their grief, women will often work themselves into the grave. I go so far only out of concern for your family, you understand?"

"No. I don't understand." His tone grew decidedly colder, his eyes hardened. "Who are you to us? You claim to be here because you are a friend of Dare. Well, where is he? He's gone and you've taken his place. But you don't live on Crescent Slough, you don't work at your own affairs. Instead, you meddle in mine. What's worse, you expect me to be grateful."

"Not grateful, only sensible. I'm here because I have no reason to be anywhere else until my friend returns. Naturally, as a doctor, I notice the condition of those around me. I would no more let your wife work herself to death without saying anything than I would have let those Chinese drown without trying to help. It's not in my nature to be a passive observer of life when I can help someone."

"It is in your nature, it seems, to offer help where no help is required. The Chinamen no doubt screamed to be saved. I'm not aware that my wife has made any such plea."

"No? But you were at the table last night, you saw her distress. What was all that if not a plea for help?"

Thomas Lansdowne grinned unpleasantly. "Ah, well, it's obviously never occurred to you that my wife might have a very good reason for her behaviour last night. Perhaps you did not hear the dog barking? A dog does not bark like that without cause, just as a woman does not react as my wife did without cause."

Anson spoke quietly now, for the subject was delicate. "You and your wife lost a child recently, yes? In my experience, a woman's grief runs deeper and lasts longer. That is cause enough to account for her behaviour at the evening's end, as well as for her obvious fatigue and distraction throughout."

Thomas Lansdowne's eyes opened wide. His jaw set and his neck tensed. "You would speak of my grief! Mine! What gives you the right? I'll speak plainly, since my brother is not present to check my tongue. You're not wanted here. You're a friend of Dare and he's no friend of ours. You wanted to know why I should insult the man? Because he's a damned scoundrel without morals or religion or family, a man who'd stoop to anything to achieve his ends. And you give his name to us as a recommendation? On that basis you expect me to stand here wasting time when there's work to be done, listening to you, a stranger, tell me how much grief I've felt at the loss of my child. It will not do!"

His chest rose and fell in great heaves. But he did not shift his braced legs. He lowered his voice, but the tone remained hostile.

"I would advise you to leave, doctor, on the next ferry. In the meantime, stay out of my business. Dare has not heeded this advice and he'll be sorry for the lack. You'd be unwise to join him in his folly."

With that, the Englishman stepped forward and smacked the horse on its flank, setting the animal straining at the ropes again. Then he squelched back into position behind the stump and threw his weight against it as if it was, in fact, William Dare, and he was trying to hurl the man into oblivion.

Anson was still reeling as if struck by a fist. It was not the Englishman's anger that shocked him, but the wholly unwarranted and violent attack on Dare's character, an attack that he now felt unable to repel. William Dare without morals? A scoundrel? The man who'd risked his life repeatedly in battle to save his comrades, who'd nursed the wounded until he himself was but a shadow on the tent walls? It was as close to blasphemy as Anson had ever experienced.

He stood on the wet earth under a blue sky alive with only the occasional bird and the dull echo of the tin press and felt as if he'd been reduced to the same level as the horse, struggling in vain to free itself of a burden it could not even begin to comprehend. At least it was obvious that Thomas Lansdowne had attempted to reduce him to that level. It was a vile attempt, and all of Anson's sympathies for the man evaporated.

"I'm not done, sir!" Grabbing the bridle of the horse, Anson stopped the animal's efforts. As the ropes slackened, he turned and faced the furious Englishman, who had clambered out from behind the stump, breathing raggedly, his cheeks blood-full. "I don't know how such matters are conducted in your country, but in mine, when you attack the character of a man's friend, you attack the man himself. You'll have the decency at least to stand up behind your words a moment before returning to your work."

With Thomas Lansdowne glaring at him, hands on his hips, Anson forged ahead.

"I would no more defend the character of William Dare than you would the character of your own brother. Dare is a business adversary of yours. I understand that. You do not know him as I do. I understand that as well. So I'll put your attack down to ignorance and move on. Your wife, whether you wish to hear this or not, is in grave danger of harming herself and her baby. If a tragedy occurs, that will fall hard upon you. But I fear it will fall harder upon your other children, and one in particular."

Anson did not flinch as Thomas Lansdowne raised one great fist and stepped forward, spluttering rage.

"Calm yourself, man, and listen! Your daughter, Louisa . . ."

"Louisa? What of her?"

"I said be calm. The girl is fine. Indeed, she's much more than that. You know, of course, of her musical gifts. But perhaps you don't fully grasp the extent of them."

The rage slowly drained from the Englishman's face. He unclenched his fist and lowered it. "She likes music, yes. It's a pleasing quality in a female."

Anson considered him at length. *Ka-thunk-ka-thunk-ka-thunk.* The tin press did not let up. Thomas Lansdowne's face had softened and was now almost quizzical in its expression. But he did not speak.

At last, Anson said, "Your daughter has a rare talent. Though I am no expert, I believe her to be a prodigy."

"A prodigy? Nay, she has but rarely touched a piano."

"This is why I call her a prodigy. The piano on the wharf? I came upon her playing it. And she was playing Chopin."

"Louisa?" His bewilderment was genuine, but Anson detected a small amount of pride and pleasure in it. The man might just have said, "My Louisa, my lamb," instead of what he did say, which was merely a nod to social convention. "She'll be of use at services, then. The Lord does not require Chopin for worship."

"Perhaps not. But beauty of any kind is a gift from God and is meant to inspire us to higher thoughts and feelings. Your daughter can be a servant of that rare kind, given the opportunity. At the very least, you could find the time to move the piano indoors for her."

Thomas Lansdowne's round, wondering face resembled a clock missing its hands. Anson could almost hear the futile grinding of the works in the body.

The horse lifted its head and nickered. A dark flock rose on the horizon and fell away without sound.

"You heard my daughter play? When was this?"

Ah, now I've done it, Anson thought, I've made trouble for her. But it was too late.

"Last night, on the wharf. She and Edward had removed the front board of the crate. It was to be expected. The child loves music as you love her. To know a piano is near and not be able to play it—you must allow her the impatience."

"Impatience is not a virtue. It's to be discouraged."

"Yes, well, I ask only that the discouragement isn't severe. I wouldn't wish to be responsible for having the child punished for what is as natural to her as the song is in a bird."

"How I discipline my children is not your business." But Thomas Lansdowne had more wonderment than severity in his tone now. Anson knew that the revelation about Louisa had unsettled him.

"Of course it's not, nor is your wife's health. I ask only that you consider both matters carefully. You are, after all, a fortunate man."

Anson paused, embarrassed to find his voice breaking, his eyes watering. He composed himself and continued.

"I have no family myself. Perhaps if you think me overly concerned with the welfare of yours, you might take that fact into account."

But Thomas Lansdowne appeared to be listening to the far-off sound coming from the direction of the river. It would have been almost an act of violence to disturb his silence. Anson felt he had done enough, in any case.

"Good day," he said and took a few steps backward before turning his back on the sky-searching fathom of the Englishman's gaze and returning to his own solitude and unprofound meditations of the day's slow light.

VII

July 1881, Chilukthan, British Columbia

Sunlight rarely penetrated the parlour, or perhaps Edney had simply not noticed it doing so for many months. As she poured a fresh cup of tea for the American guest, the sunlight appeared to flow from her hand as well and descend to the bunched bottoms of the velvet drapes. Had she even parted them since May's illness? Edney could hardly believe the room contained a window that looked out on something as ordinary as this world.

As she placed the teapot on the table, her eyes remained on the sunlit glass—if she held the gaze long enough, surely May would appear, fresh as the last spring of her health. For the child had not vanished in the days succeeding the dinner at Henry and Mary's; she hovered so close, just a whisper away. It *must* happen any time, the contact.

Mr. Richardson, sitting serenely on the ottoman beside her, his long legs crossed at the ankles, shared the opinion. No, not Mr. Richardson—Ambrose. Edney tried to remember his admonition that she address him so, but despite the pleasure of his conversation and sympathy she found it difficult. He was not a member of the family, nor even of the settlement. Yet he hardly seemed a stranger either. Hour by hour, in fact, Edney began to know a greater ease in his presence.

"It is," he went on, lowering his teacup, "the one matter over which I disagreed with many of my countrymen, then and now. I took the view of our president, Jefferson Davis, who, upon hearing of the boy's death, sent a note of condolence to the White House. This was in the second year of the war, mind. He did not have to do it. Lincoln was the sworn enemy of all we cherished, but even so, his profound grief touched me deeply. And this was before Sharpsburg, before my own devastating loss."

His voice flowed easily as the light, despite the pain behind the words. Edney felt the warmth of the teacup in her hand diminish: the coolness, like any change, no matter how small, signalled an arrival. Her breathing came easy. She thought of the late American president with a small sense of shame: Lincoln's murder, though tragic, had been very remote to her. She'd been a young mother then, with May and the baby Edward taking most of her attention. In truth, Edney could not remember hearing of Lincoln's grief over the death of his son. She must have, of course, but her great joy at the time would not have been dampened by a distant misery, no matter how famous.

"We heard the rumours," Ambrose Richardson said. "Many scoffed at the idea that the great man would participate in a seance, especially during wartime, but I understood perfectly. Perhaps, in some way, my sympathy for our enemy's leader was a kind of prophetic vision of my own future. I have thought of this often. Lincoln's grief, had I but known it at the time, was a gift from God; it helped to prepare the ground for my own tears."

He sighed and raised the cup to his lips. Lowering it again, he looked at Edney with watery eyes.

"They say he returned to the crypt on three separate occasions, wanting one last look at the boy. The embalming had been remarkable. They say the child looked to be only asleep. That man destroyed the hopes of my country, yet I cannot, before God, deny that I would embrace him in compassion for his lonely returns to that crypt. What I wouldn't give, even now, for one last look upon my own dear boy's face."

He put the cup down and pulled a handkerchief from his vest. Dabbing his eyes, he said quietly, "I did try, I tried even to the point of risking my own life." His voice caught, but he continued. "I couldn't get to him. He lay in contested ground after the battle. When I could finally search the field, there was no sign of . . . I . . . even now it pains me to think of the poor boys whose bodies I turned over to see their faces, always in great hope, only to have my hopes dashed."

His hand trembled as he tried to place the handkerchief neatly in his breast pocket. Finally, he gave up and let the handkerchief hang limp from his hand.

"Shovelled into a mass grave by negroes who probably treated him like a slab of fouled meat. That was my boy's fate. I walked that battle-field for hours, blind with tears, and came to feel that I was searching for the child he had been. I thought if I listened for a baby's cry, it would lead me to his body. It is most strange . . ." He glanced at his left sleeve and sighed. "It is most strange how time and sense are altered by death. For years, I consoled myself with the fancy that my arm had somehow joined my child in his unmarked grave, that it was whole and well and cradled the head of that little boy." He broke off. His head dropped to his chest.

A part of Edney wanted to reach out and touch him, as if, by doing so, she could comfort the child he had lost. But his openness froze her; it was almost a sin to respond to something that she had wanted so desperately since May's death.

Finally the American raised his head and spoke again.

"I would ask you to forgive me, but I know it would be an imper-tinence. Your feelings are fresh. I cannot claim as much of mine from such a world as this, but I know that I can from you."

For a moment, Edney feared that he was about to reach out and take her hand. But he merely leaned closer.

"I've given much thought to your grieving. I've asked myself repeat-edly how I can help you to come back to God's fold. Believe me, I, too, have known the sin of anger, I, too, have doubted His mercy. But He knows this, He expects it. And I believe with all my heart that He has given us the means to return to Him. He has, in His great mercy, provided a way for us to love this life again before we are reunited in Glory with our own lost lambs. Ah, but lost only to us, only briefly, because of our own weakness. Madam, if you will permit me, I can arrange for you to reach her, to go beyond the veil. In Victoria, I know of the gentle services of a lady well versed in these matters. And I am certain that, at my request, she would be willing to come here and help you to find some of the peace that I've known."

Edney drew back. His eyes seemed to have taken all the sunlight into them, and his moustache quivered as his lips moved. What he had said hardly reached her; she was still thinking of her undiminished desire to see May's face one last time. But this mention of a lady in Victoria—what could this mean?

"Please, don't be alarmed. Perhaps I move too swiftly. But it is only out of my sincere desire to bring you comfort. I often wish, indeed, that someone had led me to this special and most providential of balms much sooner, though perhaps I would have been too angry yet in my grief at the time."

He leaned back but did not move his searching eyes from Edney's face. She felt the strange hunger in his look and it confused her. If he had anything to gain, it would only be the Christian comfort of having helped to ease another's suffering. She could give him nothing else. She could not even promise to give him that comfort. But if she did, perhaps the gift would be a renewing of her faith and a cooling of her terrible hatred, a gift her Maker might reward with that one last contact she so desired. It was the teaching she had always known—for the soul to be at peace, the life must do good. Why not let this gracious American, alone, wounded in heart rather than in body, try to help her?

"I don't understand," she said at last. "What are the services this lady in Victoria provides?"

He smiled and sat up straight. The watery blue of his eyes suddenly brightened. He brought his one hand around and rested it on his thigh. The fingers were long and thin and yellowed with tobacco.

"Ah, she is an expert in the ways of bringing the living into contact with the dead. A medium, a clairvoyant, a spiritualist—but there is no earthbound word that can do justice to those who have the gift of parting the veil. For our purpose, she is the one hope we have of communicating with your child while she is still so close to her corporeal time. Oh, that I had but spoken with Robert sooner! How richer the conversation would have been, how fresher the feeling." He stared sadly away.

On reflex, Edney looked after him and seeing his empty teacup on the table moved quickly to fill it. The physical act, simple and repetitive, helped to orient her. For the truth was, she could not imagine how anyone could reach May if she, who had loved her so deeply, who, indeed, perhaps loved her even more now, could not do so on her own. But these matters were profound, more so than she could fathom. That someone dedicated to finding ways of contacting the dead could succeed where she had failed was not an impossible idea—Edney did not pretend any great knowledge of life and death. She knew her heart and she knew her duty; if the first was broken, the second could not be properly carried out. So what choice did she have? For her dead and living children, she must repair the break. And if a woman in Victoria, upon the recommendation of the sympathetic soul sitting in the parlour where May's body had lain, could be an agent in that lonely work, Edney knew that she'd be foolish and irresponsible to resist.

The clock ticked heavily. Ambrose Richardson lifted his cup and took a silent sip of tea. The sunlight no longer flowed through the room, but it had the same trembling quality as the American's eyes as he spoke again.

"Of course, I'll make all the arrangements on your behalf. The fee is minimal, considering the great peace that results. However, should you require any assistance . . ." He made the slightest of bows and courteously dropped his eyes.

Edney absently pulled at the end of one of her tight braids. The fee? It was difficult for her to think of money or any other worldly concern in relation to May. But she tried hard, recognizing the intensity of his feelings and the honourable manner in which he expressed them. Not all the Americans she had met—and there were several on the delta—possessed such gentlemanly graces.

"Thank you, but that won't be necessary. As for the other arrangements, I'd be most grateful for your assistance."

"I'll leave for Victoria on the next steamer. Madam, your faith will be rewarded in the only way that can truly help you. You will speak with your beloved child again."

The words were so dazzling, his tone so convincing in its promise, that she did not notice for several seconds that they were no longer alone in the parlour. Only when Ambrose Richardson stood, rather suddenly, and a few drops of tea spilled from his cup onto her hand, which rested on the ottoman between them, did she awaken to the world of flesh.

"Arrangements? For what?"

Edney turned at the sound of Thomas's voice, as if yoked to it. But she was not alarmed by his presence or his question, merely surprised by the former as he was generally at work all day in the fields.

"Good day, sir," Ambrose Richardson said. "Your wife and I have been enjoying a cup of tea and some most uplifting conversation. Why don't you join us?"

Edney watched Thomas carefully but with little emotion. He seemed very far away, even though he was so palpably present. The world that he carried with him, he carried in the same way that a horse did. His face was red and slick with sweat. A few strands of hair were stuck to his brow, and his thick beard was smoulder waiting to flame at the quick light in his eyes. But he had removed his boots and held his hat like a limp pelt in one hand.

"No. No, thank you," he said awkwardly, and Edney knew that his discomfort came from the simple confusion created by a guest acting as a host. Her husband was not a man who took even a slight change in the proprieties with calm. It was no surprise to her, then, when he pressed on with his questions in an abrupt manner.

"I heard my wife mention arrangements, sir. If they concern your interest in the cannery, it would be best if you discussed such matters with me. And if they concern something else . . ."

Edney felt his darkness shift heavily toward her as he continued.

". . . well, I cannot think of anything that does not require you to speak with me first. I heard mention of a child. What child did you mean, sir?"

Edney sensed the American's attention settle lightly and briefly on her, but she did not look at him. He cleared his throat. Edney was surprised to find herself hoping that he would answer the question directly, as in "Your dead daughter, sir." Suddenly she wanted all the surfaces gone, wanted her truth to be the only one. It saddened her that not even her own husband was prepared to stand at her side on that painful, clarifying ground.

But Ambrose Richardson gracefully deflected the question. "My sincere apologies. I realize that I've yet to accompany you on your rounds of the cannery. Perhaps you're free now? It's a fine day and a walk would be most satisfying."

Thomas's silence spread thickly through the air. His eyes blinked like an owl's but did not appear to take anything in. Edney might even have felt sorry for him, had there not been a kind of savagery in his confusion. But once she had regarded his coiled strength as comforting, a protection against so many dangers. If that same strength seemed dangerous now, she understood that that was as much a result of her own fragility as of any change in him. In truth, he had not changed; the death had not changed him, and therein lay the great danger.

The seconds dragged by. Edney almost believed that Thomas was going to dismiss the mention of the cannery and insist upon an answer to his question about the child. It would have been like a cleansing breeze blowing through the stale parlour; the walls would have collapsed and the three of them would have stood in an open relationship to the insistence of death. Instead, to her strange mixture of relief and disappointment, Thomas finally took the bait of commerce. He shifted his hat from one hand to the other and said, almost meekly, "As you wish. The Chinese will be well at work on the cans, and the Indians are making more nets."

Ambrose Richardson stood. His smile was so broad that it gathered the skin into bunches on his cheeks.

"Excellent. I'll just retire to my room for a few moments and meet you on the veranda." He extended his hand to Edney.

She took it, noting the soothing white coolness, which seemed nothing less than an extension of his presence.

"Madam, I thank you again for your most gracious hospitality. Why, I could be treated no better in the finest of Virginia society."

He did not wink, yet Edney felt, behind his words, a promise that he would not fail either her or May. And, strangely, when he had left the parlour, the child's hovering spirit seemed to depart as well. Edney almost cried out, she almost rose to plead with the slightest trembling of the sunlight that signalled May's flight, but Thomas had stepped in front of her, his body's motion like the swinging of a barn door on darkness. Now it would come, she thought, now his confusion would demand answers. What child? Our daughter. What arrangements? To speak with her again, to know her again. Edney waited, her breath held. Just then, the new child moved inside her, as if a stone had been dropped into the parlour's sunlit stillness.

"I had hoped that you were discussing the cannery with him. You know how important it is that we secure his investment."

The ripples of the stone's fall did not leave her body. Edney closed her eyes as the ripples returned deeper into her. Quietly, she said, "We weren't discussing business."

He settled his weight onto the ottoman beside her and took both her hands in one of his, which was as warm as a clench of the sun. "Mother, listen to me. We are in difficulties. I have told you of the debt. You must not dwell on what can never be again. We must live. This man, he is . . . he is our salvation. If he comes in with me, and if the season is even half as good as most predict, our future is secure. I'll be able to compete with Dare and anyone else. You must do what you can to convince him."

Edney could not even find the will to nod. Her whole body went numb; ice lodged in her joints as she struggled to remember her duty to the dark and pleading man beside her. The child moved again. The clock ticked. The sunlight was bereft of presence. God, she saw clearly, was in her daughter, and her daughter was gone. If she could not bring her back, God, too, was absent forever. A surge of will lifted Edney's eyes to his.

"Soon it will be a year, Thomas. I cannot think of business so close to the time."

"A year?" He blinked at her, his face rough and raw as split cedar, his wet lips parted.

Edney could hardly bear the sight of him. The mud smell rising off his thick arms could have been his daughter's own grave-dirt and he would not have noticed.

His blinking stopped. He held his eyelids closed and slowly leaned his head back until his face was raised to the ceiling. Then, as if some force lowered his head on a string, he met Edney's gaze.

"You think I do not grieve for her? You think I have forgotten?" He pushed his thick thumb slowly up his brow. "Our first child? You think I do not miss her every . . ."

Edney could not bring herself to pity him. If he missed May as she did, then how could he possibly care so much for business? Some feelings destroyed the world; they were meant to destroy it. And only a long, careful humility before the awe of the destruction and a proper attendance on the gap a child's death left in the spirit could hope to save a family. The American gentleman understood. It had been fifteen years for him. Thomas would not adjust for even one turn of the calendar. No, Edney could not pity him. She could hardly look at him; he seemed so much smaller and weaker than his material form. All she wanted was to be alone in the parlour with May's spirit.

Coldly and clearly, she said, "I'll discuss with Mr. Richardson what is most important to us."

Her husband's relief was horrible. He slumped back against the ottoman and almost gasped, "Thank you, Mother."

Edney heard his heartbeat pounding, saw it break the parlour's sunlight into pieces. But it would not break her heart the same way. She almost smiled at the thought of the woman from Victoria, gifted in the byways between life and death, crossing the waters. At last the long suffering would be altered. At last she could mother the life she had not mothered well enough on earth. Then perhaps she could work on the future again. Not before.

VIII

Unable to read or sleep, the taste of opium in the air as palpable on his tongue as spit, Anson once again found himself on the wharf outside the Lansdowne house. He stood, his back to the China House and its long, soothing pipes, and listened to the plaintive crying of a seal pup. One of the Indians, so the boy Edward had told him, had caught the pup and was keeping it for a pet. Tied for days to a post near the Indian's driftwood lean-to, eventually the seal would be tame enough to swim with the Indian children. That seemed innocent enough, almost cozily domestic, yet the seal's cry, remarkably akin to a human baby's, was disturbing. Anson moved on.

For several minutes he stood in the side yard of the Lansdowne house, trying to convince himself to return to bed. But the smoke on the air from an Indian's fire further whet his old longing for opium and he began to walk downriver toward the China House.

The sound that stopped him came as less of a surprise than previously. He listened. It was the girl again. She had not taken his advice. When Anson had come upon her in the middle of the day while she was meant to be at her chores, she had been so rapt in her piano playing that interference seemed more than cruel; it was like turning off the sun. But for her sake he had urged her to be patient. If her father or uncle knew of her passion for the piano—he had not used the word to the child, though he had thought it—they might send the instrument back to Victoria. Ah, but the girl could no more resist the lure of the music than Anson could quell the past. Why not let her run the risk? It maddened him that the Lansdowne brothers had managed only to move the piano from the wharf to the nearby barn. He understood, of course, that they were busy men, but they clearly had no idea of how to treat a piano. Either that, or they simply didn't care. Anson had thought that his heated exchange with Thomas Lansdowne out in the field would have resulted in the piano's removal to the man's house, not just to the nearest barn. Yes, it was maddening. But then, what of the Lansdownes did not madden him?

He walked to the barn and slid in through the thin gap in the doors. Straw chaff and dust on the planks and in the air almost made him cough. For a few seconds, as his eyes adjusted to the dimness, he saw only some worn tack—harnesses, bridles, saddles—hanging like strips of beef on a wall near the stable. Then he saw the girl. As before, she had not bothered to find a crate or anything else to sit on. In the fractured light falling through the beams, she stood, wreathed in the stench of manure, and played with unsophisticated energy the lovely Chopin music she had no business, but every right, to play.

Anson swallowed hard. More moving to him than her talent was the purity of her will. She must play. It wasn't a question of rules and authority. It almost brought him to tears how little she seemed to be aware of her own vulnerability. But when she played, even he could recognize that, in some mysterious way, she was inviolate.

The wind shifted the thin starlight a little. Anson turned and coughed deep in his chest. Up from the river came the high-pitched cry of the seal pup, followed by another sound, not so high but just as tortured. Anson realized that it must be the pup's mother swimming along the bank. Sadly, he turned back just in time to see the child collapse, one hand dragging across the keys before her body hit the ground.

"Louisa!"

He rushed forward and lifted her in his arms. She was sweating profusely, on fire, trembling. He staggered into the darkness and moved as rapidly as possible over the soft ground, the whole time thinking, What's wrong with her, how can I stop it, how can I help her?

He laboured up the half-dozen steps and across the veranda, then banged the front door of the house open with his foot and shouted as he carried the girl into the parlour and laid her on the ottoman. From above him came quick footsteps that pattered along the ceiling and down the staircase.

"Light a lamp," Anson ordered without looking up.

"What is it? What's happened?" came Mary Lansdowne's strained voice.

"It's Louisa. She's sick."

"Louisa?"

"I need light," Anson said, not waiting even to see his concern mirrored in another's face. "And my case. In my room. On the dresser."

The footsteps started again, climbed, and crossed the ceiling. They were like a pulse. The child moaned but did not open her eyes. In the darkness Anson could barely discern her features, but she was like a live coal to his touch.

There were more footsteps, then Mary's voice and fluttering descent in the sizzling spread of light.

"Dear God, dear God, what's happened to her?" Mary's hand descended to Louisa's brow. "Doctor? She's burning with fever."

"Yes." Anson sent Mary away for a cool cloth. The girl's pulse in his fingers was quick and slippery as rain.

Henry Lansdowne appeared. He stood still as a piling.

"I don't understand. How is it that the child's here, doctor?"

"The piano, of course. You and your brother wouldn't take it into the house."

Angrily, Anson grabbed his case and opened it. The oil light fell and splashed on his instruments.

"The piano?"

"She's been coming out at night to play it. And obviously she hasn't been looking after herself. Just look at how she's dressed."

Anson noted the man's incomprehension: it was like a block of

194

lead dropped on the floor. To keep himself from losing his temper completely, he said, "You'd better notify the child's parents. The danger's not immediate, but it is grave."

"Oh, poor Edney," said Mary Lansdowne and placed the cloth in Anson's hand. "Hurry, Father. You must hurry."

Once Henry Lansdowne had gone, his wife knelt beside Anson. Her voice was hushed, her white face framed by grey braids.

"Is it the scarlet fever, doctor?"

"I don't believe so. But I can't say with certainty." He placed the cloth gently on the child's brow and turned to the window at the sound of hooves striking the ground. At least the man appreciates the gravity, he thought.

Mary Lansdowne, however, took Anson's turning for something more ominous.

"What do you suspect? Not . . ."

The child moaned, her eyes opened wide, with that seeing that sees more than the surroundings. Then the eyes flickered and shut again.

"It could be any number of illnesses." Anson read the pale face for answers he suspected that time alone would provide. And yet, he had a suspicion. The high fever, the periodic moans, the look of delirium: these symptoms pointed to typhoid fever. If the girl, on waking, complained of headaches or stomach pain . . . yet she had been strong enough to come across the fields and slough to play the piano. The mother, no doubt, could provide some useful information.

Anson cursed beneath his breath. For now, there was little he could do. Treating disease, even during the war, had the effect of reminding him of how little his skill and knowledge mattered. At least a shotgun wound, for instance, required immediate action of a most absorbing kind. For the sake of his sanity, a man could not feel hopeless or powerless as he sawed through flesh into a bone.

Mary Lansdowne, who had slipped quietly away, returned with a blanket. But as she laid it over the still form on the ottoman, the girl suddenly rose up, her eyes wild, and the blanket slid off.

"Louisa, dear, it's Aunt Mary. Your mother's on her way. Oh, child."

The girl's dark eyes flared, then rolled back. She opened her mouth, but no sound came.

Anson sent Mary away with the cloth, which was already warm and damp. Lightly he touched the girl's brow. The fever was very high. The blanket on the floor might have been a skin shed by fire. Seconds accumulated very slowly, heavily. Mary returned. Anson placed the cloth on Louisa's burning brow. Then he listened to the pulse again until the rapid hoof beats struck the ground outside and the child's mother rushed into the parlour, a whirling descent of black in the yellow light, her long hair loose, her eyes almost as wild as her daughter's. She smelled thickly of rain and mud. Her skirt bottom was drenched and splattered from the half-mile ride along the slough bank. Anson rose and withdrew a few steps to give Edney a clear path to her child's side. In a silence much more disturbing than cries would have been, she threw herself on the girl's breast. Anson watched Edney's shoulders shake violently and a sense of horror rose in him. Why didn't she cry out? Why didn't she speak the child's name? She looked like some animal feeding off its kill. Anson fought to quell the gruesome image.

"Edney. Oh, Edney, please," Mary Lansdowne moaned.

Anson turned and saw that Mary's hands were at her mouth. Where was the girl's father? It would be his duty to lift the mother from the girl. Anson could hardly bring himself to consider doing so, but if the woman didn't raise herself soon . . .

Henry Lansdowne entered the room and spoke softly in his wife's ear.

"Not back?" Mary said, then lowered her head at her husband's stern look.

The two returned quietly into the shadows.

Anson could no longer abide the mother's terrible, almost silent grief.

"Madam, compose yourself."

But even as he spoke, he felt foolish and very far removed. It was as if he stood above a woman slowly transforming into an open grave. He almost expected the floor to give way and all of them to be swallowed by the earth. Some terrible moment was at hand, more than illness, more than a human death. Now Anson did not want the woman to rise. Any change would trigger the greater death he could not even imagine.

Then Henry Lansdowne emerged from the shadows and brusquely took Edney by the shoulders and lifted her. "Mary," he said to his wife, who then supported Edney on the other side. Together, they sought to remove her from the parlour, turned her slumped figure doorward.

Anson tried not to see, but it was as if his eyelids were pinned up. The mother's face floated into the dim light like something dead that had been trapped a long time on the bottom of the sea, yet as it rose it seemed, inch by inch, to be shocked back into sentience by a grinning blackness whose silent mirth trembled all around them. But the thought and feeling that flooded into the eyes were blank in their fathomless searchings. Anson, though he had witnessed similar suffering before, had never become immured to it. The sense of an intense misery just withheld was almost too much to bear, especially here, when he had already imagined himself on the way back to Antietam. The room was like a surface of water out of which, at any instant, a powerful force must explode. If there was skin on the mother's face, Anson couldn't see it. If there was a woman in the features, it was a woman Anson had never encountered, not even in a nightmare. Yet the grief was human. That was the most awful part of it. Fifty thousand dying men, fifty thousand grieving mothers, were screaming without sound in the brief bone frame that hung before his eyes, eyes that he could not close.

Then she was gone and Anson stood alone above the child's fitful fire, wondering if even the music of Chopin could ever wash that screaming from his sight.

They moved the child to an upstairs room, the uncle cradling her and walking slowly, as if leading a procession. But Anson alone attended the move, for the mother remained bone-white and trembling in a chair, with her sister-in-law dutifully at her side. Alone with Henry Lansdowne, Anson waited for the man's questions: What illness? How serious? What about quarantine? But even now the Englishman remained mostly mute. He did thank Anson for his help, but implied in his manner and tone was a criticism—no doubt he suspected Anson of knowing more about his niece's piano playing than he was admitting to.

For his part, Anson cared only about the girl's condition. Though almost in shock himself at the terrifying image of the mother's grief, he settled into a bedside chair and prepared for a night-long vigil. Even if he could do nothing to prevent a sudden death, or even if the crisis was yet weeks away, he realized that a doctor's presence, at least, might comfort the patient's family. And then, oddly, he felt that the mother's grief was itself a threat, as if her initial black descent upon the child would, if given another opportunity, usher in the permanent darkness.

The night passed slowly. At times, Anson thought he heard a weeping in the air but suspected his imagination had been stirred by the proximity of death. Toward daybreak, with the girl's fever unchanged, he stood and went to the open window. The sky was a blood-tinged gauze to the north, but the river and near distance were still a rich, impenetrable black. As far as he was concerned, it couldn't lift fast enough. Night seemed a smothering contagion, a poxed blanket, not a sanctuary of calm. It was always so when a child lay sick. Somehow daylight was the earth's equivalent of bracing health, perhaps because the sun draws children out as a field of flowers draws honeybees. For the old, of course, the night becomes almost a welcoming portal to whatever lies beyond the grave.

Shortly after the tin press began its usual thunking of the silence several rods downriver at the cannery, the girl's mother and aunt appeared. They came in as softly as gusts of black snow and settled on each side of the girl, their drawn, chalk-white faces like twin moons. Anson knew his presence was superfluous. But before he retired to his own room for perhaps a few hours of broken sleep, he studied the mother's manner.

Standing at her daughter's bedside, bent over at the waist, she was certainly changed from the terrible, almost inhuman creature of earlier: her dark eyes had resumed their focus on the surroundings, her hair, in two tight braids, reflected the general control that had come into her body, and she looked, more or less, like any woman in the throes of concern for a child. Even the way she rubbed her hands together in her lap, one palm circling the knuckles of the other hand, was familiar to Anson, almost like an action taken from a primer on maternal behaviour.

And yet he could not forget the face as it had been revealed in the parlour. A slight trace, evident in the quivering of the nostrils, which looked unusually pallid in the dimness, suggested an almost failing balance on the side of sanity. And so, before retiring, Anson took Mary Lansdowne aside and pressed on her the importance of not leaving the mother alone with the patient.

"In my experience," he said, "shock combined with solitude is a highly dangerous mixture."

The woman nodded dumbly, but Anson felt he could depend on her.

Moments later, he lay on his bed and tried to find the memory of sleep among all the other memories that flitted through his consciousness, memories of dying men far from their mothers' or wives' attendance or even the comfort of familiar smells and sounds, memories of his own frail mother on her deathbed thirty years before, followed by the more painful memories of his beloved Elizabeth on hers.

What woke him, he did not know. But something drew him to the window and made him witness to a strange scene. On the wharf, in full morning light, the Lansdowne brothers stood profiled, face to face. Henry Lansdowne suddenly waved one arm dismissively, in a pushing away gesture that caused Thomas to lift his arm as if to fend off a blow. The older man, with surprising speed, turned and pointed at the house. Anson flinched. It seemed he was seeing something that should not have been conducted anywhere but behind closed doors. The fire of Henry Lansdowne's distorted visage, however, might have burned away all privacy. Thomas Lansdowne appeared to step back from it, scorched.

Then he shook his head roughly and, at last, sagged in all his joints. With desperation he reached out and grabbed his brother on both shoulders. But Henry swept his arms away. He seemed to loom even larger above Thomas before finally striding off in the direction of the cannery.

For a few seconds, Thomas did not move. Anson realized what news the man had just received, and he pitied him. If he had been away from home for some inessential reason, he was still not to blame: illness can come on very suddenly, and he was obviously the sort of father who would rather die than be absent when his child was in danger. But the tension had been building around the Lansdownes ever since Anson's arrival. Perhaps the child's condition had brought matters to a climax. Something final certainly seemed to attend the motionless figure on the wharf.

Then, as if shot, Thomas Lansdowne dropped to his knees. He flung his head back, his posture like that of a wolf about to howl.

Anson couldn't stop himself. He opened the window, as though to admit the man's pain, but only the dull, relentless pulse of the tin press disturbed the silence.

At last, Thomas Lansdowne got to his feet and, like a blinded bull, lumbered down the gangway and into the yard. In a moment, Anson knew, he'd be wild at the girl's bedside, feverish with questions.

Turning exhausted from the window, Anson braced himself for the charge.

PART THREE

I

July 1881, the mouth of the Fraser River

All day he had felt the salmon coming, sure as nightfall. He stood, his long legs braced, in a flat-bottomed skiff in the middle of the broad, silty river and gazed toward the ocean. Out there, by the millions, the salmon waited, hanging like ripe fruit in the salt depths, ready to make their last fierce rush to the spawning grounds far inland. The brinish air trembled with the weight of the fish's will, the sun burned yellow-white as it crept between the horizons, and Dare often had to raise one of his muscle-knotted forearms to his eyes to wipe away the sweat. All around him the delta of sloughs, sandbars, and marshes held its breath; the tall reeds and grasses close to where the river met the ocean shivered slightly, like the fine filaments beneath the gills of the salmon, and, behind him, along both banks, the serried rows of great firs and cedars silently pulled in their shadows as if they did not want to contribute their black nets to the harvest that would soon follow.

Dare knew he had done all he could. He had gone to Victoria and secured another crew of Chinese. He had readied the cannery for the great run of salmon that would soon begin. But the forces against him were strong, and he knew that his time in this place was ending. Even knowing that the doctor had come was just a beginning in the next part of his own journey, just as Orlett's death had been an ending and a beginning as well. As everything was an ending and a beginning.

Dare looked at his forearms, already browned from the sun, and wondered at the blood flowing in the veins. That wonder had mostly gone, driven under by labour, by the ceaseless chase for fortune. But it could still surface, like whaleback on a calm sea, to shatter whatever peace his mind and spirit had found. Orlett's desperate lie—"You're white, boy, you're not a nigger"—and the relentless pounding of the hooves of the mulatto's horse mostly resided under his blood, but the world would not be still, it would not let the lie and the hoof beats fall completely silent. Dare had to take care of that himself.

The sun bloodied and the dusk fell and the first wave of fish struck the corklines of the linen nets spread across the rivermouth. The tide was approaching slack. Dare slipped the oars and let the skiff settle. He glanced at his shotgun resting in the thwarts and then stared downriver for the Englishman. They were still some distance apart, more than a hundred fathoms, but Dare knew Thomas Lansdowne by his barrel shape and slouch hat. It had become a familiar sight over the years, the Englishman, with his shotgun at his chest, glaring across the sun-dazzle of water.

Dare waited. Eventually the Englishman would cross the boundary and would have to be driven off. Usually it was just his Indians who let their nets drift over the line, and they picked up and left at the first raising of a gun. Lately, however, the Englishman himself tested the limits. He did not go so far as to stay over the boundary when approached, but he patrolled it with his gun visible, protecting his skiffs as his Indians picked salmon from the nets. Salmon that didn't belong to them. The Englishman grew bolder by the day.

Dusk was settling fast. The sun, like a gutted fish, spilled its crimson as it sank. Large flocks of fowl bruised the sky at the horizons. Dare watched them over the grey-white sails of his competitors' skiffs—there must have been a hundred boats, a hundred dingy canvas sails catching the last of the breeze that had come up with the tide change. The birds rose and spread like black smoke above them.

He floated on the middle of the river, the banks miles off to either side. But the war and the doctor felt close, almost at his shoulder, whispering. The sky and river darkened. A salmon thrashed in a nearby net, pulling the tins on the corkline down. Three of his own skiffs formed a loose and drawing-in circle around him. One of the Indians softly chanted as he picked fish from the linen meshes. Brine hung heavy on the air. Dare breathed it in with the smell of the blood and slime of the catch. The chanting stopped, resumed; it was like the chanting the negro contrabands had done when they buried the dead.

Now the river turned black, the sky blue-black. The Englishman grew faint, but Dare knew he was there, waiting. All the skiffs on the river, all the dirty sails, were drifting to the one point. The fleets of the Scotsmen and the Swede and the other Americans. The workers of the men who wanted to drive him out. But there was time yet. He could sit still on his stretch of river, the stretch he had protected for seven years, and watch. And when he was forced to move, he wouldn't hesitate; he would be smarter, quicker, stronger. Again.

Dare rubbed the soreness deeper into his eyes and watched the pilot star brighten far over the delta. As always, the night sky calmed his blood; how often he had relied on the stars' loyal patterns when life seemed only a roiling confusion. Another salmon thrashed, its death throes deepening the briny flavour of the air. Dare tasted the salt; it sat heavily on his tongue. The water near him broke again, louder this time. He tried but he could not keep what was behind him from rising up in the echoes of the sound.

They'd travelled several miles a day, he remembered, in a general southwesterly direction, with their meagre clothes offering little protection from the cold. McElvane, though not as cruel as the overseer had been, was nonetheless a negro driver, and he drove them hard. That he was able to do so without resorting to violence or even threats was on account of his generosity to Daney; all the slaves realized that he had purchased her out of mercy in order to allow her to remain with her daughters. But they also knew that mercy was a fleeting quality in those who bought and sold them. The trader, they did not forget, viewed them as merchandise to be brought to market. No matter how often he let them rest or take a drink of water, he always remained the man driving them south.

There was little conversation. They each seemed locked in their own forebodings as they were locked in their own chains. The monotony of the slightly swelling fields and dark woodlots was punctuated by rare plumes of smoke from isolated houses and by the occasional small herd of cattle or sheep. The air was crisp and clean, the sky pewter with a blurred sun that gave minimal warmth. If there was birdsong, they could not hear it over the dragging of their chains and the dull hoof-clop of the trader's horse.

The men led the way, the women trying hard to keep up. He— John they called him then, and he had never tried to separate the name from the memory—had little chance to observe Daney and her daughters, but he suspected that they maintained the pace, again out of a curious blend of gratitude and terror. Nights, they slept around large fires, fires over which McElvane parched the corn that constituted the main meal of the day. Still no one talked much, though the women tried to soothe the young boys. McElvane repeatedly stared into a small book that he drew nervously from his shirt pocket. Muttering, he'd push a stub of pencil across a page, then look up at the starless sky and shake his head. A few times he spoke to the blacks, almost as if to himself, saying that a good nigger brings both a tall price and a good home. Whip marks, he said, generally send you to the rice fields, and that's a hard lot.

John remembered keeping silent then, like everyone else. The chains were heavy, and once he'd eaten and lain by the fire, all he wanted was for sleep to blank out the world. With the others, he remained in a state of shock. Everything had happened so quickly, from the overseer's arrival to Caleb's whipping to the escape attempt of Daney's girls and finally to this drive south. Only his burning hatred for Orlett sometimes stirred him out of his numb despair and gave him thoughts of escape. He didn't even think of a future apart from revenge, for he did not wish to escape anywhere except to the satisfaction of squeezing his hands around the overseer's throat. Whenever the hatred abated, the letters on his cheek began to burn. He felt them even more than the iron around his neck.

Late one afternoon they crossed a wide river, the Patuxent, and it was on the other side of it that everything changed. They reached a small village, not unlike Sharpsburg, and on a dirt road before a grey-planked building with iron-barred windows joined up with a much larger coffle. Fifty or so other blacks, mostly men, boys and young women, including one who was pregnant and one carrying a baby, were similarly chained and roped. But their driver was a different sort of man. He carried a black snake whip across his shoulders and kept up a steady torrent of threats and insults. He rode up and down the line, cracking the whip and yanking back on the reins so that the horse would rear up and snort great breaths in the air between its flailing front legs. Meanwhile, his two assistants, much younger men, scruffy and sullen, rode close by, shotguns at their chests.

McElvane deferred to the new driver. From what John could gather, both men worked for a Mr. Wych, a slave dealer in South Carolina. But it was what they all learned that night—after the drive had finally stopped, exhausted, at a shabby public house that the new driver called an "ordinary"—that brought the terror back in force.

They were driven into a bare room and made to sleep on the straw-covered dirt floor, the men on one side, the women on the other. The new driver, Jensen, forbade any conversation. "I don't want you niggers giving each other any foolish ideas," he said and shut the door, leaving them in darkness.

Over the weeping and the praying, the grunts and sighs of bodies adjusting to the crammed space, John was surprised to hear voices almost as plain as day. Through the thin walls came McElvane's voice imploring the new driver to leave his coffles unwhipped.

"They're good niggers, and I especially don't want the bright girls marked at all."

"Yeah, I noticed them. Right pretty. Wych has told me there's most money in the handsome ones right now. The houses in Atlanta can't get enough."

"It's the talk of war does it. It makes some men mad that way."

"Nothing mad about it," Jensen said. "A man's got to take his pleasure. Can't work hard with no promise of pleasure afterwards."

McElvane said, "I expect as much as two thousand for each and so I need their faces clear."

"Nobody cares about the face, eh, Matt," Jensen said and snickered. "It's not the face that gives the pleasure. But I won't deny that the lighter skin's an attraction."

The voices seemed to float around the room.

"Well, I'd appreciate it if . . ."

"Sure. By the way, what's the story with the boy with the brand on his cheek?"

"He's a good worker. A house servant, but he was hired out too. Knows some carpentry and tinsmithing. A prime boy. I expect no less than a thousand for him."

"All right you don't have to tell me. It don't matter. I've sold Indians to free niggers before. The money's the same colour, even if the niggers don't have so much of it."

"It's a strange world, that's so," McElvane said.

And then came the sound of chairs scraping back. A door slammed. The voices ceased. Now the air over the blacks hung thick.

The hatred rose in his throat again and he tried to choke it down. But he couldn't. It came out in quick, violent gasps. After a while, he curled into himself and tried to press the letters on his cheek into the dirt. But the iron collar and padlock kept his skin from the floor. Across the room, he heard crying. But something else caught his notice, something he recognized because it burned with the same intense energy that had risen up in him. And he didn't have to see clearly to know who the energy came from. It was frightening. He lay inside it all night, waiting for it to subside so that he could sleep. But it did not subside. He rubbed the worn leather on the little pouch between his fingers, thinking that he could calm the energy that way. But it flowed on; he could not slow it. Daybreak found him trembling, his skin as cold as his chains.

Across the room in the grey air he saw Daney. She sat upright against the wall, Jancey's head in her lap. He wanted to tell her that it was no good, there was no way she could save the girl now. She should have made the attempt when it was just McElvane. Because even if the attempt had failed, he would not have been severe in his punishment. But now, with the new driver and his assistants, escape was unlikely, and there was no telling what the punishment might be for trying. Don't, the boy heard himself say. Just wait. Maybe I'll be able to help. After all, Jancey means as much to me . . . But he did not speak. Daney's face, fierce in the grey light, rigid as iron, had gone beyond anything he could say. She was a mother. She wouldn't wait.

They moved on again just after first light, without breakfast. Jensen dashed along the line, cracking the whip and shouting. "Come on, you niggers."

McElvane's coffle set the pace because the blacks belonging to Jensen had been driven harder and treated more cruelly. John had never seen such listless people. He wondered where in Maryland they had come from. Perhaps they had been purchased farther afield and had entered Maryland simply as a way to reach South Carolina. Their clothes were little more than coarse pieces of hemp and thin cotton. Most of the men wore old scars as well as open whip marks; several had elaborate iron collars with spikes sticking out. But it was the women who lagged behind. Jensen kept riding back and threatening them that if they didn't keep up he'd soon put a stop to their damned tricks.

"Pregnant one's trying to take advantage," he said to McElvane as he rode forward to the lead coffle. "But if she thinks I'll be soft on account of her belly . . ."

"We're making good time," McElvane said. "We can stop a while."

"Hell, no! I want to make the Potomac by sundown. The faster the journey, the higher the profits. I've a good mind to go by rail the next drive. It's getting so this way's hardly a savings. Heeyah!"

Jensen kicked his horse's flanks and turned back down the line.

A half-hour later, he ordered all the blacks to stop. John figured that they had finally earned a rest, but Jensen's blood-flushed and contorted face told him otherwise.

"You niggers are going to see this! And then you'll know to keep up!"

They were on a dirt road in the middle of the country. Treeless rolling hills stretched away to either side for miles.

"Matt, start driving the stakes. Billy, keep your gun on the niggers. I'll take care of the rest myself."

Jensen dismounted and strode to his cart. He took a spade from the back. Just off the road on a flat piece of grass, the assistant began driving in wooden stakes.

The pregnant woman, very black, her head scarved in dirty red, began to cry, "No marse please marse I'll keep up I promise marse please."

The baby in the mother's arms wailed and she tried desperately to hush it. Jensen took no notice. He feverishly dug a hole in the centre of what turned out to be four stakes. His breath swirled around him.

John looked at Daney. She had almost vanished in a loose circle of women seated on the ground around her, but he could see the intensity of her eyes. Their fire was a stark contrast to the dull cast of the other blacks' eyes.

Jensen finished digging and marched over to the coffle of women. He roughly undid the pregnant woman's ropes and dragged her to the stakes.

"Take off that shift!"

"No marse please marse!"

"I said take it off!"

Still pleading, the woman did so, revealing a dark belly smooth and tight as a drum skin. Her breasts were large, the nipples erect with the cold.

Jensen forced her onto her knees.

"Shut up and lie down there! You hear!"

When the woman merely covered her face with her hands, he grabbed her arm and dragged her and pushed her face down so that her belly fit into the hole. She whimpered as he roped her limbs to the four stakes. At last he stood back, breathing hard, and said to the blacks, "I told you what I'd do. And it's gonna be worse for you from now on."

All this time McElvane sat on his haunches at the side of the road, chewing a piece of bark. He wore a pained expression but did not interfere.

John felt the restlessness of the men travel along the chains. Their faces were wet masks. He tried to take their hatred into him, thinking it would increase and strengthen his own. But he also knew that there was a greater force at work and his eyes kept returning to it. Even when Jensen began to whip the pregnant woman's bare back, even as she cried out and the men's chains shifted and all their breath rose as if it came from the earth itself, even then he stared at Daney. She was not watching. She was holding her daughters close. Her eyes were struck flint. He could not believe that the whites didn't notice.

After twenty lashes, Jensen stopped. His hard breathing and the woman's weeping hung in the air together. Nothing else stirred for miles. Despite keeping his attention on Daney, John found that he'd clenched his fists so hard that his fingernails had dug into his palms.

McElvane returned to his horse. He led it by the bridle up to Jensen. "Better hurry if we want to make the river by dark."

Then he mounted.

Jensen untied the woman. He dragged her to her feet, her belly dripping bits of earth and grass, her back torn and bloody. Meekly, she pulled on her shift and returned to the coffle.

Once the whites were all on horseback again, the drive resumed at a faster pace. The boy held his chains and jogged over the hard ground, his eyes on the horizon. But it was Daney's eyes that were searching; he felt them on his back but he could not see what they were seeing. The air was rich with sweat and wet earth.

By dusk, they had reached the Potomac, at a point of considerable width. Coming out of a clump of oaks, they were driven straight to the river's edge and told to rest. John gaped at the pewtery expanse of water stretching several hundred yards to a far bank of oaks and other hardwood, bare and black like twisted iron. A low, broken mist slid slowly off the water and over the bank. The icy cold of it set his teeth chattering.

"You'll have to signal," McElvane said to Jensen. "He won't hear us."

"Matt's a powerful voice. Give a holler, Matt."

The assistant's shout rolled along the banks and died away.

"It's too far," McElvane said, "and the river's up."

They waited, listening. The current under the ghostly mist made a low, rushing sound.

"I'll light a torch," McElvane said and busied himself about his cart. In a few minutes he raised a burning stick high in the grey light. After a while, a lantern flashed on the opposite bank.

John stared at the grey, darkening water. It gave nothing back, not even the dull sky. McElvane took out his little book and pencil stub and scratched away while a small light in the distance grew larger, its edges yellow and blurred.

Jensen said, "Some take the chains off as soon as Virginia, but I have to see the town limits of Columbia before I'm comfortable. Even so, I feel better over the Potomac."

"Any body of water slows a runaway down," McElvane said.

Though it was almost dark, the day was warmer. The breath of the blacks no longer hung visibly. John tensed and turned. But the dusk had hidden Daney's face among the women's. It had been only days and miles, yet his old life seemed a distant memory, effaced by the hatred building in his veins. He could imagine seeing Orlett's doglike grin in the ferryman's widening lamp glow as it spread over the black water. It seemed sometimes that the overseer had burned that grin into his brain. As the ferry reached the bank, John lifted a cuffed hand to the letters and pressed the cold iron there.

Jensen began to drive the coffles onto the scow. It was broad and flat, like a barn floor, with thick ropes low around the sides. The ferryman, pinch-faced and elderly, had two large blacks as helpers. Their job was to move the ferry by means of two long wooden poles that they wielded with powerful grace. In the glow cast by the lantern, everything appeared larger. Shadows splashed over the deck like buckets of thrown river water. A ragged mongrel chained to an anvil at the ferryman's side yipped and growled as the coffles boarded.

"We'll have to make two trips," Jensen said. "We're in a hurry. Can't you make those boys pull fast?"

The ferryman spat out a chaw of tobacco. "Never met one of you Georgia traders who weren't in a hurry. My boys pull as fast as the river allows. No hurrying a river."

The scow pushed off into the current. John stood near enough to the dog to smell it; it strained at its chain and bared its teeth. He looked away. At the opposite end of the ferry, standing behind McElvane's horse and cart, Daney seemed to look straight back at him. Her eyes caught and reflected the lantern's glow as she slowly lifted one hand and touched the rope at her neck. She shifted slightly. Now her body seemed cut in half by the board of McElvane's cart; she might have been sitting in it. The boy glanced at the dog, which leapt and threw itself forward and fell back again. McElvane's horse shied, its hooves battering the wooden deck. McElvane approached and patted the horse's neck, then bent his head to it. Beyond him, Daney's body dipped quickly and vanished. John saw her lift one of the iron balls from the cart and turn.

"No!" he shouted. "Nooo!"

The women screamed. McElvane's head shot away from the horse's as the blacks' poles hung in the air. In his effort to jump forward, John pulled Daney's eldest son, Robert, down against him. But he kept his eyes on Daney. She held the ball cradled at her stomach and pulled the coffle toward the edge. It happened so quickly that the others had no chance to resist. Before McElvane could reach the ropes, all the women had gone over. Jancey had gone over. The ferry drifted away from the rapid sequence of splashes until the ferryman heaved an anchor into the current. The women's screams continued for a few long seconds above the dog's barking as the scow turned sideways. The broken water where the women had gone under quickly healed. Frantically, McElvane ordered the blacks to sweep with their poles.

"Try to catch hold of the ropes," he shouted and bent so far over the edge that it seemed he must fall.

The ferryman rushed over with the lantern and pulled him back.

"Don't be a fool, man," he cried. "There's no chance of getting them up in time."

Robert was panting. He tried to pull the whole line of chains forward. But the men resisted. For his part, John was willing enough to join the women; at least he did not have the will to fight Robert's grief. The face of Daney's son was raw and tear-scalded. His eyes rolled back in his skull as he shouted for his mother and sisters. The ferryman ran to a wooden box near the chained dog and removed a shotgun. He trained it on the coffle.

"First one who wants to, dies."

John helped to hold Robert still. McElvane continued to direct the blacks with the poles. "She can't hold them all down," he cried.

It was impossible to see where the water had been broken. "Oh, pray! Oh, pray!" repeated the old man, Motes, as the current flowed around the scow. The dog began to howl, and McElvane, looking conflicted, finally left the edge of the scow and calmed his horse before it bolted and plunged over the side with his cart full of iron. His face shook like paper being eaten by fire.

John stared at the calm, black surface of the river. They were all dead by now. Daney always said. Except no one but her had made the separation. That was what she must have thought. They were all dead, still roped together, the iron ball spilled from Daney like the dead weight of all the children that could not be ripped from her by other hands.

The river flowed black and smooth, and the last shreds of mist and lantern light flickered over it. He touched his cheek.

Dare felt the fish hook bit of scar that stuck out from the top of his beard onto his bare skin. The mark remained, but the two letters were gone, the chains were gone, he held in his uncuffed hands a set of oars. And the shotgun, just visible in the grainy dusk, appeared to shine and rise before him in the air.

The Englishman had begun to cross the boundary.

II
July 1881, Chilukthan, British Columbia

The days passed quickly now, though fractured and fraught. Anson attended Louisa much of the time, for in her presence he did not feel such urgency about reuniting with Dare. But his concern for the girl would not let him relax. Evenings were the worst, and he fell naturally into the same broken rhythm that he'd known at Antietam, snatching an hour or two of sleep and walking to keep himself alert.

Suddenly, one morning, the settlement took the girl's fever into itself. It wasn't only the days lengthening and the sun burning brighter and hotter; it was the general pace of activity. Down at the cannery, in the mix of shadows and sunlight on the rough-planked wharves outside each building, the barefoot Indian women spent endless hours hunched over piled tresses of linen, expertly weaving them into gill-nets. Anson watched in amazement as their brown hands butterflied among the meshes; these women, short and stocky for the most part, mild and silent, with their shy smiles and fondness for colourful beads, ribbons, and braid work, turned into regular demons of industry with wooden hanging-needles in their grasp. Meanwhile, more great cedar canoes, elaborately carved with designs of various totemic creatures—bears, ravens, wolves, and killer whales—slid into the landing almost by the hour, bringing more men and women to pull the nets and row the fishing skiffs, more barely clothed children, noses green and running, to roam the muddy banks, and more scrawny, mixed-breed dogs to fill the sultry silence with their barks and howls.

Behind the main cannery building, the Chinese had stopped punching out cans. The absence of the thunking sound on the air was somehow unsettling, as if the heartbeat of the entire coast had stilled suddenly, replaced with the erratic, wandering pulse of the dogs' hunger.

There were darker changes too. Without telling anyone, the Chinese coffined one of their own and placed the plain box high in a fir tree, as apparently was their habit. Gold Mountain, the China Boss said when pressed for an explanation, gone to Gold Mountain. Fair enough, Anson thought, they could call heaven whatever they wanted, but he needed to know the cause of death because there was always a danger of epidemic. If the Chinaman had perished of typhoid, for example, the situation was suddenly more grave. Typhoid was highly contagious, but as long as he restricted Louisa's visitors to those relatives who had already been exposed to the disease, Anson felt confident he could keep it from spreading. But after considerable awkward entreaties had led the Chinese to lower the box and open it, Anson discovered that the man, so emaciated as to be only transparent skin over bone, had likely died of nutritional lack, probably of scurvy. He ordered the Lansdownes to make sure some vegetables were added to the meagre rice meals at the China House, but Thomas, at least, was unmoved by the death.

"I'll have to get another Chinaman," he muttered and lowered his shoulder into the heated air as if trying to break through an invisible door.

With the excitement of the big run playing on everyone's nerves, drink suddenly became a problem. Where the alcohol came from was never clear to Anson, but the effect was obvious enough, as several of the male Indians spent their non-fishing hours with the bottle, which led to games of chance that sometimes ended in violence. On two occasions, Anson had been called from Louisa's bedside to stitch wounds, one from a broken bottle, another from a knife.

The comings and goings at the settlement began to blur; everything became caught up in the tidal flow. The self-righteous Southerner, Richardson, took the steamer to Victoria, though not before vowing mysteriously that he'd return soon "to help ease the family's sorrows." The fiscal agent had crawled onto the scene like a colourful rat, and Anson had done his best to avoid him, which wasn't difficult, since, upon hearing of the child's illness, the agent immediately hired some Indians to row him to New Westminster.

Much more dramatic than these various events, however, was the sudden arrival of the big salmon run. The fish had struck the rivermouth in numbers greater than anyone had known. Instantly the cannery's belts and wheels and gears smoked and whirred as the now-sober fishermen returned with their skiffs heaped to the gunwales with rippling silver. The sun bloodied. The air filled with the stench of dead fish and guts as the cannery spewed offal into the river. Great swirling clouds of gulls shrieked constantly. It was an assault like nothing he'd ever seen, and Anson was sorry he could not spend more time watching the deft skills of the Chinese and Indians who slit and gutted the fish and fitted the deep-red sections into cans.

But then, even the excitement of the salmon run and the slow, tortuous drama of the child hovering between life and death became secondary to the news of Dare's return.

One morning, as Anson checked Louisa's pulse for the thousandth time, trying again to decipher her mumbled, semi-conscious words, Henry Lansdowne appeared in the doorway.

"A letter's come for you," he said.

It wasn't exactly a letter, just a few hastily penned sentences on the back of an invoice for pig tin. But Anson knew the hand well enough, and the directness of the tone.

> Back at the Slough. Come as soon as able. The diffi-
> culties I mentioned are unchanged and I have need of
> your counsel.
> Dare

At last! After all the days of tense waiting—during which the Lansdownes certainly seemed to think that their fierce competitor had not gone away at all—Anson found the note an immense relief. But it left him in the same quandary. He looked at the girl, then back at the note. In the fetid gloom of the house, he wondered if Louisa could be left in her family's care for a short while.

The girl stirred. Her teeth chattered rapidly, as if trying to keep pace with her pulse. She moaned and put a hand to her head. Anson knew she was suffering much pain there as well as throughout her limbs. Typhoid cases generally passed through three distinct phases, of which this was still the first. But with the violent chills generally came the fingertip-sized red spots on the chest and abdomen.

Anson gently lowered the top of the girl's shift. No spots yet, but he suspected they would appear soon. In the meantime, there was little to do but to keep the linens clean and the air circulating through the room and to hope. Doses of quinine, broths for combating the fever, a light diet easy on the bowels and stomach (chicken broth, mostly): he went through all the required treatments but knew that, when the crisis came, it would be the child's own will that determined the result. Anson could hardly believe, despite the slackness of the girl's mouth and her pewter-dull eyes, that she might choose death over life. But his belief in a patient's will to live had been severely tested before and had failed. So he tried not to make any predictions, even to himself.

He left the sick room, determined to head for Crescent Slough right away, determined to feel no guilt for leaving the child in the loving care of her relatives. After all, he had another loyalty to attend to, older and more powerful. And he knew he could trust the mother and aunt to follow his instructions for the child's care in his absence.

Stepping into the light almost hurt; the clarity was such that he had to hold his hand over his eyes for a moment as he walked along the riverbank, idly following the sounds of work: the whining of conveyor belts and the clunking of cans from inside the cannery, and the sporadic shouted orders of men on the wharves outside.

As always, Anson found the slaughter both repellent and oddly attractive. There were so many salmon that whole fish were routinely thrown dead into the water if they'd been left in the sun too long. Of those that were processed, often only the midsections were used to fill the cans; the rest of the fish was simply dropped on the cannery floor to join the great red pulpy mess through which the smock-clad Native women and Chinese men trod heavily from task to task. It was little wonder to Anson that the settlement had known many outbreaks of typhoid fever; with so much fouling of the drinking water, along with the infectious rottening of the air, how could it be otherwise? According to Mary Lansdowne, there had been ten cases the summer before, with four fatalities, including Thomas and Edney's eldest child. With so many guts sloshing back and forth on the tide, the atmosphere was decidedly poisonous. If he had not been so harried by recent events, Anson would have stressed more emphatically to the Lansdownes the need for improved sanitary conditions. But the English brothers themselves were too preoccupied to pay much heed to his advice on those occasions when he tried to raise the subject.

As he reached the wharf, Anson saw a thin, bare-chested young man standing in the middle of a scow loaded with still, apparently dead salmon. The stench of blood and slime was heavy and overwhelmed the usual muddy musk of the river. The man held a long wooden stick in his hand. At the end of the stick was a large curved hook. With much difficulty, the man was trying to hook the fish and flip them onto the wharf where the figure of Thomas Lansdowne, hands on hips, glowered down at him.

"For Christ's sakes, man," he shouted. "That's no way to pitch fish! Give me that pick!"

Several other men standing nearby grinned. One yelled, "Atta boy, Tom, you show him!"

Anson watched in amazement as Thomas Lansdowne threw himself off the wharf and onto the sloppy pile in the scow. Immediately he found his footing, yanked the pick away from his slack-jawed worker, and set about pitching fish. The result was impressive, at first. Anson couldn't even see the pick as the Englishman wielded it, the hook barely puncturing the head of each salmon, a steady stream of the silver fish leaping as if brought back from the dead and landing with a slosh on the mounting pile on the wharf.

The young man's jaw dropped farther. The men watching cheered and clapped; a few others emerged from nearby buildings to take in the scene. The fish continued to fly through the air. Twenty, thirty, forty, fifty.

My God, Anson thought, enough. A strange silence descended. Only the slapping of each dead fish on the pile and a quick, harsh grunt from the thrower—who now sprayed sweat from his head, which swung like a mallet—sounded along the river. Even the cannery had fallen quiet, as if sensing its own workings to be inadequate. And still the fish rose and slapped down, rose and slapped down. The spectators looked apprehensively at one another. The young worker tentatively reached to take the pick back, and he must have said something, for Thomas Lansdowne whirled and cursed, the action only the briefest pause in the fierce rhythm of the pitching.

Eighty, ninety. At last the speed slowed. A couple of fish hit the side of the wharf and splashed into the river. Thomas Lansdowne's face blazed like the sun, which hung high above him and was gradually sapping his strength. But the man did not stop. The fish must have seemed as heavy as bars of lead to him now. He laboured up from the bent position, the veins swollen in his neck, and heaved each time as if forcing something through a stream of molasses. And as his energy weakened, his grunts turned to cries. Now more fish splashed in the river than hit the wharf. He fell, got up again. The pick waved like a divining rod. The young worker had backed away as far as possible without jumping overboard.

One of the spectators said quietly, "All right, Tom. You showed him."

The great head lifted, dripping with sweat. The white shirt was drenched, as if he'd just been swimming. His chest moved like a bellows. He squinted into the sun, then lowered his eyes and, very slowly, levelled them at each man on the wharf. Finally, the eyes came to rest on Anson.

As the two men were thirty yards apart, Anson could not be certain of the expression on Thomas Lansdowne's face, but he detected a general air of blankness, as if the man had not come fully out of the dream of his own physical strength. Gradually, the blankness lifted, replaced with a deeper worry than usual. He raised a finger, which

Anson interpreted as a sign for him to wait. Then the Englishman scrambled over the fish, stood on the scow's edge, and, reaching up, hoisted himself onto the wharf.

"Doctor! She hasn't . . . she isn't . . ." He struggled to catch his breath as he walked. A trail of bloody boot prints stained the sun-baked wood.

"No, no," Anson hurried to reassure him, realizing that each of his sudden departures from the house was a potential death knell. "I have come out only for a rest. Louisa is . . ."

"Unchanged." The panic had gone from the Englishman's voice, but the one word fell heavily.

"Not exactly, no," Anson said. "The disease is progressing. I have no doubts now that it is typhoid."

The Englishman's shoulders slumped. His dark eyes took on the querying quickness of a child's. But it was not to Anson that the questions were directed. To whom, then? God? Conscience?

"It would be best to keep people from her room," Anson continued. "Be sure to keep her brother clear."

"I have sent him away. To a neighbour up the slough. With my wife tending to Louisa and the cannery in full operation, I could not leave the boy on his own. And Edney will not leave, of course." He sighed, pushed a blunt, slime-wet hand through his hair. "Edward has been insistent. He blames himself, you see."

Anson nodded. It was not the boy's fault, of course. No one could have kept the girl from the piano, but Anson was weary of explaining that to her father.

"It is very warm, doctor. Shall we move to the shade?" He held one arm out, indicating that Anson should proceed to the side of the near-est cannery building.

The coolness was indeed a relief, but Thomas Lansdowne seemed no more comfortable. Indeed, the tension of his business and domes-tic responsibilities had begun to take a noticeable toll; he had lost weight and there were dark rings beneath his eyes.

"I don't wish you to think," he began softly, "that my absence from her bedside is a choice I'm free to make. This work I'm doing here is for her, for all of them. And she's in God's hands."

The shade and the contrite tone of the man's voice gave Anson the uneasy sense that he was hearing a confession in a church. But a sudden violent keening of gull cry destroyed the impression.

"You have been too many hours in the room as it is. You can do little for her now and you will only damage your own health. You are wise to tend to your business affairs. When the crisis comes, I'll find you."

Some of the sweat had pooled in the hollows under Thomas Lansdowne's eyes and glistened in his scale-flecked beard. He might have just finished weeping. But Anson knew that such a man would never cry; when his grief became great enough, the blood inside him would burst. Anson could almost smell its heat, almost believe that this was what sent the gulls into a renewed frenzy. Yet the Englishman seemed weaker now too, not quite the force he'd been only days before when Anson had come upon him in the field removing stumps. It was becoming easier to pity him. But, as if he recoiled from pity as though it were a form of violence, Thomas Lansdowne changed his manner abruptly.

"It wouldn't be so difficult, doctor, if my business affairs were not continually threatened. Your friend, Dare, is back on the river." The Englishman's tone had become cold, his eyes took on their more characteristic probing quality.

Surprised by the sudden aggression, Anson merely replied that he had heard as much.

Thomas Lansdowne did not relent. "Louisa's illness is not the sole reason I have sent Edward away."

Anson had no interest in this subject and took a step toward the sunlight. "I am well aware of your disagreement with my friend. I would have thought, under the circumstances, that you would have set it aside."

Thomas Lansdowne scowled so fiercely that he almost bared his teeth. "How can I? It's as great a threat to my children's future as any plague! Don't you understand? I work not for myself, I work for them. And because I work for them, I have a responsibility, a moral responsibility, a responsibility to God that binds my hands in any fight. What does he have? What does he work for? Nothing but his own will to succeed at any cost. You claim he is a friend of yours. Well, what drives your friend, doctor, to work against everything that we're trying to build here? Why doesn't he co-operate with us? He has no family, he attends no service, he associates with no one. It's easy enough, then, to compete without scruples, easy enough, then, to ruin another man."

Halfway into the sunlight, Anson felt that his body had split into the grave-dark past and the dawn-bright future. He balanced uneasily there, as the Englishman continued his tirade.

"And since I cannot explain to myself how any man of decent upbringing can conduct himself in such a manner—nay, sir, don't interrupt! You have not been witness to his actions!—I can only conclude that the information lately received is true."

"Information? Sir, if you have charges against Dare, it does you no honour to hint at them. Be frank if you would prove yourself the pillar of morality that you claim to be."

The scowl eased into a hard line, but the eyes somehow found a reservoir of brightness. "I make no such claim. I am the Lord's servant, one of multitudes. A Christian, not a heathen."

"A heathen? If you mean . . ."

"We know Dare for what he is. We know he's a negro."

Anson did not fall back in any way, but shock must have registered on his face, for Thomas Lansdowne hurried to defend his words.

"It's no use denying it. We have it on good authority from an American who has lived among the race since boyhood. He assures us that there are negroes so fair-skinned that they can easily pass for white."

But Anson no longer took in the Englishman's words. Now he understood Dare's difficulties, now he appreciated the urgency of the summons; everything that Dare had made of himself since the war, all the struggles, many of which Anson could only imagine, were threatened by the revelation of his blood.

"Good authority?" Anson said. "You must be desperate indeed to take the word of someone who is no friend to Dare if you're so willing to believe such a slander."

A puzzled look crossed Thomas Lansdowne's face. He blinked several times and said, "Of course, doctor, I realize that this information might be a surprise to you. Dare has no doubt been long accustomed to hiding the truth from everyone he meets."

Anson stepped into the full sunlight, then turned. "Truth? What truth? The only truth I respect is a man's character, and there's nothing you can tell me about Dare to make me change my opinion of him. You call yourself a servant of the Lord, but you would stoop to believing base rumours about a business rival simply in order to remove him. I suggest you spend more time reflecting on your own character."

"You swear he's a white man, then?" Thomas Lansdowne also stepped into the sun. His shirt had lightened as the sweat dried. The sun deepened the redness of his beard. "On the bible, you would swear this?"

Anson almost laughed at the man's naive faith that his bible meant as much to others as it did to him. But the laugh died in his throat when he considered what he had to do, or not do, now. He closed his eyes and saw, in a flash, Dare staggering across a battlefield with a wounded soldier on his back. What little difference it made then, or now, how much of his blood derived from the negro race. A man was his actions and his courage—surely the war had been waged and won on such a principle, or else the dead were truly husks of a rotted harvest. And so, when Anson opened his eyes again, he not only swore to the truth of his friend's white blood, but he had also made up his mind to leave for Crescent Slough. The child would not reach a crisis for at least a few days; there was time to answer Dare's summons.

Thomas Lansdowne slowly extended his hand. "I would not doubt the word of a man who has been attending my daughter in her illness. My apologies for the error. The American was convincing."

Anson shook the hand and, eager to escape from his own deceit, said, "I'd best return to her now. I must leave instruction for your wife, as I'll be away briefly."

"Away?"

"There's no danger. The illness will not peak for a while yet. We can only wait. In the meantime, I must have the use of a skiff."

The sunlight seemed heavy, clotted. Anson wanted to be out of it again.

"You're going to Crescent Slough?" Thomas Lansdowne's eyes narrowed.

"It's the reason I'm here at all."

The Englishman's dark eyes probed Anson's blood one last time, then drifted away.

"Take any skiff you like. I must return to work," he said and was gone.

Anson watched his leaden progress for a while before following another peal of gull cry upriver to where Dare and the past waited, shackled together, body on body, black with white, white with black, and no God to tell them apart.

III

The water was very cold, but the poor child still burned. Edney could not reason it out. But then, did not a live woman sometimes carry a dead child in the womb? And, so, the Lord travelled the same air as Satan. Here was only common mystery, but it froze Edney in her duties. Only Mary's voice made her move.

"I think we had better not bathe her too long, sister. The doctor suggested ten minutes."

Edney rose from her knees at the edge of the bathtub and reached for a towel. "But she's so hot, Mary. It's almost as if she was not touching the water."

"I know. I know. We can only hope that there's a cooling inside. When the fever breaks, it will be sudden."

The child inside kicked. Edney dropped the towel.

"Sister, are you not well?"

Edney pushed a braid, heavy as a rope of tar, away from one eye. At least the delirium had stopped. The child no longer babbled incoherently, no longer had spittle at the corners of her mouth. In the water, her crimson spots looked innocent as fallen petals. Edney slowly reached a hand out, thinking she could just brush the spots away. But what if she removed the child with the sickness? The idea did not horrify; it was merely a practical matter. With life so fragile, inside and outside of her, in God's keeping or in His wrath, every action appeared so much larger than itself. It was easier to remain still, but stillness was not given a woman in this life. Edney retrieved the towel and helped Mary lift Louisa from the bathtub.

Moments later, with the burning girl returned to her bed, Edney watched the diminishing light run down the wall opposite the open window. How slowly and silently the earth drained the sun—there should have been a great clamour, as of a battle, at the close of each day, not this noiseless, remorseless dwindling to dark. Given the brevity of the years allotted to man, did he not deserve more ceremony? May deserved to have had a band play to mark each cycle of her days' short course.

"Edney? Are you well enough to meet our visitors now? Louisa sleeps, and I have put them off for some hours, ever since the steamer arrived. I fear there may be no better time."

Visitors? Edney brought her eyes away from the reddened wall. Mary's hands twisted in her lap, her face was ill composed, drawn, pale. Meeting these visitors might calm her sister-in-law, and Edney felt she could do that much without pause, though she could not think who the visitors might be.

"We'll have to go down to them," Mary said. "Don't worry over their needs. I have already seen to the evening meal and told them to await us in the parlour. Mr. Richardson was quite insistent that we do not indispose ourselves, but I could tell that he was most anxious to see you. A fine gentleman. He has quite convinced me that his friends can help to ease your burden, Edney. Henry and Thomas would not approve, I know, but as long as Mr. Richardson is present, I don't see any harm in their attempting to help." Her shoulders slumped suddenly, as if her whole body had sighed.

Edney went to her, took her hands in her own. Both were as cold as the child's were hot.

"Mary, I will go down presently. Mr. Richardson has been a good friend to us. If he truly believes something is for the best, I hardly think it is just of us to doubt him."

As she moved toward the door, Edney struggled to recall the exact nature of the offer. It involved her children, her daughters. He had said that he could bring May closer. But how was that possible, since May was already flesh to her bone? The absence had been filled by peril and duty: Louisa had done what God could not or would not, and May had returned. Hadn't she?

The child inside moved again, a slow turn that pushed against the heart. Returned? The price occurred to Edney with a horror that kept her from touching the doorknob. It was, after all, how life worked. But how could May ever come fully back, back in the shine of eyes and the warmth of skin, if Louisa did not die? Edney's hands flew to her mouth. Had she willed it? Could she have been so wicked? The more she thought on it, the more the horror filled her: there would have to be another death to pay for May's return. Suddenly Edney longed for the comfort of one who understood such matters so much better than she. If providence yet operated for her, this was bare proof of its workings. She took it as such and let it calm her before she proceeded, with Mary at her side, downstairs to the parlour.

Ambrose Richardson rose so smoothly and quickly at Edney's appearance that she felt she had conjured his lithe, white form from the shadows with the urgency of her need.

"Dear lady," he said and took her hands in his. Edney looked down, away from his blue eyes, the colour of a robin's egg, and into his graceful, long-fingered hand. She could not help but stare again at the one sleeve of his pale linen suit so neatly pinned over the place of his wound and then up at his lean, softly smiling face. Quickly, she looked down again. Could the warmth of his palm be the result of its singularity? Her hands seemed to have formed a prayer around a candle. She opened her mouth to plead for his consolation; he would know that she had meant no such wickedness. They had last spoken before Louisa fell ill. May had felt so distant then, even in her closeness. Edney could not reach her. Now she feared she had done so at a terrible cost. But he would understand, for had he not spoken of his own hatred of God and all Creation at the death of his boy?

But before Edney could speak, Ambrose Richardson turned her to the lamplit corner where two figures stood motionless. One detached itself from the other and approached with a feathery step.

Ambrose Richardson spoke just as gently. "Mrs. Lansdowne, may I introduce Miss Elizabeth d'Espereaux of Victoria." With a slight bow, he released Edney's hands and stepped back.

Edney was not accustomed to seeing such youth and beauty in her sex; even May, had she grown to full womanhood, would not have rivalled this woman's physical charm. Elizabeth d'Espereaux was perhaps three and twenty, at once winsome and strong, her brown eyes alive with points of light, her features small and exquisitely formed, the skin at her throat white as fresh cream and set off by a thin collar of small purple jewels. Her black hair was bobbed and formed two smooth identical waves that drew attention to her smile, which was gentle and even. Had God wanted Eve to walk again on the earth, Edney did not think he would have had to do more than remove the fine silk dress that covered this young woman's modesty. Her voice, it was no surprise to learn, had a brooklike trill.

"Madam, I am delighted to make your acquaintance, even under these trying circumstances. Ambrose has told me of your sorrows, but even his powers of expression could not convey the full impact of what is here." She raised her nose and daintily sniffed. "Your daughter's aura is as strong as any I've ever encountered. She must have an urgent need to contact you."

Edney, however, could sense nothing but cigar smoke. It swirled in gouts behind Miss d'Espereaux as a thick, burly figure emerged from it. This turned out to be a man of about thirty years, brown-suited, his face as rough hewn as the young woman's was delicate. He sported untrimmed ginger sideburns and his cheeks were badly pockmarked, but there shone the same quick light in his eyes, though they were small and set deep in his chiselled face.

Miss d'Espereaux introduced the man as Mr. Collins, her assistant, then said, "Is not the aura of unusual strength, Francis?"

"I have never known the like before," he said enthusiastically and nodded at Edney. Then he resumed puffing on his cigar.

Ambrose Richardson cleared his throat pointedly, but the man ignored him. Miss d'Espereaux hastened to continue.

"She must have been very close to her sister. I believe it's the younger girl who lies ill upstairs?"

"Louisa," Edney said and could not keep the tears from her eyes.

"Yes. Louisa. It is she who holds the veil. In her presence, I have every confidence, madam, that we will be able to lift it."

Ambrose Richardson asked if they might be allowed to go to Louisa.

"Go to her?" Mary said. The lines on her brow and at the edges of her mouth deepened. "What do you mean to do?"

Miss d'Espereaux smiled and lightly fingered the jewels at her throat.

"Yes. The portal will be widest in Louisa's presence. It's a rare thing, in my experience, to have a spirit so close and in so much need of contact. Your daughter, Mrs. Lansdowne, must love you greatly."

Edney's tears were heavy, but they would not fall from her eyes. She could hardly keep her own daughters separate. But why should a mother's love for her children be divided by their bodies and souls? A family was but a single child, after all.

Mary turned her anxious gaze to the American gentleman. She seemed to be fading in the swirls of cigar smoke.

"Louisa is very ill. I don't know that it's wise for you to . . ."

"Dearest lady," he said. "Don't be alarmed. I personally guarantee that no harm will come to the child. On my honour." With the same watery blue gaze to which Edney had become accustomed, he addressed her, his voice as tender and modest as a man's could be. "Edney, I implore you, hard though it seems, you must try to recognize in this affliction a rare opportunity. Miss d'Espereaux and I have discussed this matter at some length, and she shares my feeling that your lost daughter is using the illness to expedite contact. It has been known before. The boundary between life and death is more fragile than we dream. If we but lift the veil and let her speak, I am certain the illness will release its hold upon the child. Miss d'Espereaux is a most expert spirit healer."

This gentle yet impassioned speech was abruptly followed by a gruff voice from the corner.

"It's the Lord's gospel, ma'am. One time Lizzie removed a lady's tumour all the way in Australia."

Miss d'Espereaux smiled thinly. "Thank you, Francis. But Mrs.

Lansdowne does not require a history of our successes." She paused and floated closer. Edney could smell violets through the smoke. The young woman's face was blurring with mercy. She took Edney's hands in hers. "Will you trust me? Shall we go up to them now?"

"Them? Oh, Edney, I don't think that Henry—" Mary turned her head rapidly, as if in search of her husband's guidance. "It is not perhaps quite proper, after all . . ."

Edney hardly heard Mary's objections. She felt herself drawn upward by Miss d'Espereaux's eyes. But she managed to allay her sister-in-law's concerns.

"It's fine, Mary. What harm can be done? Dr. Baird said the crisis would come in its own time. And besides, we have Mr. Richardson's word of honour."

"No harm but rather a blessing that is not given to many," Miss d'Espereaux said as she released Edney's hands. "Your daughter has something she must communicate. We will ease her burden as well as yours. I have never known the spiritual plane to be so close. Mrs. Lansdowne, please, allow me to be your servant."

Edney had not felt such lightness in months. The sympathy of Ambrose Richardson seemed magnified in this beautiful young woman and was therefore even more to be trusted. With sincere hope, and against Mary's faltering protestations, Edney led the way out of the parlour and to Louisa's room.

The child still slept, still burned. She lay in the day's subsiding light with the rich brine of the tide flowing over her, so that she might have been adrift on the river itself. Edney touched her cheek, lifted a wet strand of hair from her dry lips.

"A lovely child," Miss d'Espereaux murmured. "Worthy of heaven, but she will remain in the material sphere a full life's course, I sense it. Please, everyone, be very still." She slowly circled the room, gazing around her, her body moving like a dowser's branch. At different points, she paused before a tall mahogany wardrobe, then before a plain deal dresser, her gaze fixed on the unblinking eyes of a small boy china doll seated on its surface. At last, she lingered before a small oval mirror on the wall, into which she stared as if seeking those same changeless eyes in the glass. Then she began to move again, almost gliding, past the wooden doll house with its eerily darkened little rooms, past the shut closet containing the child's dresses and shoes, past a table with a cracked porcelain basin on it, and finally past the simple needlework on the wall opposite the child's bed that announced in red stitches the biblical phrase, "He shall gather the lambs with his arms."

Edney's pulse quickened. She yearned to see with the younger woman's eyes, she held her breath and put a hand to the child inside, asking without words for it to be calm.

Suddenly Miss d'Espereaux froze, her body rigid, her chin raised so that the white of her throat appeared to spread. In the middle of the room, with her eyes fixed on the open window in which the curtains billowed gently, she waited. Minutes passed.

Finally, she turned slowly, as if following the flight of a bird. Now she looked at a portion of wall just beyond Edney's shoulder. Louisa moaned and twisted her head on the pillow, then fell silent. Several more minutes passed. Miss d'Espereaux did not even blink. Her lips were slightly parted. At last she spoke, but only to the air. "Yes, I understand," she said, and her voice was different, more of a monotone than the usual trill. She approached the bed. For a painfully long period, she stood there, her spine seeming to tighten as if with screws. Then she began to breathe out slowly and evenly, through pursed lips.

"It's all right, ma'am," Edney heard from behind her. "It's only the start of the insufflations. Lizzie always uses them on the sick cases."

"Sir, you must be silent," Ambrose Richardson said in a low voice.

The other man bristled. "You'd think I'd never been to a healing before. I know I need to be quiet. But the lady here was getting kind of upset."

He meant Mary. Edney glanced at her, saw that she was trembling, her eyes widening like a frightened horse's. But Edney felt no such terror, only an ever-increasing wonder. Even as Miss d'Espereaux bent to Louisa and began to breathe on her bare arms, a cloth placed between the young woman's lips and the child's skin, Edney remained calm. But Mary did not.

"Oh, what is she doing? Mr. Richardson, can this be proper?"

Francis Collins spoke up forcefully. "Oh, it's as proper as the Sabbath, ma'am. The insufflations always come before the curing passes. It's all very proper procedure. There's no harm in it. Why, I'd almost welcome the fever just to have it done to myself and that's the honest truth."

"Will you or will you not hold your tongue?"

But Edney did not look away to witness Ambrose Richardson's temper. She was, instead, entirely absorbed by Miss d'Espereaux's powers of concentration. The young woman had breathed her way up Louisa's arm to her shoulder, and now drew back. She folded the cloth and placed it to one side on the bedsheet. Her face was rapt, slightly dewed with effort: the light in her eyes had a candle-flickering quickness. Amazed, Edney stared as the young woman slowly drew the palms of her hands over Louisa's face, just above the skin. Then, suddenly, she put her hands together and shook them, a look of distaste on her features.

In a voice barely hushed, Collins said, "That's the bad magnetics she's shaking out. See. It's like washing the dirt off your hands, that's all."

Miss d'Espereaux's touch again hovered an inch from Louisa's brow, then passed all the way down her body to her feet. Again, the young woman clasped her hands and shook them. Then she picked up the cloth once more. This time, she very discreetly spat onto the cloth and placed it over one of the crimson spots at Louisa's throat.

Mary gasped. Edney noticed out of the corner of her eye that Ambrose Richardson had stepped to the side of her sister-in-law. He bent his white head to hers.

Miss d'Espereaux's hand passes resumed; it was as if she were covering the child in fine silk. Long moments passed. The room filled with dusk. From outside came the crying of gulls and the lowing of cattle, the life of.the ordinary day nearing its end. The creamy colour of Miss d'Espereaux's throat darkened. Her eyes lost their quickness. When she spat on the cloth again and prepared to lower it, the sound assailed Edney's ears as if a drunkard had hawked in a gutter. Edney couldn't move. Something had changed, but she did not possess the strength to stop the young woman's ministrations. All at once, the room was dark. Mary made soft protesting sounds, almost like whimpers. When Francis Collins began to reassure her, Ambrose Richardson hissed, "Enough!"

Suddenly Miss d'Espereaux stiffened.

"No, no, no!" she cried and put her hands over her face.

In the darkness Edney thought the young woman was striking herself.

"It was well, but there is evil here, a terrible evil."

"What?" Francis Collins exclaimed. "Liz, what are you saying? That's not the usual . . ."

"Damn it, man!" snapped Ambrose Richardson. "Have you no sense?"

"Look here, colonel, I've had about all I'm going to take from you. Can't you tell you're only wasting your time? Liz, I'm done putting up with this one. Do you hear? I wouldn't care if he was missing both his arms."

But Miss d'Espereaux had risen from the bed. Her voice was strange, shrill, her eyes glassy. "Mother! Mother!"

Edney clutched at her stomach. The cry seemed to come from inside her. The dark swirled and then rushed into her eyes. Alone at the foot of her daughter's bed, she fell.

"Watch it!" a man yelled.

Edney heard herself hit the floor. On her knees, she listened to her heartbeat running fast over the bare planks, louder and louder.

"Mother, oh, Mother," Miss d'Espereaux whimpered and slumped almost without sound or contact to the floor a few feet away from Edney.

"Lizzie! What is it? For the love of God, girl!"

Edney sensed bodies rushing toward her. A lamp sizzled on, the light burned across the floor and ceiling. Miss d'Espereaux's horror-stricken face, the beauty shocked out of it, roiled below, as if risen from a current. Then the faces of the men plunged down from above. The footsteps came closer until they reached Edney's heart. Just as the door burst open, she closed her eyes and let Mary support her weight.

IV

July 1881, Crescent Slough, British Columbia

Anson paid the Indian for his rowing services, then climbed out of the skiff onto the small wharf and looked toward Dare's operations. His cannery was oddly quiet in the mellow mid-morning sunlight. Only the constant keening of gulls—a sound that at Chilukthan seemed as continuous as the noise of the cannery workings—reminded Anson of the particular slaughter occurring along the river. But there were visual triggers too: a few square-bottomed skiffs pulled up on the dike, some Indian children running silently in the distance, a listing scow on the near bank. Yet, compared with Chilukthan, Crescent Slough seemed almost abandoned. Of course, the fishing hadn't ended; doubtless many of the skiffs Anson had seen on the river, their occupants hunched over in the sterns, picking fish out of the nets, worked for Dare. His cannery would likely explode into life as the fresh catch came in.

Anson proceeded slowly up the gangway, his eyes trained on Dare's plain house. There was no sign of life anywhere near it. But then, Dare himself would be either at the cannery or on the river.

Anson knew his old comrade-in-arms was every bit as industrious as the Englishman, and Thomas Lansdowne certainly would not have stepped foot inside any house during the past week had his daughter not lain delirious and fevered in her sickbed.

The smoke, therefore, brought Anson up short. It trickled thinly up from behind the house, its white almost transparent against the pale blue of the sky. Anson felt tethered by it, but he resisted the pull. Suddenly he realized that his eagerness to see Dare had been replaced over the past few days with dread. They had not met since shortly after the war, and there was no guarantee there'd be any ease between them. But much more disquieting than that was the old spectre of deceit that always seemed to accompany their relationship. Anson had lied to Thomas Lansdowne about Dare's blood, he had shaken hands to "prove" that his old friend was white, just as he had once forged papers to prove that a runaway slave named John was a dead and forgotten farm boy and soldier in the Union Army. That had been a simple enough deception: the dead farm boy remained dead to everyone who'd ever known him, and Anson had made certain, initially, that Dare remained out of sight in a tent with some rebel wounded. Later, as it turned out, the deception proved even simpler: the dead soldier had been a recent arrival and had kept to himself. No one seemed to notice his resurrection in the form of a tall white soldier who was, in fact, the mulatto killer of his master.

Anson drew a deep breath of the mud-heavy air. Could it be that, at the bottom of that white finger of smoke, or even nearby in the cannery or on the river, breathed another man for whom the past was such a potent mixture of pride and horror? Somehow it was easier to believe that Dare was dead, that he'd gone into the grave at Antietam with the poor white farm boy at last. Of course, Anson knew he hadn't, knew he had continued to reinvent himself, always keeping ahead of the deception until the deception itself inevitably increased the pace and caught him from behind, caught them both from behind.

But even as he walked across the yard toward the smoke, Anson knew he was lying to himself, something he had resisted doing for almost all his adult life. It wasn't punishment or capture that worried him now: what could the world do to him that would change what he'd done in another life and been proud of doing? It was a nagging sense that perhaps, just perhaps, he'd been wrong in his pride. He had sheltered a slave, turned a black man into a white man as if he'd possessed a god's power. But the Lansdownes' hatred of Dare had eaten away at Anson's confidence to the point where he had to concede that his friend, white or black, might have changed for the worse. It was at least possible. And Anson had just lied for him again on no greater basis than an old system of belief.

He stepped around the corner of the house and approached the canvas tent. It was even more familiar than before, its sag like an admission of the weight of the years. Anson walked to the fire. The coals were still red, still giving off heat. He looked around and let his eyes rest on the stand of cottonwoods just beyond the tent. The trees stood dark in the clear light. They seemed to breathe, to form something animal. Anson watched them and did not realize with how much anticipation until he heard his own short breaths.

"Hello? Is anyone here?"

Only silence returned his call. He fought off the feeling that the woods, the tent, and the absent man were part of the same unease. But the longer he stood by the fire, breathing the wood smoke, the more the feeling came back to him, intensified. So he walked to the house and knocked loudly on the front door. It opened on contact. Anson called out a greeting, then stepped in.

The air reeked of fish and sweat. He opened a door off the entrance and looked in on emptiness: no furnishings at all, just bare planks. Puzzled, he moved along the hall and tried another door. This time, he came upon a large room that looked like an Indian village of the sort he'd observed at spots along the Washington coast—clothes, hides, furs, cooking utensils, and a powerful odour, that curious mix of the human and wild that defined the riverbanks at Chilukthan and was captured here in an enclosed space. Some pieces of fishnet were stretched across the floor, no doubt for the purposes of mending. So Dare had given his house up to the workers for the duration of the season. That did not seem out of character for the man Anson remembered. Besides, Dare had never seemed like a man who'd prefer a parlour to an open field.

Outside again, Anson drew the obvious conclusion: if Dare had just left the fire, then he'd be at the cannery. He hurried toward the dike.

Now even the Indian children had vanished. He wondered if they'd really been there at all. Crescent Slough was disturbingly still. Where were the Indians? Surely not all of them went out on the boats? And the Chinese? If Dare had managed to replace his crew, they'd likely be somewhere nearby. At the very least, there should be some activity once he reached the cannery buildings.

But, at the campfire, evidence of recent activity was everywhere, from the smell of grease and oil and smoke to the slop of fish heads and guts over which buzzed clusters of flies. When Anson peered through the gaps in the wharf planks at his feet and saw a fleet figure rummaging in the muck of the low tide, he breathed a sigh of relief. It was just what the Indian children did at the Lansdownes' cannery; they scavenged for the knives that had slipped out of the workers' hands during the frenzy of making the pack.

He walked into the darkness of the main building. The sudden stifling of the gull cry was like the slamming of a door. The machines were silent, greasy with death.

"William! Are you here?"

He cried out in the same way that he'd throw a rope to a drowning man, only Anson could not shake off the feeling that he was the one struggling in the water.

But a living man did emerge from the bloodied shadows. It was the elderly Chinese with the smoky eye.

"Where is everyone?" Anson said.

"They sleep. Others fish. Much, much work to do."

"Your boss? Is he sleeping too?"

The Chinese grinned so broadly that Anson could count his three gold-capped teeth.

"He never sleep. He not need it. Maybe he get all his sleep in winter."

"Well, where is he then?"

"On the river. He just left. More trouble maybe."

"Trouble? What sort of trouble?"

The grin disappeared. The Chinese scratched his chin with a long fingernail. "Very bad this year. Others try to fish our drifts. He take his gun."

Instinctively, Anson turned toward the river. But all he could see through the open side of the cannery was a rectangle of blue sky.

"Which others?"

The Chinese shrugged. His good eye flickered. "All of them maybe."

All of them? Anson struggled to shut out the image of dozens of armed white men surrounding Dare.

"When do you expect him back?"

The Chinese turned his palms up. They were like old parchment.

"I'll wait," Anson said.

As if the words were a spell, the Chinese slipped away at the utterance of them.

But wait where? Anson decided that a shady spot under a tree would suffice. Perhaps he might even manage a few hours of sleep. Outside again under the gull cry, he passed a towering stack of wooden crates stamped with the label "Fraser River Salmon Dare Cannery." An arched silver salmon circled by bold red appeared above the words. It was a comfort to Anson to see that the season was proving productive for his old friend. Surely when the fish ran in such abundance, there'd be profits enough for all the canners. So why the trouble? Anson smiled at the question, pleased that it would even occur to him after all he'd lived through. The hope in it calmed his nerves, made death retreat. Soon, he'd ask Dare the question directly, perhaps over a campfire at the edge of a brooding wood.

He walked along the top of the long, earthen dike that, unlike the one at Chilukthan, fronted the entire settlement, until he saw a large cottonwood casting a broad net of shade over a field of knee-high grass. At the sight of the tree, a sudden weariness came over him. He descended the dike and crossed the field, grasshoppers whirring and leaping at his every step. The murmurous late morning opened so gently that all thoughts of conflict washed away as he took up a position near the thick trunk and shut his eyes. Through all the horrible suffering and deaths, through the severing and rejoining of his country, through his own losses and failures, Anson had not lost the capacity to recognize and revel in the earth's own offerings of grace.

They did not occur regularly, but he knew the fault was his—the toil of work and society, the mind's relentless worrying of the past, kept the spirit closed from most opportunities for a natural, human rest. Yet they still occurred: he could still feel himself embraced by something outside of all conscious planning, even if he no longer cared to use the name of God to describe that presence, the God that both sides in the war had used as justification for killing.

The moment did not cease, nor did Anson open his eyes. Gradually his breathing and pulse slowed, and the world—Antietam, Chilukthan, the eyes of the dying and the healing—joined him in the balm of darkness.

He woke to voices and frenzied gull cries. At first, he thought they were rapidly approaching him and he raised an arm as if to fend off a blow. But then he realized that they came from the dike and that they rose and fell in varying levels of excitement. Anson stood quickly, for the voices meant one thing: the boats had returned.

When he reached the cannery, he saw that the harvest had not abated. Two large scows—each twenty feet long and a dozen wide—squirmed with salmon. Six Indian men stood waist-deep in the fish, flinging them as if they were silver blossoms onto the main wharf, where two Chinese, their pigtails swinging in almost perfect unison, transferred them to wheeled wooden carts. These were then shoved hurriedly by other Chinese into the cannery, which had begun to hiss and grind and clatter as if on the verge of explosion.

The gulls whirled over the wharf, beating their wings as they dropped as close as possible to the fish before some human motion dampened their appetites and blew them back skyward. The din was fierce. The closer Anson came to the wharf, the harder it was to hear the voices. As he stepped out of the buildings' shadows and approached the river, he felt the equal ferocity of the heat and squinted up. The sun, just past its apex, burned small and white. Anson calculated he had slept at least two hours, but the contrast with his moment of spiritual reflection made it seem more like two years. Already he smelled that curious mixture of smoke, blood, and river that at once alerted and confused his senses. It was a potent, almost overpowering smell that quickened the pulse even as it held out the promise of nothing but carnage. No wonder the gulls had gone mad. They kept breaking like a whitecapped surf against the brown bodies sweating in the scows.

Anson looked for Dare but could not find him. He shouted out to the one Indian who had taken a brief pause in his work. "Where's your boss?" But the Indian merely pointed to the river and resumed his labours.

When Anson followed the gesture, he saw nothing but a bright sheen of empty water stretching away to the base of distant blue mountains. No doubt the fishing skiffs were out there in the glitter, and Dare with them, but the day had closed itself with light.

Again, he had to be content with waiting and watching. He found a convenient position against a piling head and settled in for a while. He tried to count the salmon as they were tossed on the wharf, but they came too fast and he grew dizzied with the effort. Then he concentrated on the gulls. Somehow their frenzied attendance appealed to his sympathies—Anson knew how they felt, so close to their goal yet maddeningly kept from it. Their screeching seemed to come up out of his own body. And when the sound stopped, the silence jolted him first. Then he heard them.

Two gunshots. Three. The Indians on the scows and in the skiffs turned to the river in one motion. The sheen on the surface dulled. Anson saw flecks of white sails in the distance, but the sight explained nothing. Even so, he instinctively reached for his medical kit, which he then cursed himself for forgetting. The fact was, he had met Dare only once after the war, only once when the possibility of violence was not palpable on the air they breathed, and this did not feel like that singular peaceful encounter. Indeed, that feeling had not been present during Anson's whole time at Chilukthan, awaiting Dare's arrival. What grace had fallen had been entirely separate from Dare.

Seconds after the gunshots' echoes had died, the gulls resumed their raucous attack on the steadily increasing supply of fish guts, the sun dragged its own viscera down the sky, and the Indians folded their torsos into the pitching. Steam poured out of every chink in the planks of the cannery: it resembled the rim of an active volcano around which savages were carrying out an ancient ritual. And the blood that leaked from it was somehow human, the result of human violence upon the body of a human past. The blood of Thermopylae and Troy as well as Bull Run and Antietam. As the blood mixed with the descending dusk and approached over the darkening river, Anson rose to meet the violence he had been tasting for weeks, the violence he did not want to believe in because, somehow, the blade of the knife was pressed against his own throat.

V

July 1881, the mouth of the Fraser River

Suddenly Dare sensed the skiffs closing around him. The dark was fast. He couldn't see the Englishman clearly, just the faintest outline of his shape. The slap of fish on wood, a sharp, wet sound, like a lash on bloodied skin, replaced the Indian's chanting. Dare raised his gun to his shoulder. Right beside him he could hear the Indians breathing as they untangled the catch.

The shot startled him. He ducked, stayed low. Waited for the pain. A second shot started in the echo of the first. He heard a cry from the closest skiff, only a dozen feet away, raised his gun high and pulled the trigger. Sound inside sound, a lit torch tearing through the dark. He saw, very close, the Englishman's face. The white shock there. Then silence. The lapping of the current. The cats in the moonlight at the shining pools. After Daney had cursed him, when he stood in the middle between the shack and the house and didn't know where he belonged.

The other skiffs pulled away. Oars splashed violently. Someone shouted that Thomas Lansdowne had been murdered.

Dare's whole body tightened. His hands twitched, and so he put down his gun and reached for the oars to pull himself forward. It was the one thing he had always done. Gone forward. It didn't seem he should do anything else, even if he could. There was nothing behind of any use. But what if going back was itself a way to go forward? He paused, took the small leather pouch that hung off a string inside his sodden cotton shirt, and rubbed it slowly, repeatedly. Was it time? For twenty years he'd been moving, convinced he did so only to make his living. But he was tired; the past was catching him. And what if it did? A splash of oars broke around him. The other skiffs pulled away in the dark. He bent into the strokes until he came alongside Lansdowne's skiff, thinking he would take the fallen and bleeding Englishman to the slough. The doctor would be there. That much he could count on. Yes. The doctor would be there. Dare clambered into Lansdowne's skiff and positioned himself at the oars.

He pulled harder now, found a rhythm to calm himself. And yet he still heard the taunts as he headed for the slough; they seemed to rise up out of the river and surround him.

The Englishman moaned from the gunwale where Dare had adjusted his body. For a moment, Dare froze, the air on his nape warm as the mulatto's breath. He knew his bullet had not struck the man; he knew he had aimed at the sky. So why did he feel the awful, descending chill of a haunting? What ghost had come for him out of the slime and salmon blood? He shook the chill off. On the horizon, a small moon hung faint and dirty, the dark pressing around it. Marbled pig's flesh. The overseer's cheek. Only the black smears on the moon were wrong; they belonged to another face. Dare drew a deep, ratcheting breath, then pulled to meet his image, the boy the overseer hadn't killed, the boy who escaped the rice fields and ran, starved and terrified, with only the stars and his hatred to guide him. But the man who had returned to Antietam could not keep what was behind from coming up with each lifting of the dark water.

The letters were gone. He had scraped them off his flesh with a dull blade not long after joining up with the great backwash of people following the Union army. But he could still feel them under the larger, messier scar he'd made, even without raising a hand to his cheek. Sometimes they burned even more than when he'd hidden in the master's house after the great battle and waited for Orlett to return. Those hours had been among his worst. Each small sound fired his blood; he was so close to the revenge that had kept him awake nights, so close to wiping out the doglike grin and Caleb's red back and the quick splashes beside the ferry. But as time passed and the overseer didn't return to the master's house, the pressure became too much. He had to act. He had to go out again and search. Sometimes it seemed that every moment of the overseer's continuing life subtracted a moment from his own. It was harder than the drive south or the long year toiling under the whip in the rice fields because then he knew he had obstacles to overcome. Now, this close, the delay felt like a failure that might prove permanent. Besides, he needed to contribute to the Union cause. Daney had been right about the war, and he was going to do all he could to make sure she'd be right about the freedom too. Waiting in the master's house to exact his private vengeance felt almost selfish. But he decided there was no reason that he couldn't do both. After all, just that morning he had removed the uniform from a dead soldier; so it was only right that he should continue the work of that soldier's army.

The war had surrounded the farm, washed up against it like a great bloody tide that, receding, had left a beach of rotting debris. Within a hundred yards of the house, the bodies lay thick, fallen almost in perfect rows. Beyond, for a half-mile north and south along the dusty turnpike, solitary figures and small groups of three and four men moved among the dead and wounded, slowly as wasps over rotted fruit. Farther to the north, banked against the woods like the ashes of a fire, the bulk of the army rested.

But he did not think in terms of armies and battles: the cries of the wounded circled his legs and threatened to pull him down, for they were cries that contained the same suffering he had witnessed in Daney and Caleb and their children. Except, in the case of these fallen soldiers, he could still do something.

So he walked the body-strewn battlefield, picking up the wounded, one after another, and taking them to the hospitals, the barns, and houses on the neighbouring Mumma and Roulette farms that had been converted for that purpose. His fear had gone. He did not feel like a fugitive slave anymore, he did not tense, waiting for the baying of a bloodhound or the shouts of a patrol. He had been through that terror. The battlefield was almost a relief, or it would have been if not for Orlett. But where was he? A black from another farm said that the overseer had not left when the battle threatened, that he was too greedy and too drunk to leave his property unprotected. So where was he?

John cradled the wounded white men and watched out for the overseer. From the bodies of the dead he took whatever food and drink he could find. When soldiers approached, he either lay low or sought to blend in. The soldiers, however, took little notice of him; most were searching the battlefield themselves or were limping away from the front lines.

Hours passed quickly. By nightfall, he had returned to the master's house, to the elaborately carved veranda running along every side of it and to the large dormered windows and turreted roof. Inside, the house seemed even emptier than before, the darkness having swallowed what shreds were left of the finest furnishings—a bunched bit of velvet drapery like a puddle of blood. If the overseer had sought to protect his property, he had failed. But then it occurred to John in a flash what the "property" referred to. He decided to search the shacks.

The battle sounds had ceased. Only the occasional crack of a picket's rifle echoed over the stillness. Across the fields he could see the flickering lights of the hospitals. The wounded would be many, and he had to fight off the urge to help. It wasn't that he cared so much for the soldiers; it was because they were Daney's army, his army too. Their survival and eventual triumph were the black man's. That was why so many blacks had attached themselves to the federal troops and why he was able to blend in with the contrabands through most of Maryland. It was also why he could slip away for his own purposes and assume the guise of a soldier. In the chaos of battle, he knew he had his chance. But he also knew that chance wouldn't last long.

The shacks were empty, stripped of their meagre tin utensils and homemade wooden furniture. He stood in Caleb's and felt the strange acceleration of time—how quickly the world had changed. The air around him even seemed cleared, as if a whirlwind had passed through. Yet the longer he stood there, the more the shack refilled with its recent miseries. As soon as he remembered Orlett's grin again and heard the unbuckling of his belt and heard his grunts and Jancey's cries, John hurried on.

Back at the master's house, he realized that he had not made a thorough search of it from top to bottom. The instant he started down the cellar stairs, he heard the low thumping. It was very faint, and he might have ignored it if he had not known the house so well. Behind a false wall, down a short flight of stone steps, he found a thick oak door chained and padlocked. A hectic search of the cellar uncovered nothing that would help, so he left the house at a run and entered the barn. There he found an axe and hurried back to the cellar.

He put all of his hatred for the overseer into his axe swings. But the last year and a half had taken its toll. Overworked and underfed, almost starved on his run from the rice plantation, he had only begun to regain his strength once he'd joined up with the federal troops. Now his arms weakened as the axe splintered the wood. With each pause, he listened to hear if his actions had brought others to the house.

But it remained silent as the axe finally struck the decisive blow. John stooped through the jagged opening into a putrid, dirt-walled room with a low ceiling. The air stank of sweat and excrement. He heard breathing. As his eyes adjusted to the dark, he made out the bodies sprawled on the dirt, their hands chained; some wore iron collars.

"Is you from de North?" a voice said weakly. Another croaked for water.

John noticed there seemed to be about a dozen bodies, all men. He quickly assured them that he was a friend as he tipped his canteen into several mouths. At the fifth mouth, he drew back, shocked by the loose-skinned, almost toothless old face. John dropped the canteen, spilling the water. It was Caleb.

He reached for the canteen as he spoke the old man's name.

"Who is dat knows me?"

He moved closer, on his knees.

"It's John."

"John?"

Caleb's eyes moved slowly, like flies in blood.

"Yes, it's John. I've come back."

Slowly the thin arms lifted their chains, then dropped them again. John placed the canteen to the split lips and tilted it. The water trickled down the grizzled chin. Caleb's Adam's apple worked rapidly. He mouthed her name and John could not speak. The others groaned for water. He crawled away with the canteen.

"I'll have to fill it at the cistern," he said. "I'll be back directly."

Outside he leaned against the house, panting. Caleb was alive. The overseer's brutality opened inside John like a raw wound. He saw the grinning face clearly as a harvest moon, felt the searing iron on his cheek. The taste of blood filled his mouth.

Back in the dirt room, he lied, as he knew he must. He told Caleb that Daney and his children were sold to a plantation in Alabama, that they were all together. The old man closed his eyes and said nothing. There was no point in lying to a clever man like Caleb, but John could not bring himself to speak the truth. Not yet. He asked about the overseer. Caleb said he was worse than ever, crazed with spirits. That he'd taken over the farm when the master had died—over two years ago, a few months after the trader had taken them away—and had sold most of the other blacks, replacing them with blacks from the Deep South who could hardly speak a word of English. When the federal army entered Maryland, the overseer left Cray, the mulatto, and several other vicious white men in charge, and disappeared for long stretches. Some said he was a spy for the Confederates. Some said he was a soul driver himself, that he made his living that way because he sure didn't work the farm.

"But where's he now?" John said. "And why are there no women here?"

"Dey somewhere near. Dey his living and his pleasure too, him and Cray together. Dey no more dan two devils. Cray? Oh, he's jes as bad.

I don't think he b'lieves he's coloured at all. He b'lieves he goin to git de overseer's place once he done drink hisself into de grave."

"But where are they? Where are they?"

Caleb sighed and dropped his head to his chest.

"What you gwan to do? Dey ain't no point in it now."

"I'm going to see that they don't hurt anyone again."

"But dey two devils, you hear? Dey evil and dey know how to stay alive."

"I've come here to kill him," John said, "and I can kill the other too. Why else would I come? He said you were dead. I believed you were dead."

"Den Daney and de chillen thought so?"

"Yes."

Caleb's tears filled his deep wrinkles. For several minutes he did not speak. At last he raised his bleary eyes and fixed them on John. A flicker of triumph touched his face.

"Jancey knows different. I got word to her."

"Jancey!" John's heart banged against his ribs. He couldn't speak.

Caleb smiled. "De overseer didn't catch her. She's clear away. In Canada."

With a sickening sensation, John understood that Caleb's mind had been damaged along with his body. The old man needed to keep one of his daughters alive in order to keep himself alive. That he chose Jancey only increased John's own pain.

"She knows de truth about dat hog too," Caleb said, reading his thoughts. "I figure she always did know. Inside. Probably her mother did too."

He slumped against the dirt wall, ran his thick tongue over his cracked lips.

The mention of Daney struck John like cold water. He remembered where he was, and when. The overseer's face crossed over Jancey's just as if he'd come up from behind and wrapped his arms around her. John knew he couldn't waste any more time.

"Orlett and Cray. Where are they, Caleb?"

But the old man just sighed and shook his head. Fortunately, one of the other blacks explained. Orlett and Cray did some kind of work for the Union army. There was money to be made from the war, he had heard Orlett say. Maybe they sold horses. They owned plenty of them, had been buying them up for months. Generally they returned to the house at nightfall, but on account of the battle, it was hard to know when they'd come back this time.

Carefully, and with much effort, John struck the irons with a mallet and chisel he'd brought from the barn and told the men he'd take them straight away to a Union camp. If they were too weak to walk, he'd carry them. He wanted to get them safely away before the overseer and the mulatto returned. Did they have any idea where the women were kept?

"Dey somewhere in de house," Caleb said. "We could hear de screaming sometimes. Jes days ago. De overseer, he like us to know what he doin with dem."

John told them to stay put until he came back. Then he ran upstairs. But a search of the other rooms revealed nothing. Finally he remembered the attic. Climbing the stairs to it, he did not think anyone was there, for the air was not so foul and there was no sound. But when he pulled his head through the hole in the floor, he saw the bodies, gagged and handcuffed with rope. The overseer must have kept the space clean because . . . he didn't want to think of it. He spoke gently to the women, told them he was a friend who had brought freedom, that he would lead them away from this place. Urging them to be quiet, John undid the gags. Light fell in thin shafts through the ceiling cracks, and he saw that the six women were mostly young and very black. They just stared at the air as he undid their ropes, trying his best to be gentle even though he could feel the overseer's foul warm breath on his neck. Whenever one of the thin cotton shifts slid away to reveal a breast or stomach, he paused. Once, he discreetly pulled the shift back up. The smell of the women's bodies stirred him despite the situation, and he was ashamed. The women began to speak to each other in a foreign tongue and he urged them again to be quiet. Hurriedly he prepared to lead them downstairs, not knowing exactly what he should do with them or the men in the cellar. The Union army would not welcome any new contrabands now, not so soon after a horrific battle. And besides, he already knew that the slaveholders of Maryland were to be respected, given that the state remained neutral. Perhaps he could find the home of a free black on the other side of the village. Caleb would know what was best.

John told the women to wait for him, then he rushed back down to the cellar. The men had already begun to stir; several had gone through the broken door into the cellar itself. But Caleb had not moved. John bent over him, urged him to stand. Caleb shook his head.

"Dey's no hurry for me. I knowed the truth long ago. I could feel it happen."

"What truth?"

"Doan lie to me, son. I know dey gone. All of dem gone 'cept . . . I could always tell when something bad happen fo us. I'd have been dead since dat time if word hadn't come down de underground about Jancey. Listen, now, you take dese people as far away as you can, dat's what you got to do."

"But Orlett. I want to . . ."

"If dat's goin to be, den it will come. But you get dese people away."

And Caleb told of the house of a free black man south of the village, a man who'd been harbouring runaways since before the war and knew all about the underground railroad. That man would know best how to protect the blacks.

"But you can't stay here," he told Caleb. "When Orlett comes back and finds the others gone, he'll kill you."

Caleb's face was blank; the tears had gone from his wrinkles.

"You think dey's anything dose devils can do worse dan what's been done. It's too late for me. But you get dose people away and yourself too. Never mind de overseer. Dat evil jes keeps comin' if you kill it."

He ran a trembling hand across his lips and blinked slowly, as if his eyelids were made of iron.

"Dey's always evil. You can't kill it by killin' one man. Den you be jes as bad. But you're not a killer, John. Dat ain't your way. You get dose people clear. Go on! I'll get myself to my cabin. Dat overseer, he too busy now to bother about one old nigger. Go on now!"

So he gathered the men onto the main floor and explained that he would take them to safety. Running back to the attic, however, he found only four women; the other two had run off on their own. Now the sounds of the old house and the starting rain on the roof seemed to contain hoof beats and footfalls. He hastened to get the blacks outside.

The air still burned with the acrid chemical smoke of battle, but the rain brought a welcome freshness. John gulped several breaths down and surveyed the immediate area. No one appeared, so he set off, hoping for the one thing contrary to what he'd been focused on for so long: that Orlett would remain absent.

It took the rest of the day to reach the free black's house and relieve himself of the responsibility for the men and women. His success strengthened his resolve; when he moved on, he was surprised to find how much his body had lightened.

Not until after midnight, however, did he reach the farm again, coming at it slowly. The house was dark and empty. Orlett had not returned. John moved on to Caleb's cabin to take him what food he had managed to gather during the day's travels. There had been bodies everywhere, the cries of wounded for water, wagons and men clustered around almost every building, which, he discovered, had been turned into hospitals. Soon, perhaps, this farm, too, would be used for a similar purpose.

He had not slept in a long while. The excitement of the morning's battle and the tension of the aftermath suddenly weighed him down. He entered Caleb's cabin heavily.

The old man was curled into himself in a corner, without even a covering blanket. John touched him gently on the shoulder, eager to tell him that he had succeeded in reaching the free black's house. But when he turned him slightly, he knew that Caleb was dead. His eyes were half-closed, his face cold, but there was no mark of violence upon him save the whip marks scarred into his back.

John wrapped his arms around him and lay there on the bare floor. His tears flowed freely, but they were no relief. He felt them form the two letters on his cheek, and his cheek seemed to blaze, to become a beacon that the overseer could not fail to notice. But the cabin's silence and his own great fatigue closed his eyes. Though there was no peace in the brief sleep he found pressed against Caleb's cold body, he felt stronger when he woke. He lifted Caleb in his arms and carried him to the blacks' graveyard and buried him, not even caring what attention he drew, hoping in fact that his grief would bring Orlett to him.

Afterwards, he found he could not sit and wait. There was much work to do. If Daney and Caleb were denied the benefits of freedom, many others would not be, but only if the Union won the war. He decided he could help the cause and look for the overseer at the same time. For there was no guarantee Orlett or Cray would return anytime soon or at all. Perhaps both were dead out there among all the other bodies. Perhaps he would come upon one or both of their corpses on the battlefield.

Daybreak approached as he skirted the dark woods and walked out among the groaning wounded. In the thick grey-black light, among the wreckage of knapsacks and overcoats, smashed limbers, discarded weapons, and smoking holes, he discovered a young soldier with blood caked on his eyelids and the bridge of his nose. He looked to be sleeping. John put his head to the soldier's chest and thought he heard a faint beating. He picked the soldier up and gazed to the east; somewhere in that direction he expected to see activity, evidence of a hospital at work or a campsite of soldiers stirring with the dawn. Instead he saw a single black tree, its branches shattered but for one, the air a slightly fainter black around it. He moved on, the soldier's head cradled in the crook of his arm. The white face, stained with blood and powder, moved him strangely. It was young enough to be one of Daney's children.

A groan just off to the left broke his odd reverie. It came from a much older soldier, a middle-aged, rough-bearded man with a wound in his neck. He lay on his back, his eyes fluttering. John laid the young soldier down and, on his knees, took the older man onto his back and shoulders. Then, with as much care as possible, he clasped the lighter soldier to his waist, letting the feet drag along the ground. Hunched over, he proceeded slowly, stopping every minute to catch his breath.

More grey light spread over the field and sky. The one tree loomed on the horizon yet never seemed to come any closer. Already the air was poisonous with the gases of the dead. He kept going. Over the pounding of the blood in his temples and his laboured breathing, he heard little. Once, panicked, he thought he heard several quick retorts, like musket fire. He lifted his head and peered around him, but he could see nothing except the same shattered ground of dead horses and tipped-over wagons. Again he moved on.

At last he stopped, figuring that he must have come abreast of the tree because he could not see it. Suddenly he knew he was being watched. The idea that it was Orlett flashed into his mind, but he could not react quickly on account of the wounded he carried. He turned his head slowly, his muscles taut.

A man stood almost directly against the black tree. He wore a kind of smock covered in gore. His face, though mostly hidden under a thick beard, was kind and vaguely familiar, the eyes dark and wet. They were like Caleb's eyes.

"Let me take the other man, soldier," he said and stepped around John to tend to the body he had laid on the ground.

"Thank you, sir."

"The hospital's back there." The man, who must have been a surgeon, pointed eastward. Then he tended to the young soldier, taking up one of his wrists, leaning to his chest, touching his eyelids. The man's shoulders sagged. He looked up.

John recognized him now as one of the surgeons from the day of the battle. Comforted, he lowered the other soldier to the ground. The doctor probed the wound in the neck with his finger, then muttered something John did not catch.

"Sir?"

"Your name?" he said gently.

John touched the letters on his cheek. His name? When was the last time a white man had even asked him for it?

"John."

"John? What's the rest of it?"

Suddenly a voice cried, "Don't move!"

His heart lurched. It was the cry he had dreaded hearing the whole way from South Carolina, the cry of recapture. He turned and saw two Union soldiers pointing their muskets at him.

The doctor said, "It's all right, I'm a surgeon. We're taking this wounded man to the hospital."

The soldiers stepped closer. They stared at the doctor a while, then nodded and withdrew into the shreds of remaining dark.

John controlled his breathing. "Just the one man, sir?"

The doctor sighed.

"The other's dead. A burial party will take care of him. Was he a comrade of yours?"

"No. But I reckoned he'd make it." But what he wanted to say was, I couldn't leave him, he's just a child, his mother will be missing him. Because the doctor looked as if he'd understand, he looked as if he'd do anything to save a child's life. Now he raised his face to the sky and scowled.

"Pick him up and follow me," he said softly.

John did so, thinking, this man will help me if I need it, this man with Caleb's eyes. Caleb. A cluster of hospital tents emerged from the ground. Then a bugle sounded. John stopped and swung around. He almost expected Orlett and Cray to come galloping across the battlefield.

"Baird! Where the hell have you been?"

An elderly man in a smock drenched with blood strode through the tents toward them. John lowered the soldier to the ground and slipped away. Behind him he could hear the same man shouting. His voice carried through the dawn stillness, then stopped.

John kept as low as possible to the ground, fearing that the uniform might not be enough of a shield. From a safe distance he saw Union troops gathering into lines, saw other buildings that had been turned into makeshift hospitals. The dead and wounded lay everywhere in the grass. He had to take several detours to avoid others who were searching the battlefield, but then he realized that he was almost invisible. At least no one seemed to find his wandering presence unusual. Whatever soldiers had been posted as lookouts must have been ordered to concentrate their attention closer to where the confederates held the line. He had been so focused on his own doings that it came as a sudden shock to think that the battle might be renewed. A periodic crackle of rifle fire served as a sharp reminder. He kept low, and trusted to his instincts to alert him to the overseer's presence.

The day grew warm, then hot. He dispensed what water he had found in the canteens of the dead to the suffering wounded, those who had fallen outside of the disputed ground, and carried several other fallen soldiers to hospitals. The whole time he kept Daney's fiery eyes before him, but they kept turning into Caleb's unseeing ones with the dirt showering down. And as that grave filled, it became a black depth of water from which the bodies of Daney and her girls and the other women slowly surfaced. He could shut the image out only by concentrating on the one face that, more than all things, had brought him this far. He sometimes wondered if he would have been able to escape the South if not for his hatred of the overseer.

In the afternoon, the heavens opened. For an hour the rain poured down so that the battlefield indeed seemed like a river bottom crowded with sodden bodies. He took shelter in a canvas tent in which two wounded soldiers lay; neither moved, but he could hear their breathing. The air stank of rot and chemicals. The rain beat heavily against the canvas and then, all of a sudden, stopped.

When he emerged, he saw that he was very near to the field hospital where he'd walked with the doctor at daybreak. It was midday. There'd been no sign of the overseer or the mulatto. Several civilians, including some women dressed in fine clothes, had appeared on the battlefield. Mostly they just held their hands up to their noses and gazed around, wide-eyed. It seemed, by the time that he approached the hospital again, that Orlett and Cray must have left Sharpsburg or been killed. The idea both disappointed and relieved him. Despite his hatred, he remained uncertain of his ability to kill, knowing that Caleb, right about so many things, could be right about that too. And besides, he knew the overseer would not be easy to kill; that much evil couldn't be overcome without a struggle. He wondered if he possessed the courage and the strength to do the job. But one thing was clear enough: he could do his part for the future that Daney had predicted.

When he walked across the barnyard, he saw the doctor, bent over a body, holding a long strip of dirty bandage in one hand. Just beyond him, caught suddenly in the re-emerging sunlight, was a sloppy, sickening, waist-high pile of arms and legs. For a moment, the doctor looked stunned, defeated. He blinked at the long, growing line of waiting wounded and seemed unable to move. He lifted a gore-covered hand and brushed it over his thick beard. A small cluster of flies buzzed near his face. Then he turned and made a sweeping gesture toward a group of civilians standing a few feet away, their hands over their mouths.

"Go on," he said wearily. "If you're not going to help, then clear out of the way. For Christ's sake, this isn't a circus. Clear out."

But his voice had grown increasingly weak. He stared at the limb in his hand as if surprised to find it there, then tossed it on the pile and shouted, "Next!"

John offered his assistance and the doctor immediately put him to work.

"Good man. I need you to keep a firm grip on the patient. Here, at the shoulders. Have you ever seen chloroform used before?"

"I've seen how it's done."

"Not too many drops," the doctor said, demonstrating with a cloth. "Like this, over the mouth and nose."

John nodded. A soldier was led forward and he helped him onto the table.

"It'll be fine," John said low to the terrified, powder-burned face while keeping a firm grip on a shoulder with one hand and administering the anaesthetic with the other.

"Good man," the doctor said. "That's it."

Time vanished, became a steady succession of torn flesh and broken bone. The stench was awful. It seemed to be a part of the hot sun; the flies seemed to breed out of the light and heat. The doctor no longer put his knife down or even rinsed it; he held it between his teeth as John calmed another soldier and applied the anaesthetic. At some point, the doctor asked him to put pressure on the patient's arteries, and he did so, calmly, buoyed by his usefulness and the doctor's confidence in him. The work kept the painful memories away as well as the tension of the immediate future. Not once did he see the overseer's doglike grin hovering in the air, nor did he feel the letters burning on his cheek.

Darkness came. Candles flickered around the table as the stars emerged. The air was colder but still putrid. Now the doctor's fatigue was clear; his hand became less sure, the knife cuts ragged. John could not bring himself to point these errors out, but he found that when he lightly coughed or shifted his body, the doctor seemed to come awake and realize what he was doing. Once, when John saw that the doctor was cutting away a great deal more tissue than usual, he had no choice but to speak before the damage was done.

The doctor shook his head and ran his bloody forearm across his eyes.

"Could you lower the candle," he said. After a brief pause, he sighed and went on. "Thank you. You've just saved this man a great deal of grief."

John did not think that he'd ever felt so alive. Despite the blood and the stench and the fatigue, despite the pitiable pleading of some soldiers to have their limbs cut off, he was almost euphoric. From time to time, meeting the doctor's dark eyes in the candle glow, he almost believed he was helping Caleb. As the hours passed, this belief deepened, until at last he could not keep his past or his purpose back; both rushed at him in sudden waves that he tried in vain to fight off. He paused, listening. A continuous low rumble spilled out of the night—the sound of troops on the move. All at once his own stillness seemed wrong, a terrible mistake. He was meant to go forward. It was the only way that the brutal memories would not overtake him, the only way that the overseer and the mulatto and his own parentless past would not strike the decisive blow. He had a disturbing sensation that the overseer, too, would move in the night. He couldn't explain it; it wasn't a matter of reason, it was a stirring in his blood, a prickling along his nape. He looked one last time at the doctor. He was exhausted and bloodied, yet he kept on. The doctor was white and from the North, he already had freedom. So what was he driving himself for? The doctor's will suddenly seemed even more miraculous than his own. For a few more moments John remained at the man's side; it seemed, oddly, the safest place he'd ever known. But the overseer was on the move. He could see him riding. And the image fired his dormant hatred. The letters burned. When the doctor stepped over to the pile of bloody limbs, John quietly slipped away.

Twenty minutes later, he ascended a hollow and approached the house. The closer he drew to it, the more he felt the overseer's presence, which seeped like a stain out of the walls and across the ground and further blackened the night. John's mouth was dry, his brow and hands cold. He could not quiet his blood; it rushed in great currents that swept him on. In the yard, moving at a crouch, he suddenly stopped, realizing that he had no plan and no weapon. It was likely he'd be confronting two men—two men long conditioned to being on their guard. They would probably be better fed and rested too. He did not move. His breathing and his heartbeat were too fast, too loud. He forced himself to see the overseer's face, to hear his voice, to smell his skin greasy with goose and pork fat. He needed the hatred even though it only increased the pounding of his blood.

A light flickered in the parlour window. He crept closer, needing to be sure. Before he even peered through the glass, he knew. His whole body told him. At the table the two faces hung side by side in the faint candlelight, almost touching, the overseer's rounder and flaccid, like a melon gone to rot, the mulatto's just the same as ever, round but hard, the forehead ridged and prominent, hanging above the deep-set eyes and full mouth. The two men were tearing into a cooked chicken. John could smell it. The grease of the meat made the overseer's face shine. Silently the two sets of jawbones worked up and down, almost in unison. He watched, unable to pull away. To kill them seemed as impossible as it was desirable.

Done with the chicken, Orlett lifted a small sack off the floor and dropped it on the table. The mulatto nodded like an excited dog. Orlett began to remove the contents—coins and folded bills. There was a great deal of money. The two men bent so low to the table that they seemed to be lapping water off the surface.

John stared at the shine of the silver and gold as if he was seated at the table, as if the wealth belonged to him. And then he realized that death was not enough, that it was not a practical compensation for all that he'd suffered and witnessed. All his life he'd been property, even when the fact wasn't so brutal as it had been for the past two years. Suddenly the wealth heaped in front of him was more of his future than the overseer's death. But the one had to happen so that the other could begin. He began to pant and knew it was starting.

But before he could pull away from the window, he saw Orlett and Cray stiffen and look toward the window. Just then, something struck the glass. A ferocious barking ensued. John fell back, the dog's teeth inches from his own. He scrambled to his feet and ran. The barn loomed in front of him. Inside, he looked desperately around. If he hid in the hayloft, he'd be trapped there like a treed raccoon, especially if Orlett came out with the dog. He decided instead to crouch in a dark corner behind a barrel. Picking up a shovel from the ground, he hurried into his hiding place, his mind racing. They might not come out with the dog. After all, this was a war zone; the night was tense, they might not bother to check every time the animal barked. He fought to still his blood. A minute passed. His hands clenched the handle of the shovel. Thin shafts of moonlight fell between him and the open barn door.

Then he heard the horses. Smelled them. They were stabled across the dark. He took a chance and sprinted over. If the overseer came with the dog, then a horse would provide a useful means of escape.

John approached the animals cautiously but without fear. He had worked with horses; their power had often seemed to contain a promise, as if they, too, would one day break free of their bondage.

There were only two of them. He recognized the overseer's bay, but the large white charger was unfamiliar. He stroked the horse's necks. Both were warm, the mouths frothed. Then Orlett and Cray had very recently returned. Had they even checked on the blacks in the cellar and attic and found them gone? Likely not. He stood between the horses, his panic subsiding. Something in the animals' calm clarified his thoughts. He was much taller and thinner than two years before, and he wore the uniform of a Union soldier; if he kept his face hidden, they might not recognize him until it was too late. The element of surprise might not have been lost. If only he had the courage and calm . . .

The night remained still. The dog's barking had faded away. Several minutes passed before he allowed himself to believe that Orlett and Cray were not coming out to investigate the dog's alarm. Confirmed in that belief, he yet remained unsure of his next move. Somehow he would have to separate the two.

Then he heard a faint sound. Someone was crossing the yard. He returned to his hiding place and watched as the mulatto entered the barn and headed for the horses. He untethered the bay and walked it toward the door. When Cray had gone through it, John followed, hardly able to believe his good fortune. If the mulatto rode away, leaving the overseer . . . John stood just inside the barn door as Orlett left the house and crossed the yard; the dog was not with him.

"They won't have gotten far," the overseer said. "I'll join you when I can. If they're with the Federals, you tell the officer in charge whose they are. We'll have them back. Tomorrow I'll get a start with the contrabands if I have to."

Then he put his two hands to the side of the mulatto's great head and shook it roughly, the way a man does to a favourite dog.

Cray mounted.

"I'll get them," he said. "Don't you worry, honey."

For a long moment, John was alone with the overseer in the same yard where Orlett had given Caleb the whipping, where Caleb's blood had dripped into shining pools. The stars were many but dim, the moonlight faint. For a long moment, his body tensed; he almost ran out, risking all. But something held him back, some instinct of patience that had developed in the long, sun-scorched hours in the rice fields. He looked past the overseer to the house rising beyond like a black cliff. He'd spent most of his life there, but the house held almost no emotion for him except numbness, a numbness that quickly became rage. His old master was dead, buried in the family graveyard. Daney and Caleb were dead. Jancey and all the children were gone. He had nothing to attach himself to this place but his hatred. And he knew his hatred would have to play out inside the house.

When Orlett finally walked toward it and pulled the door shut behind him, John followed. He still had no plan, but the mulatto's absence came as such a gift that he believed the night would contain others, that he would be given the courage and strength he needed if only he did not weaken. On the ground near the door, he saw two large rocks. He pocketed one and clenched the other in his fist. With luck, maybe he could separate the dog from the overseer, shut it in one room while he took on its master. If that luck didn't come, maybe a well-placed throw of the rock would at least stun the animal until he could escape it. The overseer would be armed; he always was.

For another moment, John hesitated, wondering why he had not taken a weapon from the battlefield. But he saw his hands around the overseer's throat just as he had seen them there a thousand times and knew that the killing would be intimate; that's why the idea of a gun or knife had not even occurred to him. From the moment Caleb had been tied to the whipping post, John had watched the overseer's face redden, his eyes bulge, his tongue flail in his foul, rotten mouth. It would happen that way or it wouldn't happen at all, he was sure of it.

He opened the door and slipped inside, tensed for the dog's bark. It didn't come, so he continued to the staircase, thinking that he'd hide upstairs and wait for Orlett to come up alone. But a heavy boot fall told him that the overseer was already above. Now a ferocious barking broke out from the parlour behind him. With relief, he saw that the door was shut, heard the dog scratch at the wood. He looked up the staircase, debating whether to go up or to hide somewhere and wait for Orlett to come down and check on the dog.

In the end, he couldn't wait for the strategic advantage of remaining downstairs to unfold. His blood decided him, drove him on. His fate had begun at last, it was on his lips like salt. He needed to get upstairs before the overseer started down. The rock was cold in his palm, rough like grizzled skin. He took the stairs at a sprint, his feet barely touching the wood.

The blow fell before he'd even stopped running. It glanced off his skull and sent him sideways into the wall at the top of the case. On his hands and knees, facing the floor, he struggled to stay conscious as a lantern light puddled around him.

"You'll find nothing here, soldier," Orlett said. "Better forage among your dead comrades."

A breech clicked.

"You're lucky I don't kill you and drag you out there with them. No one would know the difference."

He laughed.

"Didn't expect a dog, did you? Thought you'd slip in and take the fine silver? Get up!"

He could feel the overseer's shadow heavy on his back. His vision blurred, came clear again. Then his hand closed around the rock's cold. Slowly he began to rise, Orlett's rank smell in his nostrils.

He'd be grinning, almost panting, his rotten breath, the shine of grease . . . John threw the stone and rolled to one side as the gunshot blasted into the ceiling. Orlett had reeled back, dazed, and kicked over the lantern. In a flare of pale light John saw the blood on the overseer's forehead before the blood and the man vanished. The shot echoed in the dark. Bits of plaster and dust floated whitely down. John leapt forward, his hands already closing in a tight circle. The dog howled below, scratched frantically at the door. John struck nothing. There was a flurry to one side. He ducked as the overseer's gun swung toward him. But he did not avoid the kick. It hit him hard in the stomach. He collapsed to his knees, bent over, gasping. Then his head was yanked up by the hair and the overseer's fist struck him only a glancing blow as he found a burst of strength to pull away. At the same time he reached out and grabbed the overseer's leg and jerked him off balance. In seconds John was on top of him, his knees pressing into his chest, his hands on his throat. But he did not close them tight. It was too soon. Orlett didn't even know who he was; he thought he was only a soldier out foraging. John struggled to control himself. He kept a firm pressure on the overseer and said, "I'm not a soldier."

The overseer's eyes swept across him. Suddenly his body relaxed. He grinned. His lips pulled back from the rotted teeth.

"Welcome home, bright boy. You've grown since I saw you last. What did you do to your cheek?"

He laughed hoarsely, and John had to increase the pressure to stop the sound.

Orlett gasped. "Go on. What you waiting for?"

He squeezed harder. Now he heard only the dog's howls and his own quick breaths. It was what he had wanted, it was everything, he needed only to shut out Caleb's voice, but you're not a killer, John, dat ain't your way, he needed only to bring his hands as close together as possible, to cuff them to the overseer's throbbing blood. Why couldn't he do it? He had to; there wasn't a choice. So why couldn't he squeeze harder? Why had his grip weakened?

Orlett said in a rasp, "Goddamn ignorant not even a nigger you're not even . . ."

"What?" John eased the pressure a little.

The overseer's lip curled. "Sold by your white trash . . . not even a nigger . . ."

"What?"

"You heard. He told me. Bought you in Baltimore. Poor white trash. But I made you a slave. More of a slave than any nigger. You think you'd know."

He wheezed laughter between his rotten teeth. "You'd think a body could just tell something like that."

John's grip loosened. "You're lying!"

"Not an ounce of nigger blood in you, bright boy. But maybe there's some just born to be niggers anyway."

John lifted one hand to his cheek. Caleb and Daney would have said if they had known. And they would have known. It couldn't be true. Orlett would say anything to . . .

Then it was too late. The overseer bucked him off and rolled clear. When John recovered, he found the shotgun pointed at him, the doglike grin wider than ever. In the splay of light the blood shone in streaks on the overseer's face. His foul breath came rapidly. He swayed. There was a lot of blood.

"You missed your one chance, bright boy. Goddamn ignorant, white or black. For some it don't matter, I reckon." He placed his arm against the wall for support but kept the gun fixed straight ahead.

John saw the motion at the same instant he heard the screams. It was a sound unlike anything he'd ever heard, closer to the shriek of a wildcat than anything human. The overseer shrank under it, the gun knocked clear. It clattered down the first few stairs. John did not spring for it. He was frozen at the sight of the two women's wild faces as they tore at the overseer's body. In seconds they had him on the ground, and seconds later they had his breeches down. Something dull-bright flashed in one of the women's hands. Orlett's screams were terrible.

John leapt forward. This was not how it was supposed to happen. This was not his revenge. It took all of his remaining strength to pull just one of the women clear. She scratched and flailed at him but stopped once the other woman, with a savage cry of triumph, raised a chunk of bloody flesh in her hand and ran down the hallway, her screams a kind of cadenced singing that descended to a moaning as she vanished from the lamp glow, the other woman running behind.

Screaming, his face dissolved with blood, Orlett suddenly called out, "Cray! Cray! Help me! Cray! Where are you?"

John should have watched without pity, with a pleasing sense that the overseer had received what he had deserved for so long. But he was not pleased, he was sickened. It had all happened so fast, like a whirlwind from those bible stories Motes had liked to tell. There was something unworldly about the women's revenge, something final that seemed to involve more than just the overseer. John found he could not remain near the place where the attack had occurred. Bile rising in his throat, he followed the overseer down the stairs and outside, watched him stagger into the barn. A moment later, the white charger galloped out, Orlett slumped in the saddle, arms wrapped around the horse's neck, the reins flailing over his shoulders. The sky was beginning to lighten. As the charger passed him, the boy saw that its flank was drenched in black blood. Orlett's weak cries for the mulatto hung in the festering air. John dropped to his knees, put his hands over his eyes. Not even a nigger . . . Poor white trash . . . But you're not a killer, John . . . Goddamn ignorant . . . Dat ain't your way . . . Not a nigger but a slave . . .

He raised his face to the fading stars, the dead air cool on his cheek. It was the second day after the great battle and he did not even know who had won. But he knew where he'd felt the most victorious, he knew where there would be sanctuary for him, if there could ever be. But not yet.

Dazed, he went back to the house. He had no energy left, his body weakened with every step. He needed just a little sleep. And then he'd find his way back to the hospital and the doctor with Caleb's eyes.

He did not sleep long, perhaps an hour. At a sudden eruption from downstairs, he woke with a start and immediately crept to the head of the stairs. The dog was not barking in the shut parlour. Perhaps the mulatto had returned? John started down. All at once voices broke over the stillness.

"In here. Set the tables up. And for Christ's sakes drag that dog's carcass out. We don't need to attract any extra flies."

He breathed easier, relieved that it was not the mulatto. A flurry of boot steps. He crouched on the stairs and watched men carry in stretchers of wounded. There were a great many stretchers. Doctors in stained gowns hurried about, shouting instructions. Many of the wounded wore grey uniforms. Had the enemy not left the field after all? But then he saw a number of blue-uniformed wounded and realized that the Union doctors were tending to both sides. As the moans and cries of the wounded filled the house and the strong smells of decaying flesh and chloroform floated up to him, he decided that it was safe to descend. His uniform, torn as it was, protected him, and in any case the doctors and soldiers were too preoccupied setting up the hospital to take much notice of him.

Without difficulty, he made his way outside. Just beside the back door lay the dog; it had been shot in the side. Flies crawled in the wound and along the muzzle. He could not take his eyes off its mouth, the bared teeth, the too-familiar human grin. But he looked away at last. The sun hung just above the tree lines to the east, the sky was pale blue. Out in the fields the troops moved, heading away from him. Closer, a single black wagon, pulled by a horse, bounced among the shell holes and rotting bodies. Closer still, a group of blacks with spades over their shoulders walked slowly across the battlefield. Other lone figures dotted the landscape. It was quiet except for the constant low buzzing of flies rising off the dog's bloodied fur.

He tried to let the daylight clear his mind. Too much had happened too quickly. He needed to think. The overseer had ridden off, likely with the sack of money on his person. The mulatto would come back. But to find what? With such a wound, Orlett would not have survived long unless he'd found help. Where? At a hospital. John looked to the north where the overseer had gone. It was the same direction in which lay the hospital where he had helped the doctor.

He began to walk to the north, but then stopped, frozen by the sound of a horse's hooves. From the other side of the barnyard approached a single rider. John did not need a closer look to know it was the mulatto. Now, more than ever, the doctor's sanctuary beckoned. He increased his pace, every second feeling Cray's hands around his throat; the mulatto would not hesitate in his vengeance. Every heartbeat became a pursuing hoof beat. He expected even the dead dog to rise up and sink its jaws into his flesh. He began to run, tripped and sprawled face down in the dirt. He got up and ran faster, the black of the woods a bobbing blur as he crossed the torn field, his blood thrashing in his throat and temples and his destination seeming to slip away each time he looked down to secure his footing on the blasted earth. At last, after ten minutes, he arrived gasping at the hospital.

The doctor stood at the operating table. No part of his smock was unstained. His beard and face were flecked with blood and pus. John approached. The doctor blinked at him, then smiled broadly. It seemed to take all of his energy.

"Ah, John," he said. "Come to lend a hand again? Good man."

And they resumed their work of the night before, and little had changed except perhaps his blood. Orlett had said he was white. Like this doctor. Could it be true? John put his finger on an artery and stared at the red blood flooding over his hand. It didn't matter. He had been a slave but now he was free. But freedom required more; it required a future. And that, he understood, would be possible only with money. If there was a chance of recovering that sack, he would do so. And then he would somehow put the mulatto and his own memories and Maryland itself behind him forever.

When the doctor clutched his stomach and said he needed to go into the field a moment, John slipped away. The sun was well up. It was already hot. His face dripped sweat. The battlefield became a buzzing blur as he searched among the fallen. The bodies had begun to bloat and turn black. He gagged on the putrid air as he looked into the dead faces and as he negotiated the shell holes. Out of the corner of his eye, he saw a thin man in a clean suit approaching gingerly, a white cloth held over his mouth and nose. His hands were white-gloved and he wore a bowler. John stood motionless as the man stopped a few feet in front of him and lowered the cloth.

"You're searching for a comrade?" He sighed. His lips were wet and pink and he seemed to hold his breath as he spoke. "A sad duty. Very sad." He dabbed the cloth to his shining brow. Little beads of sweat hung off the ends of his elegant moustache. "But perhaps," he said almost shyly, "you'd be willing to ease the suffering of others even as you carry out your duty?"

When John did not respond, the man removed a small white card from his breast pocket and offered it.

"This is a coupon. If, in your searches today, you should find any soldiers with this card on their persons, you can earn a considerable sum by transporting the soldiers to that tent, just there."

He pointed to a small, dark encampment in the near distance.

"My employer, Mr. Horace Greaver, is a respected surgeon of the embalming arts."

John blinked, his hands twitched at his sides. The man, who had lifted the cloth to his nose again, lowered it and winked.

"A soldier must always think of his family at home. I'm sure you are no different. Wouldn't you like to be able to send more money to your beloved parents? Or, perhaps"—he smiled and the pink tip of his tongue emerged from between his pink lips—"your sweetheart? Listen."

He stepped closer. His voice was hushed.

"I tell you this in confidence. The work's more than I can handle alone. There are so many valiant dead. Such a sad day." He bowed his head briefly. "But why should a soldier not benefit from it? The sadness is a fact. But so is life. And life requires industry and imagination. I can tell at a glance that you are intelligent. I tell you this in strict confidence." He leaned forward, his chin seemed to be propped on the air of decayed flesh. "Officers. My employer will pay handsomely for officers. North or South. If you transport them to that tent. And tell him that Tomkins sent you."

John did not fully understand, but the thought of the money appealed to him. If it turned out that he could not find the overseer's body or that the sack of money was not on it, he would be happy for the . . . a sudden thought stopped the others.

"Are many bodies being taken to that tent?" he said.

"Oh, yes, there are others doing this work. It is a competitive venture indeed. But you are not, I can tell, a young man to shrink from competition."

John considered. Perhaps the overseer's body was at the tent? He turned away from the man without a word and headed south, his eyes scanning the ground for the overseer just in case. Within five minutes, he came upon an elderly Confederate soldier lying on his back. His face was fine-boned, and powder burns had darkened the neatly trimmed white moustache. His large, brown eyes fluttered. As John bent closer, the soldier's lips moved, struggling to form words.

"Are you a soldier?"

"Yes, sir."

The mouth opened again without sound. The eyes closed, opened.

"A federal?"

"Sir?"

"It doesn't matter. Not if you're a soldier." The old man's eyes remained open. "You'll understand. I won't recover from this fight. I do not wish to survive if I cannot fight. Please." His lips hardly moved. His blackened skin ran in rivulets of sweat. A fly crawled along one eyebrow. "Please." A tear formed in his open eye.

John looked around. No one was within a hundred yards. He could do this. This was not the same as what he'd faced with the overseer. This was more like the feeling he had standing beside the doctor. But as he moved his hands toward the old man's throat, the horrifying image of Orlett's doglike grin appeared on the face. Nigger. Goddamn ignorant. John hesitated. He watched the old man's eyes close and not open. Then he knelt, gently pushed his arms under the old man's back and legs, and lifted. The corpse was light, easy to carry in a cradled position. He hurried toward the embalmer's tent.

❖ ❖ ❖

An hour later, not far from the field hospital, he found the overseer in a neat line of dead Union soldiers. Jubilant, John searched the body. But the sack was not there. As he stood dumbfounded over the corpse, he had an overwhelming sensation that someone was watching him. Fearing it was the mulatto, he looked around wildly. Two hundred yards away sat the same single black cart and horse. A man stood near the cart, some kind of black object in front of him. John could feel the intensity of the man's stare; it burned two circles of heat into his brow. He thought quickly. If the overseer's body disappeared, others might believe he had simply left the area. The mulatto, especially, might believe it, he might leave to search. Without a corpse, John realized that he'd be safer. And the man staring at him would just think that he was carrying off a dead comrade for a private burial. Other soldiers were doing just that, either for themselves or for one of the embalming surgeons. And civilians also wandered over the broken field. His actions could not be regarded as suspicious.

He bent again to the overseer's body but reeled back in shock as his eyes locked on the face. It still wore its living grin. John waited for the taunting to start, but only the drone of flies rose from the bloated lips. He waited longer than was safe. The man by the cart would be growing more suspicious; he might even decide to come closer to investigate.

At last, John took the overseer onto his back and headed for the woods hunched darkly on the horizon.

PART FOUR

I

July 1881, Crescent Slough, British Columbia

Standing on the small black wharf just upstream from Dare's cannery, Anson knew almost immediately which of the three skiffs approaching over the darkening water had his old friend at the oars. It was the lead boat, the one putting so much distance between it and the others, the one that drew the last few crimson shreds of light around it. As the skiff came close enough to the wharf for figures to be distinguished, as the smooth, steady power of the oar strokes replicated the most efficient machine in the cannery behind him, Anson saw that the years had not greatly diminished his friend's strength. Dare pulled without pause, his shoulders level, his head raised. Anson could hear each quick grunt that accompanied the stroking, a natural sound, as of the day itself winding down with the light. Then the oars stopped.

As the skiff glided the last few feet to the wharf, Dare stood, still as tall and lean as Anson remembered. Sweat glistened on his sunburned forearms. He wore a white cotton shirt, the thick sleeves pushed up, crushed like the petals of great flowers around his biceps. A wiry, grey-flecked tangle of beard hid most of the lower half of his face but focused attention on the eyes. They seemed even larger than Anson remembered, darker and worn, as if two mixed handfuls of river and blood were continually breaking apart and being replaced. Except, Dare's face also possessed a curious repose. Anson sickened at the contrast; it spoke too clearly of grave-grass pushing through the bars of a cradle.

He had expected the years to alter his friend's appearance. The deep lines on the brow, the grey flecks in the grizzle; these were predictable enough, almost comforting in the way they bound the man to his kind. But the alarming condition of the eyes! It seemed that at any second they'd break apart and no amount of river or blood could be gathered to return them to sight.

Anson's relief that the gunshots had not deprived him of their reunion quickly evaporated. At the edge of the wharf, a groan made him look away before speaking, down into the skiff. Thomas Lansdowne lay stretched along the thwart. His shirt was ripped open at the chest, and a chunk of the fabric served as a tourniquet around his upper right arm. He was conscious and moaning, but his eyes flickered constantly and his face was pale. Thin shafts of light cut across his body. Already a cloud of mosquitoes had begun to drip onto his exposed skin.

Anson locked eyes with Dare and all the finer distinctions between past and present dissolved into one long, continuous moment.

"John?"

Dare didn't smile. This close to him, Anson could see the deep lines etched into his sunburned face and the tightness of the skin pulled over the cheekbones. The eyes, however, possessed some spirit yet.

"He's lost a lot of blood. I got him here as fast as I could."

"Leave him there. I'll come down."

Anson lowered himself into the skiff and quickly studied the wound. It was a large spatter but clean, and no vital area seemed compromised. Unfortunately there was no obvious spot where the lead had exited the body. Even so, the situation was not hopeless. At Antietam and for years afterwards, the arm would have had to come off below the shoulder, but now, with the proper attention, things might go better, though there was always a risk that the wound might prove fatal. So much depended on the degree of the fracture and, of course, on the patient's strength. Thomas Lansdowne, Anson reflected grimly, had been in a weakened, worn-down condition of late.

The Englishman moaned. His blue eyes opened for a few seconds, glassy, apparently unseeing. Anson was sorry he did not have anything to give him for the pain.

"I'll send for some whisky," Dare said with unnerving prescience, then, without using his fingers, he emitted a high, piercing whistle.

The sound startled the hovering gulls and set off an even wilder chorus of shrieks.

Meanwhile, the plashing of other oars sounded nearby. Soon the tiny, still scene of Antietam, like something captured in a daguerreotype, would be invaded. Anson felt a rush of disappointment that he and Dare would not be given time for a reflective reunion, that they would have no immediate opportunity for a detailed talk. And yet, somehow the fact did not surprise him, was almost a natural extension of the haste and suffering they had known on the battlefield so long ago.

But Dare's face showed no sign that he, too, was disappointed. It flared, as always, with an attendance on the welfare of others.

"I brought him here because I knew you'd be here," he said.

Anson nodded as he stood. "Yes. I've had some experience with gunshot wounds."

Dare didn't appear to notice the irony. He clenched and unclenched his huge hands, which hung fish-scaled and brinish at his sides, and slowly turned his head in all directions. When the elderly Chinese, thin as a heron's leg, drifted over the wharf, Dare instructed him to bring some whisky. The Chinese drifted away.

"I'll carry him to the house." Dare stepped toward the wounded man.

Anson gently touched Dare's elbow. "I left my bag at Chilukthan. We'll have to go there."

Dare's eyes turned downriver but not his head. His corneas were as blood-streaked as Thomas Lansdowne's arm.

"I'm not welcome there," he said.

"That much I know. But I'm not asking you to come to the house, just to the wharf. Besides, the circumstances . . ."

Dare turned to face the incoming skiffs. When he turned back, his face was blank.

"He's already killed one of my Indians."

"Killed? Who?"

"The bullet was meant for me."

The last daylight trembled on the water. Only a bent sabre of red showed in the west. The seagulls began to fly inland, silently, in a loose formation. Anson shivered. If Thomas Lansdowne died or even lost his arm . . . Suddenly Anson realized why his old friend would be especially unwelcome at Chilukthan now.

"It wasn't your shot?"

"My shot?" Dare spoke with the same uninflected tone he'd used at the height of battle, as if matter-of-factness was the only sane way to face what couldn't be faced. "Not first. Not even second."

Anson searched Dare's eyes for the truth; it was like seeing a long way down a country road at dusk—there was a great calm but also the pressure of darkness coming in, a sense of things disappearing that might not return at dawn. Anson didn't need to ask what had happened—Thomas Lansdowne had shot the Indian by mistake, had shot again, and would have kept shooting unless someone had stopped him. But for Dare, the first shot had done the damage. His presence on the river almost certainly wouldn't be abided after such violence, especially given the knowledge of his blood.

The elderly Chinese returned with the whisky and a blazing oil lamp. Its frayed glow, lowered into the skiff, cast the scene in sharp relief. Thomas Lansdowne was very white, trembling the whole length of his body. Anson looked up from him and down into the first of the other skiffs as it glided past. The dead Indian—a man of early middle age—lay on his back, his face a pulpy mess half blown away. The silent, implacable manner of the woman at the oars—husband and wife usually fished together—was somehow more disturbing than screams. A dozen silver salmon lay beside the body like an offering. Anson watched the fish slip out of the oil light's glow before he took the whisky bottle and knelt to the wounded man again. He managed to pour a little liquid between the trembling lips, then a little more. This close, he couldn't help but note the resemblance between father and daughter: the strong

nose and brow, the distance between the eyes, and, more than anything, the proximity to death.

"Quickly, John," he said.

In minutes they had left the slough mouth and joined the current
of the main channel. With the tide not against him, Dare pulled the
skiff along at a tremendous pace. His breathing was level but oddly
rasping. The powerful muscles in his neck and arms moved rhythmi-
cally. Anson, seated beside the wounded man, keeping firm pressure
on the wound, took a slug of whisky for himself, then gazed upward.
There was no moon, but the stars had begun to emerge in the blue-
black, most of them as faint as scales on wood.

A heron rose off the bank with a loud squawk and winged slowly
away, as if dragging the slabs for two graves through the air. The smell
of the river suggested the same final heaviness. With a chill, Anson
recalled the gravediggers working the bloody Antietam ground after the
sudden, heavy rain. Then he saw the corpse again, vivid, gore-spattered.
Thomas Lansdowne floated away into the soft edges of the coastal dark,
replaced by Dare's defining act. The blood glistened at the groin. The
terrible rictus came alive in a grin. Anson closed his eyes, but Dare's
old words still reached him: "He did not deserve to live. He was evil."

Anson opened his eyes. Dare had paused in his rowing. He seemed
to be studying Anson's face. That unsettling, uncanny prescience!
Anson fought it off. He spoke clearly and calmly.

"They know, don't they?"

Now the silence gathered from all sides. The seconds passed. In
the shimmering oil light, it appeared that a smile came to Dare's face,
but that couldn't be; the situation did not call for amusement. When
Anson looked again, the expression was gone.

"What is there to know?" Dare said evenly, his arms akimbo, resting on the oars.

"Why, who you are. They know who you are."

"Who I am." Dare spoke the words with a slight pause between
each one. He straightened up, his knuckles tightened on the oars.

This should not have been so awkward. After all, Dare had asked
Anson to come, he had summoned him for help. He knew the answer.
But it appeared that he wanted to hear it spoken aloud.

"They know you're black, John." Suddenly, Anson felt no reason to use the name he had given his friend at Antietam. The artifice seemed pointless now. "Some Southerner saw you in Victoria and—"

"I never knew my parents."

Dare blinked slowly, as though his eyelids were crusted with salt brine. He seemed to speak to himself.

"The overseer told me they were white. That I was born of white trash and only raised as a nigger."

He held the oars so tightly that his two fists were against his chest.

Anson swallowed dryly. The glass of the whisky bottle was cold in his palm, but he didn't raise the bottle to his mouth. White? Both parents? The idea staggered him. He had looked past the colour of Dare's skin for so long that it simply never occurred to him that there was any question of his mulatto ancestry. Dare was black, an escaped slave who looked white. And Anson had saved him. To doubt these facts was worse than to lose faith in God; it was to abandon everything, to find nothing in life but deceit and shadows. He gave another drink of whisky to the gasping Englishman, who seemed even paler than before. Then Anson forced himself to address Dare's last statement.

"Did you believe him?"

Now Dare did smile, a slow unwinding of skin that revealed the slightest glimpse of teeth.

"For a time. Then I knew it didn't matter. Not if I owned myself. That was all I had to do. The owning's what matters."

Anson tried to assess the conviction in Dare's tone. What struggles he must have endured to reach so blunt a philosophy! Yet Anson couldn't deny the stark truth of it. Was the North's ambition in the war any different? He decided to address the situation at hand.

"I don't see that this changes anything, John. Even if you're white but they believe you're not, that's trouble enough. These people want you gone. That's the point, isn't it? That's why I'm here. To help you stop them from getting their way."

Dare made small circles with one oar by slightly moving one fist. Water dripped off the blade. "Yes. It was why I cabled."

"Was?"

His nostrils flared. Several mosquitoes settled on his upper lip, but he did not brush them away; they sat there like a crooked stitch. Or another scar. The rough, whitened edges of an earlier one showed just above his beard on the right side; it looked as if Dare had been scratching desperately to get at the old wound but without success.

But his voice contained only a chilling calm.

"There's no help now. I thought I could fight and stay this time.".

Dare rowed swiftly for a dozen strokes, then let the skiff glide again. Finally he spoke. "I'll have to get myself away. But you can still do something for me. I need someone to protect my property."

"Protect? But I can't—"

"It's all right. My Chinese knows the business. I'm asking only that you sell what you can. You won't get much, but it should be enough to give me another start."

As Anson began to protest, Dare cut him off.

"You've put your own money into this. And . . ." He dropped the blades lightly to the river. "And we've known each other a long time."

Anson bowed his head. All his unshakeable trust in Dare flooded back at the reference to their old bond. Here was a man, likely of mixed blood, once white in the eyes of this place, now black, for whom the past was more than merely inescapable; it was deadly. Yet he would not let the blade be driven into his back. He would pick up his gun and turn and then keep moving.

"Where will you go?" Anson said.

Dare began to stroke rapidly. "South" was the only word that slid between his breaths.

"South?" Anson could not keep the alarm from his voice.

"South of here. I have a piece of land in California."

Dare bent to the oars again as another moan escaped Thomas Lansdowne's lips.

"Louisa," he said, his eyes opening.

"She's fine." Anson gave him some more whisky. "You'll see her soon."

The eyes flickered shut again.

Dare suddenly stopped mid-stroke and began to cough violently. The muscles in his neck tightened and his eyes seemed to loosen in their sockets. Even the white edge of his scar appeared to expand toward his shaken look. After ten seconds he wiped a forearm over his brow, muttered something to himself, then picked up the stroke rate. He rowed so quickly now that Anson tensed, expecting another harsh fit of coughing to cut off the rhythm. But it remained steady as the Chilukthan wharf came into view and the clattering and hissing of the cannery echoed in the darkness. Anson noted the light blazing in Louisa's room. Her mother and aunt, no doubt, had been vigilant in their attendance.

As Dare moored the skiff to the wharf, the gravity of the situation settled over Anson's mood. Someone, perhaps Thomas Lansdowne, had murdered an Indian. And while it was likely the Englishman would never be charged with the crime, it might very well unhinge him; that is, if he didn't succumb to his own wound or at the very least lose his arm. Meanwhile, his daughter was very ill and might die, and there was no guarantee that her mother, pregnant, grieving, and already on the verge of hysteria, could survive further losses.

Matters were no better for Dare. If Thomas Lansdowne died, Dare, guilty or not, would be a murderer and a fugitive. Even if the Englishman survived, Dare's fate on the river was sealed. Nor was it likely that any of his competitors would feel the need to pay full value for a nigger's property, especially not a nigger who'd shot Tom Lansdowne and been forced to flee.

Heavily, Anson positioned himself to lift the wounded man to the wharf.

Dare stopped him. "I'll carry him to the house. All seems quiet enough."

It was true. Other than the cannery's relentless noises, there were no sounds along the riverbank; most of the fleet must not have returned yet. Anson hesitated. He knew so little of Dare's life, where he'd been, what he'd endured; mostly their correspondence had been of business, and even that had been infrequent. Until this moment, it had always seemed enough, the bond they had forged at Antietam. It had pulsed behind everything, like the sun, even long after it had gone down, pulsed with the promise of more light. And now it seemed that that promise surrounding his friendship with Dare might never be fulfilled. In any case, there was no time to ask everything that might be asked.

Wearily, Anson helped position the wounded man in Dare's arms and struggled not to see the old images but to hold on to the present, for the Englishman's sake, and even more for the sake of his gifted daughter.

A few moments later the men crossed the wharf, Dare breathing heavily with the effort of bearing Thomas Lansdowne's bulk, Anson holding the oil lamp just ahead of them. As they came down to the yard, Anson looked up at the bright window of Louisa's room and saw two shadows cross the pane. For some reason, the sight alarmed him. The women, after all, rarely moved from their chairs. He quickened his pace, knowing that Dare would manage to keep up, despite his burden.

At last they reached the veranda. The first floor of the house was in darkness. With the women upstairs and Henry Lansdowne likely at the cannery, it would be quite safe for Dare to carry the wounded man inside. At Anson's suggestion, he did so, laying Thomas Lansdowne gently on the ottoman in the parlour. Then he stood and faced Anson in the shimmering oil light.

"I'm grateful to you, doctor," he said and extended his hand. "I always have been."

Anson gripped the hand firmly in return. "I know it, John. I just wish I could be more help to you now. It isn't right. I wish . . ." Anson stopped. What did it matter what he wished? His wishes wouldn't help Dare or anyone. "I'll do what I can for him," he said and nodded at the prone figure on the ottoman. "And I'll do my best to see that your property receives fair value."

"My Chinese will help. I'll leave instructions with him."

"How soon will you leave?"

Dare looked over his shoulder toward the front entrance. When he turned back, his eyes blazed with a strange light. He was almost smiling.

"That depends."

"On what?"

"On others. There's no moving in life doesn't speed up or slow down except for others getting in the way. Or out."

He didn't sound bitter or frightened, only resigned. Anson had a sudden impulse to lay a hand gently on his shoulder.

But just then, a flurry of footsteps crossed the ceiling. Raised voices could be heard. Anson's chest tightened as he glanced upwards and then down again. His mouth was bone-dry.

Dare began to back away.

"John?"

Anson took a step after him, but this felt like he was leaving the sick girl behind. He stepped back.

"My bag's upstairs," he said. "I'd better go up."

Dare stopped. A rush of river smell poured off his sweat-slickened face. He might have been standing in the bow of a skiff, the sun fading along his arms.

There was too much to say, too much to go over. Anson faltered, then pushed ahead. "They've been saying slanderous things about you."

Dare was unmoving, his eyes vivid with will.

Anson had an awful foreboding that this might be their last meeting, that Dare would disappear and never contact him again. He thought a few seconds, then said, "Fighting a war's no use if it takes your belief away. I can't afford to doubt you, John."

The voices upstairs grew louder. Something hit the floor with a loud bang and made Anson start. But Dare remained motionless. His eyes, fixed on the staircase, filled with a strange longing. He touched something at his throat, under the collar, and spoke with a curious, almost questioning tenderness as he stepped back.

"A man can doubt everything. Even a good man."

This time, as Dare withdrew, Anson did not call his name. In a matter of seconds, he had slipped silently from the house.

Immediately Anson raced up the stairs, the practical demands of living and dying a spur to his purpose. But even so, Dare's last words echoed on the air. What did they mean? That a man could learn to doubt goodness? Or that even a good man could learn to doubt? Anson had done the latter and he'd come dangerously close to doing the former. But seeing Dare again, even under these tense circumstances, or perhaps because of them, had saved him from that most fatal wound.

He reached the second floor just as the voices in Louisa's room rose to a crescendo.

II
July 1881, Chilukthan, British Columbia

At first Anson couldn't believe what he saw. The room appeared full of people; their shadows stained the walls in grotesque patterns. One lamp spilled a crackling yellow against the mildewed wallpaper of faint roses and over the planks of the floor. His eyes remained fixed there, on the bodies clustered almost in a circle, as if in worship. But what faith could explain the prone young woman with the frozen gaze and Thomas Lansdowne's wife, on her knees, propped up under the arms like a limp puppet?

"What is this? What's happened?"

He didn't even wait for a response from the startled faces. The girl groaned and he hurried to her bedside, stepping over the young woman who had not turned at his rapid approach. As he passed, he recognized the Southerner, Richardson, his white-framed features flushed and wavering in the dimness, his mouth open as if he was about to speak. But Anson's immediate thought was for the child.

She burned as hot as ever, the spots along her collarbone and chest like circles of flame. A linen cloth, slightly damp, lay like an infected scab on one shoulder; much of her body, including her feet, was exposed. Anson could hardly register the meaning of what he'd come upon; it was like some sort of dark ritual. And yet the girl's mother and aunt were present. Confused and outraged at once, Anson quickly checked the girl's pulse. It was rapid. He found a clean cloth on the bedside table and doused it in a basin of lukewarm water. Then he pressed it lightly to the child's brow.

From behind him came the sounds of motion. Anson pulled the sheet up the child's body and turned, ready to order the room cleared immediately. But the two Lansdowne women, their pathetic postures like those of statues melted by their own tears, cooled his wrath. He went to them.

Mary Lansdowne cried openly, her round face slick and red.

"Oh, doctor," she said. "Thank goodness you've come! Edney's had a spell. I don't know what it is, but . . . oh, doctor, I shouldn't have allowed them up, I knew it was wrong!"

"Calm yourself, now. Bring me a chair." Anson held Thomas Lansdowne's wife against his chest as she seemed about to collapse. She was rank with sweat, and her heart thudded against him as if he'd wrapped a bat in a towel. Yet as she pulled her head back, Anson saw that her face also wore a strange repose. The contrast was terrible. If not for the heartbeat throbbing along his lower chest, Anson might have thought her dead.

As he guided the woman into the chair, he realized he didn't have time for either explanations or apologies. Thomas Lansdowne lay bleeding in the parlour. The best time to operate would be while he remained in shock. Anson looked into the woman's eyes. She did not look back. He touched her stomach, feeling for the child. When it moved, he did not know if it was a good thing or not.

"I had meant to help," a recognizable voice spoke at his shoulder. "If I had possibly known of the presence of the evil . . . doctor, I assure you, I wouldn't have brought Miss d'Espereaux into such a house."

The Southerner's face appeared ravaged; he might have aged twenty years. The blue in his eyes was washed out. A muscle in his cheek twitched repeatedly. He clutched a handkerchief like a limp dove in his hand and spoke with a deference that took Anson by surprise.

"If you would be so kind, doctor, to attend to Miss d'Espereaux, I would consider it a great favour. I fear she has been quite overcome."

Anson looked down. The young woman remained still, but her eyes opened and closed slowly, her chest moved in an easy rhythm under her finery. She had a remarkable beauty. Her white skin shone with it. The rough character kneeling at her side and fanning her face only made her fragile charms more evident.

"Who is she?" Anson said, moving closer. "What's she doing here?"

"Miss Elizabeth d'Espereaux," Richardson said brokenly. "One of the world's most gifted spiritualists."

So that was it. Anson had heard of spiritualism, of course, knew how popular it was in certain quarters of society. He had even read attacks against it in medical journals: spiritualism, according to these articles, was a haven for quacks and frauds of the most villainous kind. But this young woman was clearly not acting. Something had terrified her. She had, however, begun to emerge from her fright.

"Lizzie? Can you hear me? Are you all right now?"

The rough character's sincerity softened his crudely hewn face. He turned, perplexed, to Anson.

"She's never done that before, doc. Never. Has she hurt herself any? I couldn't catch her before she fell. The colonel there . . ." He glowered at Richardson. "He got in my way. But it's the only time he's going to touch her, I'll vouch for that."

Much to Anson's surprise, Richardson did not even defend his honour. He merely sighed, his shoulders sagging.

"If I'd known about the evil," the man said at last, "I'd not have brought her here. But she'd have come anyway. She is so good, you see, that she would risk her life to help a spirit find peace. The fever meant nothing to her."

The young woman had a slight bump at the back of her head but was otherwise unhurt. As Anson examined her, she kept repeating, "It's gone now. It was here, but it's gone." There was no longer any fear in her voice, however—just a confused kind of wonder. Anson instructed Mary Lansdowne to find suitable places of rest for the two women. Then he took Richardson aside.

"I need your assistance. Some good may yet come out of your return to this house."

Anson briefly explained the situation that awaited in the parlour. The Southerner took the news without interest; the words hardly seemed to reach him. He was no more substantial than the long shadow he cast. But he nodded gravely once Anson had finished.

From downstairs came a mournful howling. Thomas Lansdowne's dog, Anson supposed. Somehow the creature's misery affected him as deeply as the human suffering around him.

"Meet me in the parlour," he said and hurried off to get his bag.

Ten minutes later, with Thomas Lansdowne shirtless and laid out on the dining room table, Anson carefully examined the wound. It was bad, high up in the shoulder, the humerus fractured. Anson removed what bone fragments he could, all the while desperately trying to convince himself that he could avoid amputation. It had been years since he'd performed one, and he hardly trusted himself even to make the correct diagnosis, let alone to carry out the surgery. Circumstances were decidedly against him.

Thomas Lansdowne's dog continued to howl outside, as if about to crash through the window at any moment, and the sound, along with the smell of chlorophorm, to which he was no longer so accustomed, had a powerful effect on Anson's imagination. He kept looking at the long, thin fingers of Ambrose Richardson, pressed, upon instruction, on the subclavian artery, and seeing instead the hand of Dare, as if it had reached out of the mud-clotted darkness to help as it had done so many times before. But Anson knew his current assistant had once been his enemy on those distant battlegrounds and knew, moreover, that this same long-grieving man had endured the loss of his own left arm. The conjunction of images and memories worked against Anson's concentration as much as the strange mixture of fatigue and exhilaration had focused it in the past. As if guided, he searched rapidly through the gore and shadows . . . there was something he'd seen in . . . what was it? . . . an amputation at the shoulder joint had not proved necessary because enough of the upper humerus remained intact. He asked for the light to be brought closer.

Mary Lansdowne lowered the taper over the wound. Good woman, she had recovered her senses and could now be depended upon. Anson felt encouraged. He let his thoughts remain in the past, in a barnyard open to the elements and crowded with wounded. A senior surgeon, a very experienced man who wasted no energy on saving limbs, had surprisingly saved a young soldier's arm in just such a case as this, by . . .

Anson peered at the bloodied gash as if he could see through it. What was it that man had done? He had made an incision . . . yes . . . and extracted the splintered head of the humerus. If there was enough upper bone . . . Anson probed with his fingers. The breathing of his assistants faded into the dog's howls, then even the howls diminished. Anson picked up his knife.

"Wipe, please," he said.

Mary Lansdowne quickly mopped the sweat from his brow.

Anson's hand was firm as he made the incision, firm as he removed the head of the humerus, firm as he sewed the wound shut and positioned the arm upwards, indicating to Mary Lansdowne how a sling would be required to keep the bone as high as possible. Only when Anson stepped away from the table and the lived years rushed together into the strange, living present, and the voices of the wounded were replaced with other voices at the dining room door, did his whole body go so limp that he almost lost his balance. He found a chair and gingerly lowered himself into it. His lower back ached and his hands were weak. He let his eyelids fall.

"You have carried out your duties nobly, sir," Richardson said with unusual warmth. "I will deal with this."

Anson opened his eyes and looked after the Southerner. An Indian couple stood in the doorway. The smell of fish blood and the river poured off them as they spoke quietly to Richardson and Mary Lansdowne. Suddenly she reeled and Richardson, with much difficulty, caught and held her in his one arm. Anson rushed forward.

The Indians' faces were blank as they withdrew. Outside, the dog's howls had turned to ferocious barks.

Richardson said, "They spoke a strange mix of words. I couldn't understand much . . ."

"Henry's gone after him!" Mary Lansdowne cried. "He'll be killed!"

Richardson stared at her, then at Anson; it seemed that the idea of revenge, despite his own sorrows, had grown cold in him.

But Anson was not alarmed for Henry Lansdowne's sake. The Englishman obviously had blood vengeance and a cool intellect on his side. He was not a man quick to act, but when he did so, he was undoubtedly dangerous. Anson realized that he had no choice.

"I entrust the patient . . . the patients . . . to your care," he said over his shoulder as he left the room.

From the wall in Thomas Lansdowne's den, Anson removed a shotgun and loaded it. Then he hurried to catch up to the Indians.

They had not gone far, but only the dog's incessant barking and growling indicated their whereabouts. The darkness had closed as though sewn to the earth. To the west along the riverbank, the cannery beat remorselessly on, spewing smoke and yellow shards of light, but even its hissings and clankings seemed smothered by the thick night. A wind had come up from the east, but it wasn't strong enough to freshen the air of its heavy blood, slime, and low tide taste.

The Indians stopped at Anson's call. The dog, whimpering, ran to his side, as if seeking permission to return to her master. She moved heavily, her belly swollen.

"It's all right, girl, go on now, go on back."

Anson shouldered the gun and spoke plainly to the man.

"I need to get to Crescent Slough right away."

The Indian's face was noncommittal in the darkness. He spoke softly to the woman. She nodded.

"I'll go," he said. "But not stay."

Anson understood. He also wasn't keen to follow any farther in the wake of Henry Lansdowne's vengeance than was necessary. Unfortunately, the necessity was ultimate, he could not pretend otherwise. The heavy smell of blood wafting over the damp earth was more than sobering fact; it was the unassailable truth that had replaced faith and memory. He could no more turn away from it than Henry Lansdowne could turn away from his vengeance. And it was a truth whose darkness could be penetrated only by a different belief. That Dare stood at the centre of it meant that Anson had no illusions about his journey. More than even the child's survival, it was, at last, the reason he had come to this place—to prevent a murder. But the knowledge was like a gun at his back.

Past the wharf in the direction of the slough mouth, they neared the Indian settlement, their way dimly lit by burning bulrushes he'd been told were dipped in oolichan grease. A cluster of barking dogs ran out of the shadows but retreated immediately at the male Indian's command. Though they moved steadily, Anson and the Indian couple's progress seemed imperceptible. The smell of fish and tide deepened, the river sucked at its banks, the stars brightened but cast no greater light: the distance to Crescent Slough might have been the distance between planets. By the time Anson and the male Indian had veered off to the riverbank, boarded a skiff, and set off into the current, only minutes had passed, but Anson could not stop himself from thinking in years; each pull of the oars was like a tear in the thin fabric between a life's experiences, between the child's and the man's sense of time. From the Indian, Anson learned little, only that Henry Lansdowne had left just before the Indian and his wife had come to the house: if he pulled hard and steadily, the Indian believed he could close the gap. Anson settled into the bow, and his body tensed, set to the trigger of Henry Lansdowne's anger. The canoe seemed to plunge through panes of glass that broke silently again and again. Other than the almost soundless motion of the oars, only the occasional cry of a hunting owl disturbed the still air.

They entered the mouth of Crescent Slough without seeing or hearing another skiff ahead of them. Yet Anson's whole body tightened. It was as if they floated on a bloodstream. Earth and sky fell away, the small black wharf loomed ahead like a clot. The tide had fallen and begun its rise again since he had sped downriver with Dare. The going was now smooth, rhythmical. The Indian, however, did not relax until the skiff pulled alongside the wharf, directly behind another already moored there. With haste, Anson scrambled onto the wharf and gazed along the bank.

Dare's cannery pounded steadily not far away, its noises erupting in sudden spurts, its smoke and lights spewing the same broken energy as the Lansdownes' cannery. Together, they were like the inflamed lungs of some great beast that had crawled to the river to die. Anson could see dozens of shadows in the faint lamplight; they fell swiftly back and forth, flung like dead salmon. For the air was thick with their creaturely death; like a wind, it touched everything, from the silt of the low tide to the sweat on Anson's brow. It seemed to him that the fish, in their dying, only continued their ecstatic journey in another form, one invisible to the ordinary senses. But he took no hope from the thought. He ducked his head repeatedly as he ran up the gangway, convinced the air would crack and bleed above him at any second. He had no idea where to go. Should he try to ward off Henry Lansdowne somehow or look for Dare and warn him? The night offered no guidance. For now, it mattered more that he reach the dike.

Once there, his breath came raggedly, a cramp pierced his side. He stopped and bent at the waist. The clanks and hisses seemed farther off, as if the cannery was drifting away on the very smell that it was swallowing.

Then he heard it. A single word, shouted. "Dare!" And it was like a cipher into which everything plunged: river, stars, sky, even memory. The darkness began to flow. Anson felt himself moving with it, heavy as a sodden stump, roots torn away from the earth. But when the word came again, it stopped him short. *Dare.* Now it was quieter. Anson wondered if he'd really heard the name a second time or merely an echo. Then he realized that the voice was not quieter, the word had fallen in unison with a sudden eruption of noise from the cannery, which now opened before him like a side of bleeding flesh. The blue-smocked Chinese, their pigtails cracking, tossed chunks of salmon from them like burning armour. The greased and bloodied conveyor belts whined. Rows of Indian women wielding knives bent so far over that they appeared headless—their elbows sliced the air as sharply as the blades they held. Steam and smoke travelled in great scuds underlit with blood. Everywhere workers trundled wooden barrows heaped with fish, as if delivering souls to the furnaces of hell. Anson stared at one worker and his burden: the living man and the dead salmon shared the same agonized expression of nothing. The planks underfoot ran slick with slime and entrails. Anson slipped as he rounded a large, pulsating boiler into which a bare-chested, wickery Chinese grinned as he tossed in chunks of cedar. The wood, like the fish, seemed recently dead. The absence of screams was as nightmarish as the sudden appearance of two Indian children, a boy and a girl no more than eight years old. Naked except for a cloth at the loins, their skin speckled with blood, they stood laughing and chewing on raw gouts of flesh. The boy had his hand inside a severed fish-head, working the jaw open and closed as if it were a puppet. Then a thick retch of steam hid them from view.

Anson stood in the midst of the chaotic order and looked desperately around. The pounding of the gears, shafts, and pistons reverberated up from the floor straight into his skull. Slowly his stinging eyes came to rest on the open wall of the building fronting the river. A tiny stitching of stars shone just below the roof beams. He started toward the light, vaguely thinking that he could regain his bearings outside and make a rational decision. But before he could escape the damp, blood-soaked interior, Anson glimpsed a dark figure slipping to the right of his vision. This time, however, the word did not come. Perhaps, he thought with horror, there was no longer any need for it. Though he had heard no shot, he knew that Henry Lansdowne was capable of a more intimate revenge. Anson began to move, the blue-smocked Chinese sliding away to either side of him as if they'd been stabbed by the grim labours of the Indian women invisible in the dirty steam. Now the word was on Anson's lips, but he could not utter it. The letters were weighted down with blood. Anson waded through fathoms of stench with dead fish swimming around his legs, their entrails clutching like seaweed, threatening to pull him under.

The night air helped. Outside again, the name became a whisper he could hear a long way down, where he had helped to join it to flesh in the vague years already spent. He listened to himself as if the past were a compass. Then he knew where Dare would be. The knowledge came to him in a burst of clarity, the whole night's hood thrown back off the shoulders of an indifferent, because nonexistent, god. Dare would be where he had always been, where he had died even as he started to run, where Anson himself had died, where the salmon wanted to die even beyond the meaningless physical phase of their brief lives.

Anson hoped only that Henry Lansdowne would continue to search in the wrong place. If Dare could be warned, even moments ahead, he could yet prolong his dead run, as the salmon did, out of the inexorable hope of purpose inherent in generation, to pass on, if nothing else, the thrill of surviving until the blank eyes were torn by an equal hunger from the skull.

Away from the cannery, the darkness thickened as the air ran fresher. Time grew young. Despite the unceasing cramp in his side, Anson hurried along the dike and then down toward Dare's house, which sat on the depressed earth like a doused coal. No one stirred as Anson passed. The night was suddenly fragile. Anson held the shotgun before him, pushing the seconds away like cobwebs.

The shot rang out just as the campfire winked its red at his approach. Anson covered the dark ground as fast as he could, keeping the trickle of white smoke straight before him. The gun seemed to come alive as he ran. He grasped the stock; it was slick as horse flesh.

A man stood beside the open tent, his arm lengthened by the weapon he held at his side. Feet away lay a body crumpled at odd angles: it looked like two halves of a body struggling to reconnect itself.

Anson came close, stared into the face of the standing man, who spoke with neither sadness nor disappointment.

"It isn't him. I thought it was but it isn't." Henry Lansdowne was calm as only a man can be who has released his violence at last. "I should have known he'd be gone. But I thought more of him than that. I thought he'd face up to it."

Anson bent to the now-still body, saw that it was the elderly Chinese, saw the hole in his abdomen and the long knife fallen from his hand onto the grass. And all that Anson could think was: that should have been my price, for my loyalty was older. As the last life of the Chinese drained into the ground, Anson's scalp prickled. Slowly he looked around.

"John?"

Lansdowne tensed and brought his gun up. The campfire hissed, a fish spine of smoke stood against the dark. A throbbing of flies dripped out of the air and onto the corpse.

There was no answer except an old and ravaged echo of the voice of a trembling, runaway slave: "He did not deserve to live. He was evil." And inside the echo, "A man can doubt everything. Even a good man."

Anson peered into the darkness beyond where the flies were feeding. He could see no purpose there, hard as he looked. And the stars themselves were faint, sucked clean of light by the same murmurous flies near the grass.

"If he's here, I'll kill him." Henry Lansdowne's face shone pale in the starlight.

Suddenly Anson saw a trail, clear and direct and mysterious as the salmon's trail from sea to river. It was lit with bloodshine and Dare walked it, and would keep walking it until his breath came no more and perhaps beyond that. It didn't matter how it was walked, in what name—justice, truth, faith—Dare would walk and his feet would be covered in blood, his or others', and that hardly mattered either.

Anson, however, still had a useful service to perform.

"Your brother's recovering," he said and rose. "But I must return to your niece. We'll have to tend to this later."

Henry Lansdowne nodded. Together they turned from the corpse of the old Chinese and walked with intent toward the river. They had not gone twenty paces before Lansdowne stopped and whirled around, his gun aimed in the direction of the black woodlot.

"Dare!" he shouted. "Come out and show yourself!"

There was no response.

Anson strained to make out the thousand tense faces between the trees, his body went rigid waiting for the burst of noise and motion.

Lansdowne lowered his gun very slowly. "I do not doubt," he said in a level voice, "that he would shoot me in the back. Or . . ."

His jaw dropped and his eyes widened. He whirled around to the west and stared downriver.

Anson understood what the "Or" implied, but he could no longer be sure if the implication was unfounded. Henry Lansdowne had killed Dare's Chinese, a man who'd clearly been in Dare's employ long enough for a certain loyalty to accrue. And yet, to mete out vengeance on a slave owner who'd destroyed all you'd ever known of family, to so lose yourself in that act of vengeance to be reduced to savagery, was a particular brand of justice. Anson knew that Dare was not that same man—twenty years would cool any blood, white or black, but he couldn't be sure how Dare would respond to the murder of the Chinese.

Henry Lansdowne obviously had no such doubt. He began to run toward the river.

Anson hesitated.

"John?" he said, facing the woodlot. "Are you there?"

He hoped for a response without really expecting one. The air bristled. Seconds passed. When Anson finally turned away, he saw that the darkness had already swallowed Lansdowne's figure. There would be no catching him.

The smoke of the campfire had vanished. Near the ashes, a body lay under the faint stars, on the cool grass, with the dead salmon's open-eyed vision on its face. It was there because of Dare, regardless of right and wrong, good and evil. It had been there since Antietam and it was never going to be buried. All the bones in Anson's body felt the ache of the knowledge—it was like a dull saw blade scraping the memory off his skeleton.

Clutching his side as he ran, he hoped he could find an Indian to row him downriver again.

❖ ❖ ❖

At first the red glow in the distance looked like nothing more than a soldier's campfire on a hillside, a flicker of light in the surrounding dark. But as the skiff drifted in to the Chilukthan wharf, the glow became a fierce ball of crackling flame. Then Anson heard the frantic shouts of men. But it wasn't until the skiff had landed and he was rushing along the dike that he connected Henry Lansdowne's open-jawed panic with the fire. To connect the two, however, was not the same as accepting the cause and effect. Anson had seen the cannery in full operation, had seen the careless work in the boiler room where the hot ashes were not hosed down as regularly as they should have been. Even so, he was not a fool, not quite; he recognized that the timing was a damnation not even a friend of Dare could dismiss lightly.

When Anson reached the cannery, the heat was intense even though the fire had been contained to one corner of the building. Madly, the processing continued inside. Anson watched in disbelief as the dark, hunched figures of the Indian women continued to slice away at the silver fish even as the smoke and flames crept closer. Outside, a long line of men and women—Chinese and Indian mostly, but also some whites who oversaw the cannery operations— had formed a bucket brigade down to the river. Each person stood about twenty feet from his neighbour and raced two buckets of sloshing water up the line where they were thrown on the flames by Henry Lansdowne himself. The Englishman hurled each bucketful with such ferocity that he might have been a devil driving a pitchfork into sinning flesh.

With his arm over his face, Anson ran forward.

Lansdowne did not pause. The fire glow in his beard made him look as if he'd been feeding on a piece of bloody meat. He shouted, "Get a bucket, man! Hurry!"

Anson staggered away from the heat. He found a place in the line and reached for the handles of the buckets. The Indian who handed them to him seemed to find nothing unusual in the emergency, but the man who burst out of the darkness below, his face greasy and red, was shouting as if on fire.

"Move it! Move it, there! For God's sakes, hurry!"

It was Thomas Lansdowne. His blackened sling hung loosely from him as he ran. Anson opened his mouth to protest, but the next buckets were in his hands and the person above him was urging him on. With a heave of his sore shoulders, he set to the task.

To Anson's amazed relief, the bucket brigade proved effective. After what seemed like hours, the fire was out, but not before the cannery crew had been forced to flee. Only the use of the steam pumps, in fact, had saved the building.

The riverbank hushed. Anson stood beside a barrow of salmon, the top layer of which was charred. Little flecks of red ash floated past him. He watched one rise until it disappeared against the stars. The night quickly recovered its rhythm. The river chewed almost docilely against the bank, an owl hooted somewhere beyond the smoking cedar of the ruined section of the cannery. Men and women trod heavily through the restored rhythm, their heads down. A few pairs of gumboots sloshed through the inches of water on the cannery floor. Buckets were strewn about like severed fish heads. A man kicked savagely at one. It was Thomas Lansdowne. His brother stood at his side, sniffing disgustedly at the smoking char. Anson did not have to approach them. In unison, they turned to him, and Henry Lansdowne said, "Now he'll be running. At least he'd better be. And if he's intelligent at all, he won't stop."

He never has stopped, Anson reflected, not since Antietam. Now Dare was gone, plunged somewhere into that darkness of the earth from which he had emerged, and would emerge again, with or without the imprimatur of goodness bestowed upon him by the diminishing belief of one for whom almost twenty years was enough of a church. But if the bricks had collapsed, the beams might yet remain; if it could be done, Anson vowed to transfer what belief he still possessed to where it might prove of greater benefit. There was no point in talking to Thomas Lansdowne about his arm; the man would not listen to him now. Without a word, Anson turned his back on the cannery and set out to resume his vigil at the child's bedside.

As he neared the house, however, the sudden snorted breath of a horse startled him. But Anson did not see the animal; its hoof beats struck the ground almost immediately and died away in the opposite direction, to the south. When Anson reached the veranda stairs, a strange whimpering sound stopped him before he could fully absorb the idea of connecting Dare with the horse. He knelt and peered into the close, warm darkness beneath the stairs. The smell of blood and wet fur flowed up. It was the Lansdownes' dog. She'd given birth to at least six puppies; he could hear them suckling, hear the mother licking and breathing. One of the pups was curious, already pushing its nose into the greater world. Anson reached out his hand and collected the soft creature. Then he stood and gazed in the direction the horse had gone.

A good man. What was he? Not vengeful, not remorselessly responding to misery and pain by inflicting it on others, most of whom, like most people, were innocent. The smell of charred wood on the air was suddenly the burnt evidence of an ideal Anson could no longer carry. To accept this revenge as an extension of the mutilation of the corpse almost twenty years before was to do more than allow his old friend to disappear without explanation of either the present or the past; it was to know himself, at last, for a fool, naive as those Southern planters had been in their romantic attachments to a non-existent code of chivalry. Now he had to accept what all the years of graft and scandal and retribution after Appomattox had held out to him, that the achieved glory was cold, blunt, and efficiently ruthless. Even so, it was not an occasion for tears, even if he could shed them: if he had not cried over the operating tables of the war, he would not cry over this final failed surgery of his antique values.

The wind blew over the ruined cannery and the battlefields of the slain. The pup wriggled in Anson's hands. He gazed into the dark and let the small animal's warmth sink into his chest.

Crescent Slough

Dare directed the horse over the marshy ground and let the briny air dissipate the smells of wood smoke and his own sweat. But if he breathed too deeply, he began to cough from very deep in his chest, so that he had to pull up on the reins and lie gasping along the horse's neck for several seconds before he could continue on his way to Chilukthan.

He did not have a clear purpose. The Lansdownes were not the real enemy; he knew it was the Scots canners, Craig or Owen. They were certainly behind the current plotting against him; one or both of them were responsible for the shooting of Thomas Lansdowne, just as they had almost managed to block him from hiring another canning crew in Victoria. If he hadn't been willing and able to pay twice the going wage, if he hadn't made his own connections in the city, he'd not have been able to put up a pack at all.

But it didn't matter now. The fact that the Lansdownes—and others—believed he was a nigger, and a violent one, only hastened the end that had to come. But the end could be different. It would have to be. Even if the words were the same. Goddamn ignorant. More of a slave than any nigger.

But a slave was not free to leave a place, and he had left many. A slave did not have property to sell, and he would sell. Or, at least, the doctor, his friend, would sell for him. And a slave did not have white friends. So Orlett was as much of a liar as ever.

Dare urged his horse along the slough bank, and thought, I will go to the house of Henry Lansdowne, I will tell him that I did not shoot his brother, that I will agree to sell at a fair price and leave the delta. Because he could not stay. There always came a point when the world required his hands on the throat of something that couldn't be killed even if he used all his strength. That point had come again. It was no use fighting beyond it. There were always other places. But this time it had to be the last place, the piece of isolated California land he'd bought ten years before. He was dying from the poisons in his lungs. How long it would take he did not know; perhaps he had no more time than the salmon who struck into the river from the sea, perhaps more than that, but certainly not enough to waste.

The narrowest portion of slough approached in the dim starlight. Dare kicked the horse's flanks and circled away from the bank, preparing for the jump. As he rode, the motion confirmed his decision, cleared him of all doubts and worries, as motion always did. He saw Daney's face before him, Caleb's eyes, he saw his own branded cheek.

As he moved, he felt his skin darken. Perhaps if he moved fast enough and with enough purpose, he'd grow so dark there'd never be any question of it. Then he could walk comfortably among men, his head raised, his whole scar open to the air, then he could lay to rest the ghost of the overseer's grinning face.

By the time the horse lifted from the ground, Dare was hardly even flesh and blood; he was pure black and free even of memory and time. And when the horse landed softly on the far bank, Dare knew exactly what to do: he would wait for the doctor and tell him that he was leaving the delta, that he would contact him when he could. No matter the wrenching cough from his lead-filled lungs, he was still strong enough to move clear. A slave who had moved clear, who could move, was a free man. And a free man could choose his own place to die.

Dare noted the fire glow on the horizon and slowed the horse. He watched, unsurprised, for five minutes, ten. Once, a long time ago, the crackling fires of a burning nation had been at his back, and almost three years of hard survival had been behind him too. Somehow he had survived the worst of the fighting and the diseases and had even come slowly to a greater understanding of himself and of the nature and purpose of the war. But though he had witnessed many terrible things, nothing ever touched him as deeply as the sight of Daney dragging her daughters and the coffle of women to their deaths. The man couldn't shake the image the boy had seen; it haunted him more than the overseer's revelations about his parentage. But the war cured him also of any illusions about seeing the world in so simple a fashion. Blood was well mixed in America, and suffering wasn't limited to those of a single skin colour, no more than were the nobler qualities—a poor white farmboy, after all, a shy and gentle soul with some learning, had taught Dare to read on the dreary, dull bivouacs of the seemingly endless campaigns.

For he had no intention of failing at the war's end, that much he knew almost from the moment he marched out of Sharpsburg with a new name. And with that conviction, pressed continually against the image of Daney's final act, came the desire to prove himself against white men, to better them simply by escaping their traps again and again. Each time he moved on from a place, taking his tinsmithing skills with him, the smell of solder like a shield, he moved farther away from the burning brand that had left the scars of the insulting letters on his face. Now the final move had come, and he was not even sorry for it, as long as he could leave as a free man, with the money his skill and sweat had earned, with the knowledge that he had escaped the closing trap of the overseer's grin once more.

The fire widened like daybreak down along the river. Dare lightly tapped the horse's flanks with the heels of his boots and continued on toward the Lansdownes' cannery. As he rode, shouts rolled up from the riverbank and across the flat ground and died. Approaching the Englishman's house, he saw a dark shape move against the darkness. At the same time, a dog began barking. The sound chilled him. He dismounted and tethered his horse to a stump, vowing that he would not see the overseer's grin, not look over from the smell of wet dog to Daney's iron face above the trader's wagon, not watch the black flies lift again from the bloodied muzzle.

But before he came close enough to see the live animal, the barking stopped. Somewhere in the dark a horse whinnied low.

As soon as he had made the connection between the fire and the shouts and the horse, Dare sprinted back.

He untethered and mounted, his blood pounding to join the hoof beats that came rapidly his way. He waited until the rider was nearly upon him before he kicked the horse forward and blocked the path. The other rider reined quickly, his head dropping. Dare jumped off his horse and, in seconds, grabbed the rider around the midsection and threw him to the ground. The horses neighed wildly and galloped into the darkness.

The man, pinned on his back, cried, "Who are you? What do you want with me?" His small eyes swam in his doughy face.

Dare pushed his knee down into the man's chest and placed one hand near his neck. "Who are you working for?"

The man's eyes filled with knowledge. His nostrils dilated. "My God, it's you." His voice shared the horses' wildness. "What are you going to do to me?"

Dare closed his fingers slightly. The man began to choke. He tried to buck but Dare held firm.

"Who is it?" he said.

"Craig. It's Craig."

He could do it this time. He felt the will in his hand but even more in his blood. He tightened his grip. The man gave a gargling sound, like that of a salmon strangled in a net. Dare stared at him. This man had plotted against him for money, he had set a fire and had probably even shot Thomas Lansdowne, and all for money.

The letters on his face burned under the old scars. As if he were still property, still a nigger. But the burning meant slavery; why should it burn? He was not a slave. He had a home, on his own land. He had a place to die free. He pressed down until the man's eyes fluttered and the choking sounds ceased.

At last he stopped and stood, his chest heaving, the fingers of his hand tingling, his cheek aflame. He could not kill when he was a slave, so how could he kill now? As a free man, a dying man? The idea froze him. He looked down. The man's jaw worked slowly, his breath came in rasps.

"Please," he said. "My child . . ."

The man touched his throat in wonder.

Dare gaped at him, at the naked word on his mouth. "A child?"

"A boy. He's just nine. Please. I can't leave him alone. His mother's gone already."

Nine? Once he'd been that age too. A boy. A son. Dare tried to look far down into himself, but there was only darkness, a darkness that seemed to pull him in. He felt his body succumb to the warm pressure until he lost awareness of his surroundings. Vaguely he whistled for his horse. It trotted out of the field toward him.

Dare took a step, then looked at the stars. Once he had been both things. The idea was so strange that it stopped him from taking another step. The horse nickered softly, the musk of its damp flesh reached out of the dark. But very briefly a son. And it did not seem he'd ever been a boy. Perhaps, if he had become a father, his own boyhood would have grown clearer to him. But he'd never stayed long enough in one place, and how could he have risked a family, never knowing with certainty the colour he would pass on?

He lifted the well-worn pouch from under his shirt and carefully emptied the contents into one hand. They shone like a constellation, near and farther away than anything. His milk teeth. Not even an ounce worth. And yet what he held was all he really possessed. It didn't even matter about his name or his skin. Not now. A man couldn't own them. What mattered was that the blood had to be cool enough for a man to die properly.

The teeth were so light, as light as the past was becoming. Dare looked at the clustered stars. It wasn't only the Englishmen who could plant themselves in this place. The teeth were as small as the stars; he understood that he no longer needed the guidance of either. With a graceful sweep of his arm, he sowed the teeth into the fields.

A second later, he heard the chilling shout of the past and the present—"Goddamned nigger!"—and whirled just as the near-simultaneous blast of the shotgun struck.

Then the earth rose rapidly to meet him and the darkness, no longer inviting, but cold and unyielding, rushed in.

EPILOGUE
New Westminster, British Columbia

Jacob Craig stood at a second-floor window of the hotel on Columbia Street and looked down at a drunken Indian weaving along the board-walk. Near him, a grey mare tethered to a pole weakly flapped her tail at a cloud of flies, and two ravens pecked at a clump of dung. Craig counted carefully. Five seconds, six seconds, seven. Time enough.

He turned, slowly removing the toothpick from where it hung on his bottom lip, and took his chair again. He glared at the American doctor but immediately realized it was no use; he might just as well try to intimidate Owen sitting there across the table like some kind of statue filled with lava rather than stone.

"That's a steep price for but a single cannery," Craig said. He narrowed his eyes as the doctor blinked his heavy eyelids and smiled slightly. His lips were a red smear in his unkempt grizzle.

"That includes the pack. And you know how large that is."

"Do I?" Craig reached for his glass and took a short swallow of whisky. "It seems to me that, with your friend gone and not likely coming back, there'd be some effect on production."

The doctor hardly reacted. His face was loose-skinned above the beard, and his eyes had all the vitality of a whipped spaniel's. He ought to medicate himself, Craig thought, then recollected the gossip that Smith, the agent, had passed on. The story was that this Yankee doctor had taken a keen interest in the Lansdowne girl, the one he'd carried through the typhoid. Smith said that with the mother nursing her sickly newborn and Thomas Lansdowne even more preoccupied with getting his cannery running again the doctor planned to take the daughter back east on the proceeds of the sale of Dare's property and wait the appropriate four or five years until she was old enough to marry. Well, men had done stupider things, but Craig didn't think this fellow, Baird, looked lovesick. In fact, he looked much the way a man does in a slump of the market when all his stocks prove worthless and he finds that he's ruined. Then again, some men took love the same way, apparently. It'd be useful if Owen did, but Craig still hadn't found a chink in that armour.

The doctor suddenly fell into a coughing spasm. His face reddened and he seemed to retch into the handkerchief he'd pulled from his vest. After several seconds, he stopped and, with a shaking hand, drank from his glass of water.

Owen spoke, his mouth hardly moving.

"How do we know he isn't back already, Craig? He might never have left. Say what you will of his character, but Dare possesses a considerable talent for remaining unseen."

Craig felt the smart to his intelligence. Owen never missed an opportunity to belittle him. It would have been so much easier if Dare's body had been dumped in the slough. But you couldn't trust an Irishman to finish anything, except a bottle. For all Craig knew, the mick was even lying about shooting Dare. Well, better to be safe, then, and play along.

"What of it?" he said, staring hard at the doctor and feeling himself competing with Owen for whatever information was writ on the man's haggard face.

The American blinked so slowly that his lids seemed to draw the blood up into his eyes, which were red and wet around each small circle of brown. "No more doubt his absence than God's presence," he said dully.

Craig felt Owen's grey eyes settle briefly on him, but he could not decipher the message. He knew that Owen had no more time for God-talk than he did. It was no asset in business, except for the connections a man could make in church, but they were as easily made in hotels and saloons. Easier, in fact, since worship happened but once a week. Craig almost allowed himself a grin at his witticism, but he wasn't about to give Owen any more advantage than he already had.

From the direction of the bar came a volley of laughter followed by a clink of glasses. Craig waited. Just when it seemed that no one was going to speak again, the doctor stood, one hand flat, the other limp at his side.

"It matters little to me, gentlemen, if you believe what I say about Dare, except as it interferes with our business here. He's no longer on the delta, or indeed in this country. And it's not likely he'll return. He's not a fool, nor is he a spirit able to remain unseen permanently, despite your appreciation of his talent. And, that being so, I have a responsibility as an investor to seek what compensation I can. Clearly you recognize that?"

Owen nodded and the doctor continued.

"I don't know how you've kept the other canners from this meeting, but that means nothing to me as long as you meet my price. If you don't, I'll consult the others directly."

Craig relaxed. Now the conversation was comfortable again. He replaced the toothpick in his mouth, probed gingerly near his sore molar, then said, "The market in England is glutted. You have only to smell the air to know why. I'll be fortunate to sell my own pack, let alone whatever slop Dare's squaws and Chinamen have managed to stuff into tins."

The doctor shrugged and pointed the limp hand at Owen, who looked at it as if seeing a fish whose flesh had turned too ripe to be canned.

"Consult whoever you wish," Owen said. "There'll be no takers." His voice fell like a block of salted granite. If Craig hadn't already known that Owen had pressured the other canners into keeping their hands off Dare's holdings, the cold voice would have chilled him straight through. As it was, he shuddered a little as he studied the doctor's reaction.

To Craig's surprise, the man stiffened. Something of Owen's hardness settled into his jaw and bloodshot eyes.

"So that's how it is?" he said and turned to face Craig. "A blood bond, gentlemen, or just greed?"

Craig repressed the desire to tell the fool everything, that Owen had even paid off the steamships—Dare's whole pack for this last big run would just sit and rust on the wharf.

Owen's grey eyes iced over, but no flush came to his skin. It was always a disadvantage to show too much; his genius lay in knowing that even better than Craig himself did.

"What you call greed, sir," Owen said, "is what we call business in this province."

"Business?" The doctor convulsed into another coughing fit. He pulled a small bottle from his pocket, poured some pills into his hand, and swallowed them. Finally, he said, "You won't get away with it. I'll see to it that you don't." But his voice lacked conviction. After all, Craig knew there was little the man could do. He was only a visitor here, and a doctor, not a businessman with the necessary connections. And no doubt Dare's disappearance had come as a shock, especially as it followed so quickly upon the revelation of his being a nigger. Of course, a sensible man ought to expect a nigger to run. Just as a sensible man knew that a nigger, once he'd run, wouldn't turn and rejoin the fight. No. If Dare wasn't, in fact, dead, he was as good as dead. It wasn't even necessary to guard his pack. Even if the nigger did the unthinkable and returned, he'd have a hell of a time selling his fish with no buyers and no shipping companies willing to transport the cans.

Owen reached for his coat on the back of his chair. "When you have a reasonable price in mind," he said, "I'll join you for another drink."

"I wouldn't drink with the likes of you if I was dying of thirst," the doctor said and turned his back.

It was a handsome and noble gesture, Craig had to admit, as useless as it was foolish, as such things generally were. But just perhaps it left an opening.

When Owen had gone, Craig cleared his throat and threw a low number at the doctor's back. If the man was indeed lovesick and needing funds to get away, he'd be apt to accept anything that wasn't an outright insult. Dare's pack would be large. Nigger or not, he'd built the biggest packs on the river over the past three seasons.

The doctor turned slowly as if caught on the breeze of rotted fish guts blowing through the open window. His face was haggard but fortunately not livid. Craig believed that he had just won himself a significant gain in his battle with Owen. It hardly seemed possible.

"I must thank you," the doctor said. "You have made matters very clear for me. If the choice is between the desperation of a good man and the snivelling, underhanded grasping of those for whom goodness doesn't even exist, I know where I stand."

Ah, well. Craig slid his toothpick back to the safe side of his mouth and watched the American stride out of the bar. Salmon have gone bad in their tins before. And the English market, while not exactly glutted, was tight. Besides, men who make grandiose statements about goodness usually come back to earth once their tempers cool and the realities of the world press in on them. If they don't come back, they lose. Simple.

Craig dropped the toothpick from his tongue into his palm, then carefully pocketed it for later.

Chilukthan

The riverbank was a gruel of rotting guts. Anson no longer took much notice of the loud smell or the mizzling layer of flies heavy on the mud as a matted scalp. He had the crushing weight of leaving upon him, which was not simply a matter of place but of time. And leaving time—or at least a particular inflection of it—was a more painful and palpable death than what the summer and the river had strewn around him.

Downriver the rebuilt cannery continued to pound, as if rendering the ghosts of all the flesh it had consumed. Anson blinked toward it, the cry of gulls washing lightly against him. He could hardly imagine that he had searched for Dare in such fierce workings, just as he could hardly recall his own right arm sawing off the limbs of a thousand soldiers. Everything he had lived, including his love for Elizabeth and his grief at her dying, shimmered with the same urgent unreality as the crimson, sunlit landscape. Yet the present was forceful enough. It still had the strength to pain him when he resumed his place there.

The other canners had frozen Dare out, even in his absence. They weren't content just to ruin a man, they had to destroy whatever good his wealth might do for others. Well, Anson wasn't about to let that happen. He wasn't without means—if he couldn't sell Dare's property, he'd see to it somehow that Louisa would have the money for proper music instruction.

As always, the thought of the girl cheered him. She had recovered well. And it even seemed that the trial of the illness had deepened her musical talent, as if the nearness of death had imbued her with an even greater responsiveness to life. Every day she practised. And though Anson had left explicit instructions for her to rest, he knew that the parents were too busy with the new child and the cannery to pay much heed to Louisa's care. But it didn't much matter. The child's health lay in her music; the more she played, the better and faster she'd recover.

He walked along the wharf slowly, to avoid bringing on another coughing spell. The mountains to the north shone luminous in the bright sun. With his eyes fixed on them, Anson could almost forget about the killing that continued on the river, continued despite the inability of the canners to process the catch. It was little wonder that Henry Lansdowne's cattle were dying from the contaminated water. Anson suspected there'd be fresh cases of typhoid fever before the summer's end too. The whole coast was awash in an indolent sensuality; it lay like an infected film upon the mud and the guts and the slowly blinking eyelids of the Indians who no longer even bothered to go out in the skiffs, but instead sat, hour after hour, gazing northward, no doubt thinking of more familiar, less repellent waters. Anson felt that he stood on the threshold of a brothel after a busy night's debauch; the slack, flesh-drugged quality of the air and the overwhelming presence of something noble and precious bought cheaply sickened him and turned his thoughts also to home.

But could America be less repellent to him, now that the past, the very best of it, had sold itself just as cheaply and vanished into the common, present corruption? A weight pressed on his shoulders. Anson resisted, but the natal impulse in him—the love for the country whose ideals he still believed he would die for, even if the country had dishonoured them—was too much.

When he turned at last to the south, it was as if all the hands of the wounded men he'd tended were directing him, laid one upon the other in gory ranks from his shoulder into the still, blue air. And then only one hand was touching him. A strange music vibrated at the touch, music of no regiment or nation or acknowledged genius, the music of what it meant to accept certain truths as given and to live in their service. Anson could almost hear it; it seemed to ring out from the bright air and rise in a shimmering reflection off the summer-drugged waters.

So when Louisa herself ran up, shouting, "Dr. Baird! Dr. Baird! You have a telegram!" he wasn't so much surprised as confirmed in his appreciation for the music that the ancient Greeks and Romans must have absorbed in order to capture it in their poetry. Even so, when Anson took the cable from the smiling child, when he saw who it was from and what it meant, his hand trembled a little.

"Louisa," he said and knelt to look closely at her. "Will you promise me something? Will you promise to meet me backstage after your first concert in New York?"

Her laughter flowed high and rippling, as if she played it with her fingers. "Oh, Dr. Baird, you're so funny."

But Anson had already looked over the girl's shoulder, upriver, toward Crescent Slough.

"Yes," he said. "But will you promise?"

When she realized that he was serious, Louisa paused a few seconds, her brow furrowing. She was, after all, a highly intelligent child, old beyond her years. Finally, she nodded. "I promise."

"Then let's shake on it." Anson extended his hand and took the girl's warmth into his palm. But already he was making his plans for Victoria; the cable had become a knife that he could wield with his old confidence and every expectation of success.

He knew even better than his enemies did what they expected of a nigger. If a nigger somehow managed to survive a murder attempt, he'd never stop running. So Dare, when he regained consciousness, lay on his back under the bunched stars and the flitting of bats, waiting for enough strength to return to his body. At last, very slowly, he pulled himself up, pain flashing in his shoulder. It took a long while, but he managed to remove his shirt and use the arm of it to stanch his wound. All the patience and care of his youth on the battlefields returned to him. He could almost see the ghost of his young face, calm, steady, looking down at him from just above and whispering, "Go slow, easy, there's time enough."

He knew it was true. He knew that he would not lie to himself, not now, so close to the end that was coming. The poisons sloshed in his lungs as he forced himself up, gasping and coughing raggedly. Then he whistled. No sound came back across the churned ground, but he did not worry. He whistled again. A rippling neigh broke to the south, in the direction of the marsh. It would take a while, but he would recover the horse. And when he had done so, he would not return to Crescent Slough until enough time had passed for the other canners to believe him dead. Five days or a week should do it. Long enough for him to make his private arrangements. One thing you could count on with the canners: their loyalty was to profit first, and to each other not even second. Five days to recover with the Indians in their camp at the ocean's edge, where Chilukthan Slough spills into the Gulf.

❖ ❖ ❖

And he waited just that long to return to his cannery. As he suspected, the other canners hadn't even bothered to steal his pack; no doubt they believed him dead and saw no reason to take time away from their own operations to visit Crescent Slough. Perhaps they had sent someone out to investigate the settlement shortly after the attack. It didn't matter. Dare was so confident in his timing, and in the reports of the Indians he'd sent ahead as scouts, that he did not even feel the need for a weapon as he set to work.

It took hours of sweat and labour, but whenever his shoulder throbbed the pain was almost pleasing because it was not on his cheek. At last the long scows were ready, securely roped together. The tins, stacked ten feet high and twelve wide on each scow, made an impressive sight, glistening a little in the moon glow. The red salmon on the labels were crowded close, as in a huge school, waiting only for the mysterious rush of instinct that would drive them forward. But it was the owner of the name on each tin who controlled this mystery.

He had paid off the few Indians he'd hired and sent them away the night before. By now the doctor would be in Victoria, making the necessary arrangements at the harbour. All except one. Dare would handle the shipping of old Kim's body back to China himself.

He boarded the front scow and stared downriver. Moonlight slid and rippled on the great, fast-flowing dark. A strong breeze blew into his face, carrying the pungent decays of the season and scouring the stars high over the Gulf. Behind him, the three broad mountains of tins, the whole pack for the last run, shivered and whistled as he pushed the scows into the current.

Within minutes, he was drifting rapidly toward the sea, past the Englishmen's landing, the whistling in the tins louder with every minute. Only once did he look over his torn shoulder at the gleaming pack, tens of thousands of tins, all the fortune he would need. A few empties shook loose and plunged into the roiling current, but that didn't matter; he'd only stacked them at the last moment, not wanting to leave them to Craig or Owen.

He smiled. It was too bad that the river wouldn't carry him past the canneries of the two Scotsmen. But they'd find out soon enough that their control of the industry wasn't complete. And by then it would be too late; his pack would already be on Wadhams' wharf at the very edge of the Gulf, sold and ready for shipment to Victoria, and from there to England. After that, he could leave the fighting and man-oeuvring to the others. After that, he would be home.

The stars were as many as the tins. They seemed to whistle and shake too as the shimmering scows slid under them. Just as the salmon below, as multiple as the stars, whistled and shook as they plunged out of the salt into the fresh waters. The whole night was alive and yet still, fixed, unchanging in its purpose to become dawn. In the marsh grasses, the sloughs, the black folds where the bats hunted, everywhere drifted the same old desire. And part of it was his; he was a part of it, the river, the marshes, the salmon's faithful return. He had stayed and fought longer here than anywhere else, long enough to justify the seeding of all that remained from his childhood into this wet ground. And what would grow from that seed would be superior to what the Scots and the English grew, because it was more than money to him, it was the victory of his own death.

The tins whistled as the scows drifted past the last silt island before the sea.

Dare stood listening at the front of what his skill had wrought, his legs braced, his eyes open, and did not look back.

Acknowledgments

ta Foundation for the Arts, the Edmonton Arts
imon Guggenheim Memorial Foundation for
My late agent, Frances Hanna, contributed
(I miss her intelligence and good humour). I
doubt very much that there is a finer and more generous editor of fiction in this country than Jack Hodgins. It was a pleasure and a great gift to have the help of such an esteemed author, and a fellow native of the West Coast, on this novel.

TIM BOWLING is the author of ten poetry collections, two works of non-fiction, and four novels. Tim's most recent books are the poetry collections *Tenderman* and *The Annotated Bee & Me*, and the non-fiction titles *In the Suicide's Library: A Book Lover's Journey* and *The Lost Coast: Salmon, Memory and the Death of Wild Culture*. A native of the West Coast who now lives in Edmonton, he has received many honours for his writing, including a Canadian Authors Association Award, two Governor General's Award nominations, a fellowship for his entire body of work in prose and poetry from the John Simon Guggenheim Memorial Foundation, and four Alberta Book Awards.